I0687268

THE BRIGHT LOGIC OF WILMA SCHUH

ALSO BY SHIRLEY GLUBKA

End into Opening: six sestinas and their humble companion poems
Echoes and Links: poems
Return to a Meadow: a novel
All the Difference: poems of unconventional motherhood
Green Surprise of Passion: Writings of a Trauma Therapist

SHIRLEY GLUBKA

THE BRIGHT LOGIC OF WILMA SCHUH

A NOVEL

BLADE OF GRASS PRESS
PROSPECT, MAINE
2017

Copyright © 2017 by Shirley Glubka

The Bright Logic of Wilma Schuh
a novel by Shirley Glubka
paperback

published by

Blade of Grass Press
85 Bowden Point Road
Prospect, Maine 04981-3000
bladeofgrasspress@gmail.com
http://shirleyglubka.weebly.com/

Front cover painting: *Machtzentrum* (*Power Center*)
courtesy of Mattes
https://commons.wikimedia.org/wiki/File:Machtzentrum_visualisiert_-
_Mattes_2009.JPG

ISBN 978-0-9666481-8-8

Gratitude

I owe more than I can express to the ongoing generosity of my manuscript readers. They catch errors, awkwardness, excess. They make great suggestions, large and small, many of which I happily use. For their interest, their encouragement, their time, their intelligence, and their loving forbearance when I stubbornly go my own way, I humbly say thank you to:

Laura Levenson
Rae Dumont
Sonia Gernes
Virginia Holmes

Dedicated to the memory of my mother,
her philosophical and spiritual leanings,
her lifelong passion for learning,
and the great hugs she gave.

Harriet Glubka
(1918—2015)

There's a blaze of light
In every word
It doesn't matter which you heard
The holy or the broken Hallelujah
—Leonard Cohen, "Halleluja"

Beneath the story of cause and consequence
Another story is pointing another way.
—Carl Dennis, "Not the End"

Contents

One: Wilma

Of these three I am concocted

Wilma Schuh intends to acquire mystical experience, well aware that the god she seeks is somewhat unclear as to qualities. Surely this is a minor consideration. A few words do come to mind. *Infinite* is acceptable, as is *eternal*, but she puts little stock in descriptors. Determination, on the other hand, is essential. The god will be contacted, no question about it.

Determination takes its own form in a woman approaching the age of seventy. Younger, she would have called on "will power," assuming such a thing to be direct and effective. She did accomplish, in her own mild-seeming way, what she chose to accomplish. If Lorraine, for example, demanded the unthinkable, a decision would be made, yes or no. Yes was simpler and generally prevailed. After that, will bullied through. But today, sitting on the plain brown couch in her living room, agreeably alone, Wilma is content with indirection, with delay. The business of the god waits, but determination is not undone, not at all.

She sits holding an urn.

Can a cube be an urn? Shape might matter. Perhaps the shiny ceramic container with its greens and its browns—essence of forest, moonlit—does not strictly qualify. But let us not quibble, the cube has an urn's function. As urn, it wants to be held. Or the ashes within want to be held. The ashes are those of Alma Schuh, Wilma's mother, recently deceased.

"Demand to be held" might be more accurate. Lightly, though. Alma's ashes demand lightly.

We have perhaps left the realm of fact, entered fantasy. If so, it is persuasive fantasy. Wilma sits. It's been well over an hour. She does not mind her task. She appreciates the smooth feel of the surfaces of the container which is perhaps not quite an urn.

Lorraine was Wilma's lover. Odd designation, but there it was. Domestic partner seemed a bit cold, though lover was, at least toward the end, a tad heated. Spouse applied only to the heterosexual element, of course. Lover was the word, even unto death.

Long gone, at any rate, is lover Lorraine.

Not so with mother Alma. It's been only a week. Every death has its singular demand. Alma's is this daily holding. When will she agree to be scattered? Perhaps she had enough of scattering, thinks Wilma. Alma Schuh was lovingly designated "scatterbrained" within the tiny family. It

1

let her off most hooks, this way of hers. Thus the development of will, or perhaps discipline, in daughter Wilma, for who else would hold daily life to a shape? Not the philosopher father. Deep into books or lost in a project around the house, Henry was off the track of time. Even Lorraine, requiring practicality, was not quite able herself. This is a heretical thought, thoroughly satisfying. But who did notice suppertime? Who cooked, cleaned, shopped? Only little Wilma.

Like Lorraine, lover, Henry the father is long gone.

Decades dead, both of them.

Alma, Henry, Lorraine. Mother, father, lover. Of these three I am concocted, thinks Wilma, caressing the container filled with her mother's ashes. Of these three, and now god. Or perhaps GOD. It's one way or the other, isn't it? Short modest syllable, all lower case, or a shout. But the shout seems unlikely.

Well.

Rise up, old girl, and put your mother in her place.

She sets her mother on the kitchen table, at the center. This is a small rectangular table, bare good oak oiled weekly. Alma was fond of the kitchen which is sunny yellow with two windows, southern exposure —windows kept clean for twenty-five years by Wilma. Candles, one green, one brown, accompany the glossy box. The effect is serene and orderly. Lorraine Benedict, deceased lover, would approve.

Wilma would not want you to think her god, shout or not, is the controlling sort. She had enough of that with Lorraine. Agreed to enough of that, no one forced her. Still, this god: unclear as to qualities but definitely not one who commands. Nor does this god punish, we are not in the Middle Ages. Nor are we, here in this apartment, in the territory of the religiously fundamental; or, to be clear, the religious of any ilk. Wilma's god will not be a god of religion.

She stands looking at the table. A single cloth placemat now, thick and deeply ridged, warm rusty brown, hers. She sighs, turns briskly away. Time to leave the apartment and purchase a few groceries.

Take the back steps, off the kitchen. Fourteen worn steps, down, down, down. These she does not sweep quite often enough any more, but no matter. It's been many months since Alma bumped down on her bottom, determined to see the sky entire. One must, said Alma. But the

2

time came when one couldn't, a deprivation accepted, windows would suffice. Adjustable Alma. Mother.

Emerge at the driveway, loved for its cracks, for the tough grass inhabiting the cracks. New concrete would be disconcerting, smooth and unbelonging, an invasive laying-over. Perhaps the workers wouldn't see it that way.

Onto the bicycle, grateful for good legs, for balance, grateful for warm spring, for leaves once again agreeing to appear. Beyond the high leaves, the reliable sky. Wilma is feeling quite fit in mind and body as she pedals the streets of Bangor, Maine.

~ ~ ~

One jar of natural style extra chunky peanut butter which she stirs thoroughly. One bunch of celery. A shopping to be proud of, uniquely hers. She cycles daily to the store, comes home with modest packages whose contents are cherished for their specificity. She eats by whim but not carelessly, feeling her way. On the stove, boiling for one minute, celery, cut to small pieces. Drain it now, palest tint of green in steaming water descending, descending. Into the small bowl go the bits. Butter them, salt them, add pepper. On the table beside the bowl put the jar of peanut butter. The oil is now integrated, invisible. Two serviceable teaspoons, one for celery, one for peanut butter, are already in place. Sit to eat. Nod to Alma in her box. The celery is hot, with a delicate crunch. What is *celerity*, though? Something to do with speed. Is there a root in common, the food and the pace? Unlikely.

Ah, language.

Next come the spoonfuls of peanut butter, two of them, generous. This is for contrast in color and texture and by way of a bit of protein. Someday a piece of meat, a baked potato. Not yet. Is she losing weight? A few pounds. Nothing to worry over, her bones are well-cushioned.

It is when she runs warm water for her meager dishes that Wilma notices the pattern. Food, ceramic cube, candles: her life is made of green and brown.

This is hardly true. Will she have to cleave to reality more firmly some time soon?

3

The patterns have been appearing. A robin's song in the early morning yesterday and then on the radio, before the news, a singer named Robin, never mind the raw scratch in her voice. More crow than robin, that one. Wilma has never objected to the caw, caw, caw. Some do. As the song ended an old Volkswagen the exact color of a robin's springtime breast—recently painted for a cheerful owner, she decided—pulled into the parking space across the street. Robin number three. Why was she passing the window just then, peering down from the second floor of this apartment where she, daughter of recently deceased Alma, lives in unaccustomed but not unwelcome solitude? In case there was something to see on a pleasant spring morning. For whimsy, and perhaps for pattern.

Twenty-five years is a considerable time to live with one's older and older mother. Death finally arrives. Is Wilma grieving? Is she relieved? Questions arise and recede, arise and recede.

But life: life insists. And time, that peculiar vast atmosphere, life's genie, insists also. Or is the situation reversed? Does time own the genie called life? Either way, there seems to be a lot of escaping just now, and from a rather large bottle.

And Alma. Has she escaped? If so, she hasn't run far.

But this day is going, going. Wilma has a plan. She will look into the first notebook. Alma will appreciate that, having extracted a promise. *Wilma, you do intend to see what's there, after I'm dead.* It was one of the last times Alma headed for the back steps. Perhaps it was the final time. Leaning on Wilma, still walking a little at that point, Alma had her intention. Down the steps she would bump on her bottom, out into the air she would go. But first a sudden turn to the right as they were about to leave the living room, Wilma almost losing her balance as her mother, abruptly strong, pulled toward the boxes and stood there, staring, silent. And then the demand. You do intend. After I'm dead. Which Wilma will now honor.

Yesterday she opened the boxes. Notebook A stared up at her from Box One. From Box Two, the flat gaze of Notebook S. Under each, more notebooks. The spiral bindings were respected, the notebooks set meticulously this way and that to preserve balance. She noted the care. Her father's? Her mother's? She lifted Notebook A. Under it was not B but W.

W?

She closed the boxes. She found herself reluctant to look into the spiral-bound contents of her father's mind.

Hundreds of times through the years—thousands—Henry Schuh went to work his thought: *I'm going to work my thought now.* Privately, modestly, mysteriously, for hours at a time. He would emerge with shining eyes. He would emerge with ravaged look.

Alma cautioned. *He's been wrestling with his angels. Wait a while, child, and he'll tend to you.* Wilma, good child, waited. It wasn't long before Henry held out his hand and the two of them approached the other work, Our Work. Fix-it projects, carpentry. The old house on the land offered plenty of opportunity. Or someone would order a bookcase to be built, or a table, chairs. Her father was a patient, careful teacher. Together they loved their tools and their hands and their fine, steady minds. Always the mind and the tool, alive together. *Do not bother yourself over mistakes, little Wilma, mistakes are a help to the mind.* Side by side they lived, except when he was at his desk. At desk time, hush.

Alma, meanwhile, was in the garden, looking into the sky, digging into the earth. Alma communed with clouds and loved earthworms who helped her grow good things to eat. Henry worked his thought and Alma worked the earth and the worms helped her. Alma loved a poet named Rilke. "There were cliffs there / and forests made of mist." This was on the way to the underworld. "There were bridges / Spanning the void, and that gray blind lake." Alma was not much suited to daily mother work, wife work. Alma was their soul, Pa said.

Alma's Rilke made a strange world spun from words, but education was largely the province of Henry. No school would be up to teaching his daughter, he did not quite believe in schools. For Henry everything must be cast in High Terms. They read at the edge of Wilma's understanding, but not beyond. Or the books were beyond her, but she was taught to glean, to pick up what fell to her level, pocket it.

And silence. She was taught silence. She was taught the time of her own mind. Neither parent hovered, they were not suited.

But Alma seems to be hovering right this minute. Spirit now, she is apparently finally suited to nearness, to attending. She must be wildly curious. All those years of not-looking, not-reading her deceased

5

husband's writing. The feared and joked-over Henry Journals. In the boxes. Over there in the corner.

The Time Has Come.

Come along, then, Alma.

It should be noted that Wilma does not *believe* this nonsense—spirits hovering, deep simultaneity erupting into visible pattern—but a certain pleasure, like a tap-dance down the brain's most provocative pathways, accompanies what we shall call for the time being her inclination toward spiritual whimsy. Her intention to garner mystical experience—let us be straightforward about this—exceeds whimsy.

She kneels on the living room floor. She faces the corner where two cardboard boxes hold her father's life work, companions in patience. She has dusted the taped-shut boxes week after week, year after year. After the third element of yesterday's robin convergence—the Volkswagen precisely parked—she cut the tape. And opened the boxes, saw the notebooks, held the first one in her hand. Put it back, closed the boxes. Unready.

But here she is again. She will look into her father's mind. She ignores Alma's skepticism, oft expressed, echoing now: *They might be ridiculous, those notebooks. They might be Henry's Folly.* Then, too, sometimes her mother had suspected the opposite, that her husband's great effort was the work of genius. In Wilma herself, all these years, a steady resistance to curiosity. Also, the strangest fear.

But is she ready? Yes, of course she is, she's barely trembling.

~ ~ ~

Spiritual-Intellectual Autobiography of Henry Schuh

(Exile from Rollingstone, Minnesota. Mainer now, newly fathering)

A baby born. Alma's. Mine insofar as fathers in the minor way contribute. Wilma, tiny. Wilma, new.

I give greetings to the someday grown human, the woman. Greetings to the fully formed mind, the expected amalgam,

6

philosophy-infused, poetry-saturated, mind of a daughter grown no doubt beyond her genitors.

Thus I write again, my nights unsleeping, my long abstention from language work now ending. Prolonged fasting, word-nourishment eschewed, fasting that began in flame, now ending. Is it possible? It is possible.

All numbers will be allowed their invisibility. Dates and ages yield to Eternity. In the Presence they step back. Invisible, they exist. From the platform—point of time, point of space—a call out to every when and every where, as in the oldest days, as in the most promising present—and to the adult child, a greeting. Well Come, Wilma.

Wilma must breathe and wipe the tears and steady the trembling hands that hold the notebook in which her father greets her, a woman nearing seventy, his pen reaching from her infancy, from his young manhood. She must read this page many times and not go beyond it. At his desk he wrote to her. Pa, so long dead. Now, here, alive.

Excessively alive.

She puts the notebook down on the floor, she is kneeling on the floor still, kneeling at the corner of the living room where the boxes have been waiting for decades for attention beyond the dust cloth. She lays her hands over the words, tries to press them back into the page, flatten them. They are fat and wormy. Alma, wife of Henry, mother of Wilma, is loving them, they are making holes in the earth, they will be a good help. The earth is being plowed for planting by the good wormy words of good Henry Schuh.

All of which is rather grotesquely metaphorical and quite inaccurate as Alma herself would surely point out. *Humans plow, Wilma. Worms aerate.*

Excessive life bulging from words on a page is not a new experience for Wilma, nor is the act of laying hands on the page and pressing and pressing. Sometimes it's an unruly beast, language. Aside from the fact that her father wrote to *her*, aside from the implication that her infant nighttime needs kept him awake and thus prompted him to write again

7

after some hitherto unsuspected first burning (there was another, the Alzheimer's burning, the one she and Alma stopped part-way through, thus saving these notebooks, but she knows nothing of a first burning, nothing at all)—aside from all of this, look at the way his very mind was pressed—yes, pressed—pressed out into the language, arduously. Her own hands now press back.

Well, well. Henry appears to have worked his thought, just as he said. Already we can see it, can we not?

Yes, Alma. Yes, we can.

Read further, dear.

Wilma tenses, resists, but reads on.

The houses were made of stone in which we lived. I was the boy who left the stone houses, houses rigid with practical Catholicism, bound tight. I was bound another way, bounding forth. Call of Theosophy, child. A Siren's call, but all temptations are opportunities, remember that. The Madame herself in my hand, pages bound and bursting, The Secret Doctrine *was the book's title. Esoteric milk and honey from the mind of Madame Helena Blavatsky.*

Myself, so young. Boxcar riding, therefore. What else? On the journey east, inside one dark car among many, another book-reader. In a frenzy of wine-poison he thrust at me better salvation, though I could not yet know it. Deep ethics reaching into the brain, reaching inward and outward—both! to infinity! —and the least Godly god of all, god to whom commandment is foreign, obedience irrelevant, punishment unknown. God of reason and mystery, believable. Spinoza, as you will have guessed, his Ethics, *gift from a stranger in a boxcar. For the future, my future, when I was ready. May he, most essential philosopher, endure to the end of our days. My days and your days. Never trust those who hold he was an atheist. Never deprive our Baruch, our Benedict—Blessed is the very name— of his perfect eternal unGodly god-joy, Wilma.*

8

This is Henry Schuh, her Pa, talking god, god, god? And uncapitalized! Was she never told? Did Alma know? She cannot remember a single admonition in the direction of any god whatsoever. There were oddities after the Alzheimer's developed, regressions, confusions, Catholic fragments from the past thrown up, but in his right mind—

And the inevitable, unwanted question: is it because of her *father* that she finds herself bent in this mystical direction? His god sounds suspiciously like the very god she intends to encounter.

Henry's passion for philosophy, and for Spinoza above all, was no secret. She remembers the day she pronounced the name correctly for the first time. *Who is the first modern philosopher, little Wilma? Spinoza, Pa. Very good. Even the pronunciation, dear. Excellent.* She was four years old.

Spinoza was an element of the family air, but—

Spinoza: his architectural Ethics. Inside them, inside the building he made from mere words, mere human thought: secrets beyond all religion. The book was unread on my long journey East. Unread until the need came, daughter.

She remembers Spinoza's *Ethics.* It perished in the Alzheimer's burning, already a blackened sacrifice, unsalvageable by the time wife and daughter discovered Henry in action. Then, long after his death, she and Alma found a copy in the crowded aisles of Lyle's bookstore. *Henry's obsession*, said Alma. *Don't you think we ought to buy it?* They looked at each other, burst into giggles, and bought it.

It must be here somewhere.

Wilma is thus released from kneeling. Notebook A in hand, she approaches the bookcases. She and Henry made these. They follow the model of the sturdy, exact, practical carpentry her father produced for income now and then, bringing in just enough to supplement Alma's trust fund from her grandmother. Henry would say, did say again and again, that he was wealthy. The world would say otherwise, but he believed it. He had his mind and he had his hands and he had his tools.

Then he lost his mind.

He had us, Wilma.

9

Yes, Alma. His little hermit family.
That's right, dear.

The movers, struggling up the stairs to the apartment the day she and Alma moved in, damaged one of the bookcases, but the other three are unmarred. All are well-dusted, filled with books. The books are a blur. She's kept them clean, but somehow managed not to notice—

Here it is, *The Ethics*, by Baruch Spinoza who was apparently also called Benedict. She opens the book.

Part I

Concerning God

Definitions

1. By that which is self-caused I mean that whose essence involves existence; or that whose nature can be conceived only as existing.

The great philosopher starts with God. She must have known this. But did she? Henry was never effusive or even explicit about Spinoza's teachings, or those of any other philosopher. Was there any other, for him? He believed philosophy was the most individual of pursuits and directed Wilma to follow her own nose. *Sniff your way around the library, child.* He meant the Bangor Public Library, the family's mecca, half an hour's drive from home then (but only a lucky five-minute cycle from this apartment). *Sniff out your elixir, Wilma.* Sniff? Yes, that's what he said. Odd and solitary, Henry was not without humor. And never not serious.

Her nose was insufficient, but the librarian was delighted to recommend a starting place. She proceeded to read Will Durant's *Story of Philosophy*, pleased when Durant, who sounded like a smart nice man, expressed respect for Spinoza and quoted the great and difficult Georg Wilhelm Friedrich Hegel: "You are either a Spinozist or not a philosopher at all." Perhaps her father was not entirely eccentric. She could feel it herself—how philosophy might pull a person's mind to strange and creative places. Still, it would be years before she read more philosophy. She never read systematically, never quite seriously, and she's forgotten most of what she read. She forgot that Spinoza placed God at the very start. Durant must have conveyed this, but she forgot.

She reads again: "...whose essence involves existence—"

And again.

What God is and *that* God is are inextricable. For Spinoza, God's essence, she concludes, demands, needs, *sings* existence. Here is the being that cannot not-be.

Essence. Existence.

The dry words rise up, shimmer, enter each other. She watches, allows, does not try to press them back into the page. She endures, almost accepts, as if this were a sudden grace, a wind from nowhere. In fact, doesn't she feel such a wind?

And then not.

UnGodly god-joy wrote young Henry Schuh, father of infant Wilma.

Which is a suitable way to speak of it, thinks grown Wilma, as if she could judge. Truth: she is shaken. Shaken and suddenly aware of mundane matters. Her knuckles ache from their tight hold on the book. Her lumbar region—

These bones want to move.

Wilma has had a troublesome back for years. A graceless fall on an icy walk one hurried morning was all it took to change her pain-free physical life. A set of stretching exercises pulled her slowly out of real distress and if she's faithful to them they keep her comfortable enough. She's gotten accustomed to the frame they give her days, the way they guide her to work with muscles and tendons and ligaments. Inside the stretch a subtle and strangely buoyant energy is sometimes released, like a clear note expanding. Or, of course, the whole thing can be annoying. Down on the floor how many times now over the years, and yet again? She can become quite irritable over the necessity.

Now, however, it's only a relief to have a known thing to do. She gets her old blankets, folds them to form. They are her mat. Down she goes, one knee under her chest. She sinks, letting gravity stretch her left hip's muscles. And then the other side. Faithfully, scrupulously, she performs the entire routine. When she has put the blankets away she looks at Alma resting on the table. Or at the ceramic cube, container of Alma's ashes. Alma herself is not there on the table, she does know this.

Still, she feels the presence as she runs a glass of cold clear water and stands drinking it. For a quarter of a century—after Henry died, after Lorraine died and the house and land were sold—she and Alma lived here together. She can remember the rich taste of well water from the family home, her only other home, but city water is good enough, she's used to it now. Since Alma died, her thirst has increased. All day at intervals, a glass of water. There must be worse symptoms of grief, if that's what this is. She washes the glass and places it upside down in the drainer. Ridiculous work, this washing of the glass. She'll reuse it soon. Nevertheless, it satisfies. She dries her hands. The towel is green, a match to one of the candles standing sentry over Alma's cube. She has no brown towel, or she'd be displaying it, too, to give the candles equal echoes. Should she purchase a brown hand towel?

Certainly not.

Now, what else is this young father wanting to say?

I would leave. My determination was firm. Reversing the common route, I went east. Your mother was there, I could sense her in my deepest mind. Learning, too, was there. Let the others go west, or stay planted.

Much planting in the days of my youth. Planting and harvesting and stone-working and churchgoing. I come from Luxembourgers. Your mother does not. Our origins differ.

Unseen magnets exerted force: Steven. Alma. Your mother will tell you the entirety when she turns your way, when she sees her daughter in readiness. Of Steven I will not write. Nor of Theosophy, I see that now. Let it dissolve.

Steven. This must be the man she met, the one Alma searched and searched for, as if finding the priest could somehow reverse Alzheimer's. When was that? Soon after Henry was locked up in Pooler Pavilion among old Mainers with senile dementia and those not so old, struck early by Alzheimer's, like Henry himself. He would live there until he died. Alma, obsessed, looked for Steven Builder for months. One day he arrived, charismatic, upper class, a perfect visitor. He sat with Henry. They held hands. Alma smiled and let tears run down her cheeks, Hart Crane's *White Buildings* in one hand. Poems, held like a talisman. An aura with a boundary surrounded the three, a trio in their sixties. Wilma left to get herself a Pepsi from the machine down the hall.

As for Theosophy, it certainly dissolved. Never a word about *that*, at least not one she can remember. Henry's youthful Siren Song. Rather nice to know he had one.

But this attempt: the difficulty of Spinoza for my untaught mind. I, solitary reader, thrust thought-ward into the definitions, the axioms, the propositions, the proofs, corollaries, scholia. Digging, digging, digging into work that was meant never to finish itself. A frame I found, then: Natura Naturans, Natura Naturata. *The making and the made. Inside which, and ever forward, you come, newest one, and my own mind follows. You: made. You: born.*

Goodness, how opaque. Axioms. Corollaries. And the Latin phrases.

But doesn't she remember the rhythm of that Latin? Wasn't it almost a fundamental of her early childhood? *Natura Naturans. Natura Naturata.* Was her father more forthcoming about his Spinoza than she remembers? Perhaps when she was very young? And will she have to, now, follow? Her mind feels untaught, like Henry's, but even as she ponders the depth of her ignorance a fact comes running at her like a child barreling into a long-absent parent, head butting into belly of arriving mother or father, screech of agonized welcome erupting from young lungs.

Which experience Wilma Schuh never had, not as a child and not of course as a mother since she has no child. But here it is, the barreling fact: she was somehow prepared long ago. Prepared for this moment. As if she already knows her father's deepest mind.

Of course you do, Wilma.

No 'of course' about it, Alma.

Just read, dear.

So she reads.

Ah, to move against the page again. To anticipate a reader—if this be not burned. Let this not become burn-worthy, I beg it, I who do not beg. May this effort, may these pages, survive for

13

the sake of the mind of a father and for his daughter. A daughter new, and someday grown. Wilma. To work down into the page again! Out of the inner mind! Out! And to imagine— ah, Child—even such a reader as you, who might gather to yourself, to your mind's heart—

The page breaks off. Wilma is breathing heavily. Her father's emotions are filling and stressing her lungs. This is of course Henry Schuh in a very particular moment. The man is sleep-deprived, for one thing. And allowing himself a pleasure apparently long-denied: to write his thoughts. He does seem to take to the fact of her early existence. One might assume he's baby-wakened on more than one level.

What can we say now about this daughter, all grown up and reading the packed pages? She is filling up, but with what? Unanchored intensities, she might tell us. A phrase sufficiently indefinite. Was that the tiniest visit from a god a moment ago? Henry's or her own? Are they one and the same? The wind from nowhere—essence, existence—the ecstatic whirl of their union. This is the result of reading her father's writing? Of opening a book by his favorite philosopher? It is as if something wild has invaded her deliberate, practical soul.

Wilma Schuh's late-life project might be taking an unexpected turn.

She had her plan: after they all died—Henry, Lorraine, Alma—she would find again a path discovered in childhood. The plan was made during Lorraine's illness, shortly after the diagnosis. Henry had died years before, Lorraine would die within the year, Alma was already seventy-five years old. When all three were gone, when she was alone, she would proceed. That her mother would live to be a hundred was not anticipated, but Wilma is not inclined toward impatience and a long incubation for such a project might be best, she's often thought so.

The plan was to find and follow the childhood path, the one the god lived on, the one those three would find inconsequential. Inconsequential? What she meant was *silly*. They would find it silly, or so she thought.

The plan was to proceed in solitude. Unaccompanied. Unaccompanied by any of the three human beings—Henry, Alma, Lorraine—who sometimes seem to be all she is made of.

Wilma Schuh, concoction of others.

14

Untrue, and she knows it. The invisible ingredient in Wilma—and, frankly, the most cherished, the most delicious—is something entirely private. When she tastes herself it is there. She would tell you, if she spoke of such a thing, that her particularity has never lost its flavor. She would link this to her childhood god.

If she were to speak of such a thing.

But here is Henry—

Inside the little hermit family, much space opened up. The psyches were quite separate. Attentions went to individual interests. Then came Lorraine, but Lorraine did not see everything, though she saw much. Wilma guarded her invisible ingredient. When she made her plan, she envisioned a stride out on her own—toward a god of her own.

But here is her father's notebook—passionate—god-seeking—

On with it, girl. Alma is looking over her shoulder, impatient as a child to have the page turned.

It is a wrestle begun. A few years now of reading his book—not even a decade—the wine-poisoned gift-giving boxcar rider's book. The Ethics. *I fear he's dead now, that boxcar rider. He claimed his eyes could no longer—*

Perhaps he knew I needed the hard bread of philosophy. I thank him.

The book. Authored by Spinoza, exiled Jew, fresh from the centuries. Some write into, out of, eternity. Simultaneously here-embedded. Spinoza is one, the one who is mine. Will your days remember a man named Albert Einstein? Scientist. Seems to have an interesting brain. Believes in the god of Spinoza.

Ah, this century! How it proceeds, spreading backward and forward.

And Spinoza, embracing Time as he stands firm upon Eternity. I see him reaching round, one arm stretched over the past, the other over the future, all of it pulled to his heart. Joy! Intuitive intellectual joy from god-knowledge that escapes the bindings

15

of religion! Living necessity, bursting through to godly freedom!

If I could convey, Baby Wilma—

If I could give to you—

A life's work.

There stops the worked thought of the opening pages of Notebook A. Blank pages follow. Wilma knows she has consumed enough. More, today, would certainly constitute excess. She hopes the ghost of her mother agrees.

~ ~ ~

Alive but old, old, and older, Alma Jones Schuh faded to an absence in her final years. As Wilma sees it, the arc of Alma's life moved from absence to presence to absence. Absent was the young mother, off working the garden under her hat, or gazing at the sky, or reading her Rilke. Absent was the wife of the man with early Alzheimer's, sitting with her institutionalized husband who had come to the end of his useable mind, occasionally reading a poem to him in a blank voice, expecting no response, a woman dulled at the end of her difficult days, staring into her own middle distance. Absent even the widow in her early seventies, a solitary woman walking the land, still reading, reading, reading poetry.

But with the jolt of Lorraine's death, Alma came to vivid presence and stayed—stayed until very old age when she finally faded away, as absent as her younger selves ever were. Toward the end, in bed, eyes closed, a flutter of shallow breaths, Alma was barely a wisp in the room, though there were times—exceptions—when the eyes of the mother brightened, or hardened, or softened, demanded, or released, astonishing the watchful daughter. But for the most part, a wisp in the room.

Wilma was quite busy, tending her fading mother, but as Alma slept hour after daytime hour, a version of solitude would sometimes enter the apartment like a character from an old story set down South—a stranger

16

come to tea, eccentric, keeping her veiled hat on, failing to speak but sipping from a thin small cup politely enough. Solitude as companion then, thought Wilma.

Alma's death seemed to complete the long arc. Home from the grocery store, Wilma bent to kiss her mother's cheek and found it cold. More than anything else, the moment was simple. The simplicity was a comfort. Now would come total absence. Alma, gone.

Instead: presence! Alma as ashes, demanding to be held. Alma the ghost, hovering, commenting. But reality is various, as Wilma has observed from childhood on. The days since Alma died, haunted enough, have also been abundant with solitude—real solitude, which is nothing like a woman with a veiled hat sipping tea from a delicate cup. It is robust, full of possibility. Soon—after Alma agrees to be scattered—Wilma will set out, alone, to find the god she glimpsed in childhood. Or such was the plan.

Now this plunge into Henry's writing. A threat. A plain threat. Her father's mind endures, his worked thought. Henry's hand is offered again —as if the two of them will work together, tackle another project around the house, only this one is a bit different. Contacting a god is not like building a bookcase.

Or is it?

Enough of that. Wilma has risen to a new day. Alma in her cube will be held, her quiet insistence will be honored. Involved with Alma, Wilma expects to be happily delayed. Impossible while thus occupied to approach the dreaded second notebook, labeled not B but W. Let the W stand for anything other than her own name, prays Wilma to no god at all.

So she sits and holds the glossy box. Almost absentmindedly, she removes the lid, begins to sift through. The ash is soft, a comfort of sorts. She takes a sharp breath when she feels the unexpected fragments of bone. Her mother's bones are in her hands.

But aren't they quite lovely? Gifts from a ghost, then. She chooses three of the tiny sculptures, sets them aside. They will rest on the bedroom dresser, joining the stones and shells collected on trips to the ocean. Lorraine, who had quickly decided to broaden the lives of the little Maine women she found herself living with (Wilma, Alma) insisted they go to Schoodic Point, see the pale pink granite with its striations of

17

black; took them there three times, then never again. Why never again? A question unasked. Perhaps she forgot about the ocean. She did tend to set out in a direction, go forward, then turn another way and seem never to look back. Classical music was a brief interest, a new album every month, listened to repeatedly. All three of them, sitting and listening. Then not. Her poor mind was busy, that was it. But are the stones and shells from another place, not Schoodic, after all? Up so high above the water, did Schoodic yield such things? Perhaps the gulls dropped them.

Wilma closes the ceramic cube, sets it on the table, gently washes the three pieces of bone, and dries them. On the dresser she sees the feather. She hasn't noticed it lately. The scene comes to her in that movie-like way, action rolling out in clear colors, Lorraine arriving home with an eagle feather, child-thrilled. "Look! Look what I found!" The woman had a sharp and innocent sense of the beautiful. The thought pleases her surviving lover. At this moment it pleases her greatly, a stream of freedom rushing through.

She places Alma's three bone fragments on their own little doily. There was a period after Lorraine's death when Alma crocheted while the two of them, mother and daughter, listened to the news from National Public Radio after their "early repast." Alma liked to twist an old word back into use. *Repast*, she'd say, and smile.

The time has come. Wilma will approach the cardboard box, retrieve Notebook W. She sets out in that direction as if starting on a long trek, then swerves and finds herself at the bookcases. Alma's favorite translation of Rilke's work was by Stephen Mitchell. Lyle, sitting at his old scratched desk, was reading when they entered the underlit bookstore one winter day. He looked up. His eye pulled Alma over, his one good eye. He handed her the book. No words. None needed. Lyle knew his customer. Toward the end, Alma would sometimes suggest that Wilma read to her. "Let's have a bit of Stephen's Rilke, shall we?" The poems were a potion. They quickened memory, foretold the future. They were pain-killers, they were sleeping pills whose side-effect was splendid dreaming. "I've had a splendid dream, dear. It's the Rilke." The briefly alert but mostly absent mother would drift back to sleep. Or to some state near sleep, a state preferred to presence. Or was it a state beyond preference, something entirely other than willful departure?

Yes, that would be it, dear. Only the unwilled, at the end.

18

Pondering Rilke's various uses, distracted by her mother's ghost, Wilma is almost able to ignore the pulsations in her tensed hand. Even closed, the book has power. There is a lively residue here from Alma's fingers tracing the lines year after year after year.

And from my mind, dear, which is moving about among the living words, spilling itself just a bit. Containment can be difficult. You won't be bothered, not once you've gotten accustomed.

Wilma wonders if she will somehow find herself meeting her mother's actual mind, after she lets go of this ghostly whimsy.

What on earth does she mean by such a question, though?

Minds, in the family, were somewhat separate from the person. "I notice my mind wants go to the old field today," Alma would say, and put on her wide-brimmed straw hat and walk away, an apple and a book of poetry—not always Rilke or Hart Crane, there were others—inside the small backpack she took from its nail in the hall where jackets, sweaters, and a practical selection of hats also hung, hats for each season, kept there year round. The frayed and faded canvas backpack was essential. Alma needed her hands for touching tree trunks, grasses, the warm dark ground; or, in winter, ice against the edge of a rut in the road. During the years following Lorraine's death, Wilma might join her mother on a walk. Conversation would be much in progress until the abrupt moment when Alma had to stoop and touch. Wilma, feeling a little large, a little stolid, almost elderly beside such behavior, waited. Alma—seventy-five, eighty, eighty-five—stooping and touching, looked up at her daughter then, smiling. It was the time of presence.

And now again. Alma in ghost form, even more present and certainly more demanding than in the years after Lorraine's death, though she was far from absent then. When Lorraine died it was as if the mother aspect of Alma flew in from another dimension, arriving for the very first time in sudden color, friendly, and tall. Noticeably tall. Grown mother and grown daughter would henceforth approach reality as working partners.

Alma *was* tall, the only one in the family with any height. This was true in absent periods also. Certainly it was.

Get on with it, girl.

What a demanding mother you've become.

Yes, dear.

Impossible to sit with Rilke, untouched since the day before Alma died, without, too, bringing Henry. A parent in each hand, obviously necessary. Wilma approaches the boxes, takes Notebook W, sits on the couch. But doesn't she need a drink of water? She does.

Set Rilke down. Set Notebook W down. Leave a generous space between the two for the return of the daughter who will settle and read. In a minute. Run the glass of water full, drink it down. Decide while drinking who is to be tackled first, the father with his worked thought or the mother's poet who cannot be separated from the mother's soul.

We need a bit of Rilke just now, dear.

I suppose we do, Alma.

Truth be told, Henry is the greater threat, though why this should be is not only an unanswered question but one Wilma has no time to ask since Rilke vibrates again in her hand. And of course Alma is right. This is after all her time. Dying produces that: a *time*. Attentions go to the recently departed or even, as in this case, to the not quite fully departed. Alma is perched on Wilma's right shoulder. She is not exactly impatient. Entitled might be the better word. Or queenly. The mother knows that if she wants Rilke she will get Rilke.

Wilma takes a deep breath. She is making a good attempt, trying to please her ghost mother, but her shoulders suddenly collapse. Alma slips from queenly mode. No harm done. She lands nicely, stands, pats herself firm. Now she is the motherly encourager. Versatile Alma. *Open it like a Bible, dear. Remember the Bible? Those lovely neighbors. You must invite them, Wilma.* Wilma squares her shoulders. She remembers the Bible and the lovely neighbors. But as for inviting them—she hasn't spoken to them in years, nor even driven past the old place. *That hardly matters, dear. We need the land, for the scattering of me. Didn't I instruct you?*

Thus it is that, opening Rilke like a Bible, letting her eyes fall as fated, Wilma understands that the scattering of her mother's ashes will take place on the family's old land, sold to the neighbors after Lorraine died; and that the neighbors, fervent Catholics, will be invited to the event. *But not too soon, Wilma. No, Alma, not too soon.* Her eyes have fallen on the first of the *Duino Elegies.*

being dead is hard work

20

*and full of retrieval before one can gradually feel
a trace of eternity.*

She lays her hand over the passage but feels no need to press the poet's words back into the page. In fact the words, which she has after all read and reread to her mother, are a comfort. Possibly, whimsy aside, Alma *is* here. Possibly Alma has work to do, hard retrieval work. Perhaps—here is the startling thought—what Alma needs to retrieve, more than Rilke, is her Henry. Could this be?

Yes, dear.

Wilma Schuh, devoted daughter, puts Rilke down and opens her father's Notebook W. The first page is a list—a table of contents perhaps —or a series of intentions—a roadmap—

Who
What
When
Where
Why

At the bottom of the page is a determined, pressed out, stomping line of letters.

WILMA SCHUH, DAUGHTER

Which letters Wilma has to stare at for some long moments and then cover with both hands and press; thereby flattening them back into mere print.

~ ~ ~

Wilma is on her bicycle, peddling toward the storefront on Third Street where the words above the unwashed window fade from their original red a little more each year. She feels a need to decipher them every time—*Lyle's Bookstore*—as if to assure herself she's in the right place. She is carrying the news, unless Lyle reads the obituaries, which possibility she doubts.

21

One-eyed Lyle. Bit of a hunched back, overly thin. Frayed at the edges, the sleeves and pant-legs. Is he frayed in some other way, too? He doesn't wear an eye-patch. His lid is scarred and glued down, so much a part of his wrinkled face that it's scarcely an ugliness. The thing about Lyle is that he's basically immaterial, hardly a matter of an actual bodied being at all. So said Alma more than once. His role today will be to distract. Who can endure the ghost of a mother and the written remains of a father without looking elsewhere from time to time? A modicum of conversation with the living is required. Besides, Lyle must be informed, and invited to the scattering. He might even agree to come. Wilma finds, somewhat to her surprise, that she would welcome him. She intends to read Rilke's sonnet, as directed by Alma, and to Lyle the poem might even be comprehensible. Or he might be appalled at the idea of getting into a car with her, the two of them alone, driving out to the country; appalled, too, at the intensity of the event, preferring to remain in his store with its back room "where a narrow bed and other necessities reside," as Alma phrased it. Wilma stays astride her bicycle, unable to move, looking at the tired but persistent letters. *Lyle's Bookstore*. The man should not be surprised at the death of a centenarian. But perhaps he doesn't believe in death, or is inclined to doubt the particular death of the eternal Alma Schuh. Perhaps. She parks the bicycle.

It's one of his good days. He looks up when she enters and almost smiles. He stands near his desk, book open, as if the reading impulse overtook him before he could sit, but he often reads standing, at random locations around the store.

"Wilma."

"I have news, Lyle."

This is unusual enough to keep his attention from his book. What is his book? She can't quite see. But he can see her. See into, when he wants to. He'll wait forever, silent, until she can—

But she can't.

"I lack the words," she says finally. This is unexpected, as are the tears that rise and drip.

"Gone, then," is Lyle's response. He hands her a tissue, pulled from the desk drawer as if it were part of the bookstore's service, along with recommendations for reading, making change, tearing off the register's

22

receipt, and at the end of the transaction—only at Lyle's—a handshake brief and dry. All that and tissues, too.

"Did you know?"

"How would I know?"

"Well, the obituary."

"I forego the paper. I have a speech about that, a decade or so old. Care to hear it?"

"Well."

"When?"

"Two weeks today."

"No wonder then."

He must mean her tears: no wonder tears appear and wash over your naked face. But it's a wonder to her, this unanticipated wash, this nakedness. She receives a second tissue.

"I'll sit," Lyle says.

So Wilma sits too, in the chair for the customer next to the stacks. Lyle's store is like a library, the shelves like stacks, using space efficiently. She estimates the distance between this man and herself. Seven feet, desk chair to customer chair. They can converse but need not mingle their exhalations. They are not permitted to collapse, either of them, for both chairs are straight-backed. This is an advantage.

The silence goes on. Alma would say, "With Lyle Franklin a person can be alone." This was a compliment. The tears dry up after a while. Nose-blowing stops. It occurs to Wilma that someone else might be in the store, some quiet other customer tucked in toward the back, reading and rereading the same dense page. There are a lot of dense pages here, incomprehensible at first reading.

"The air is emptier without her," Lyle says.

Wilma ponders this. The air at home is quite occupied.

Here we are, she thinks, Wilma Schuh and Lyle Franklin. How odd.

But not as odd as if Alma's ghost were to join them, what a thought.

"You might have a book for me," she says.

Lyle looks at her, nods, and limps into the stacks. His is a minor, familiar, undisturbing limp. Perhaps it's only that his legs don't quite match, or it could be some old injury. She doesn't know him well. Always it was Alma and Lyle, the two of them like puppies going over the ground together, stopping to sniff the same spot. Henry, who sent

23

twelve-year-old Wilma out to sniff her way around the library, might have one day sent Alma out too, but Alma chose not to be on her own, she found Lyle, companion seeker of the world's literary odors.

Wilma, dry enough now to notice her own thoughts, ponders the canine species, how dogs will work a neighborhood, sniffing, lifting legs, producing streams. Not exactly like Alma or Lyle. Though there *was* a way they were like puppies, those two. Innocence, maybe. That could be the connection. Still, the image is a strange one. No doubt it's inappropriate. If not hilarious. Or hysterical. Well, never mind.

Lyle is known for acute recommendations—as if he enters the mind of a customer, then exits and flies over his substantial stock, locates the exact book, flies back with it, hands it over. Generally no eye contact is offered, but the book is purchased by a pleased, or at least intrigued, customer—and then the handshake, quick and complete. But Wilma has never been the customer, she was only here with Alma. When Alma could no longer leave the apartment, she came on behalf of Alma. Still, Lyle has been a sort of step-father, though he's closer to her age than Alma's. "He's only six years older than you, dear, but I don't suppose you're interested." Interested in Lyle? What a thought. Lyle was the wrong gender, and essentially the wrong generation, no matter his actual birthdate. Besides, he was *Lyle*. But Alma was only clearing the path for herself. Not that she would seduce him in any obvious or carnal way— she was still a married woman with a living husband. That her husband was chained inside Alzheimer's disease and now suddenly locked up further in that unlikely place in Bangor gave no leave for immoral doings, but she needed a flirtation of the mind and she needed it with a person of the male variety. Was Wilma shocked? No, she assured her mother, she was not shocked.

But was she? It was a rupture: Alma reaching out and taking.

Here's Lyle, book in hand. *Keep This Deep and Velvet Night: A Self-Portrait*. Wilma accepts the book, stares at the title. Death as a deep and velvet night? The author is Michael Chaim Solomon. Solomon: wise man. A bit obvious. Lyle's standards might be slipping. Of course he did just learn of the death of his perhaps best friend.

"Explain," she says.

Lyle looks at her for a long time. "Poems in there about losing someone who got sewn into his life, how the rip out was rough. Gay fellow, from the sound of it. It says on the back that he's a psychotherapist. Seemed amiable enough when he brought the copies in. Courteous. Surprised to find himself with a published book, if I remember right. I only read bits here and there. I don't know, Wilma, it's a stretch. I have no skill for you yet."

She nods and buys the book and they make their arrangements because, yes, he would appreciate the opportunity to see Alma put to rest. Saturday will be fine, he'll close the store, a worthy reason. He'll be happy to meet the O'Connors, Alma spoke well of them. And the quick dry handshake, no extra squeeze.

~ ~ ~

Wilma bikes a circuitous route home. The compact little volume resting inside Alma's small frayed pack bounces lightly against her back. Here and there she spots them—pansies, nature's velvet. This is not a spontaneous emergence of pattern, it is sought, constructed. Mr. Solomon's title has brought forth a clarity: she is in need of pansies, deep and velvet. Alma grew them long ago.

Pedaling along, she lets her mind wander over the realities. Alma's ashes will be scattered on Saturday, this Saturday, as has been arranged with the benevolent former neighbors, current owners of the old Schuh land and house. The O'Connors still live their own house, rent out the one full of her childhood and so much of her adult life. Lyle, whose presence is apparently necessary for both mother and daughter, will be there. Lyle and Wilma and the tolerant Catholics, a modest gathering. Perhaps a flake or two of Alma will settle on a pansy. But will the garden be kept up?

Never mind, dear. I feel a need for the essential shelter of trees. Rely on a breeze to carry a small particle to the garden. You remember that impressive pine not far along the path into the woods. Nothing sturdier could be wanted. Perhaps a little handful of my ash just where it rises out of the ground, and then fling me. Don't fuss, Wilma.

Alma is right. Wilma's plan—that the tiny group would stand in the field near the garden, exposed to open sky—just stand there, spiritually naked—suddenly seems beyond contemplating. This mother, whose writing (hidden, unexpected) she has discovered, requires a protected

25

resting place. Beyond the blank pages of Henry's autobiographical Notebook A were more entries, some having to do with Alma. Then came anguished paragraphs on Alzheimer's. Alma placed her own writing, ten or twelve pages—her own version of an autobiography—deep in toward the back. She wrote, not without difficulty it would seem, long after Henry himself was gone. Wilma imagines a blind insertion, the wife with closed eyes opening the notebook and tucking her writing in quickly—as if slipping between the sheets of the marital bed, a shy bride. Did she read Henry's work? Did she at least glance? Her writing claims she did not.

Wilma has in the last few days been inside every notebook her father left. At times, for pages, she has read seriously. Often she has glanced and moved elsewhere. True to his word, Henry did not date entries, nor did he offer any other obeisance to time as an organizing factor. Like Spinoza, he was writing into and out of eternity. Entries from various stages of life sit side by side. The notebooks have topics but lose track of them readily. Stones are a theme. One page read only, "Inside stone houses, stone life." Another: "Low creek taking sun. Wet stones. Dark shine." Notebook A ended with Henry's contemplation of a photograph of the extended Schuh family. He was the well-behaved toddler in the front row, quite as expressionless as the rest of the family: stony. The precise handwriting became shaky. Primary entries and marginalia both show this change—a clue that helps to satisfy an unexpected historical curiosity in his daughter. No matter how shaky it becomes, the penmanship never fails to convey a sense of heedfulness. *Careful hand and careful mind, little Wilma. Remember that.*

The dreaded Notebook W—dreaded for reasons now partly understood—did in fact focus on Wilma. First tooth and first step and first word were recorded and pondered, as if the notebook were a philosophical version of a Baby Book, a thing commonly used to record the progress of a childhood, as Wilma learned when Lorraine, bringing her own, moved in. It was Lorraine's role to educate the Schuh women, teach them how normal humans lived. Surely there had never been a Baby Book like this one. The first tooth led to a meditation on intake and elimination and a broad set of thoughts on the interconnectedness of species and other biological facets of *extension* which was—Wilma, reading, was reminded—an attribute of Spinoza's God, along with

26

thought. Thought and extension, those two: the only divine attributes humans are capable of knowing. But Spinoza insists there has to be an infinity of others. So wrote Henry. A short paragraph on a page all its own, told of a day Wilma wore a red dress, fell against a rough rock, and cried. Henry came upon her, a sobbing disintegrating young human with a skinned knee. *Oh my little god*, he said as he took her into his arms. Henry's older mind found space on the page to return and comment, return and comment. In less and less steady handwriting he added his precise thought to the initial story. It had not been pity, he wrote. Pity reduced. Spinoza was right, one must never pour such a thing over another being. Neither was it worship—Spinoza's God evoked no worship, not as active, in-forming *Natura Naturans*, not as receptive, in-formed *Natura Naturata*. The young father had been in tears when he named his daughter god. He reported the tears in the margin in shaky penmanship, as if the older, much older, mind needed this detail confessed at last. The least competent hand wrote: "She, Wilma, is. As the great god of Israel, the I Am, is. She. Is."

And here she is indeed, a woman nearing seventy years of age who has gotten off her bicycle and now sits cross-legged on the cracked sidewalk of a questionable neighborhood in Bangor, Maine in the season of spring. She is giving one little patch of pansies its due attention. The pansies also exist. Someone planted them. Someone cares for them. The party appears not to be home. No sign of life disturbs her solitude. The street is empty.

Perhaps she contemplates the pansies on behalf of her mother who (this must be admitted) now lacks the human eye. She who used sight for the purposes of her own soul can no longer see. Her eyes are ash.

Wilma sits numbly on the sidewalk, then shakes herself to full consciousness. Henry was the writer, never Alma. But there they were, Alma's pages. An entire mother poured herself out in a smoother, looser, more comfortable hand than Henry's. The material itself was, in its own style, as intense and intelligent as Henry's own, and it was definitely more succinct. True, Alma's writing meandered—according to a certain whimsy, if Wilma is not mistaken—but it got its business completed and it stopped. It lacked Henry's insistence, his ongoing demand. It allowed, as a pansy allows the eye, freely offering its existence. She reaches out to touch a petal, but directs her hand instead to the ground, to the pansy's grey city dirt which is a tad dry, a bit like ash. She rubs the dirt between thumb and fingers. It is more substantial than ash, really. Ash is so finely textured—it occupies the border—the boundary where substance stops— one step further and it would enter the invisible.

A physicist would disagree, dear.

I know that, Alma.

But *is* the business of Alma's writing completed? The last paragraph breaks off. Alma leaves the reader—the daughter—hanging there, unsatisfied. Perhaps it's a matter of discretion. Whatever the reason, Alma never managed to approach Lorraine's death, falling to silence or veering to distraction despite stated intentions, and she broke off before writing about the year Wilma turned twelve. Perhaps it's best. There might be limits, natural limits.

Sitting next to the pansies, looking into their depths, breathing cautiously, Wilma remembers taking her mother's pages into her hands. It was sufficient for a while simply to *hold* the unexpected pages and refrain from placing them on the floor and flattening the loose and lovely unread lines. But soon it became necessary to read what Alma had written.

~ ~ ~

Alma's Writing

It is five years since I participated in the death of my daughter's lesbian lover, Lorraine. It is autumn and I will soon achieve eighty years of life. Death and endurance meet in my mind. I think to write. But writing was Henry's sphere. With some trepidation I enter his sphere.

"I think to write." Did Henry once say the reverse, that a human writes to think? Will matters here become a bit topsy-turvy? Never mind. I proceed despite.

On this anniversary of Lorraine's death, Adam comes to my dream. Death is the link. I discover myself at his small grave with the little marble marker, a place much visited throughout my childhood. Each blade of grass is carved to clarity. The green stuns my sight and I fall back in time. I am floating to the house, floating up the steps of the wide porch with its columns. It is the Hour Between. Adam is not alive, nor is

28

he buried. He is dead in the house. I stand at the foot of the tiny coffin in the Great Parlor of the house I am to grow up in.

Surely I cannot remember the dimensions of my twin's coffin, nor would it have seemed tiny to me. I was a child of eighteen months.

But the dream insists. I see the gray shine of the tiny coffin, how it stands on its thin metal legs in the parlor, how the adults sit on the straight chairs that line the walls, watching and silently weeping. I toddle and reach out to touch the black-clad knees one by one by one. Adam is there, over in the corner. He wants a drink. No one else can hear him, only I. Dink, dink. Dink, dink.

Perhaps we never heard Lorraine as she expressed her thirst? Such thirst! And all of it for the intangible. Expelled from the Catholic convent, what rivers of shame ran beneath that parched surface? An overabundance of reaching plants sprouted from Lorraine, even if a bit spindly, white where they ought to be greening. Thirsty plants, with unreachable rivers beneath. Such things are possible, are they not?

Lorraine. Not a moment of boredom with that woman. Not for me, not for Wilma. On this we agree. But the depths. I do suspect entire rivers far inside the vast territory of that being—from which no one could drink, in which no one could swim. Unless of course at night, my daughter and her lover, together—information I was not privy to, nor should I have been. Finally, as ever in life, there is mystery. I will say this. I am pleased to think Wilma has not lived a life deprived of the sexual. I am greatly pleased to contemplate this simple fact. She knows the surge.

Well.

In the womb we melded, Adam and I. After birth we lived in Mother's two arms or in the wide cradle carpentered for us. The cradle, the solid fact of it, is memory, not at all imagined. It never left us, though we twins left it, moving to the short wide crib. Everything for us was designed, unusual, suited to twinship. After Adam died I rolled in the wide crib, side to side, side to side. I believe, with unfounded ongoing insistence, that this happened. Perhaps Father told me. In time I moved to my sleigh bed, sized for a single child. Many dolls were needed then to fill the empty cradle and the wide crib in my large room full of beds never removed. It was a way of living, to leave nothing behind, to preserve. Adam was thus preserved.

29

In Mother's dullness, in every slow gesture of hers, Adam is kept. When he comes in dreams, Mother is hovering. She is an undulating mother-ghost surrounding her bright baby. She is the Mother of After Adam Died, a long dirge.

Father explains. Your mother is grieving. I am age five, age six. I belong to Father now, while Mother grieves.

No, that is not accurate. I assume five or six only because I am unwilling to credit my own mind. Thinking now—writing, this moment—I understand. I had to be much younger. It was when I turned three that Mother came back to daily life. She looked at me, a shine upon her, a burnishing. The time of her hidden face was ended.

The dark and the bright control my childhood memories, as if life then were filmed in black and white, strong contrast, chiaroscuro. It was much before the age of technicolor, we knew nothing of that. Even the dolls are darkly grumpy now, or they smile with a surfeit of shine, but I give one a red and perky dress and set her in the center of the short wide crib. She stays there.

And, yes, there is the green of the cemetery grass. There is that.

Mother's brightness was turned on me, a blaze of attention. I was now her child. I lived in the little sailor outfit, Mother's boy. I have a photo somewhere.

Here. Here I am, in my sailor suit and here is the date. I am in fact three years of age.

When Father is away Mother calls me Adam which is a secret and Father must never know. I am proud when I am Adam. I extend my child height and act my part. Does Father suspect?

The years blur. Father needed a graceful delicate girl child. Never would another child enter this family, so he must make the best of it and I must play for him my feminine part. This I had no talent for. When Father called, I stumbled, coughed, placed my feet wrong. He meant no harm.

By the time I turned twelve I understood—consciously, I grasped— that I could not offer a proper presence to either parent. The great gift of withdrawal had come to me. Alone, I watched the sky. Never again would I watch the sky with Mother.

In earlier years Mother and I go often to the orchard to look upward. I am her companion then and do not have to be Adam, he is in the high distance. It is a rest from the honor and the striving. Not being

Adam is a rest. Now I am definitely five or six years of age. Seven. Eight. Nine. I train my eyes toward the point in the sky Mother indicates. I try to see. I do see—once—what Mother sees each time, the ghostly essence of a toddling boy child. He smiles a sweet young ghost smile. Very young.

It was difficult for Mother, I now realize, when I began to resist. I remember my tenth birthday. What I wanted as my birthday gift, for that one day, was to stay indoors. I wanted not to look for Adam in the sky. It saddened her. She understood I was beginning my departure. By twelve I had completed it.

All this time I, too, kept Adam. This was my secret. He lived in me and grew with me.

I am twelve, taking my solitude which includes Adam. We watch the real sky. Unlike Mother, we have no need for the ghostly apparition. Together, over the years—age thirteen, fourteen, fifteen, and on and on—Adam and I will come to understand that the real sky is a blend of the given and the stolen, icon of unpredictability, of shift and change. Also of constancy, of the eternal. All elements play in the sky which is mood-maker, tease, and comforter.

When the days of the dust bowl arrive and I hear of the faraway troubles, I in my safe place at the eastern edge of this great land nurture a secret excitement that only Adam can understand. Even earth is in the sky now, as we always knew it would be. Earth, air, fire, water. The whirl of all, in the sky.

The dust bowl days. Was it then, when times were hard for many but somehow not for my family, that Steven entered my life? Yes, when the college men came for dances. I, privileged college girl, met Steven, privileged college boy. Steven gave me Rilke, a great gift. He took from me, too. He took the better part of Henry. Considerable complications developed that year. Steven was older, but still in college. I think that is accurate. Yes, there had been his year in the Catholic seminary and perhaps a year to recover from that before he was firmly on his way as a non-seminarian, a simple student. He intended never to go back, never to pursue the priesthood. The young do not know their futures.

Henry was not a registered student but along he came, wandering the campuses, whether the men's or the women's, breathing intellectually saturated ungendered air, as he put it. He was a ragged campus eccentric, sublimely intriguing. Eros struck me. I learned that what I felt

31

for Steven was human awe, but for Henry I felt plain fatal love. Smitten. We were age-mates but I do not think Henry came to replace Adam.

No, it was Rilke who replaced Adam and for that I remain in Steven's debt, for it was time. Steven brought the poets. Not only Rilke. Hart Crane was in fact his passion. How we poured over White Buildings, *the three of us.*

Steven and I gathered to our mutual bosom this strange pilgrim Henry, this penniless traveler who could quote Spinoza. There was an upspringing of interest in Spinoza at the time. The forgotten philosopher had been found. No one could understand Spinoza but everyone knew he was of utmost importance. Then came Henry who appeared ready to devote his life to reading a single book by this singular philosopher. The Ethics.

Neither Steven nor I possessed a philosophical mind but we lived to watch Henry exercise his. Already he was working his thought, off by himself, scribbling away, indoors and out, emerging from hidden corners in wretched ecstasy. And talking. At that point Henry was driven to speech. "Listen to this," he would say. "Spinoza says, 'By reality and perfection I mean the same thing.' How can he say that? He believes it. Everything spins to a new level! And all he's doing here is giving his definitions. He hasn't even made his argument. The axioms, the propositions..." He would look with hungry expectation from Steven to me, and back to Steven. We felt the depth as readers of poetry will feel the depth of what they cannot understand. And of course we were both in love with Henry.

*

To make a seamless narration must be the mind's delight. But perhaps not Nature's. I have let this little effort of mine lie in the drawer for an entire month. It roused me to discomfort and a set of sleepless nights. I thought to let it cool. It cooled. I might say it congealed, unpleasantly. There were days when I remembered it with distaste. Days, too, when I forgot it entirely, only to wake in the night with a sense of the unfinished upon me. Now I have read it through and laughed at the bulge in our history that memory refused to bring forth. Even as I prepare to confess, I doubt my own mind. Could we three have bonded in the

32

strange regions of—theosophy? It seems to do justice to none of us. And yet—

I suppose I find it embarrassing. Why else would I give theosophy the unpleasant designation of a "bulge"?

Such good minds my boys had, and I thought my own quite sophisticated by then. A college education, after all, even of the female variety, included a bit of exposure to Great Thinkers.

But it is true. I remember now. When Henry first appeared, the book in his hand was not Spinoza's Ethics. *It was Madame Blavatsky's* The Secret Doctrine. *Spinoza waited in Henry's dusty satchel. It was there, it had traveled with him, but it was not his first offering.*

So. Theosophy, the embarrassing bulge, or appendage, that does not attach with grace to any part of our fine intellectual history. We spent a few months—or perhaps it was only weeks?—immersed. But was Henry not already disenchanted? Straddling the ways, did he not, even in our first days, begin to quote what he called the cleaner thought? Spinoza, with his deliberate discipline, gave a high pure philosophical air to breathe. So said Henry. Madame Blavatsky began to choke him with her plethora of specificities. And such claims she made to esoteric certainty!

Still, I do wonder if Henry saw the ghost of theosophy playing, calling to him through the years like a mischievous child from hidden places inside the careful structures of Spinoza's argument. I know he aligned with those who declared his philosopher God-intoxicated and scorned those who thought him an atheist. I remember Spinoza was a Jew, banished by the leaders of his own congregation.

Banished with vehemence, for independent thought. How Henry loved that about him.

But first there was theosophy. I would open Henry's copy of The Secret Doctrine *at random. One day I found reference to a goose. A goose! It became clear she was a symbol of Divine Wisdom. I laughed out loud. The Hindu name was Hansa. This is my only firmly-held piece of esoteric trivia. The dear goose is offered milk mixed with water. She wisely separates the two, drinks the nourishing milk, and rejects the thin, colorless water. I suppose the good Madame then found a path from milk to breast to goddess, or perhaps to Mother Earth. There was an abundance of imagery in the book, some of it quite lovely. But the glut and hubris of it, the chaos!*

Steven liked Blavatsky better than I. He, after all, appreciated the density of his beloved Hart Crane, the crowded stanzas, the braided images that so often snarled, tangled, at least for me. But they could be combed to shining beauty, those images, each strand glistening. I learned.

Also, Steven had the religious thirst. Oh, yes, he had that. Which theosophy might have satisfied more adequately than the stringent Spinoza whom he could not read. Well, neither could I. I believe Wilma managed, for a while. She was not her father, though, and did not persist.

Nor was she her mother.

At any rate, one day we all threw up our hands, our theosophy phase ended. Steven then led us through Crane. One green and sunny afternoon as we sat together in the shade of a large tree he read Crane's "Legend" to us. This was not the esoteric goose with her explicit lesson to teach. This was truly mystery upon mystery. I stared into the poem's silent mirror, was stunned by the realities in silence plunging by. And, oh yes—I remember now—the flame and the moth, their mutual attraction and parallel stubborn resistances. I pondered that image.

Steven was besotted, enamored of every line. I remember how he stood up suddenly, proclaiming to the students passing by: "drop by caustic drop"! He was in Cranian ecstasy.

For Henry it was Crane's striving—"twice and twice and yet again"—it was the effort—the terrible effort—"until the bright logic is won."

Ah, we were young.

It might have been that day—

I can almost see it in Henry's dear dark eyes. Yes. He fell in love with Steven that very day. If this is not accurate I shall eat my favorite hat. But who would require that of me? No one alive can challenge my assertions. I could record things upside down or inside out with no consequence.

Goodness. Is this what Henry was doing in his many pages? Wandering like this? I don't suppose so. I shall never find out. He told me once, while enough clarity remained in his poor mind for me to credit the statement, that he intended the writings for Wilma, that I needn't bother with them. He meant to spare me. I am certain he meant to spare, not

34

exile, me. I honor his intention. And, as I have already written, I do not have the philosophical mind.

What sort of mind does Wilma have, I wonder. Lorraine tried to ferret out the answer to this very question, did she not? I doubt she penetrated beyond my daughter's clear mild surface. A surface I admire. If I have a creed, it is this: one's mind is one's own.

*

It was necessary to stop again. Two months have passed. A new year begins, if one attends to calendar time. Spring is in the unimaginable distance. We are encased in snow, snow, snow. Wilma and I conduct our days in routine companionship. Neither of us complains. A grim endurance rules. Perhaps the pen against the white page will effect a shift in me. I would appreciate the sensation of juices moving through again—a pleasing fantasy in these frozen Maine days. And poor Wilma might lap up the spill.

Which makes her sound like a dog. She is loyal enough, my faithful companion. But, no, Wilma is quite completely an upright walker, full of the human.

Lest I sound pitiful, let me clarify. My daughter and I have found, I believe, the unusual—friendship. Not that we gaze into one another's eyes, piercing souls. We proceed day by day, side by side, domestic, in peaceful simplicity. Would she agree? It is not a matter for discussion, but I have some confidence. I believe we enjoy each other's company. Minor irritations erupt, of course they do. Nevertheless.

It has occurred to me to slip these pages into a notebook of Henry's. Chance would then offer them to Wilma some day. If I were gone, why not?

But it is not for Wilma that I write. It is for mystery.

Now there, right there, I have turned things upside down. I meant to say clarity and the pen produced mystery. I shall let it stand.

Lorraine's death sprouted both. Perhaps all intensities—and every death is an intensity, is it not?—produce a share of the clear and another of the mysterious. And is there pulsation? Clarity pulsing forward out of mystery? And then from the clear moment come further mysteries? One feels such things, reading Rilke.

35

A perfect narrative line is not materializing. So be it.

When Steven presented me with my own copy of Rilke's Notebooks of Malte Laurids Brigge *my very hands felt the rightness. This was strange prose from the poet, but I needed it as description essential to my progress. My own childhood emerged—formed and displayed, entire—from the womb that was Rilke's mind.*

Womb. Would he be bothered by the word? The feminine implication? I think not.

I had entire paragraphs of The Notebook *by heart. Even now—*

"It would be difficult to persuade me that the story of the Prodigal Son is not the legend of a man who didn't want to be loved." Rilke's Prodigal is loved to excess as a child, wrapped in a suffocation of tenderness. The poor boy cannot make a move without causing either pleasure or pain. What he learns to crave is "profound indifference of heart." Scenes come to me now. The boy is outdoors, in dear solitude. An exultation of childish freedom drives him to run through a field, arms outspread. But he must reenter the house, for it is supper time. He is drawn in by the covetous family—a group of adults, hungry for his soul—and placed under a lamp. Light falls on him. The others are in shadow. He, only he, is required to endure "the shame of having a face." Entering manhood, he left home. Of course he did. He resolved never to love, never to place anyone "in the terrible position of being loved." I understood every word. I might have been reading about myself. I pondered the phrases—"terrible position of being loved"—"shame of having a face"—"profound indifference of heart." In the eye of a hurricane of insight, I resolved never to marry. I told Steven we ought to spend less time together. Then Henry appeared and my resolution was unraveled, my heart shaken open.

When I understood that Henry's own heart was yearning toward Steven, that what Henry felt for me was friendship but no movement of the blood, I turned again to Rilke. I read and reread the poems. I pondered the original German though I knew no German. I compared translations, held the lines to the light, turned them this way and that, tried to see into mystery. Perhaps I should have learned German. I believe I preferred the maze of translation. My Rilke is my own accumulation. May he forgive me. In the end I settled on Stephen Mitchell, translator who offers clear water running over the sandy, stony

36

bottoms—all the glints of sunlight on a windy day—never the same vision twice. The weather changes. One walks along. Wilma listens politely. She has not adopted my passion for Rilke, poet of poets. This is best, I sometimes think.

Henry and I did marry, of course. A storm of events led to our marriage. Hart Crane committed suicide. Crane's leap from the ship killed all that was poetic in the world for Steven, and all that was courageously homosexual. He walked in a daze, quoting. Something about light—he was longing for it, Steven was—I can almost hear him— the lines he whispered again and again—his wrenched heart—"Light wrestling there incessantly with light, / Star kissing star through wave on wave unto / Your body rocking!" If the poet who wrote "Voyages" could not live in the world, neither could Steven. But he would not kill himself. He renounced the world in favor of the unworldly, the religious. In particular he renounced the gaze of Henry Schuh.

From me he parted, I fear, rather lightly.

So there we stood like two orphans, Henry and myself, holding hands. It was one month after Hart Crane's death. Steven was returning to the seminary, leaving us at the train station. I was left with both Rilke and Henry, my essentials. Henry was left with Spinoza and the fondness he had for me. We made the best of it. We ran North—to rural Maine— after marrying in haste.

I entered marriage shorn of illusion, bare. I clung to Rilke's profound indifference of the heart. I had the sky. Henry? He stiffened, then broke. I held him at night as he sobbed over the loss of Steven. I looked over his shoulder, out the window where often enough there were stars. Time led us along and after some years we decided to try sex. After all, we were married. Along came Wilma. She was for Henry.

I see that this writing path is circuitous. I set out to honor poor Lorraine. Five years dead, after all. And the return of Adam to my dreams. I seem to have produced an autobiography. Perhaps it is enough.

*

But, no. Apparently it is not enough. Autumn has come again. I mean to add just this a bit more, for the parallels are cogent. Adam had

37

died. Mother was confused, as I have indicated, and in her grief needed me to become Adam. A strangeness, but I was not the only child thus burdened. Rilke, too, was taken for a dead sibling. I had my sailor suit, he had his little dresses. We had our distressed and enveloping mothers. Like the Prodigal Son, we left home. Like him, we strove for indifference of heart.

Which prevented neither of us from ongoing human entanglement.

Perhaps only Henry could have given me sufficient distance. Had Steven not left us for God, had Henry and I not been abandoned to each other—

I might have lost myself.

Hiding in the recesses of convention, married to some other man, my essential being might never have known to sit and ponder skies, read poetry, respect the earthworm.

Or participate in the death her lesbian daughter's lover.

Well.

So.

Insert here, by way of my unruly mind, a third human who endured a childhood shaped strangely by a sibling's death. Was it Steven who introduced me to Dalí? Salvador Domingo Felipe Jacinto Dalí, the surrealist painter. But, no. It was not Steven. Could not have been. It was later, much later—

It was Lorraine—

I feel the fact rise up—

I shudder.

Dalí is five years old. He stands with the adults at his brother's graveside. He is instructed to think of himself as the incarnation of his dead brother. He complies.

Dalí was nothing like Rilke whose soul sings to mine, but Dalí's melting clocks—yes, those clocks. Persistence of Memory *is the painting I cannot exorcize. It appears in dreams, time bent and distorted, time in the form of a clock hanging over the table's edge, over the dead tree's limb, over the headless fallen form of the anonymous animal—the bleak desert floor—the devastation—and yet the precision, the clean lines and pure colors—the collision of clarity and distortion—all in service of a deliberate disturbance of the viewer's mundane mind.*

38

I do know why this painting haunts me. It was shown to the world in 1932, as dear Lorraine informed us. 1932 was the year Hart Crane leapt from the boat, the year Steven turned from us, the year Henry and I married.

When Lorraine, who brought many things to Wilma and me, brought Dalí, told us the year, instructed us to look and look and look again—

I must have blanched. The date struck home, of course it did. Add to this the fact of my own clock.

Had I meant to arrive at the visions? What has all of this to do with Lorraine?

Before the clock came the angel.

*

That stopped me, but only overnight. I had to put the pen down but I pick it up in morning light. Filtered light, this morning. Gentle. Perhaps that will help.

Yes, I will do this.

As I approach the visions I must credit my Rilke. Rainer Maria Rilke. The very name is part of my soul. I climb into his tree, perch and wait. I am smallest of the birds nesting there, tiniest sparrow for whom the sky breaks open on occasion.

I did see the angel, once only. Quite distressing it was, too, this angel. Laden with symbols. Armored, you might say. It was male, which was unfortunate—what about us girls? I suppose it was thus gendered because born from the brain of Rilke who was, despite everything, a man.

I see that I have confused the metaphor, misplaced elements, crisscrossed the generating forces. Rilke is my tree. I wait within him, I look to the sky. The angel, however, seems to be born from Rilke's brain which is presumably inside my own. Perhaps Dalí, though dead, would like to paint the incongruities.

Never mind. In Rilke's own great sonnets a tree sprouts from the ear of Orpheus. Or possibly it is in the ear. I have never resonated with the image. But his angels—his angels have great strength—each one terrifying, as he says. A wonder of terror the poet produces. As for gender, did not Athena emerge from the head of Zeus? There is no need

39

to match the sex of the brain to what emerges therefrom. At any rate, the angel I saw was male.

I delay.

I was looking skyward as was my habit and the angel appeared. He stood on the air, solid as could be, and nodded politely, then turned and walked into the sun. I saw him enter the sun. I could pretend I was imagining, which is, I understand, a common response to the experience of seeing what is not seen by others. I could pretend I was terrified. I was neither imagining nor terrified. I have implied that the vision was caused —should I say inspired?—by Rilke. Perhaps I had been reading too much of him. But this is no explanation. There is no explanation. I saw the angel. He entered the sun.

I meant to say how old I was at the time. Old enough to know better, as they say. It was 1942. Wilma was four years old. Henry and I were thirty-four, married ten years. I have always valued the evenness of our numbers.

Lorraine was born that year. Of course I knew nothing then of Lorraine.

Pearl Harbor had been struck. We had entered the war.

The country was excited, energy was heightened, and along came my angel.

I should not dismiss the possibility of Rilke's involvement. Perhaps the angel was in fact a visitor from the far origins of poetry about which we know little in our contracted state. Perhaps truth hides for its own protection. We do tend toward violence as a species. Not least is our violence against truth.

Twice more I "saw"—twice in one week—this was years after the angel. I am referring to my clock now. I believe it was the same clock, entering time, re-entering time. Twice it shimmered in the sky with substance beyond light and gave on both occasions comfort such as I had never known. Wilma was turning twelve. Henry and I were forty-two. A change had come upon our little hermit family but I was unable to grasp its nature—and the clock from beyond—

~ ~ ~

40

Wilma has remained sitting cross-legged on city cement for perhaps longer than is prudent. Pansies are satisfying company but not of the essence. She ought to move. Her mind, however, seems a centipede whose legs cannot agree on their direction. Thus, she sits.

She cannot deny it. This period of time is not developing as planned. Where is her solitude? Her parents are, as the sonnet has it, too much with her. But in the sonnet it is the world that is overly present, isn't it? Henry and Alma did not indulge in much getting and spending. She can see them now, standing on Wordsworth's lea just as he would advise, windblown, holding hands. Proteus rises from the sea. Triton sounds his wreathéd horn.

Which gives us yet more gods.

Wilma sighs. Dear William Wordsworth.

It does appear to be the Schuh way, this business of gods. Henry, obsessed with god-intoxicated Spinoza, calls his own daughter a little god. Alma sees angels in the sky, and eternal clocks.

Wilma admonishes herself. It was one angel, and one clock seen twice. She really must cleave to reality a bit more.

But why?

A change in the little hermit family—is that what her mother wrote? Just as she, Wilma, turned twelve. If only Alma had persisted, written more. Or perhaps less. Fact upon fact in those pages, never revealed to the daughter. A twin brother, dead at eighteen months—a cross-dressed childhood—a love triangle—and visions. Alma had visions.

Also, her mother wrestled with Lorraine's—

Let that be.

She has now read at random from the small volume Lyle chose for her. Aloud. To the pansies. "Death is a solitary act," says the poet. But consider Alma, dearly departed, who flits around the apartment, perches on her daughter's shoulder, refuses solitude.

Well, yes.

Will Alma agree to *go* to the memorial service? Will she still be in residence when Wilma, who might foolishly expect to find herself alone, walks back into the apartment afterward? More to the point, will Wilma, who is after all the most likely creator of her mother's ghost, agree, finally, to enter her own solitude?

41

She riffles the pages of Mr. Solomon's book: "Foolishly furnished with wings is he—improbable, undeniable, white-hot wings—"

Alma appears to accomplish flight without such appendages. Wilma, daughter, is irritated. She turns pages, glances. Why on earth would Lyle imagine that this book—

> *The hands of the mother, the hands of the father,*
> *the embarrassed hearts held in those hands—*
> *pulsing hearts in the piteous hands*
> *and the shy offering they made.*

She shuts the book. She stares at the tears dropping and beading on the book's shiny cover. She wipes her eyes, takes a few deep breaths, shakes her head. She could leave it right here. Perhaps pansies appreciate poetry more than is evident. Pansies might be interested in parents whose hearts reside in their hands. She could leave the book, rise up onto her own two feet, mount her bicycle, and leave. That would be possible.

Neither Henry nor Alma would have been described as demonstrative, though Henry's hand, gently clasping, as father and daughter went to do their work together, was friendly enough.

But on the page—

On Mr. Solomon's page, parents expose—offer—in their hands— their hearts.

The written word is another reality, little Wilma. Never deny the reality of the word on the page.

I won't, Pa.

Good girl.

Enough.

Wilma is preparing to stand, sensibly placing the book into the little backpack, when the girls arrive. There are three of them. As there are three Fates, as she has known from a young age.

Clotho spins life's thread, Wilma. Lachesis decides how long the thread will be. Atropos cuts the thread, which is death and nothing to be feared. Now you tell me.

Clotho. She spins.

Good.

La—

42

Lachesis. And the last one?
Atropos, Pa.
And all them together, child?
The Fates, from Greek mythology.
Very good. And their other name?
Moirae, Pa.
Excellent, my little scholar.

But these are only young girls from the neighborhood, a bit mussed in their persons, chewing gum and giggling. Twelve years old, no doubt. What other age could they be? She is still sitting on the sidewalk. They are standing, which gives them a definite advantage. One is of a stern disposition. She asks, "What's the matter with *you*?" The others are followers. "Yeah," they say, keeping themselves a bit behind their leader. They chew their gum.

"Perhaps it's that my mother died," Wilma offers. A tentative reply, but in what other way could she explain herself? It might be an important question these young goddesses ply her with. *Is* something the matter with her? Why, for example, has she been unable—truly unable—to look into the final pages of her father's Notebook W?

But here are the Moirae. Or, quite as likely, here are three ordinary young humans, residents of Bangor, Maine, out on a spring afternoon. One of them, not the leader, will be a quiet beauty in a few years. She tries to pout but it doesn't suit her. A slip of kindness in her eyes, held carefully, not squandered, can be discerned.

"May I ask if you girls are about the age of twelve?"

"What d'you want to know for?" This is the third girl, neither leader nor future beauty, trying for approval from the leader. It's a hard task for her. She loses stamina with her last two words. Wilma could spill additional tears over such effort.

"A good question. I suppose I've come to think that twelve is an age unlike other ages. It's a recent thought. Possibly it's unformed still."

It's the leader's turn. She pulls herself taller, takes her preparatory breath, steps closer. Wilma prepares for cruelty.

"That ain't no answer, old lady."

She looks up at the girl, gathers her resources. "How right you are. Answers are a mite scarce in the current circumstances. Perhaps you'd help me stand? I seem to have gotten myself stuck down here."

The request evokes a period of pondering, but then, with considerable noblesse oblige, the leader offers her hand. Wilma takes it. The girl pulls. She is stronger than she looks, and more benevolent.

"Thank you, dear. I'll be on my way now."

Trembling only slightly, Wilma climbs onto her bicycle and pedals, one, two, three, four, breathing hard—then hears the girls cry out in alarming unison. "You left your pack, old lady!"

She stops. They run at her. The future beauty with kindness in reserve hands over Alma's backpack. The girls start to leave, turn back, and recite their next line. "We're *all* twelve." They turn and run, whooping. Wilma Schuh, old lady, has been an adventure.

And had one. She was, she understands now, quite frightened. Silly, but there it is. *Quite* frightened. Of children.

Well.

Onward.

Pedal and breathe, pedal and breathe.

Is she going home? Yes, but first a little detour.

~ ~ ~

Walking her bicycle now, Wilma threads her way among pedestrians, pulling the string of Fate through downtown Bangor. On the radio this morning came an announcement. Noon was the time, wasn't it? And that open space near the Grasshopper Shop was the place.

Yes, there he is: Henry Whitsun, mime from Massachusetts, as advertised. But shorter than she expected him to be. How unreasonably surprised she is, as if a mime must be a type, tall, thin, ascetic.

Well, he is himself, short. A small man. Light brown unremarkable hair. His eyes are no doubt blue. He looks like a Mainer, plain and clean and wearing blue jeans. No white makeup, no painted-on features, and not a hint of the ascetic. Bangor workers and shoppers pause to watch young Henry Whitsun. They toss a coin into his soft cap, move on or stay planted. A few sit, cross-legged. They open their brown bag lunches. We are in a city moment.

From across the street, Wilma observes. Her bicycle leans against the window of what was in former years the Bagel Shop. It's something else now, a name she cannot keep in mind. She reads the writing on the

44

window. Oh, yes. A Thai restaurant. But for her this will forever be the Bagel Shop. Here she and Alma and Lorraine stopped after trips to the library. Henry's extreme frugality was gone, along with Henry himself. Was there money for a lunch out? Lorraine was the one to decide such things and Lorraine enjoyed her bagel and cream cheese. Sometimes, feeling daring, the ex-nun from Minnesota ordered lox. For Alma and Wilma it was plain cream cheese. Eating out was adventure enough.

Henry Whitsun is no amateur. So observes Wilma Schuh who, truth be told, knows nothing about the art of mime. But this young fellow's moves are mesmerizing, he cannot be a beginner. From onlookers he draws lines of energy, weaves them, and hands them back. He's playing with the threads of the Moirae. Spin, weave, snip, spin, weave, snip. Alma should be here.

But she is not.

In the midst of the improvisation, or perhaps beneath it, come steady beats of movement, repetitive. But there's an odd tilt to Mr. Whitsun's body from time to time. It seems to become more pronounced. Is this planned? To offer an alternate rhythm, perhaps—for flavor—

Oh, a faint!

He's very good. Everyone hovers over him—excellent audience participation.

Wilma is thinking about the bent backs, how we bend over the fallen, the pathos of it. Mime evokes the pathetic, doesn't it? Is there something in Aristotle? Not about mimes specifically perhaps—but pathos—tragedy—catharsis—even in comic moments, the shadow—or was that Plato? Plato, the poet philosopher hostile to poetry.

She knows a bit about Aristotle and Plato, possibly from Will Durant, that nice writer whose book the librarian found for her when she was a searching adolescent. And there must have been something in the venerable *Harvard Classics*. But her mind blurs. Did Henry himself introduce her, in the years before she turned twelve?

Here is another Henry, young, hovered over.

Maybe Plato and Aristotle were even part of that class—Lorraine, college professor, insisted she attend a class—

Or did she gather most of what she knows about the classic philosophers from public radio which threads through every decade and can't be separated from—

Can't be separated from Alma.

She closes her eyes. She is sitting with her mother, listening, listening—to lectures, to music. Mother and daughter sit in the living room, the daughter almost an old woman herself as the years go on, on, on.

And now no more.

Oh, Alma.

The siren rises and falls and halts. The ambulance is here.

Ambulance?

Henry Whitsun, mime, is on a stretcher, his audience having parted like a miniature Red Sea, allowing rescue. The poor boy really did faint. Others, more anchored to the present than Wilma Schuh—and to plain fact—could distinguish human need from art.

She takes a breath and nods her head. Yes, she is somewhat peculiar today. And yes, it has to be her mother's death that does this to her. Expected for such a length of time, Alma's dying is nevertheless not nothing, is it?

No, dear. In fact, it's quite something.

The ambulance leaves. The audience disperses. Wilma gathers herself. She walks her bicycle up Hammond, away from noon hour pedestrians. At Sixth Street she mounts, pedals, and considers an early afternoon nap. With pillow and blanket, curling up like any motherless child, she will sink—down, down, down. That will suit, won't it?

And then, rested, she will—she absolutely will—approach the final pages of her father's Notebook W. This must be done before the memorial service, must it not?

Yes, dear. I appreciate the effort. Remember what Rilke said.

Wilma remembers what Rilke said. "Being dead is hard work and full of retrieval before one can gradually feel a trace of eternity." Alma needs those pages read. Retrieved. It is possible Wilma herself would benefit. She is quite well aware this might be the case as she pedals home, in need of a nap.

~ ~ ~

46

I will endure separation. My final teaching: that she must abandon me. This has long been the plan. Age twelve, she is able. Look how she changes, no longer truly a child. I comfort myself with the thought of the chrysalis. Young Wilma forms even now the structures of the adult mind. My daughter will emerge—butterfly!

I give to her what I took from my own parents. Stole from them. Not at twelve. Older, but too young still in their eyes. Abandoning family, I absconded, stole freedom. How I had chafed, being held. Years, I waited. Then left. Took myself from them. Rode the rails. Found what was needed.

I, father and teacher, must now withdraw. This is my agony, that I am excluded. I turn to Spinoza, as ever. God will burst upon Wilma. Her own path. She need not chafe. I spare her that.

Ah, my little butterfly-to-be—

I have come upon the proper term for my own pupal stage. Encased, alone, I was "tumbler." I, no butterfly, emerged in the form of mosquito. This is today's small thought. It amuses me, as it would amuse Spinoza. Perhaps he knew the term. Perhaps he was one himself—tumbler, who became mosquito. Adult, he pierced, in need of the essential blood. I also.

My mind is trivial today, possibly a necessary state.

The truth teaches itself. I have not directed her to him, my Spinoza. It has been a discipline, to refrain from imposing. Now another discipline, to sacrifice the bond, to permit, even to require.

Truth reveals itself. To her mind, her singular possession, it will come, despite her startled look, quickly contained for she is good girl.

Startled, that her father would—so suddenly—release.

This chrysalis stage she must have. Later the metamorphosis, sudden blood running through wing veins, the wings spread and dried, the flight. Will I be permitted to see? I think not. Hers, hers, hers.

Mine: to turn back now, lacking a daughter.

I am mosquito indeed. Here is my high whine, annoying should anyone hear. My blessing, then: no one to hear. Once, long ago, I thought my child might delve into her father's written productions. Now, though: clarity. She goes her own way. Set free at twelve. Away. Away. What would return her to me? Only trouble beyond her capacity. Let there be none of that.

Look how I've neglected eternity today, attached myself to number, attached number to pain. Tumbler again, I regress.

Alma knows nothing of my decision.

I am no longer the teacher, barely even the father.

Will Alma, wife, notice?

*

Erupting into eternity, time nevertheless—

I add this note—one year gone, since I last wrote. This note: appendage, confession, outcry. To whom?

48

My daughter is not lepidopteran. Was not chrysalis, did not become butterfly. She has been for one year, my wife tells me, a sad human, too young for the task of the autodidact.

I thought I had achieved, in the matter of Wilma's education, a grasp of a child's need, a clear and distinct idea. But Alma has come to me. The child is still a child, she says. A child cannot educate herself. I am told that an entire year has been lost. I am informed that I have made a grievous error. This, the informing, is done with evident care, as if I am fragile, as if the news might grip and break me.

So Alma reveals herself as Watcher, Time-Keeper. I thought she was elsewhere, my Alma. Friend of my soul, soul of the family, I thought she lived in the ether, in the soil, in lines of language soldered to beauty, away from us.

She tells me our daughter has been neglected, striving, stumbling. Suffering. And too much alone. She has enrolled Wilma in public school. I grind my teeth. I comprehend the Book of Job. I bow my head.

I turned away from my own daughter. I saw not. I see now. I see many things. One is the sad fact that I am an ordinary man.

Enough. I lay my pen on the desk, needing both hands to hold my hurting head.

*

I have received the diagnosis of Alzheimer's disease. In this notebook devoted to Wilma—grown daughter now—I report this fact. My useless mind. My gnashed teeth. Already the straight line cannot be achieved. Suspicions were experienced. Was the mind, was the burden—

Stones in a sack, a bent back, the bent man hauls—

49

An old, old story. Both hands needed, the load heavy, the footsteps a labor—

My daughter was to carry the mind.

I catch the tangles, plaque-ridden. I can untangle, at times. I saw, today, ghost upon ghost. No. Saw my two women, how they merged. Wifechild, holograph, singleton—

I fumble—

Try again. Confusion is the word I seek. I confused them, my wife and my daughter. Abandonment bound them. I, abandoner of both.

Confusion abounding. To sort—

To sort will become more difficult than I could have imagined.

I suspected, I did suspect. Saw signs. The mind separating. Strange compartments holding elements of—unidentified, foreign—

As if a giant infant put this and that—playthings—here and there.

Organization will be lost. My wife, whom I was unable to—

Child, I turned away—

I can no longer read Spinoza. How shall I live?

*

Oh, but I was wrong. I am able! I read him! Time passes. I live with Alzheimer's. If I call to myself the thought of Wilma's clear and steady mind—for I have seen it in her—I can for long minutes take him up, see word after word, remember—

*

Another day and yet I live. He untangles, my Benedict, my Baruch. Will he send me his god? Oh, my Wilma, my little one. One day you fell and in your red dress, I believe I remember, I believe I reme—

*

I—

Breaking, how will the brain—

Think the effort toward—

Twice and twice—

*

To wrest from confusion the adequate idea, adequate to god: clear and distinct—the third kind, striving—knowledge, the third kind, intuitive, from which joy—to know with the adequate, the absolute—to know—pull forth from mere passivity, mere suffering, pull forth into the light: action! My Spinoza teaches.

Active the soul saturated thus—the mind—

Third kind of knowledge—

But the poor plaqued and tangled brain—ah, pity—the curves and tunnels, matter encased—brain, diseased—

How receive, shape, to action, manage—such as fear—

Twice and twice—

Long longing—

Years—decades—Steven—lost, unreleased—Steven—

Here, held, Alma, poor wife of the damaged mind—

Wilma, child—grown, grown—

And the sad mind unminded, descends to—

*

Grasp the descent—handholds all the way down—the way— yes, quick the handholds—the fall and the handholds—hold, lose—next—see—this is understanding, possible, this—new knowledge—grasp, lose—rumble of strangest—joy—new—

*

Until the bright logic—

*

Wilma: listen! For this is a good day. It might be the last. A sentence! Two! Look: sentences are still possible. Always they might be the last. But this is a good day, Wilma. This is a good day. A sentence can be wrested from confusion. Now, today, again, this is possible. I see. Active, I see. Child, this is joy.

*

But will she read?

*

52

Time—

I—

*

Do not forget the sacraments. Do not forget—

Baptism—

Penance—

Holy Euchar—

We are Catholics. Wilma, we must—

I believe in God, the Father Almigh—

Matrimony—

Extreme Unct—

Trinity—

One in all, Father, Son, Holy Gho—

Three-in-one of these—

Catholic—

Holy Catholic Ch—

We—

Two: Wilma

Down come cones of sun, hard against the ground

It is an old, old Volkswagen bug—dull burnt red—that carries Wilma and Lyle. Everything is a little loose, a little weary, in this car. The gear lever and clutch pedal in particular would like a rest, if you please. Maybe later they'll get back to work but today they would rather not continue. Nevertheless, they have continued. Clutch, shift, clutch, shift. Like the tangled and plaque-ridden Alzheimer's brain striving for a few final sentences, thinks Wilma. Or maybe not like that at all.

Wilma is the driver of this faithful tired vehicle which she and Alma purchased long ago from the son of the neighbors—the same neighbors who now own the old Schuh land on which Alma will this day be left as a scattering of ash and bone bits. The car is not frequently driven. Both hands on the steering wheel, Wilma is focused, doing her job, continuing. Perhaps she, too, is somewhat loosened in her workings, somewhat in need of rest. It does take effort to hold the wheel firmly.

The wordless drive from Lyle's bookstore through the streets of Bangor has been accomplished. It required much shifting, much tending to traffic, but they are beyond the city limits now, on a straight stretch. Fifty miles an hour, no other cars. She begins to feel the green of things, blades and leaves emerging. The day is a delicate one, carefully temperate. Let us go gently, let us be cautious, says this day. Nevertheless, a sudden rebellious freedom rises up in Wilma, almost a giddiness. She finds herself speaking.

"When I was twelve years old my father turned me loose."

Whether the words are directed to her silent passenger or only meant to fly out the open window into rushing air over fields and stands of trees, over the hill just ahead, she knows not.

"Loose?"

Lyle is in charge of the ceramic cube that holds Alma's ashes. He sits in the passenger seat, his reverent hands around the remains, serge-clad thighs pressed together beneath their burden. He has resurrected an ancient suit for this day and smells a tad musty, but never mind. The open window helps.

Wilma too pulled an old garment from the closet, her last remaining dress. She laundered and even ironed it, then tried it on. She saw something alien in the mirror, an oldish woman, almost severe. The dress, dark blue, satisfied. The day will not be a common one, why should apparel be ordinary or even comfortable? She located a pair of nylon stockings, not without difficulty. And now this driving. How long has it been since she drove anywhere at all? Alma's last doctor appointment? When was that? They let go of the burden toward the end, stayed home. The doctor had no solution.

"Loose, Wilma?"

Explanation. Lyle needs explanation. Very well, then, she will explain herself to the man in the passenger seat, kind companion on this uncommon drive toward an uncommon event.

"Henry decided, quite abruptly from my point of view, though I now understand it was his plan from the beginning, that I, having reached the advanced age of twelve, was to take charge of my own education. The entire Bangor Public Library was at my disposal, he reminded me, as well our Five-Foot Shelf."

Lyle says nothing.

Wilma and Lyle have never been in an enclosed space alone together. They have never been anywhere together outside the bookstore. Wilma sighs, watches a battered pickup pass her, honking. Where did it come from? She grips the wheel more tightly. What is her complaint? Didn't Henry give her enough? All the way to age twelve, all those years when most children barely see their fathers, there he was. And books in the house and regular transportation to the library in town—

"I sometimes think it should have been enough."

"Five-foot shelf," says Lyle, but surely he is familiar with *The Harvard Classics*. Or was the importance of owning the *HC* another idiosyncrasy of the Schuh family? Approaching her eighth decade, Wilma has not yet sorted the peculiar from the ordinary in her upbringing though Lorraine did not hesitate to speak on the matter.

The road carries them forward, rising, falling, curving. The view opens and closes. Henry was not satisfied with the philosophy selections in the *Harvard Classics* but kept his dissatisfaction to himself until his mind loosened and his secrets slid out. He had no problem with the science, the literature, the rest of it.

"Perhaps one is only discontented with what one knows best," Wilma says.

"Five-foot shelf," says Lyle.

"*The Harvard Classics*."

58

"Ah, yes. Rings a bell. Faint, though." He moves Alma just slightly. Is it too much for him, holding her like this? How quiet the mother ghost has become. Hardly a word from her for several days. She might be ready.

That's right, dear. Tend to your driving.

An unnecessary admonition. She is doing just fine now.

"We owned them. A certain Mr. Charles Eliot decided early in the last century—I believe it was around 1910—that any reasonably intelligent human could acquire a liberal education by reading for fifteen minutes each day from books that would fit on a five-foot bookshelf. Henry labored, saved, and purchased. The volumes were to assure me, I think, adequate intellectual nourishment—and variety beyond my father's scope."

Lyle nods, staring straight ahead. It is apparent his mind is not firmly on the topic of a liberal education compressed to five feet. Still, it steadies a person to form and speak sentences. Last night Alma offered one solitary sentence of her own. *I hand the work of retrieval over to you, dear.*

Which handover was Wilma's reward for finally reading, in concert with her ghost mother, the concluding words of Henry's Notebook W. When Wilma closed the notebook Alma slipped into her ceramic cube and remained there. Wilma sat until midnight staring into the blank air at the center of her living room, Henry's words coming and going, coming and going.

I turned away from my own daughter.

I saw not.

Until the bright logic.

The apartment was coldly quiet this morning. Only as she locked the door behind her did she realize she had forgotten even to play the radio. She lives alone for the first time in her life. She has her solitude.

But here she is inside an undersized vehicle with a little man beside her. Still, as Alma would say, with Lyle Franklin a person can be alone.

Odd, isn't it, that out of the plethora—the notebooks with Henry's earnest, agonized, sometimes ecstatic, and finally disintegrating mind on display—Alma's unanticipated inserted pages with their revelations—the strivings and the visions of the parental minds, of their souls—that out of all of this, and in the wake of the death of her mother, what stands up and claims attention is a little crisis in her own education? Truly, it is bewildering.

The countryside spreads out. Sudden flatness reveals itself. Wilma blinks against the sun which has lost its tender discretion, its delicacy.

I can no longer read Spinoza. How shall I live?

"Spinoza of course was Mr. Eliot's most disturbing omission, as Henry saw things."

Lyle maintains silence. Possibly he didn't hear her. Possibly she didn't say it aloud.

"Alma signed me up for school when I failed."

Lyle says nothing.

"*Lyle.*"

He startles, looks at her, squints with his one good eye. "Failed?"

"I was too young. Alma has told me, but I believe I see it myself."

"Alma told you. What are you talking about, Wilma?"

What is she talking about? And to whom?

"I was unable to educate myself. A dire failure, you understand. Focus and purpose eluded me. I lost solidity, I suppose. I was sent to school, then, where I felt myself a foreigner."

"Better pay attention to the road, Wilma," says Lyle Franklin, friend of Alma Schuh, his voice a bit thickened.

She glances at him. He has pressed the box with Alma's ashes against his heart. Her hands grip the wheel. She is the driver. The lives of the still-living—hers, Lyle's—dangle from her tense, aging fingers.

~ ~ ~

It had not occurred to Wilma that a memorial service might be—in fact must be—a social occasion. She herself arranged this, she does understand the facts of the case. Still.

There it is, across the field, a social occasion readying itself in the form of quite a number of O'Connors who wait, milling, near where the path to the great pine begins. How like them to be so firmly in the designated place, dependable and neighborly. She sets the parking brake, though the graveled drive is flat and there is no need. How many of them *are* there? They blur at this distance. The light is a glare. Also, the windshield is none too clean.

60

Your means of transportation has been a mite neglected, dear.
Alma?

Still here, daughter.

Wilma cannot say whether this is annoying or comforting.

No need to decide, child. I'm almost finished.

Child? But Alma is right. Wilma is at the moment more child than anything else. Which will not do. She emerges from the car in a stern frame of mind, and glances across the sun-struck field toward the O'Connors and the woods. She does not—cannot—look in the direction of the old Schuh house.

Lyle, passenger, sits in place. He is a statue holding a ceramic box. Apparently he needs help. Around the car she goes, and opens his door and takes Alma's ashes from him. "Come," she says. He comes, a small old man with a limp, squinting with his single good eye. His serge suit shines. We are a brave pair, thinks Wilma. Lyle grunts, so perhaps her thought was audible.

A brief wave of a hand is cast across the field, and then another. The O'Connors don't come running and they don't shout. They are here to attend a solemn service and will act properly. Also, they are actual people, living human beings, coming clearer as the distance lessens. Time has changed them as time changes all, a phenomenon to be expected. Still, to see that Peggy and Robert are grayed, and beyond graying—it must be Peggy and Robert who lean against one another, with perhaps the help of a cane in the hand of Robert though that might be an illusion—to see those two bent and small and truly old—

One, two, three, four—

Wilma is counting steps, and persons, and generations. But the people move about, which muddles the count. The names—at least the names of her own generation—

She should have made a list last night, prepared herself—

Catherine. She remembers Catherine well, the oldest, four years her senior. And Paul. Didn't he go off to Bass Harbor and get himself hired onto a fishing boat? Ann, who said little but seemed forever sweet. Dickie, the live wire, never married, never quite settled, unless later, after she lost contact. Dickie was a miracle-worker in the mechanical realm. And, finally, Marlene, the baby in Peggy's arms.

61

Later Marlene was the young woman in the arms of Lorraine, but never mind that.

Catherine, Paul, Ann, Dickie, Marlene. Very good. Now keep walking and don't drop your mother. This is self-admonition. Alma, who might say such a thing, is not speaking—has, very likely, spoken her last.

Wilma glances at Lyle. He gestures toward the cube. She shakes her head, no, she will carry her mother. They trudge on, closer, closer to this gathering which is not primarily a test of one's memory. How good, though, to call up the names, she must be doing quite well considering the circumstances, but of course there are the younger ones and husbands, wives, she isn't expected to know all of them, is she?

She sees Catherine, gray-haired now and rounder than she used to be, and still so firmly attractive. Catherine, center of the family, hub around which everything moves—one knows it instantly—who was once dubbed Wilma's First Crush by watchful Lorraine. They sat in the kitchen after a visit to the neighbors, just the two of them with their glasses of milk. Lorraine had decided milk would be good for their bones. It must have been early in her time with Lorraine who was entertaining herself, labeling the O'Connors. Shy-as-a-Deer Ann. Upright, Frightened Robert. Perceptive Peggy. Darling Dickie. Pragmatic Paul. Marlene, adult but not yet seduced, was Sexy Irish Slut. When she came to Catherine, Lorraine said—as if she knew, though it was only a guess—Wilma's First Crush. No hesitation, no emphasis. A throwaway designation it might have been, but wasn't. Consider the speaker.

As was so often true, Lorraine was right, though Wilma herself until that moment, finishing her milk, could not have named the intense sensation that came over her at the age of twelve—yes, it was that same troublesome year—whenever she saw Catherine. But what had Lorraine seen during this visit?

"You blushed, dear," said Lorraine, answering the unspoken question.

What a memory to call back while carrying one's mother's ashes and approaching that very same Catherine O'Connor who must have a married name now. Catherine at sixteen was already solid, already almost the Maine farm woman she was destined to become, competent, focused, intelligent, kind, and in every way admirable in the eyes of twelve year old Wilma. Hank, future husband—what *was* his last name?—was

62

already a fixture around the O'Connor house and land. He would become Robert's farming "son" while Paul went to the water and Dickie left and returned, left and returned, and tinkered brilliantly. Catherine married well, as they say, but the saying wanders for Wilma. What might the implication be? Better to say Catherine married completely.

Yes, that's the word. Not one readily applied to the marriage of Alma and Henry. Nor would it have described her own partnership with Lorraine. Something incomplete around the edges. Or were there little gaps here and there all through the fabric?

She hadn't intended to bring Lorraine to this day's doings.

It is Dickie who breaks from the milling O'Connors, stretching out his hand. "We're so sorry for your loss, Wilma." He turns to Lyle. "I'm Dickie." All Lyle has to do is give his name in return and the event is begun.

"I see you still have the car," Dickie says, as they walk the final steps toward the family.

"I suppose I ought to ask you to conjure another."

"Got you here, I notice."

"Yes. Is that enough?"

"For folks like you and me, Wilma, that's usually enough." Dickie sends a wink in Lyle's direction, including him in the Plain Folks Club, and says Paul sends his condolences, regrets he can't be here. He looks out over the field as if Marlene, who is expected, might materialize out of the air; which, being Marlene, she might do, if Wilma remembers her ways.

Catherine comes forward. The hug she gives could not be more natural, more comfortable. It even manages gracefully to include Alma, silent inside in her cube. Peggy approaches slowly, arms outstretched, tiny, wrinkled, determined. She opens her arms wider as she gets closer, not as if to hug but as if to express astonishment, and then her little hands come together around Wilma's which are holding the ceramic cube. "Is this Alma? How lovely, Wilma, to think of taking Alma into the woods in a container that blends so beautifully, just the right colors, good for you!" Robert, standing upright and solemn with his cane, gives a quick nod to Wilma, another to Lyle.

"Robert would rather this were in church," Peggy says, "But he's here. You're here, aren't you, dear?"

"I'm happy to honor Alma. Don't misrepresent me, Peg. Sorry for your loss, Wilma. You remember Ann."

Ann, nearly hidden behind her father, says, "Hello, Wilma. I'm sorry I don't remember you."

"Ann has Alzheimer's, as did your father, I remember," Peggy says. "She'll stay for as much of the service as she can manage and then go back to the house, won't you, dear?"

Ann nods slowly and says, "Goodbye, then," and starts across the field.

"Wrong direction, Annie," say the O'Connors in unison. A teen-ager runs to guide the wanderer home.

"Well," says Catherine. This simple word brings those still milling to attention. "Wilma, Lyle, here are the young folks. This is Delia, my daughter, and her kids, Thomas, Annie, and Little Jonathan. That's Cecilia helping Ann back to the house. Marlene is late as usual. Hank, get yourself over here and say hello. There are more of us, but we're the ones in residence at the moment. Delia's husband died last month. Heart attack. So she and the kids are here for now until they figure out..."

"I'm here!"

Marlene, who cannot be as young as she looks, has materialized, bulky in a colorful long skirt, running across the field, calling out.

The stories begin, memories of Alma. There is laughter, gentle and loving, and tears mark the faces of some O'Connors. The death of Delia's husband is fresh for the entire family. In the midst of this, Wilma allows herself a full breath and a moment of private wonderment. The childhood vision has been glimpsed. As the group approached the tree, the sun struck through. There, where the path widened—she did not expect—but she ought to have known—after all, the great pine—

But here is Lyle, right beside her, streaming tears.

And here is Peggy, too, recalling the moment Alma and her eight-year-old daughter appeared on the porch. Robert was waiting in the cave of the living room, a man in need of religion. "It was to be our very first sacred reading. We had just begun and here comes a knock at the door and these two waifs—forgive me, Wilma, but you and your mother did present such need—and there was my Robert, still suffering from the war —the nightmares!—and we had finally understood what would help. Oh, how well I remember. Marlene was wriggling in my arms and I was in

64

tatters myself—in my mind, I mean—and how to be hospitable was my dilemma. I asked you in, the two of you, and gave you chairs, and on we went with our reading, just like that. What was that first text, Robert? I know you repeat it often enough."

"'In the shadow of his hand he hath protected me, and hath made me as a chosen arrow: in his quiver he hath hidden me.' *Isaiah*, chapter forty-nine."

"Yes. I ought to have it memorized myself by now. You said the *New Testament* would be overly intimate. I thought that such a strange adjective."

"I might have meant familiar."

"That would have been a more expected word, but not your very own, of course. Robert does have his very own ways—don't you, dear?—for which we love him. What a time that was. So there you were, Wilma, you and Alma, introduced to our family by way of a Bible reading. What you must have thought!"

Lyle looks at Wilma and then down at the green and brown cube which he now holds. She sees the tiny grin he's hoping to hide. Alma must never have told him. She herself had almost forgotten that religion, a decidedly foreign element, snuck into the little hermit family—though not of course into the interstices of the Schuh culture—by way of the Catholic neighbors. Henry had been fussing, his women might be overly isolated. Perhaps they would benefit from socializing, that seemed the normal way to live. The children next door were washed and well-regulated, the mother was a quiet pleasant little person, the father a diligent worker from the look of things. He suggested that Alma and Wilma might go across the field. They knocked on the door and Peggy invited them in, waifs that they were. And so it began. Week after week they listened to the readings: a passage from the Bible, a selection from *Lives of the Saints*, every Thursday evening. And it seems—suddenly she thinks this this might be the case—that her vision came around the time of that first visit.

It is becoming obvious to everyone that Dickie is trying to contain himself.

Catherine says, "Speak, brother. You might as well."

"Remember that saint—" But he can't continue, he's in the grip of giggles. The ridiculous, Wilma remembers, always held sway over Dickie, but what on earth—

Dickie manages a single word: "Christina—"

At which hint all those in the know begin to chuckle, even Robert. Catherine explains for the benefit of the others. "Christina the Astonishing. She was Dickie's kind of saint. At her own funeral she sat up in her coffin and levitated to the rafters of the church, isn't that right?"

"And the reason—" But Dickie still can't manage a sentence.

It comes back to Wilma. "I remember," she says. "It was because the people stank! The stink of sinful humanity was too much for the saint and up to the rafters she rose. I was thrilled to the innards of my little heathen soul."

"She went high and she went low, that one," Dickie says, wiping his eyes. "Took advantage of being dead to have a little chat with some friends in hell. Best story I ever heard about hell. I suppose she was crazy. The villagers were terrified, I remember, but they fed her."

Wilma looks at Marlene who smiles and winks. Well, good. Marlene has been disturbingly quiet since her dramatic arrival.

"But couldn't Christina climb! To the treetops! To the crown of the local tower! I envied that with sinful intensity," Catherine says.

"And she handled fire and was never burned," Wilma remembers, "and spent hours in the freezing river with no consequence to her health. Oh, my." The energy of the moment overtakes her. She turns and kisses Lyle's wrinkled cheek. He tolerates this with only a clearing of the throat. His cheek tastes salty.

The group has fallen silent.

Wilma takes a deep breath and pulls the piece of paper from her skirt pocket. "As many of you know, my mother loved poetry. Above all she loved the poems of Rainer Maria Rilke and she asked that when the moment arrived—this moment—I—well—"

Without warning even to herself, she sits on the ground. In her last remaining dress, careful to cover her knees, she does this. There is a flurry of consternation. "Oh. No, no need for concern. I require the earth, that's all. Perhaps everyone could sit. Why have we been standing? Here, Lyle, give her to me."

66

Everyone except Robert, whose knees won't agree to it, sits. The great pine stands. The sun beams down. Wilma removes the cover from the ceramic cube. She takes some ash, holds it cupped in one hand, and reads.

Be ahead of all parting, as though it were
already behind you, like the winter that has just gone by.
For among these winters there is one so endlessly winter
that only by wintering through it will your heart survive.

Be forever dead in Eurydice—more gladly arise
into the seamless life proclaimed in your song.
Here, in the realm of decline, among momentary days,
be the crystal cup that shattered even as it rang.

Be—and yet know the great void where all things begin,
the infinite source of your own most intense vibration,
so that, this once, you may give it your perfect assent.

To all that is used-up, and to all the muffled and dumb
creatures in the world's full reserve, the unsayable sums,
joyfully add yourself, and cancel the count.

"Alma was greatly attached to that crystal cup. She would blink at the sound of the word, and then smile. Sometimes she joined in with what frail voice she still had—our voices together—the cup—how it shattered —how it rang and shattered. But her own end—her death—wasn't a bit like that. It was gradual. I want to say it was gentle. I believe it was—" She stops and looks at the sky. "What an uncommon day this is. Perhaps I'm wrong about—the actual moment. I can't claim to—I was at Shaw's —getting groceries—groceries!—for myself—food held no interest for her. She—faded—and then she was—gone. When I returned—" She stops again. The others are silent. "Still, the crystal cup. I find it— elegant. And quite severe. Yes. Well."

She looks at the O'Connors, at Lyle. The ashes in her hand are so light. Alma, so very, very light now. She lets the ashes fall back into the cube.

67

Robert says "Amen."

All of the O'Connors say "Amen."

Lyle looks up at the sky and mutters assent.

Wilma, tears coming, nods. She gives the cube to Lyle, gets herself to her feet, takes the cube from him. When everyone is again standing, she approaches the pine and scoops out a handful of ash and a few tiny pieces of bone. She lets Alma fall bit by bit around the tree's base, over soil and raised roots. A short way further into the woods she drops ash under the old maple. Next, out to the field, to the garden, the others following, a silent procession.

No pansies. No sign of anything growing yet. Mulch. From the remnants of ash comes the voice of Alma. *What could be better than mulch, dear? We don't require pansies. Let me go.* So she empties the ceramic cube, shaking it vigorously over the garden, and for the first time allows herself to look over at the old Schuh house. There she grew up and there she stayed, always planning to leave until it became impossible to do so. Henry was diagnosed with Alzheimer's. They cared for him together, his wife and his daughter. Then it was too much. Alma was distraught. Henry, her brilliant husband, locked in a ward for the demented. Henry died and Lorraine entered their lives. Another threesome living here. After Lorraine's death it was aging mother and middle-aged daughter. They sold the house and the land to these obliging O'Connors and moved to Bangor, to the apartment which is now hers. Hers alone.

What a classic farm house it is, recently painted. White, as it always was. Catherine tells her they have excellent tenants at present. Well, good. She turns away from the house, Alma's empty cube held to her body. She wonders if she'll wash this container, use it for new purposes. Where has she left the cover, though? It must be back at the pine. She starts in that direction but Lyle stops her, producing the cover.

Not until she and Lyle are once again negotiating the streets of Bangor does it occur to her that the ashes of the dead might not be a welcome addition to one's vegetable garden. Catherine told them it was Delia who planted and mulched the garden, insisting on vegetables only, no damn flowers, she'd had enough of flowers at her husband's damn funeral. The garden was, as Wilma could see, a tad late. The family had waited until Delia felt sufficiently organized. "Grief slows a person down," said Catherine.

"Perhaps Delia would have preferred not to have Alma mixed with her vegetables," Wilma says as they wait at a stoplight.

Lyle nods. "Perhaps."

"Oh, well," says Wilma and they look at each other and chuckle. "We did it, Lyle."

The light turns green. She tends to her driving.

~ ~ ~

Dusty summer on the woods path. Dry dirt cracking and crumbling next to tree roots that show their top parts. Eight years old, walking her Wilma walk. Six steps, one skip, six steps, one skip. Mother in the garden. Pa in his study working his thought. Work, work, work.

Down come cones of sun, hard against the ground. She pretends to hear their firm hum. She steps around them, respectful. She puts her feet into the welcoming leaf shadows. Maple, birch, poplar. Maple, birch, poplar. The leaves could use a wash, no rain for a while. Mother waters the garden every evening. The spruce trees, little and big, have their dark needles.

Now comes the venerable pine with its trunk like a giant elephant's leg, old weathered hide, very tough. The limbs are huge and strong, reaching in their different directions. The needles spread the sun. Look up. Look up and up and up. Mother loves this tree with a special cherishing. Pa honors it.

The child Wilma bows to the pine tree, an extravagant fine low bow. When she straightens up she sees beyond. A cone of sun is coming on the path. It is almost walking, but has no legs. She knows to look. She knows to be still. No humming now. Quiet, quiet, quiet.

The cone of sun is coming, scary and good. Stay here. Don't run.

Now you are inside it. Don't breathe too much. Wait. More will happen.

Quiet, quiet, quiet.

Wait for the answer. That's a good girl.

Now it is a piece of sun inside you, like a new thought all your own. Now you know more.

Sit down on the path. Breathe and breathe. Look at the pine. Root, trunk, branches, needles. All the parts. Stay and get used to things. Feel the air.

OK. Get up and brush off.

Whisper the tiniest whisper in the world: God.

Walk back to the house slowly, no skipping.

Step, step, step.

Step, step, step.

Never tell.

~ ~ ~

So it comes back, her very own god moment. All one need do, apparently, is scatter a few handfuls of ash, remnants of a centenarian mother—do this in the presence of friendly humans—and then turn to solitude. It is deep night. She has slept for a few hours and is now sharply awake. The moon has set, the stars astonish, the kitchen floor is cold under her bare and grateful feet. This is the beginning.

How long does she stand at the kitchen sink, cold water running into the glass, the overflow stinging her hand?

Is this the beginning?

The water runs colder and colder. Her hand will be numb.

It was a simple vision. She trusts what happened, has always trusted it. But it was a child's experience and she is no longer a child. What now?

Lorraine, former nun, scholar, would occasionally show her a passage from some mystical text, or read a page aloud. *The Clowde of Unknowyng* was an esteemed source. The *nakid entent* of the human, the *nakid beyng* of God, the *clowde of unknowyng* that hovers between the two—and the precious, unpredictable, occasional *peersyng* of the cloud —these were the basic ingredients of the mystical experience, said the anonymous fourteenth century author. Lorraine seemed weirdly fascinated and oddly distanced—scholarly, perhaps—when she read from these mystical writings. Wilma listened, unsure of her own response. She did not feel distanced.

"Stripped," said Lorraine one night as they got into bed. "God and the human, both. Stripped to nudity. Come here." It was one of their early

70

"sex nights"—that was Lorraine's bald phrase for them—nights that would begin with a stern tone and escalate to steamy intensities kept as quiet as possible, for Alma had excellent hearing. Muffled giggles were their denouement night after night. No one would imagine Lorraine, so tall and thin and tightly directive in the daytime, whispering terms such as *polymorphous perversity* into her lover's ear as she shed layer after layer of inhibition. And then in the morning: stiff and formal as she bade good-day to Alma and Wilma and left for her work, college professor, part-time but hoping for better.

Lorraine, then. Add her in.

Wilma turns off the tap, puts the glass down, rubs her numb hand dry. She shakes it through pins and needles to usefulness, drinks the water, rinses the glass, puts it in the dish drainer.

Add Lorraine in?

Never mind. The childhood vision is surely enough for now, it is nearly three in the morning. Impossible to return to bed, though. She sits at the table. No light but starlight. The box is resting empty between unlit candles. She pulls it toward herself, strokes the sides, and ponders the day just passed. All those O'Connors. And Lyle. Tears running down the poor fellow's face. Who grieves more for Alma departed, the daughter or the one-eyed friend?

Is it grief at all that rises up in the daughter?

We don't require pansies. Let me go. Last words of ghost Alma. But can Wilma call back Alma's actual last spoken words? She hasn't even thought to try.

She was leaving to do the shopping. She kissed the fragile skin of the aged cheek and wiped away a runnel of water. Alma's eyes leaked steadily in her last days, a phenomenon, Wilma learned, due to a condition paradoxically termed "dry eye." Tears ran down and gathered in the deep creases that framed the poor dry lips. Eye drops helped but did not eliminate the problem. Could they have been real tears, though, that last morning? Meaningful? No way to tell. Wilma wiped them away, whatever their nature. Alma was alert, responsive, said something— something simple. It takes a moment, but she remembers. "Nothing for me, dear. No hunger now. Have a happy journey." More words than had been spoken for a while. *Have a happy journey.* Such a generous final wish. How could it have slipped from her mind? But after Alma died,

71

even after the cremation, she was so oddly busy—busy with the lively ghost, and the parental writings, and the hours of holding this cube, which could use a wash, like the leaves on that dry summer childhood day.

She did have a vision, didn't she?

She absolutely did. And then, solemn at the age of eight, she sat down, right where she was, to contemplate the fact. As she rinses away the last remnants of Alma's ashes and reaches for the dish towel, Wilma erupts into laughter—full, solitary, pre-dawn laughter—laughter to the point of tears because what did she do at her mother's memorial service? Abruptly and inexplicably sat down. And where did she do this ridiculous sitting? Precisely where she sat and pondered God-inside-her at the age of eight. She wipes her tears with her sleeve, shaking her head, catching her breath. And just the other day, on the sidewalk beside the pansies—

She holds the ceramic cube to her body, dish towel in hand, cold floor under her feet. The crystal stars give bare light. She takes a breath. She takes another breath. These are deliberate, steadying breaths. She sits down at the table.

So. Sitting.

Well, yes. Sitting. Why not? Is it Buddhists who call their practice "sitting"? Eastern religions have appealed to her no more than any other, but perhaps a Schuh version of "sitting"? It seems as good a way as any for an experimental beginning. A sort of meditation, then, minus unwanted elements. No master with stick in hand striking the shoulders of the exhausted novice who slumps as she kneels, buttocks on her heels. A position which must become terribly uncomfortable. Is the term novice? As in the Catholic convent? It is still a bit unbelievable that she, Wilma Schuh, daughter of parents with no religion at all, found herself with Lorraine, a woman who dropped religious jargon into daily conversation, always making sure the Latin derivation was understood. Novice, for example: new to the life, but not as wet behind the ears as the postulant. Postulant: asker, requesting admittance. Wilma might be a novice, but she is surely not a postulant. Of whom would she humbly, with bowed head, ask admittance—and admittance to what?

Perhaps she lacks the bowed head.

Perhaps such a thing is not needed.

So: no master for Wilma, and no companionable clutch of postulants or novices. This much she knows. Solitude is of the essence.

She knows, too, that Alma's ceramic cube will remain on the table, contented between candles, awaiting its next task. She places it there *sans* Alma, its new state. Not unlike her own new state.

Her own disconcertingly new state.

But never mind that. What else does she know about this mysticism project?

Several things. No marathons of physical discomfort of any kind, she's much too old for such nonsense. She'll eat what she wants, when she wants it, and sleep when she chooses to, as much as she chooses to, within the limits of occasional insomnia. Absolutely no asceticism. And no mountain tops. No wandering the desert. No caves.

Good. Throw out an entire tradition. What fine work for the first night. She reaches around, pats herself on the back. She's getting a little giddy. Fatigue, no doubt.

But what else? Does she know *anything* else?

Something about words.

Words?

Yes, something about words. Something—

She is far too tired to know what it might be. Possibly she will know tomorrow.

It is already tomorrow, though. It is several hours past midnight on the day after Alma's service.

Possibly today then. Possibly later today she will discover what it is she knows about words, after some sleep, and a shower, and a good breakfast. And then what? She has no plan for this entire long-stretching day ahead. This is neither frightening nor exciting to her tired mind or her yawning mouth or her wide-stretching arms, but her bowels are disconcerted.

Her bowels are *very* disconcerted.

Wilma rushes to the bathroom.

~ ~ ~

73

Her bowels having emptied themselves, she slept. Dreams came, a hoard of dreams—attacking, taking over—but they fled, phantoms that they were, as day struck, sunlight at the window invading, superseding.

Wait, though. She almost—

The O'Connors, yes—entertaining Christina the Astonishing, feeding the saint good O'Connor food—and then—yes—a Christian martyr or two—Lawrence roasting on a red-hot gridiron, declaring he was quite done on this side and they might as well turn him over—and the Crusades, the terrible Crusades—Christians out to kill Muslims, murdering a few Jews along the way. How violent the religious can be.

Well.

She has already showered and fed herself and laid her folded blanket on the floor and stretched and held and released her various muscles. Some routines remain in place. Now she will sit. The brown couch is as good a place as any. She will place a firm pillow at her back, set her feet flat against the floor. She will be upright, serious, full of intention, and ready for whatever hilarity might come.

Hilarity?

As she arranges the pillow and adjusts her body, she has to ask: is it possible this god project will be—entertaining?

A wave of glee—*glee*—passes through her and she's laughing out loud again, as she did in the wee hours, bending forward as she sits, tears running down her cheeks.

Ridiculous, but isn't this whole thing a bit ridiculous? Who does this in daylight?

She does.

She settles herself. She takes a deep happy breath. So, here she is.

She knows that some sitters, or meditators, or whatever they might call themselves, focus on breathing. She knows, too, that such will not be her way. Let the breathing take care of itself, it's done a fine job for almost seventy years.

Perhaps a mantra. But how do those lacking a guru—she knows about gurus and intends to lack one forever—acquire such?

Try closing your eyes, old lady, says Wilma to herself.

It should be noted that she does not feel like an old lady. It was one of the scruffy Bangor Moirae who threw that designation her way, wasn't it? Yes. Well, the creature was young and easily forgiven.

74

Wilma closes her eyes. She waits.

She is in the desert, where she has never been and never plans to be, walking easily, so perhaps there is a firm path in the sand. She requests a little manna and, by the way, a mantra. Up she looks. Down looks the sun. Manna arrives. She eats. All around her are thin seekers holding the white hems of the long skirts of strolling gurus. A glow of Hollywood holiness—Lorraine had a moment of enthusiasm for movies in bad taste —surrounds the gurus and even the seekers. The seekers attend only to their leaders. They fail to notice the abundance of manna. Poor things, they are so hungry in their sacred subservience. Wilma herself is finely fed.

Do we detect a note of superiority—the cardinal sin of pride—in this woman?

For shame, Wilma Schuh.

She shakes her head, chuckles, opens her eyes, spreads her arms wide. Here she *is*. She quite radically does not know what she's doing. Which fact seems as fine as any other.

Think, though, Wilma.

Manna, but no mantra. Where is her mantra?

Om? Om, om, om...

Surely not. Overused.

But she's following some faint trail, no matter how peculiar. The mind is moving along.

Perhaps it ought to be staying still.

But no. *Following* is right. The very word has resonance. Think of the food, real food in the refrigerator, in the cupboard, in pots, on plates, eaten with the aid of silverware. Following, she has expanded the elements of her daily diet beyond peanut butter and celery. Bread, potatoes, green vegetables are now consumed. She is on the verge of eating meat. Next shopping, red meat. This she knows.

Alma died while she, Wilma, shopped, a fact not insignificant. Now, in the arena of shopping, she follows.

Yes, well.

So there is shopping and there is sitting. Sitting beside pansies she met the three Fates. What could be more significant? Those girls must have had a little story to tell at supper time. Or is twelve an age when nothing is told to parents?

She does need a mantra. A sound or a word. With or without meaning? There are probably different schools of thought on this point. Her way? Wedge herself between the two, refuse to choose a school.

Refuse / to choose / a school.

Poetry!

So much silliness, but no matter. She likes the idea of the wedge. She likes the word itself: wedge. It would lose and regain meaning, play at its task, change shape and function as needed. It would have its own mind.

Nonsense.

Nevertheless.

Wilma leaves her post and takes another drink of cold, cold water, goes to the bathroom and empties her bladder, glances out the window, spies the Volkswagen painted to match a robin's breast. Her own car might be the poor relation, faded but sufficient. The two cars, alike and unlike, might suggest a story, a little vehicular drama to entertain passersby.

She sits down on the comforting brown couch. "Wedge" is unpredictable, isn't it? It might hold firm one day, disintegrate the next. She likes this. Already she can barely remember how she came upon the word, which is perhaps more sound than word. A satisfying sound, a single syllable and more than a single syllable. *Wedge.* She can think of no religious tradition it would be attached to. Good.

Wedge.

It will suffice.

~ ~ ~

Having decided *wedge* would be her mantra, Wilma found herself at loose ends. She napped and fretted the hours away. Day turned to night. She slept, sunk in a perplexing void, and woke up early—as if there were a vague and curious appointment to keep. She sits now in determined comfort on her brown couch. She closes her eyes. Is she ready?

Wedge, wedge, wedge, goes the mind. A great wedge of cheese with great holes and a great pale yellow essence appears. She herself is the tiniest mouse, overwhelmed by her task: to eat the huge wedge.

Food, food, food, thinks Wilma. Peanut butter, manna, cheese. Is she hungry? She is not hungry.

The cheese is unreasonably dense where not, in its holes, excessively empty. She crawls around, takes a bite here and there, chews and swallows.

Wedge, wedge, wedge.

She manages to climb into a hole and rest in the curve of it.

Wedge, wedge.

Perhaps she sleeps briefly, a tired mouse.

Wedge.

Her back hurts. She shifts around, undoes the discomfort, looks for the cheese but it's gone.

Wedge, wedge, wedge, wedge, wedge.

Wedge, wedge, wedge, wedge, wedge, wedge.

She's faintly bored. Is this enough for the first try?

Not quite.

Wedge, wedge, wedge. The clock ticks. A truck in need of a muffler passes by. The Robin-breasted Volkswagen waits in its place across the street, quietly parked. Or was, just a while ago. She somehow hopes it hasn't moved. The car must belong to a neighbor, it seems to feel at home. She herself feels at home, able.

Wedge, wedge, wedge.

Her breathing slows.

Wedge, wedge. A slight loosening around her head, a band of ease, like those hippy headbands of years gone by, not that she ever wore one. Colorful, they were. Pleasant.

Wedge, wedge, wedge. The cheese returns, but quickly leaves. The little mouse slips into a slit in the wall. Wilma coughs. Her eyes water. She wipes them.

Wedge.

Her eyes itch to open. Enough now?

Yes.

She stretches, blinks, looks around. What a fine apartment she lives in. Is the air a bit brighter? Perhaps.

She walks, yawning, to the kitchen. So God, on first acquaintance at this stage of life, is a piece of cheese. Possibly this meditation was not a complete success. She does appreciate a bite of good cheese, though.

She runs a glass of water. She herself was a mouse. Well, they're cute little things, not that she's ever been happy to see them in her living quarters, or elsewhere.

She drinks.

Wait. Something about mice—

Ah, yes. Those old cartoon dreams.

When Lorraine Benedict, first and only lover, entered her life, so did a series of dreams. Whimsical or frightening, these were vivid, highly colored, but there was always a small mouse, a newsreel sort of mouse from the 50s, grainy in black and white. It would appear in a corner, separate, an observer, curious, prudently cautious but never seriously frightened. No matter the tone of the dream, no matter that each scene threatened to explode into the unexpected, the little creature understood that the outcome would be harmless. A philosophical mouse.

Wilma has not thought of those dreams for years. Her entire dream life went underground as Alma slid into very old age. But now she has crazy Christina in rags, Lawrence on the grill, the appalling Crusades. An onslaught. Or a homecoming. Alma's ashes having been scattered, she, Wilma, is carried back into the homeland of her own nights. Carried, as if she were a child.

A child?

Let that be. She will not drift, neither will she dither. Today she wants none of the uncertain strangeness of yesterday and has had the good sense to make a plan. She will bicycle to the waterfront and then to Shaw's. She will buy meat and perhaps even something sweet from the bakery. She ignores the dark clouds in the sky. A plan is a plan.

~ ~ ~

The waterfront is deserted. Good. She sits on the grass, appreciating Bangor's decision to save the river's edge for moments such as this, for humans such as herself. She watches the somber Penobscot, its slow workings. Perhaps the meditation was entirely successful. What constitutes success, after all? The very question is most likely out of order. A few gulls fly down the path of the river toward her. They land. Do they expect food? How large they are as they walk by. How white and gray and *real*. As if—

78

But her thought is interrupted by another, for Wilma has just understood that her meditation gave her—oh, dear—a Big Cheese. She sits shaking her head. A god with an inflated ego? God forbid!

But she wonders if she herself has sufficient humility as she approaches the god. Is she a bit too confident about her rights? Her capacities?

She doesn't like the idea of the Big Cheese who is, look at him, strutting around with chest puffed out and wearing, it seems, a red plaid shirt. Banish him.

But "the god"—

"True singing is a different breath, about / nothing. A gust inside the god. A wind." Rilke. His song was his poetry. She's no poet, but can't she sing in her own way? Will this mean meditating? About nothing?

Well, possibly.

What a plunge this seems.

Plunge. "Nothing is so mute / as a god's mouth. As lovely as a swan / on its eternity of unfathomed surface, / the god glides by, plunges, and spares his whiteness." More Rilke. Alma would faintly repeat, "and spares his whiteness." Then the contented sigh and the declaration: "Lovely. Isn't it lovely, Wilma?"

Yes, but what does it mean, Alma?

Alma had no answer. Needed none, most likely.

Alma, listen. I am setting out to encounter the god. Imagine.

Silence. Alma is not. Exists not. Not in any form her daughter can perceive. Nothing is so mute as a mother's mouth. A lump of sorrow tangled with liberation stops the daughter's breath. Her life has changed. Her *life*: the days, the hours, the minutes. When did she last feel she could pedal to the Penobscot, lay her bicycle on the grass, and sit for as long as she liked? And when was she so utterly, utterly alone? Should she be terrified? Should she rise up and dance a jig?

Neither. She'll sit here until she is moved to stand, at which point she will shop. It occurs to her—she's breathing again—that perhaps meditation enhances memory. Those cartoon dreams coming to mind, with their observant little mouse. And the lines from Rilke. She'll become a paragon.

Well, let us not be carried away. One meditation and some momentary prowess in the sphere of memory do not a paragon make.

Still, it's very pleasant to find the mind able. Poor Pa. He endured the disabling. That mind, so disciplined, so faithfully—even ecstatically—exercised: that it would give way, crumble—

When her father was diagnosed with Alzheimer's disease, Wilma indulged in a moderate form of worry about her own mind. This lasted for some years. One day she felt a capacity within—a sudden muscularity of will—and sent the fear into exile, decisively and forever. She wondered even as she did it whether this was an experience of what the religious called *grace*. It seemed a feat both entirely hers and not at all of her own making. And now her memory—that same sudden muscularity—

"Hello, Wilma."

Marlene O'Connor, materializing from nowhere, plops herself down beside Wilma and blithely apologizes for startling her. Wilma is indeed startled, and irritated, and of course polite. Marlene has an open bag of dried fruit and offers it. Wilma finds herself courteously disinclined. Food cannot yet be consumed without forethought. Besides, she's been munching on a large wedge of cheese. She watches Marlene chew.

"Will it rain?" Marlene asks eventually, as if Wilma will know, as if she herself, childlike, must rely on the grownups for such judgments.

"It might," Wilma says, unaccountably embarrassed.

The embarrassment turns out to be prescience. Marlene plunges into discomfiting old waters, sparing neither of them: "I'm sorry about the affair with Lorraine."

Wilma scrutinizes soft, flyaway, multi-colored Marlene, all loose long skirts and scarves, and then blinks and feels the heat spread up her neck as she blushes—*blushes*—in the presence of this least tactful O'Connor. There is a crack of thunder in the distance. Is she to forgive her interlocutor? And for what? For sexual pleasures taken decades ago? For raising such a topic with no prelude and no consideration?

"I don't mean you're supposed to forgive me or anything. And I know it was a long time ago, you probably never even think about it. I suppose you know she took the lead. I worshipped her mind, is what it was. And she did demand. It was so easy to go along with her, wasn't it? I suppose you found that, too. And she could be quite the tiger in bed. Well, I guess—"

80

Wilma bursts out laughing. This at least stops the flow from Marlene's fig-sweetened mouth, but only for a moment. "Oh, Wilma, how absolutely ridiculous of me. And your mother just died. Are you sure you don't want some of this? The apricots are especially good, soft and not too tart, but no sugar added. It's just that ever since the memorial service—you were miraculous, by the way—ever since, I've had this on my mind. *You've got to make things right with Wilma*, I told myself. But —Wilma?"

Wilma has passed from laughter to tears, a time-honored passage. She saw herself do it. She was her own little mouse, peeking into a cartoon scene of simplified emotion which erupted without warning and abruptly changed shape.

"Oh, Wilma!"

Marlene folds her into a large and amazing embrace and rocks her and rocks her, murmuring, cooing, wiping tears from her own face.

~ ~ ~

The rain comes, and wind and thunder and more lightning than Wilma has seen in years, and they sit, the only humans at the riverfront, two women in their sixties, wiping their eyes—senselessly—as heavenly buckets of water pour over them.

Then they are standing up.

Marlene starts it. "Hey! Goddess! Welcome!"

Wilma stares.

Marlene tells her it's her turn.

Wilma considers, nods her head, adds her piece. "Hello! Big Cheese!"

Marlene glances sideways, makes no comment, turns to the sky and through cupped hands yells: "O Mighty Maker!"

On they go.

"Brawny Being!" "Holy Hubbub!" "You're drowning us!" "You're watering our dry edges!"

"*What* dry edges?" asks Wilma.

Which sends Marlene into helpless giggles.

Which amuses Wilma greatly.

"Spare us!" says Marlene to the sky, when she can.

81

"Mercy!" adds Wilma.

"Let up, O Great Wet One!" says Marlene, shouting her loudest.

But the Great Wet One does not let up. Shaw's is nearby, so they shop, dripping and laughing. Marlene carries the groceries and Wilma walks her bicycle and the sun comes out just as they approach Wilma's apartment.

"A sign," says Marlene, beaming.

"Of what?"

"Oh, just a sign."

"Hmm," says Wilma. She unlocks the door. Here they are. She hadn't imagined actual living guests. There seems nothing to do but offer a bath. Marlene insists on going second. "I must honor my elders," says she, bowing. "Take your time, Wilma. I see you have books. Best way to get to know a person: browse the books."

"Very well," says Wilma, bowing back. She turns and walks youngly down the hall, veers to the bedroom and takes down from the closet shelf one old gray blanket. Quite naturally therefore, having given her guest serviceable gray wool to wrap her wet body in, Wilma runs a bath for herself, gets in, soaks and muses. What stage of life has she entered? Perhaps this is a wrinkle in time, as the children's book has it. Perhaps she is starting over, a youthful person drawn to behaviors such as shouting at the sky during thunderstorms. Will she now routinely indulge in long hot baths while women she barely knows browse her books? Her body likes this day, that much is clear. She closes her eyes and sinks down. The tub is full to the brim, the water wickedly hot. Extravagance!

When she emerges in dry clothes she finds Marlene at the kitchen table, well-wrapped and reading aloud to herself from Alma's Rilke. "'Oh, this is the animal that never was.'" She sits down quietly. Marlene looks up, smiles, reads on. "'They hadn't seen one, but just the same they loved / its graceful movements, and the way it stood / looking at them calmly, with clear eyes.'" It is Rilke's unicorn sonnet, one of Alma's many favorites. Wilma listens to the familiar lines. Marlene's wet clothes—including undergarments—hang here, there, everywhere, a frightening sight.

Marlene closes the book and holds it to herself. "I've never read Rilke. I avoid poetry in translation but this is bewitching. 'They nourished it, not with grain, / but with the mere possibility of being.' I'm starving, though. In need of grain. I almost broke into the crackers, but decided I'd wait for permission."

Permission being given, Marlene takes a plateful of the newly purchased rice crackers and the poetry of Rilke and goes for her own long hot soak in the tub. Wilma picks up Spinoza's *Ethics*, as if her father's philosopher might be a help. She opens at random and reads: "If the parts of an individual thing become greater or smaller, but so proportionately that they all preserve the same mutual relation of motion-and-rest as before, the individual thing will likewise retain its own nature as before without any change in its form." It isn't Rilke. It doesn't offer a calm clear-eyed animal that never existed—an animal that never needed actual existence, is just fine without actual existence. Is Marlene O'Connor, inexplicable presence, now bathing in the tub Wilma just left, a fantasy? A creature from the realm of mere possibility? She *seems* real enough. She seems in fact stunningly real, though improbable.

Spinoza. He, at least, surely existed. Wilma has no idea what the point of this sentence is, what the context. The implication, though: if a part of a thing—or, presumably, a person—grows or shrinks on its own, separate from the other parts, then a change in the very nature of the thing, or person, will result. A grotesqueness? Or perhaps a transformation for the better? But, wait—*the same mutual relation of motion-and-rest*—

Motion? Rest? But they are one thing, as the hyphens clearly show: motion-and-rest. Meaning? Something about speed, about slowness. Nothing static here. Growing or shrinking—parts together, parts apart—every "thing"—it's very nature—it's "form"—might, perhaps disastrously, change—unless—*mutual relation of motion-and-rest*—

Think, oh daughter of Henry Schuh.

But Wilma is not so much thinking as—

Can this be?

Yes, this can be: Wilma Schuh is experiencing a physical response to the words of Baruch Spinoza. A sexual response. A new relation of motion-and-rest within her very own wrinkled-in-time body.

Thus it is that when Marlene O'Connor walks naked into the kitchen toweling her hair, abundant in flesh and exuding an unexpected but perfectly pleasant and very warm pinkness, Wilma rises up from her chair and kisses her. On the lips. In order to make things mutual, as the great philosopher Spinoza apparently preferred.

They do not have sex. They cook, as befits women of their age and fragmented acquaintance, a quick, simple meal: steak, boiled potatoes, spinach. At two-thirty in the afternoon. For dessert they indulge in doughnuts, plain cake doughnuts for Wilma and raised sugared doughnuts for Marlene, two apiece. When the dishes are finished, they go to the living room, one with Spinoza, the other with Rilke, and read in unlikely, natural, comfortable silence until Marlene looks up and speaks.

"I ought to be working."

"Working?"

"I like to work in the late afternoon."

"It's very late in the afternoon."

"I know."

"What work?"

"Oh, collage. Acrylics. Some oils. I seem to be avoiding watercolors lately. I have several things going."

"You're an artist!"

"I do seem to be. Took me a while to agree to call myself that. Decades."

"And if you went now, to work—"

"I'm supposed to be framing pencil sketches to submit for a little show. I can't stay with any one medium. Or woman."

"Oh. I hadn't assumed—"

"No, I'm not assuming you had, but—"

"Well."

"Yes. Well."

"Clarity is a fine thing. Thank you for that, Marlene. But I didn't—I mean I don't—expect—"

"No. I know. Nor I."

"Well."

"Yes. Well."

Marlene, who has been sitting blanket-wrapped, begins to don her partially dried garments. Wilma ponders. She has never known an artist. It seems rather special to know one. Should she ask to see Marlene's work? What might that lead to? Should today be considered, as it seems to want to be, a day outside of time, a day belonging to some other dimension?

Marlene is at the door when she turns and says, "Have you ever thought about acquiring a cuddle buddy, though?"

~ ~ ~

That was yesterday. Today Wilma is experimenting with the god while absorbing the new concept. Cuddle buddy. Marlene gave an understandable enough definition: cuddling, up to and including full body contact; occasional kissing; prudently spaced nights spent together; no sex. "Really and definitively, Wilma: no sex. And no massages. This is not about subterfuge. It's about friendship and comfort. It's very pleasant. If it's not pleasant it stops." She kissed Wilma on the cheek, said she'd call soon, and departed.

Wedge, wedge, wedge, wedge.

No Big Cheese today. Big Marlene instead. Very big Marlene, floating, tumbling, flirting, spreading wide her arms, flying in parabolic pattern, a trace of color on the path behind, the work of art created in the air becoming more complex and interesting with every moment's passing. *Wedge, Wedge.* A small mouse, a pale gray little thing with bright eyes, watches the show, all agog and nibbling absently on a morsel of something which might or might not be cheese. Perhaps it is only a dropped remnant of doughnut. *Wedge, wedge, wedge.*

Marlene. Expanding. More and more ethereal. *Wedge.*

Marlene. Invisible but not absent. *Wedge, wedge.*

A tingling in the body. *Wedge, wedge, wedge, wedge.*

A happy sense of lightness. *Wedge.* Lightness of body, lightness of mind. *Wedge. Wedge.*

A breeze, though the windows are closed. Slight gust inside the god, then. *Wedge, wedge, wedge.*

And nothing is required. *Wedge, wedge.*

Wilma falls asleep. When she wakes up, sitting comfortably on her couch, she smiles. Perhaps in a week or two she'll hear from Marlene.

Her "meditation" finished, she chews on a substantial piece of toast made from bread overloaded with whole grains, seeds, and nuts, Marlene's choice as they dripped their way through the aisles of Shaw's.

She chews also on the possibility: at the age of seventy—well, almost— she might acquire a "cuddle buddy." What would the god think? Perhaps the god "thinks" not at all. Perhaps thinking is a human phenomenon. Should she, would-be mystic, be cogitating a bit more assiduously than she has been? Are there decisions to be made? Will Marlene call?

She remembers the question that came to her a while back, perhaps in the first week after Alma died. Must she somehow cleave to reality more firmly now? Strange question. Had she separated from reality? Had she and her mother lived in a land apart from the rest of humanity? Is Marlene another Alma? Not another mother, hardly that. But Alma herself was barely a mother. Though as Lorraine's death loomed, then, yes, a mother. Cleave to reality. What precisely might that mean? Maybe if she capitalized it: cleave to Reality. *That* shifts things. Does it invite Marlene in, though, or exile her? What *would* the god "think"? Or, to put it more practically, what effect might Marlene have on the quest for mystical experience? For that matter, what effect might this "project" have on Marlene, or anyone entering Wilma's life?

Is Marlene another Alma?

And in what precise way might Marlene be—strange thought—a unicorn?

Wilma attacks the last bit of toast, finishes her coffee, and gets up to do the few dishes. Where is that other visitor, the one who might have stepped out of a novel set in the Deep South? She was to be the companion, the silent, not-at-all-cuddly companion. Nothing of the unicorn about *her*. Solitude was her name and she wore a veiled hat. Marlene has an unexpected capacity for silence. It was strangely Schuh-like, how the two of them sat in friendly quietude and read their books. Rilke and Spinoza! It must have been at least an hour, a late afternoon hour of quiet and magical paradox, privacy deepening in the presence of another. Spinoza made sudden sense then, though it wasn't the kind of sense that could be explained, even to the self. Still, a river of clarity ran through the mind, as if a severe and forceful intelligence had arrived, a wide rush of water carving a bed in the sand, sudden and shining, It was not a mirage, it was an insistence. One felt the need to assert to one's own skeptical self that it was no mirage.

But that was temporary. When she tried to read Spinoza later in the evening, sitting alone, he became an unrewarding chore for a spent mind.

The soul had been sucked out of him. Or out of his reader. Perhaps she was simply tired.

Well. That was yesterday. Today looms.

She finishes the dishes, wipes her hands, looks around. What next? *Will* Marlene call?

~ ~ ~

She does not want her days to loom. That she might wait in appalling anxiety for the phone to ring like an adolescent with a crush on a popular girl is a prospect so utterly ridiculous as to evoke action. She sweeps the back stairs, chanting *Go, Go, Go* until she's laughing out loud and feeling quite completely back in control. For good measure she runs a bucket of soapy hot water, and scrubs, step after step. And rinses. And *dries*. More and more in control! How good of Marlene O'Connor to act as catalyst for cleanliness, thinks Wilma Schuh as she dumps the dirty water into the toilet and sits down at the kitchen table with paper and pen to design Stage One. She feels splendidly competent as she lists the elements of her plan.

Stage One
1. Maintain self-care routines.
2. Meditate daily.
3. Read daily from Spinoza and/or Rilke; and from Henry and/or Alma.
4. Leave apartment at least once a day.
5. Speak at least minimally to another human every day.
6. Observe the progress of the season.
7. Know the look of the night sky before getting into bed.
Note: it is permitted to throw everything over in favor of a gust inside the god.

It is a document resting on reality, a simple outline of what she has already stumbled upon. Beyond this she will not venture, not yet.

Neatly penned, discreetly folded into quarters blank side out, the plan is placed on the dresser in the bedroom beside the bones of Alma.

The next two weeks are crowded with the efforts of solitude. Marlene does not call. Wilma decides this is for the best. She has folded the piece of paper on which Marlene scribbled her phone number and address and tucked it under a canister, wondering mildly if she'll remember for more than a day or two where she put it. She does remember, but never mind. At least she has not looked at it.

Marlene does not reappear in meditations, does not visit dreams, seems a bit of an apparition when remembered. Wilma thinks occasionally—most often during one of her currently varied, often spontaneous, thoroughly pleasing meals—that some line of connection between this youngest O'Connor and ghost mother Alma might be drawn. It is an intriguing, undeveloped idea, far from the center of life.

The center of life is what she has come to call The Work. She follows her plan. She is set inside its rhythms, a solitary would-be mystic. Every morning she unfolds the Stage One page, reads it, refolds it, puts it back in its place. She lightly touches the three saved fragments of her mother's skeleton, then turns and leaves the bedroom. She brushes her teeth, she prepares her meals, she does her dishes. She folds her blanket and gets down on the floor and stretches her muscles. She walks or bikes and faithfully makes conversation with the clerk at the store, the pedestrian at the stop light. She communes with the ever-larger, ever-greener leaves, visits the pansies, and admires the velvet petals even as they wither. The night sky yields a steady rhythm of clarity and cloud. The words of Spinoza, Rilke, Henry, and Alma offer themselves with moderate force and energy and only rarely does she have to press them with the palms of her hands back onto the page. Does she like this life? She does. Insights abound. To meditate, she decides, is to pry open a moment of time and peer in, hoping to catch the gleam at the core, the tiny local fountain of a vast eternity.

She muses: to pry open.

And laughs, because she intends to pry her moments open with nothing less than a sharp-edged and very firm tool, a wedge, just made for the job.

Ah, pattern.

But the image is imperfect. A wedge does not pry open. It might keep a thing from closing, or falling. It might level what was left askew.

But it will not on its own pry anything open. Perhaps some other tool will be needed, some tool of compulsion.

Compulsion?

One does prepare for the possibility: a force that would drastically alter the hitherto known self. The thought of such violence disturbs Wilma not one whit. She meditates day after day. She repeats, descending through levels of silence, the strange word: *wedge*. Stranger and stranger, this word. It gathers meaning and density, then throws both off. It holds the mind's attention, then disappears. Images come and go, framing the word or inhabiting it or blotting it away. Always there is movement and a sense of the large, a sense of the small. Lightning splits a massive solitary oak situated at the center of a flat, grassy nighttime field while a single flower barely seen, perhaps a daisy, calmly waits at its base. The next moment the sun pours down and a blond child in red and blue clothing eats ice cream on a park bench. Lick, lick, lick goes the slow, careful tongue of the child. *Wedge, wedge, wedge* goes the slow, careful mind of the meditator. The mind becomes the tongue, licking and tasting the cold delicious word.

In these two weeks, no violence to the customary self and no discernible experience of the tiny local fountain of a vast eternity. Not a single element of the Stage One list is tossed away in favor of a gust inside a god. It seems it will be a gentle, slow, undramatic, enjoyable mysticism that emerges for mature, patient, good-humored, solitary Wilma Schuh.

But one afternoon as she is pondering the ceramic box that so recently held Alma's ashes, asking if it might like to hold seeds of some sort, Marlene O'Connor opens the door to the apartment a few inches and whispers, "Wilma? Wilma?"

Mature, patient, good-humored Wilma shrivels to a dry dot. In her stead, unsure and sweating, a twelve-year-old version of herself stands there as Marlene approaches and embraces and coos and is stiffly hated. *Hated.* This is so interesting that Wilma returns to her adult self. When has she ever hated another human? And why should she hate this colorful friendly specimen of womankind? Her arms return the hug she can surely use.

Marlene releases her. They release each other and step back.

89

Marlene, who appears to be in charge, nods and speaks. "Too long, I gather. I should have called at least. I do this again and again, when will I learn? Well, I brought bagels. Are you hungry?"

~ ~ ~

Wilma sits up in bed sipping coffee, her hands around the smooth warm cup. Beside her is her new cuddle buddy. After bagels yesterday they sat, quietly reading, Marlene with Rilke, herself with Spinoza, two women fully dressed. The day was sunny. They stopped occasionally to share a quote, a smile, a simple look across the room. After an hour or so they went for a walk. "Look how clean your steps are," said Marlene. "Yes," said Wilma, "they helped me." "Helped?" "Yes." For a moment Wilma could not recall what she had needed help with. Then she remembered, descended faster, chose a direction, and walked briskly. Marlene had to scurry to keep up.

The moment passed. They let it pass. Of course they did, they are mature beings.

Then they spent the night together, as if such a thing were natural. And here they are in Wilma's bed, sharing a lazy morning.

"I think you should come today," says Marlene, yawning abundantly. She is wearing a large soft pale-yellow tee shirt of Wilma's, left over from when Wilma herself was a bit larger, and her own modest white underpants. Wilma is wearing blue and gray striped men's pajamas, long her preference.

"To the studio?"

"To my apartment, within which resides a defined space for doing art."

"Your studio."

"If you insist."

"Lyle first, though."

"I know. Tell me again why I'm forbidden to join you in the bookstore. It keeps slipping."

"I suppose it's slippery," says Wilma. But is it? Doesn't she have an unpleasantly firm grip on the reason, which is plain fear? "I can't picture it, is all," she tells Marlene.

"Is it too soon after your mother's death?"

90

"How would that enter in?"

"I don't know, Wilma. It's a stab in the dark."

"Well, then, ouch."

"Wilma."

"I suppose you meant the dark of my lack of explanation rather than the dark of my very being."

"I certainly didn't mean to puncture your—um—reserve."

Wilma feels she has no reserve left to puncture if reserve means what's kept back, saved for times of need. It should be the container, though, not the reserve itself that gets punctured. How careless the human mind becomes in circumstances of intimacy.

Why this crankiness, which shadows the morning's wide serenity?

No sex, cuddling only. That is the rule, stated by Marlene, agreed to by both. A vast relief entered Wilma with this simple frame, this clarity. Also a puzzling, surely insignificant irritation.

No sex. Fine.

But what if she comes to want it? Does she even now want at least the possibility?

After all these years! Certainly not.

Is this where violence to the known self enters? Not from the god but from—

Wilma tells herself not to borrow trouble. Marlene is familiar and safe, known since her infancy, surely no threat. She can see herself, eight years old, standing with Alma straight and proper on the neighbors' porch, the screen door barrier, the baby in the mother's arms. Inside, the family, Catholics, caught in their moment of discomfort. Yet the Schuh waifs, mother and daughter, are invited in. Baby Marlene squirms, bright-eyed.

Marlene of the present, finishing her coffee, slithers down under the covers, still bright-eyed, almost baby-fresh. Wilma puts her half-emptied cup aside and slides down beside the human who is now past sixty, mature and quite solid. Soft, too, though, and silky, and obviously appreciative of Wilma's carefully restrained but very interested hands— hands which explore face, arms, and shoulders, staying well within guidelines given yesterday by this youngest O'Connor who is soft of style but perhaps a bit of a tyrant. Marlene turns on her side. They spoon. They nap.

91

~ ~ ~

Or is she herself the tyrant? They got out of bed, washed, dressed, ate breakfast. Now they sit, parked in front of Lyle's Bookstore. She has absolutely forbidden Marlene to come in with her.

Marlene is at the wheel. The car is green, or blue, impossible to remember which. Nothing seems to be loose yet. The steering wheel looks barely worn, firm in the hands. The gear shift, too: firm. The windows do not rattle, the doors shut securely. All this solidity. Her own seatbelt is retracted. Marlene is securely seat-belted and solidly insisting. "It's all right, Wilma. Go. I'll stop by another day for the Blake. I don't even know if it's in yet, Lyle had to order it. I'll come back and wait here for you. Twenty minutes, you said."

"Or fifteen. Maybe ten. Five? How can I know?"

"OK, I'll just walk around a little, ponder things. I'll think about why I'm about to let you see my work and how said work will survive your intelligent gaze. Go!" She kisses her own fingers, pats Wilma's cheek, pushes her out.

Wilma straightens and enters Lyle's territory. Two customers. She hadn't thought about customers. Lyle has not been suspended, timeless, awaiting her visit. She stands inside the door, dismissing the vision of the dear man hanging in space, held there by stretched red suspenders attached to nothing at all. She ought to browse, but doesn't. She moves out of the way to let one customer leave, a woman near her age. They nod to each other, as such women do.

"Oh!" says Wilma, too loudly, for here is Lyle, peering with his one eye. The second customer seems to have left, a young male. He had to pass right by her. She hopes she was courteous. Why is she here?

"Wilma?"

"Hello, Lyle."

"Hello, Wilma."

She feels a bit rooted, treelike. The life of a tree does appeal. Stand and endure, and the rest happens. Leaves arrive, proceed through their green times, dry out, turn color, detach. The bark thickens. Then it's wait to see if you crack in a storm.

"Something I can do for you, Wilma?"

92

"I wondered."

Lyle waits, a patient man.

It occurs to her there are two questions. She could start with the first.

"How are you, Lyle?"

"About the same, Wilma. You?"

"Well, yes. That was the first concern. Next is this." She takes Mr. Solomon's *Keep This Deep and Velvet Night* from Alma's backpack and hands it to Lyle. She seems to have given up using a purse. The backpack reaches out every time she leaves the apartment, it might as well have little arms and hands. Take me, take me, it says. The book, too, seems to have a pressing need to go everywhere with her.

"I wondered if you might explain."

Lyle nods his head, up and down, up and down. More like an elevator than a tree. At what floor will they stop? The Floor of Understanding, apparently, for the man speaks kindly. "You asked me about that when I found it for you, if I grasp the question. I don't know what more to say, Wilma. It must have caught my eye as I passed it. I remember thinking you needed something unusual. Is it unusual? I don't remember the book itself, is the truth. I see it's poetry. Well, that seems a start. Toward what a person might need, I mean."

Generosity of language from this spare man. She feels more human, if not entirely sound.

"I hardly know what's unusual these days. I didn't know I'd feel so unsettled. Abnormal is how I feel. I knew I didn't want my friend with me, so at least we have that. A smidgen of insight, or call it prudence. But never mind. This dear poet—his words—I can't seem to—such an unnerving—I failed to anticipate. Lyle Franklin, if you were a stranger I'd apologize."

"No need."

"Yes, that's right. Rather good, isn't it?"

"You have a friend, you said. A woman, is it? Sit down, Wilma."

"We won't talk about her. Yes, it's better sitting. Was I standing long? I think it's this little book. A perplexing selection, Lyle. The poet's parents committed suicide. They didn't wait, as Alma did, for time to sift itself. His lover left him but it was nothing like—"

93

"Lorraine? Yes, well. It might have been a poor choice. Losing loved ones is not a homogenous category, I see that. Should I try again?"

"No. The problem is how relevant, besides bewildering. I can't make sense of how loudly the lines speak, though hands seem an element. I've been thinking about hands, how Henry—my father, you didn't know him —"

"No."

"He held my hand rather often. I did value that. I think it was when we were approaching our work, his work and mine. Carpentry, for example. I would have been quite small, or did it extend? Perhaps it stopped when I reached twelve, I've told you about twelve."

"Left you on your own with your studies, is that right? Along with the five-foot bookshelf."

"You were listening, even on such a day. Yes, *The Harvard Classics*. But this little book—"

"Might have been an error on my part."

"I don't mean that. Hands are featured, they have a language here. His hands say no, the lover's do. But hearts are held. A wall and a welcome, could that be it? Alma and I held hands. I was a grown woman. It wasn't the usual thing, certainly not. I can't remember the circumstance."

"The poems bring back memories."

"They do. I seem to remember—Alma and I—standing at the foot of the bed—in which lay my Lorraine—she was very ill—it comes back— we—but no—no, that's not the way to—I do apologize, there's such a crowd in my brain and, yes, I have a possible friend, very new. She can calm things or stir them. I believe you might be the closest I have to an old friend, isn't that strange? I suppose I needed to see a human who knew Alma in her final years. All this about Mr. Solomon's book might be a sidetrack, or possibly not, one can never—"

The door opens. Marlene enters cautiously, almost on tiptoe. She has a companion, a young man whose hand she holds. She seems to have pulled him along almost against his will, he looks so courteously aware that they might be intruding.

"Wilma? Is this—? Are we—? Are you all right?"

So it is that Wilma and Lyle are formally introduced to Henry Whitsun, mime from Massachusetts. "But he's not really from there,"

94

says Marlene, "he's a Mainer. I knew him way back when. He was just a boy, and here he is, returned to us in fine form after his travels. He went to Harvard!"

"I didn't even graduate, Marlene," says this self-possessed young man.

Wilma feels the frisson when they shake hands.

"I saw you faint," she says. The words escape and embarrass her. Clearly she is not quite herself.

~ ~ ~

Wilma and Marlene and young Henry Whitsun are about to leave the bookstore. Henry compliments Lyle on the range and depth of his stock. He found nothing by Gilles Deleuze, but that would hardly be expected. No, there's no need for Lyle to order anything, he actually has the key texts, he was just curious, but if ever a customer asks for a recommendation for a radical, mind-bending twentieth century philosopher—

Lyle nods. Possibly he is amused.

Wilma looks at her little book of poems. One thumb gently strokes it for a moment before she slides into it Alma's backpack. She is unaware of this.

Lyle, after a dry handshake for Marlene who has just paid for a hefty volume of William Blake's poetry and prose, and unexpected handshakes for both Henry and Wilma who have paid for nothing, accompanies the threesome to the door, limping his slight limp. He welcomes an approaching customer—female, adolescent, shy—with a subtle smile and a soft light in his one good eye. Holding the door open, he wishes Wilma and Marlene and Henry a good day, twice. He waves them onward with unexpected gallantry. Lyle Franklin in a good mood.

Three human beings proceed thus blessed to Marlene's apartment which is also, she has to admit it, her studio. Up the steps, two flights, and in they go. Art is everywhere, much of it in progress. Wilma's breath is stopped. She was so curious. What kind of artist might this Marlene O'Connor be? A scan of the space shows no clear style, no clear subject. The paintings are large, small, pale, bold, dark, light, indecipherable, or pulsing with clarity. Here a toilet, there a lovely rhythmic abstraction, and over there, finished and framed, hanging on the wall, a very large human hand.

That one pulls at Wilma until she is locked in front of it. The hand is distorted, discolored. Its bulging fingers extend beyond the boundaries of the canvas. It is a left hand with bruised palm exposed, sinister. It intends to squeeze the viewer's beating heart. The very pigment feels dangerous, the squeeze would be fatal. Wilma feels a desperate need to take the monstrosity down, force it to the floor, press it back into itself as she presses unbearable words back to flatness. She wants to make it agree to be nothing but paint. Of course she will not do this. She turns abruptly elsewhere.

Elsewhere is no better. A vagueness of shapes, colors colliding, danger rising up, pounding intensity.

Impossibility of art, she thinks, having no idea what she means.

It's just paint on canvas, she tells herself. Paint. Canvas. Harmless.

But the power—

Perhaps one ought to bow one's head, adore the Great God of Art. Her head won't bow. It needs to whirl. She feels herself sinking, feels herself held, feels herself lifted. A straight-backed chair is placed behind her and two humans urge her down onto it.

After a moment, she is minimally oriented. Marlene's studio. Art. This young version of a Henry. She has been placed on a chair as if disabled by age or some other condition. Sitting again, then. Perhaps there is something she ought to be doing. Breathing. Or thinking.

Yes, good. Breathe. Think. And best keep the eyes closed for a bit.

What is a condition? Don't we all have one? It isn't age, she knows that. Still, some sort of condition has imposed itself. What about these two, so pleased to have run into each other after a gap of years? Neither seems in a normal state. Marlene is a nervous wreck, she said so herself. The young man stands by, emitting a low glow. Eyes closed, she feels his fine soul. His intriguing soul. Quite preternaturally self-possessed is this Henry Whitsun.

Unlike herself.

Whitsun. Isn't Pentecost referred to as Whitsun? That must be in England. She can almost hear Lorraine saying such a thing. Lorraine Benedict, source of information beyond the scope of the little Schuh women.

96

Surely this young Henry wasn't born to such a name as Whitsun. Did he choose it? Is the mime religious? Should she ask? She might not like the answer. If he has to shine, let him shine beyond the stricture of religion.

As to herself, plainly named, an old shoe in fact: what stricture has her in its grip?

She sits on the chair and watches her mind, declining to see what waits for her eye. She knows, under shut lids, that she is being observed. Well, just give her a moment. Who was prepared for this? The glimpses she could not prevent, the first sight of Marlene's innards—

That's what they must be, Marlene's innards, thrust out into paint. Where are the expected pencil sketches? Are they tamer, less intent on attacking the mind? If she opened her eyes she might locate them, mere pencil marks on white paper, surely smaller and milder, less crude. At the very least, less discordantly colored.

Who is this woman she spent the night with?

The woman she spent the night with speaks. "Is there something we need to know, Wilma? Some medical condition?"

Condition.

"Give me a moment. I'll be fine. No medical condition."

When Wilma opens her eyes she sees that Marlene is standing back, cautious. The mime stands back also, this young Henry, not her father, definitely not an incarnation of her father though the thought occurred on the drive from the bookstore, the short drive to this large, sunny, bare-floored upstairs apartment in Bangor, Maine where Marlene O'Connor lives and works as, yes, a bona fide artist. Not that Wilma believes in reincarnation but what could explain the intensity—the *frisson*—when she shook hands with this young man who shares her father's given name and apparently knows nothing about sparing whiteness? *As lovely as a swan...the god glides by, plunges, and spares his whiteness.* What a compelling poet Rilke was.

"Better?"

"Thank you, Henry. Yes."

"Knocked you flat, did I, Wilma?"

Wilma stares at Marlene who must be attempting humor, always a mistake when one is as tense as this poor woman appears to be.

"With the paintings, I mean. The big ones. I— "

97

Wilma takes a very deep breath which is now possible and necessary.

"All right. Yes. I didn't expect— "

"Ugliness. You didn't expect ugliness."

Wilma sees that Henry is watching. The word makes him flinch but he knows his place. *Mute as a god's mouth.* A hiatus is in effect, a language hiatus. Wilma is watching from afar. She and Henry are now a pair of watchers. Marlene is pinned inside herself, unable to get out, occupied in trying to hold her own. Poor dear Marlene. It's her art, exposed.

"Maybe it's a different beauty from what I'm prepared to see. I'm sorry."

"That's the wrong response, Wilma."

Wilma closes her eyes. Where is she? In some reality she fails to understand. *Wedge. Wedge. Wedge.* A crowbar appears, outsized, beautifully made, floating toward her. It arrives. She leans her being over the black length of it. *Wedge.* She is prying the mysterious reality open with the help of a trusty crowbar, perfect tool for this difficult, satisfying work. *Wedge. Wedge.*

"Wilma?"

She opens her eyes. Marlene is on her knees in front of the chair and her arms are reaching forward. Wilma feels a bit stiff. Marlene is looking at her with a perhaps frightened expression. Here they are, two women, one stiff, the other frightened. Quite a contrast to their time in bed. Life moves along.

Now Marlene's head is resting on her lap and Marlene's large arms are holding her, or are they desperately holding *onto* her? Wilma softens and leans forward. She embraces Marlene and kisses the back of the sobbing head. In her peripheral vision she sees young Henry Whitsun walk quietly toward the largest painting, which is of a complete human body bent upon itself, unless there are two, or even three figures tangled there. Henry stands before the phenomenon, a young man enduring a downpour, unresisting.

~ ~ ~

98

It became possible. They looked at the art, three perfectly sane human beings. They traveled afterward in Marlene's completely comfortable and impressively solid car to Pizza Hut. They ate, they talked.

And talked.

And talked.

Two full hours.

Henry departed, making courteous, warm—even tender, almost loving—eye contact with both women. What a stunning young man. Marlene drove Wilma home. Marlene as chauffeur. Sudden lack of conversation. Wilma got out of the car, turned and said thank you. Marlene said she was welcome and drove off. Was Marlene angry? Wilma didn't think so. It seemed more a matter of disappearance.

That was two weeks ago. Disappearance indeed. Perhaps it frightened Marlene, all that conversation sprouting from the sight of her art. After the little scene that ended with sobbing into Wilma's lap, the artist had gathered herself, risen up, spoken. Questions were asked and answered. Posters taped to a wall were explained.

"No, that's not mine, that's by Francis Bacon, not the old philosopher scientist. This guy, the artist, died in 1992. British, I think, and gay. I guess you can see that. The gayness, I mean. All of these triptychs are his. Lots of weird sex, I know—such distorted bodies, even bloody, some of them, but look at the *energy,* these forms are in *motion*— and there's something sort of *innocent*—and, well, after a while they become so intensely, so entirely, *beautiful*—even the raw meat hanging there—I know, not at first—"

Once started, she needed no prompting.

"William Blake—this is *The Ghost of a Flea*—comes from a vision he had. This one is Bacon again. It started as a bird trying to land. Can't see that in the finished product, of course. A crucified steer was—um— not his original intention. This is *Plan.* By Jenny Saville. Still young, I think. Alive, at least. It's a plan for surgery, the markings the surgeon needs. Makes human fat into something amazing, doesn't it? I see the influence of Bacon, and maybe Blake. I know, they're a strange bunch and sort of off-putting. I seem to need them. I stare and I wait. Eventually something—"

There was a limit to what she could explain. They decided they were hungry. And so to Pizza Hut where Marlene was fully engaged in the talk, talk, talk. Still, did the day frighten her artist's soul?

Perhaps she'd simply had enough of Wilma Schuh.

Or perhaps she was hurt when Henry, graceful sidestepper, refused at first to release the particulars: "Are you married? Do you have anyone, then? Man or woman, Henry? Kids? No one? What have you been doing down there in the land of metropolitan America?" She did pry out of him that when he left Harvard he moved around some, spent a few years in New York City, then fled back to Cambridge. He liked the feel of performing in Harvard Square. No, he didn't finish college but it was obvious to both women that he kept reading. Seriously reading. It was from Cambridge he came now, Bangor boy returning, age thirty-five.

Everyone sipped soda. Henry offered a little anecdote about his drive up to Bangor, something to do with a hitchhiker he picked up. Then he broke his story open with a single sentence. What he was doing down in the land of metropolitan America was being gay. Marlene wanted more. He added, "And becoming a mime, as you know. Watch out, I might go mute on you." Like the god's mouth, Wilma thought. Henry reached for Marlene's hand. She scowled but accepted the gesture. After that the conversation turned lively. Marlene talked and listened and laughed and appeared to be having a very good time. In fact, she glowed.

But perhaps she'd had enough of Wilma.

If pattern were to repeat itself, she would appear now, open the door a few inches, whisper Wilma's name with a question mark. She would be bringing bagels.

Is two weeks the interval she's being trained to expect?

It is almost dusk. Marlene will not appear. Might never again appear. One day they'll meet on the street. "Hello!" "Hello! How *are* you?" Acquaintances.

Unconvincing, this line of thought. She has seen the art.

"I know nothing." That was what Wilma said about art as she sat with Marlene and young Henry, eating pizza, sipping soda, conversing. The three of them revealed themselves not by disclosure of fact and event but by an unfurling of minds. The catalyst was the art. The mode was that of altered states. Elevations, intensities. Curiosities. Kindnesses.

Confusions laughed over, tangled further, untangled. Illuminations with bewildering causes. Satisfactions of every stripe.

Three souls.

It mattered not one whit that she knew nothing, was struck down to radical ignorance, returned to infancy by the sight of the art. Into her eyes and thence to the cells of her naive tissues—into muscle, blood, and bone—had come a chaos of color and form, an assault. It was mystery with edges of horror and she still only half-believes in it. Soft, flighty, warm, smart cuddle buddy Marlene O'Connor, girl from a good Irish Catholic rural Maine family, did this? It was terrifying, exciting—

And addictive, for she feels already the need to go back, and more than once. She has not experienced such an undoing since her first weeks with Lorraine.

Lorraine, seductress, sharp-edged and sharp-minded, directly out of, unbelievably, a Catholic convent. A nun. "Ex-nun." All right then, ex-nun. Still, there she was. And there was Wilma, daughter of Henry and Alma Schuh, parents of no faith at all. Wilma Schuh and a nun. A nun who haunted the conversation at Pizza Hut, additional presence in the booth, squeezed between Marlene and Henry. Glaring, a ghost displeased, until suddenly there would slip into her peering eyes the glint of absolute approval.

"It's really only one section of the room, Wilma," Marlene had said. "One part of the work." It was true. There were tamer pieces, tender sketches of spools of thread, for example. These were "Lost Spools." Spools in a bucket of blueberries, spools in a compost pile, spools balanced precariously on fire hydrants, and a trio of poor pink spools sinking into toilet water, the hand of a human threatening to flush. Sometimes the thread was sadly, irreparably tangled. The spools were Marlene-like enough, not too difficult to attribute to the woman she'd just spent a night with. Even the collages with puzzling phrases tucked into unexpected crevices were somehow Marlene-like. Wilma, innocent of art, felt this. But the larger paintings, the terrible colors, the ugliness, the distorted bodies—that *hand*—

Well.

And then the conversation at Pizza Hut. Minds let loose! And *was* Henry Whitsun the next incarnation of poor dead Henry Schuh after all? There he sat, bringing forth philosophy. Marlene cleared the path, mentioning Wilma's interest in Spinoza—how had that come up? when? —and they tumbled in. Henry said his beloved Gilles Deleuze turned Spinoza into an Expressionist—like the artists!—and wrote two entire books about the god-intoxicated philosopher. The two thinkers were completely different, and yet not at all. Henry was in love with both, converted to Spinoza by Deleuze. Henry, they could see, was prone to falling in love with minds.

But who was Deleuze? Neither woman had heard of him. Henry quoted: "A single and same Ocean for all the drops, a single clamor of Being for all beings." He repeated it until they had it memorized and then waxed lyrical on the importance of every single one of those Deleuzian drops, on the essentially creative aspect, the forever becoming. And more Deleuze: "Individuation is mobile, strangely supple, fortuitous and endowed with fringes and margins." Fringes and margins? Again, they were required to memorize and told it would be good for their aging minds to do so.

Great good humor stirred the soup of philosophy as they laughed and teased and conversed in ways beyond anything Wilma could have imagined. They were, as a threesome, downright charismatic. This she believes, for the waitress was obviously charmed as she came laughing by from time to time, asking if there might be anything they wanted, telling them she didn't understand a word coming from this booth but weren't they having a real good time of it anyway.

Wilma could savor the memory with less ambivalence if Marlene hadn't frozen up afterward. What *was* that? Still, it was an amazing afternoon. Francis Bacon, Marlene's most disconcerting painter, was part of it. Of course he was. Henry knew about Bacon because of Deleuze— that was the link, how philosophy came in—and then Marlene mentioned Spinoza, and Henry Schuh, father of Wilma. There were links upon links. Henry, this young version, wove the pieces together just as he had woven energies in the the air when Wilma saw him perform in front of the Grasshopper Shop, a mime working with whatever was handed to him from his ever-shifting audience. And then fainting. But with Wilma and Marlene he spoke, and was far from fainting. Deleuze, he said, wrote an entire book on Francis Bacon, turning art into philosophy. He read it when he was learning mime, read it *as* a mime. He could quote whole passages, which he kindly did not ask them to memorize. Fragments float

102

to her now "...the violence of sensation...like a wrestler...the visible body...the powers of the invisible...pass through the catastrophe...." She shudders, thinking of those terrible paintings. What is all of this? But those two, Young Henry and Marlene, were only interested. And interesting. Creativity burst the seams of thought in Deleuze, said Henry. Impossible to read, of course—Henry smiled fondly here—but somehow as the complex sentences rolled along and the spiky thought turned itself over and over, Deleuze unveiled every philosopher, every writer, every artist he wrote about as a compelling phenomenon. "You should read the book, Marlene. *Francis Bacon: The Logic of Sensation.*" Marlene wrote the title on a napkin and stuffed it into her purse. Wilma wondered if that napkin would ever be found. But this Young Henry was found.

And what of Marlene? Is she lost now?

~ ~ ~

Wilma has not forgotten her god. If Marlene is gone, well, then Marlene is gone. So be it. The advantage of a god-quest: no matter how much hide-and-seek is involved, the fellow can't really get away. His essence, after all, involves existence. (Wilma knows her god is not a *fellow* but it's a friendly mood-improving term.) It's been sixteen days. No Marlene, no Young Henry. She misses them both, an irrational response since she had no time to acclimate to either. And why be unhappy about what doesn't come? She'd like to rise to the level of Spinoza. "A passive emotion ceases to be a passive emotion as soon as we form a clear and distinct idea of it." She is beginning to understand the tiniest sliver of Spinoza's thought. Passive emotions can be troublesome. Make them active and they bring joy. A clear and distinct idea produces the transformation.

A clear mind might help.

Rather nice, isn't it, that Young Henry was led to Spinoza by his Deleuze? Nothing by Deleuze in the Bangor Public Library. She checked. How far into strangeness might she have gone if those two, the bold artist and the bright mime, had remained in her life? How far into strangeness has she gone under her own suddenly diminished but still puffing steam?

103

She unfolds the page daily. She reads it and refolds it. The creases are starting to weaken but the plan itself seems solid. She follows it, or has until today.

Stage One
1. Maintain self-care routines.
2. Meditate daily.
3. Read daily from Spinoza and/or Rilke; and from Henry and/or Alma.
4. Leave apartment at least once a day.
5. Speak at least minimally to another human every day.
6. Observe the progress of the season.
7. Know the look of the night sky before getting into bed.
Note: it is permitted to throw everything over in favor of a gust inside the god.

Will she ever get past Stage One? What might Stage Two be? It hides behind a Veil of Fog. She knows it's out there—dangling—limp as a thin silk rag—unthought—in the realm of the potential.

Is there such a realm?

When she made her plan, she was concerned that over-involvement with the god might be a danger to simple self-care. It seemed prudent to guard against such a danger. Today she has failed to brush her teeth or eat a meal or stretch her aching back, but none of this is due to god-immersion. Some previously unnoticed housekeeping demon is responsible. It must have been waiting for a blank moment, a space to leap into and take charge. The moment came, the demon leapt, and she was on her knees cleaning out the cupboard under the kitchen sink. Now that she has once again read her plan—it is the third perusal of the day—she wants only to go back to that project. She does not, not, not want to go outdoors or do a single other thing on the list. She most certainly does not want to meditate. She has not forgotten the god. Nothing is more important than contacting whatever the divine might turn out to be. Nothing. Except this cupboard.

Most items under the sink were there when she and Alma moved in, left by the previous tenant who apparently could not cope. Wilma has decided to cope. Every item under the sink has been taken from the dank

104

area and set out on the floor. The idea was to put each into a category, but the task proved more difficult than anticipated. Take a break, move on to cleaning, she told herself. But, rag in hand, she finds herself unable to dip into the bleach water. The categories are clamoring. Items in need of categorizing have refused to stay put and the woman kneeling above the battle—she sees herself as such—is held in strict stasis. How can she bend and enter the dark space and hope to cleanse it when uncertainty permeates all?

Frequently Needed vs. Rarely Used.

Liquid vs. Solid.

Summer vs. Winter.

Butch vs. Femme.

The sorting went smoothly enough at first, but now every item demands double categorization. At least double. Silver polish, for example, is Femme, but also Rarely Used. Beyond that, is it Liquid or Solid? It seems unsure of itself and runs from here to there to there. The complications are multiplying: what is she to do with steel wool?

Butch and Femme are unexpected categories, but she finds them useful, at least potentially—and oddly nostalgic. She was instructed by Lorraine: "You, Wilma, are a definite but subtle butch. I am femme, but not to an embarrassing degree and certainly not of the docile variety." The topic came up at Pizza Hut. Marlene said she agreed with Lorraine. "Subtle butch, yes. Just right for a cuddle buddy, Wilma. For *my* cuddle body, that is." Henry listened and smiled. Apparently he understood this. About herself, Marlene said, "Somewhat femme and don't ask me what that means." But is her art femme? The question was asked by brave Wilma. No such thing as butch art or femme art, said Marlene. She slapped the table when she said it. Henry laughed out loud at that. When Marlene casually referred to Francis Bacon as a faggot, he responded with a mime's gesture of mock shock, then grinned. Faggot, dyke, butch, femme. Marlene and Henry were at home in a language Wilma had never truly spoken.

Silver polish belongs in Femme. This she knows. It irritates her, though, that dish washing liquid keeps trying to get there. She wants it firmly settled in Frequently Needed which is nowhere near Femme.

How far into strangeness *would* her life have gone if Marlene and Henry (they have become a pair) had become an integral part of it? Too far, most likely. Isn't Marlene's art—at least some of it—evidence of some sort of disturbance? And who is this Young Henry, eerie echo of her philosopher father? To be rid of both is perhaps necessary. Necessary and beneficial.

She decides to believe this.

For the moment.

If she can.

She places the dish washing liquid squarely into Frequently Needed, plunges her rag into the bleach water, and bends to reach the grime beneath the sink.

Lorraine looks fondly on. There's her little Wilma.

~ ~ ~

The kitchen wastebasket is bulging with items discarded. The area under the sink is bleach-clean, contents placed rationally, no categories needed. It became obvious: put this here, that there. It only required briskness, decision, action. Lorraine supervised, or her ghost did. The effect was spare and orderly. Relief flooded the room along with noontime sun.

But there lay the toothbrush.

Relief shriveled. Lorraine turned her ghostly head aside, refused to engage.

An hour passed.

Another.

The toothbrush still lingers on the floor beside the sink, resting its bristly head. Wilma is unable to rescue the little thing from the floor. She steps over it, or around it, noting the strangeness. She considers stooping down, carefully lifting it with two hands, raising it high, an offering. She thinks perhaps she needs food.

Surely a toothbrush which is essentially a relic does not belong with household cleaning products.

It ought to be discarded.

The thought is unthinkable.

All these years—this toothbrush—Lorraine's last—dropped into the trash?

When Lorraine died, Wilma and Alma dealt efficiently with her things. Books and music albums were of course kept, clothing went to Goodwill. There was little else. Lorraine's toothbrush stayed in the cup on the sink in the bathroom with the others. Such a necessary and intimate thing, how could it be heartlessly discarded? For a while it seemed almost to constitute a shrine, silly and sacred, a joke with the ghost of the recently deceased. And then the not-so-recently deceased. It was Alma who finally removed it. "I didn't throw it away, you can visit it any time you wish, Wilma. It's right there under the kitchen sink." Wilma nodded, took a deep breath, and allowed herself to forget. After all, it was only a toothbrush.

But here it is again.

Silly.

And sacred.

She runs a glass of cold water, sits at the table. She drinks the water and contemplates the middle distance. The thing rises up to fill the space, a levitating toothbrush. Perhaps it would like to meditate with her some day. She shakes her head vigorously. What is she doing with this dangling remnant of Lorraine Benedict?

She stands up, approaches the actual toothbrush. She picks it up, gives it a pat on the head, and stuffs it deep into the jumble of the wastebasket. Out of the corner of her eye she catches a glimpse: ghost Lorraine nods and winks and disappears.

A late lunch is heated and consumed. Chicken noodle soup, canned. Soda crackers, white flour and salt. Warm and digestible, this meal. Plenty of salt. Good.

A nap is achieved, with dreams.

When she wakes she does not remember the dreams. They were mild.

~ ~ ~

Was it chicken noodle soup she ate? Already now—it is a few hours later, the sun of this same interminable day is just setting—she can't be sure. It was a pale meal, she knows that. The toothbrush haunts her. She refuses to reverse course, the thing must go. She takes the trash out, descending with determination the recently-cleaned steps. Already a bit dirty but that matters not. She empties the wastebasket into the bin behind the building, looks at the mottled sky, thinks about Alma. By the time she is back in the apartment she cannot remember what she thought about Alma. Something tender. She wants the toothbrush back, but knows she must not allow that.

Perhaps she ought to read, but what? She goes to the bookcases. The pull is firm to the low shelves Lorraine claimed. She kneels and peers. *Scivias* by Hildegard of Bingen; *The Flowing Light of the Godhead* by Mechtild von Magdeburg; *The Shewings of Julian of Norwich*; *The Clowde of Unknowyng*, author anonymous; Simone Weil's *Gravity and Grace*; Evelyn Underhill's *Practical Mysticism*; Martin Buber's collection, *Ecstatic Confessions*; *The Sovereignty of the Good* by Iris Murdoch; *The Fire and the Sun*, also by Murdoch.

Lorraine Benedict, former nun. Scholar. And what was her subject, Wilma? Her subject was mysticism. A rigorous academic approach to the female philosopher-mystic was Lorraine's work. The fact quietly slipped to the back of the mind some years ago, did it not?

She sighs. This late life project, this determination to meet the god. Has it anything at all to do with her own will? Perhaps the Fates, disguised as scornful twelve-year-old girls, control all.

Another shelf. *The Bell* by Iris Murdoch; *A Severed Head*, Iris Murdoch; *The Unicorn*, Murdoch; *A Fairly Honourable Defeat*; *The Black Prince*; *The Sea, the Sea*; *Nuns and Soldiers*; *The Philosopher's Pupil*. All by Murdoch.

Wilma has dusted these books for decades. And ignored them. It appears to be her habit. Ignore the books of the dead. A nice firm protective wrapping of habit. A habit that has cracked and fallen to pieces in recent weeks. Like Humpty Dumpty's shell.

Ah, Humpty. Poor little egg. One never sees the yolk quivering where it landed, only the pieces of shell cleanly and permanently separated from each other. But what if Marlene's painter, that Francis Bacon person, were to produce the art? The yolk would be there with its surrounding horror of albumen all viscous and blotchy and spreading. The yolk itself would be fertilized, one bright red struggling dot of blood, a point of violent precision painted into the smear of things.

Oh, my. But let us be realistic. Mr. Bacon would not be commissioned to illustrate a children's book of rhymes.

Still, think of the actual rhyme. Humpty Dumpty was never an egg, just an unlucky fellow. He sat on a wall, fell, broke to pieces, and stayed broken. An irrevocable accident was poor old Humpty. In fact, Francis Bacon might have considered him an apt subject. The idea bursts upon him: paint *Humpty*—fallen, cracked, splattered—yes! And a thin and twisted (but intact) person crouching in the dark corner just beyond fallen Humpty, a witness whose thoughts cannot be guessed, while a bare light bulb hangs over the sad bloody hero of the gruesome children's rhyme. *Yes*, says Francis Bacon.

She can almost see the painting.

Most likely the thought never came to the artist. A missed opportunity.

But did he, by any chance...? She must ask Marlene.

She shakes herself. What *is* this?

She sighs. Marlene is gone. Marlene and her entertaining impulses and her intriguing mind and her soft body and her unpredictability and her frightening taste in painters. Gone.

Look at this plethora of books by Iris Murdoch. Intriguing, isn't it?

Lorraine was drawn to Murdoch. This was not a simple interest, it was an obsession—Wilma understands this for the first time—an obsession, and one that she, Wilma, was never to go near. "Better stay with George Eliot, dear. She matches your sanity."

What sanity? She bends and reaches for *The Philosopher's Pupil*, published the year Lorraine died. The title is apt. She could use a bit of instruction.

~ ~ ~

More time has passed, though it seems—still—to be this same long day. Now Wilma sits on her comfortable brown couch surrounded by the books of the dead.

Her dead.

Her dead trio, the one she is concocted of.

Beside her on the left is *The Ethics* by her father's god-intoxicated Spinoza wherein it is written: "a thing whose nature is entirely different from our own can be neither good nor evil for us." A nice neutral thought. Perhaps exactly what she needs. Is Marlene's nature entirely different from her own? It would seem so. Well, then: harmless. Marlene is a thing to be neither sought nor avoided. Marlene and her recently acquired Young Henry.

On Wilma's right, Stephen Mitchell's translation of the writings of Rainer Maria Rilke, poet of preference for Alma Schuh who saw things in the sky. Open the book as if it were a Bible, Wilma. Alma likes that technique.

Wilma opens the book.

And how bewildered is any womb-born creature
that has to fly. As if terrified and fleeing
from itself, it zigzags through the air, the way
a crack runs through a teacup. So the bat
quivers across the porcelain of evening.

These lines Wilma receives into her own quivering mind. She closes her eyes. She notes the pattern: cracks. Cracks in a nursery rhyme, cracks in a poem. She rereads the passage and experiences an infusion of terror and beauty, an insertion of forces, perhaps through a crack in the self. She sees the bat zigzagging through the air and wonders if reaching for the divine might end in the same sort of wild flight. Alma and Humpty Dumpty and the poet himself all nod, approving the comparison. Wilma moans. Her mind is not her own.

But that passes. After all, here she is, approaching the forbidden author, Lorraine's own Iris Murdoch, a writer of apparently large and varied talent who produced a whole shelf of novels and a few books worthy of being set neatly among the philosophical mystics. On her lap is *The Philosopher's Pupil*, a novel. Surely she, Wilma Schuh, is now doing the bidding of her own mind. At her feet, barely leaving a path, are the rest of Murdoch's books, each one having been taken from the bookcase, opened, closed, and placed on the floor.

Lyle ordered *The Philosopher's Pupil* the moment it was published. They did not have to ask him, or stress the urgency. Alma made the trip to the bookstore, came home, handed the substantial volume to Lorraine who welcomed it with both hands and said, "When I finish this, it will be time." Wilma was standing right there. Lorraine would die from the brain tumor about which nothing could be done. It would be less than a year.

So said the doctors, one after another, looking right at the three of them. They—Lorraine, Alma, Wilma—looked right back. The doctors did not flinch. Lorraine had achieved this. No doctor would refuse her the information she needed, she would dismiss any who tried. None tried. This was her small miracle. It wasn't a cure, but it was something.

So death would come, and soon. Lorraine would not see her forty-second birthday. Then the announcement. "When I finish this, it will be time." As if she knew, precisely, when death would come. She *would* read the book, she could still read, how lucky she was (though whether she followed or retained they knew not) and then death would arrive, as if on cue. That same day, she said. She was calm and considerate, telling them. Even gentle. Wilma and Alma had heard of such foreknowledge. They nodded, they accepted. The gentleness would be mixed with bitterness later, the calm would sometimes turn to ice or frantic heated rage, the consideration would, in the worst times, be smothered by raw selfish need. But at that moment the message was pure, loving. Also, terrifying. To both Alma and Wilma.

Open the book, dear.

Alma?

Yes, dear. We must see what is inside, must we not?

Wilma opens *The Philosopher's Pupil*. She goes through many pages, glancing, consuming in quick gulps, unable to read normally. Around the phrases, the sentences, even some paragraphs, are patches of blurred print. Crosshatches. Incomprehensibles. She is reminded of the appalling art in Marlene's studio. "...huge spongy moist fleshy face...some evil plant which he was striving to haul up by the roots...all his blood seemed to have rushed up into his head and to be bursting out there into a blazing bleeding wet red flower..."

Wilma gasps, but does not turn away. She is with Lorraine, dying of brain cancer, enduring the image of the wet red flower bursting in the head of a very strange character, George is his name, who seems caught in some nightmare from which he cannot free himself. Or he is creating the nightmare? Everything he touches *turns*, like food spoiling. Yet there is something appealing about him, he is his mother's favorite.

She reads on, a bit here, a bit there. She turns pages quickly, skips way ahead, way back, she is seeing scraps—phrases, sentences, paragraphs—dense clouds thicken, then disappear—needles of light enter

111

and exit. Nothing stays. All is not monstrous, there are small wonders floating and sinking like feathers, intriguing webs of thought, some snarled or blurred, but if she could see into the design, if she could just do that—

The conversation with Marlene and Henry at Pizza Hut comes back, and moments with Lorraine. Even after the tumor metastasized Lorraine could be a bright wonder, a sharp taste of thought, an amazement.

"Tom's capacity for happiness amazed him."

Tom is apparently Emma's amazement. Emma is apparently male. Intriguing. She really ought to read this book—when she is again capable of actual reading.

"…capacity for happiness." Such a satisfying phrase. She's reminded of Spinoza.

"…poor socks that had no partners, and buttons which might become uncherished and lost, had all a life and being of their own, and friendliness and rights…"

She instructs herself not to pity the toothbrush living in the trash.

"…as a kind of empty secret freedom, as if she were less densely made than ordinary people…"

She herself might be moving into a lesser density. Possibly she'll dematerialize completely if she simply sits and sits. Might the god appreciate that? She keeps turning pages, fascinated, unable to read any entire page, unable to stop. She sees smoky rings of thought rise up and inhabit the air for minutes at a time. She sees strangeness akin to horror slide down a page and drip into her lap. She is not appalled.

Read where your eyes fall, daughter. Read and see.

Yes, Alma.

"…a chaotic mess of flesh spread out where a face might have been…"

"…this leak of her unconscious mind into her surroundings, this theft of her vitality by malicious forces…"

"…a sacred victim awaiting the knife…"

"…had to grow up for Rufus, to carry him along like an invisible twin."

Alma? Are you—

112

Yes, dear. I see that Lorraine's writer grasped that the living twin carries the one who dies. I believe she draws her metaphor from realities. It's a comfort to me, Wilma, when elements coalesce.

Wilma closes her eyes and sits very still. After a while she starts rocking. Her dead are here, rocking her. No, now they are shaking her, harder, harder—

She is vividly awake, as if until this moment she's been asleep. She moves. Stands. Stretches and reaches. She picks up novel after novel. She opens and sees. Fragments leap, hover, fly off. Or they rise courteously, offer themselves, settle back down. Not once does she feel the need to press anything back into the page. She is reading with Lorraine. She is reading with Alma. She is reading in extreme solitude. Every idea is true, hard, honed. Everything is acceptable, accepted. Gift after gift.

Then she finds the notes pasted inside the back covers.

Have they been there all along? Impossible. Each Murdoch novel has one. All are in Lorraine's shaky tumor-distorted handwriting. Distorted, but also clear. Every word legible. This is like the art of Francis Bacon, distortions and clarity and no contradiction. How things come together!

Lorraine was already quite ill when she started asking Wilma to bring her the novels. Every day, a request for another. Wilma knew she couldn't be *reading* them. She had been a fast reader, but no one is that fast, and as the tumor advanced she was slower and slower, a fact she did not like, not at all. The books were requested according to the date of publication. Lorraine was going through time by way of Iris Murdoch. Wilma would leave her alone to do whatever it was she was doing with books she was not reading. The project was clearly a private matter, she would ask no questions.

Private at the time, but private no longer. Here in the notes she finds, piece by piece, Lorraine's distilled memoir. Step by step, book by book: her truncated adulthood, the progress of her mind, the story of her secret struggles and delights. Each book's note records when the book was read, gives salient personal events coinciding with the reading, records significant thoughts and feelings, what the book meant to her, and what it *did* to her. All very succinct, she was catching at essences. The brief paragraphs leap and shudder with Lorraine's own intensity.

Wilma stops. Thinks.

Lorraine Benedict had an entire life with another woman. She had another lover. That woman, that lover, was distant unknowing Iris Murdoch. Wilma finds this idea exceedingly interesting. She finds it rich and wonderful. It makes her want to dance. She gets up from the couch. She walks through the books, stepping carefully, for they are in disarray now, there is no real path. She goes to the kitchen. She must have a very cold, very large drink of water.

She has it.

Then she dances.

This is a modest sort of dancing, nothing wild. A Wilma sort of dancing. No music, none needed. She is well able to hear the gentle knock on the door, the turn of the knob, the whisper offered to the air: "Wilma, are you awake?" And then "There's a light on. She must be awake. Come."

~ ~ ~

"Is this too late? You're already in pajamas, are you all right, did you just get up to pee or something? You look—I mean—well, your hair—I think you're in the middle of your night—I'm so sorry, Wilma."

While Marlene is sputtering, Young Henry is making eye contact.

"She's all right, Marlene."

"I'm all right, Marlene. What time is it?"

"Well, it's 10:30. I told Henry we should take a chance. He just found—the most wonderful thing—he rushed right over to my—Wilma, are you really all right? You seem—"

"I'm quite fine. Found what? And where have you been?"

"Oh. Well. I don't know what happened to me. That day. The art. I don't know. And then Henry. I bought that book Henry said I—Deleuze —Henry's philosopher—he wrote that book on Francis Bacon, the artist — "

"Francis Bacon the artist. Yes, I know."

"We've been—"

"Found what, Marlene?"

"We've been reading that book—and talking—and we got so involved—and I've been painting—I'm bursting with ideas—and—"

114

She gives up on Marlene. "What did you find, Henry?"

Henry takes some papers from a satchel he's carrying and hands them to her. Old pages, xeroxed.

Marlene, Henry, and Wilma are all standing in the kitchen. Wilma sits down at the table and motions vaguely that the others ought to do the same but they just hover over her. She is looking at the first page. Enter Henry Schuh, Spinoza enthusiast, by way of what looks like a copy of a published article. She takes a deep breath. She closes her eyes. She opens her eyes. She looks at the ceramic box that recently held her mother's ashes. She looks at the candles, one green, one brown. She glances down at the page. If Lyle would just happen by, that would complete the circle. Her people, living and dead, gathering. Lorraine, in evidence most of the day. Marlene, never effectively absent no matter the intention to make her so. And Alma, twin to little Adam—is she still close by?

Yes, dear. I could not have left while you danced, surely you know that. Tend to your present, Wilma.

She is unsure whether this means her present moment with its present materialized company—these two who arrive unexpected (but welcome, yes, they are welcome) at 10:30 p.m.—or the present, the gift, they bring to her, which is, yes, an article by Henry Schuh published in something called *Mind*.

Published.

"I knew you'd want to see—I mean—I thought you—Henry suddenly remembered—a professor of his—this article—the professor had it for years and years and he gave it to Henry and Henry never lost it, it was in with his school stuff—he had been thinking *Henry Schuh, Henry Schuh, Henry Schuh*, and then suddenly he knew why the name was familiar—what the name *meant*—it is your father, isn't it?—so when —"

Wilma looks at Marlene, puts the stapled pages down on the table, stands and gives her a hug. This is to calm her and get her to sit down as much as anything. Marlene tears up, says thank you, and sits down. Henry sits down. Wilma picks the pages up again. They are the tiniest bit blurred, an imperfect copy, or possibly she has tears in her eyes. "Letter from a Boxcar Rider...Henry Schuh, Independent Scholar...approach to Spinoza's *Ethics* expressed herein...a high school education, an inclination toward Thought..." She closes her eyes and reaches for Henry

Whitsun's hand. It is warm and responsive. Touched thus, the young human is at ease. How this can be, she dare not think. Henry and Henry, father and friend. Gift upon gift.

She feels it: humility, that basic state, so very real—

Yes, dear, I believe that might be a definition. Neither expansion nor contraction. An accuracy pervades the self. I remember pure waters running in springtime.

Alma?

Yes, dear.

Did you know about this? His thought, published?

Facts fade, Wilma. I doubt I could answer that question. Rest your mind about such things.

She accepts this. Why fuss? She lets go of Henry's hand. They both let go, easily, naturally, as if they have a pre-established rhythm, as if they've done it many times. She still has her eyes closed. Marlene is able to be silent now. They are all silent. She feels the presence of her people. Ghost mother Alma, philosopher father Henry, ever-lurking Lorraine, Marlene, Young Henry. Everyone is here.

Except Lyle.

Lyle Franklin, sturdy relief from emotional upheaval and good friend to the Schuh women—to both Schuh women, for she is part of the structure of friendship Alma built, a thing she did not know until this grateful moment. She will take the article to him tomorrow, after she has read it, which reading she will do later, in solitude, or perhaps with Alma, though Alma seems to have faded away now, along with old facts. This seems quite acceptable, perhaps necessary. At the moment she, Wilma Schuh, daughter of Henry, has living company.

Company! How long has she been sitting here, unspeaking?

"Thank you. Thank you both."

"Well you're welcome of course. It's exciting, isn't it, Henry? I can't believe how *hungry* I suddenly am. I wonder if—"

Henry looks at Marlene, which is enough to give the message.

"Oh, right," she says. "Wilma, we can entertain ourselves if you want to read—"

"No. This is for later. I wonder what I might serve."

"I didn't mean *you* should—"

"Well—"

"*Were* you in bed, Wilma?"

Henry wanders into the living room. Wilma watches him. How firmly set inside himself he is. Something happened since he fainted in front of the Grasshopper Shop. A lovely sureness entered him, didn't it? She settles her mind around this nice gentle young man for just a moment while she thinks about answering Marlene. She supposes some version of the truth.

"I was dancing."

"Dancing," says Marlene.

"We'll leave this right here, won't we?" She gives a pat to the article and lightly touches Alma's ceramic cube as she starts to get up from the table. It occurs to her to wonder if she might be producing an unusual impression. A person might prefer a steadier sense of things.

Young Henry is in the living room looking at books, those on the shelves, those on the couch, those on the floor. He is intent and does not appear to notice the disorder, the strangeness. Marlene, however, approaching him, notices. "Oh, Wilma, what have you been doing? Look at all of this! And look at *you*. You are *not* all right."

Wilma has not gotten herself to the living room though the intention was in that direction. Her head is resting on the cool kitchen table. This is a comfort, but perhaps not for Marlene who has come near and is hovering. What might this woman, artist and sometime cuddle buddy, require?

Now Marlene is bending to embrace, which is pleasant though unwarranted.

"Wilma Schuh, what *is* going on?"

"I'm intact. Just a bit faint is all." She raises her voice but not her head. "I saw you faint, Young Henry. It was my first sighting."

Henry answers from the other room, "I remember, Wilma." He sounds a bit distracted.

Marlene, still leaning, still embracing, asks again. "What's going on, Wilma?"

Wilma ponders the question. It seems large.

"*Wilma*."

She lifts her head. Marlene must therefore reposition herself, stand, and then sit. Now they are both seated at the kitchen table like two normal women, how companionable. Marlene, however, glares. A parent

117

determined to pry truth from a recalcitrant child. This is amusing but one does understand. An explanation is owed. "I think I might have neglected to tend to supper. It's very agreeable to see you. Both of you. I wish I had food to offer. Didn't you declare your own hunger? I must have something."

"You skipped supper?"

"As you can perhaps see, I took a day off. I don't think I've ever before spent an entire day in pajamas, unless perhaps during childhood illnesses. Yes, certainly then. Which hardly matters now, does it? I suppose it's unusual, my being in nighttime attire, and with company arriving. Though the hour is unconventional for such an arrival, and a person is not always required to—and I had decided *you* would never again—but apparently you have."

"Took a day off?"

"From the god, I believe. Yes, that is a possible way to put it."

"*What?*"

A drink of water might be in order. She does feel the compulsion. She finds herself on her feet, able to walk. Marlene, on the other hand, is resting her head on the cool kitchen table.

And now she is banging the poor head just a bit. Oh, my.

Having drunk a mere half-glass of fine Bangor water, feeling wondrously but possibly only momentarily revived, Wilma is bending over Marlene, squeezing her shoulders gently.

"Oh, Wilma," says Marlene who is after all easily mollified.

Wilma whispers, "Let's just see what Young Henry is up to, shall we?" She takes Marlene by the hand.

Henry is involved in Iris Murdoch's *The Sea, the Sea.* Wilma has looked into this volume and intends to read it, but where in the order of things she might do that is undecided. Her decisiveness, or is it her determination—that characteristic she thought might lead to the god— seems to have destabilized. She must find a way to stabilize it soon. She bends to read over Young Henry's shoulder, hoping he doesn't mind. The father Henry did mind, but that was some time ago. "I was looking into the vast interior of the universe, as if the universe were quietly turning itself inside out," says the character. If she were in possession of the book at this moment she would place her hands gently over the words and feel the pulsation. She would not have the slightest need to press them back

118

into the page. This is astonishing, as if the universe were quietly turning itself inside out.

Henry turns and looks at her, turns back to the book, and reads aloud. "And then, much much farther away, stars were quietly shooting and tumbling and disappearing, silently falling and being extinguished, lost utterly silent falling stars, falling from nowhere to nowhere into an unimaginable extinction. How many of them there were, as if the heavens were crumbling at last and being dismantled. And I wanted to show all these things to my father."

Father.

Wilma breathes, and thinks the word.

Henry turns to look at her. There are tears in his eyes. "Fathers," he says.

She feels a tear roll down her cheek. Marlene stands at her shoulder, blowing her nose, her face wet.

~ ~ ~

When the trio is settled into the booth at Pizza Hut, which is luckily open to all hours, Wilma dares to ask. "Tell us about your father, Henry."

"My father. Hmm. Getting right down to it, aren't we, Wilma?" He shakes his head and smiles tolerantly. "I suppose I could say something about this current period, an unusual one for us. For example, I could tell you that I'm sleeping on his couch."

"Oh, no!" says Marlene.

"It's all right, Marlene. For now, it's good."

"You know Henry's father?" Wilma asks.

"Not well. Not now, really. But when Henry was—oh, how old?— nine or so, I think—Henry, is it OK if I—?"

"No idea where you're going with this, Marlene. I'm as curious as Wilma. Speak."

"Your dad was my mechanic. Sort of. Don't you remember?"

"Almost. Keep going."

"He took care of my car when Dickie wasn't around. You remember my brother Dickie, don't you?"

"Almost."

"Anyway, your dad was a good mechanic when—"

119

"When he wasn't drunk."

"Yes. Even sometimes when he was, actually. But mostly Dickie took care of me. Still does."

"I was about nine?"

"I guess I'm telling Wilma how I came to know you. Maybe I'm telling you, too."

"Maybe."

"This kid—you, Henry—was around the station a lot, helping his dad, reading a book, throwing a ball against the building. Or just watching. I remember you used to watch a lot. You watched your dad, you watched the traffic, you watched the sky. You'd be looking up for minutes at a time and I wondered what drew you up. You watched us customers sort of sideways. I thought about what you might be seeing when you watched me, what conclusions you might be drawing in your young brain. I could see the wheels turning. You were the most interesting combination of scruffy and bright and shy. Maybe a little eerie, too. You never said a word."

"I think there was a weekend—"

"Yes, that's what I'm getting to. Your mom had gone off with that clown, a real circus clown, but I suppose I mean the man was a clown in the pejorative sense, too, not that I ever met him and I shouldn't judge but your dad was in a bad way and off goes your mom with that—"

"He wasn't a terrible man, Marlene. Things happen."

"OK. Your life, not mine. Anyway, I had to have something done on my car—"

"Your brakes."

"You remember?"

"It comes to me."

"I'm sure you're right. I remember there was a time Dickie wasn't around when I needed my brakes fixed. But it turned out to be a good thing—because of you—you then—and now—I mean—"

Marlene is blushing. Wilma feels a surge of tenderness. And hunger. It does take time for an actual pizza to arrive at a table.

"So, anyway, I ended up taking you out to the farm, I must have been in one of my times of returning home, out of rent money, something like that. Must have been before I met Philomena, but that's another story."

More blushing. Poor Marlene, she's in territory she hadn't intended to enter. Wilma knows the feeling. How could she have mentioned the god? *Did* she mention the god?

"...so I took you with me for the weekend and—wait—Wilma, you're involved in this!—I just remembered—I was baking something —"

"Angel food cake," says Young Henry.

"That's right! Because I told you that you were *not* a weird boy, you were just an absolute angel and to prove it I'd bake you this cake except we had run out of something—"

"Sugar. You sent me across the field to the next house. Was that you, Wilma? A lady answered the door and invited me in and sat me down and gave me a cookie."

"I had to wait *forever* for you to come back with the sugar. I remember sitting and waiting and wondering if you'd run away or hurt yourself or maybe you were just waiting and waiting while no one was home but someone was always, always home over there, it was when Lorraine—"

"Wilma? Was that you?" Henry asks, reaching to quiet Marlene.

But Wilma is busy trying to put the two realities together, the boy at the door and this young man across the table. It's a bit confusing because her father who wrote a philosophy article has been overlapping with the father residing at Pooler Pavilion with Alzheimer's disease, Henry and Henry, and now the boy Henry at the door and the mime Henry at this table—two simultaneous palimpsests for her to sort, the images beneath faded or incompletely erased, though it's possible that term, palimpsest, refers only to words—but where is that pizza, she really does need something to eat—words over words, one set erased, scraped away, but never entirely, another imposed, the underlying layer constituting therefore a ghost presence, would that be it? Old papyrus, used and reused—the very image of time itself—she remembers the day Lorraine informed her of the etymology, palimpsest, from the Greek for "scraped again" or "rubbed smooth," Greek to Latin to English. And then Lorraine who was quite ill already said something about her strained brain braiding strands of time—*try saying that three times, Wilma*—and how it was sort of fun, she said, how her brain was suddenly taking off on its own, but it confused her and maybe she should be frightened because what next, but here is this Young Henry, full grown, in this late night booth—and she sees the ghost, the boy he was, materializing in her doorway, as much a waif as she herself and her mother were when they appeared at the O'Connors' screen door. Here he is, so young, quietly vivid with his uncombed hair, his slight scruffy body. Lorraine is in the bedroom reading *The Philosopher's Pupil*, a woman who is past her time of conversing about the etymologies of words such as palimpsest and who will not live much longer. The child who will became this young man sits politely eating his cookie. She tries not to watch, tries to prevent his feeling scrutinized, but steals her glances. Already there is a brightness to him, but private, a quality one ought not to notice.

"Wilma?" This is Marlene and Henry in chorus.

"What? Oh. Yes. So we are more acquainted than was apparent, Henry. Yes, I believe it was an oatmeal cookie. And milk."

The three of them have made a circle, hand holding hand. Someone must have begun this. Did she miss a beat? Well, never mind, it is a nice little triumph over time they have just achieved, a memory retrieved, a making of pattern, and they are apparently acknowledging the fact. They squeeze gently and release each other's hands. It might almost not have happened. They sit, exchanging mute and suddenly shy smiles—they are sitting with their phenomenon, their small victory over time and human separateness—until the pizza arrives.

They eat in silence except for little exclamations, mostly from Marlene, about being famished, needing this pizza, perfect food, how lucky they are that the place was open, just the thing, so glad—

The waitress clears the plates away, refills their glasses, gives them their bill, tells them to stay as long as they like. They stay. They talk about Francis Bacon and a complicated web of related things, art and philosophy and horror and beauty. Deleuze's book is at the core. Deleuze and Bacon, philosopher and artist, have so much to *say* about painting, about a "catastrophe" that has to happen, how the "figure"—Bacon liked that word, he was determinedly not an abstract artist—must "emerge" from the catastrophe, how "invisible forces" must be "made visible," there is chaos to go through, there is a sort of violence, a real danger, things don't always work out, it's thrilling and terrifying when the outcome is yet unknown, it might not work, but if it *does* work distortions become clarities and horror is peeled down to a radiance, a revelation of rhythm, form, shape, color, paint.

Paint. Marlene cradles the word in her hands, looks at it. Such wonder, and love.

Horror and wonder and love. Wilma thinks about Iris Murdoch's horror-tinted phrases sliding down the page. Will she have to read *The Severed Head*? These are private thoughts, little thought-ghosts playing around the edges, not distracting significantly from the once again astonishing conversation. How she joins in, when Marlene and Young Henry have already gathered for themselves such a bulk of fresh history by talking about these very things, how she joins in *without difficulty*, will seem on later reflection almost magical. But now, as the ideas and laughter, the hesitancies and leaps and pauses, the resumptions and confusions and revisions and new ideas and new laughter go on and on, she simply feels as if she belongs here. She, Wilma Schuh.

When she is home and settled into bed, propped against pillows with a cup of hot milk in one hand, her intention is not to sleep but to read. She picks up the beckoning pages.

~ ~ ~

Letter from a Boxcar Rider

by Henry Schuh, Independent Scholar

Editors' Note: The approach to Spinoza's *Ethics* expressed herein has not been widely explored in recent times and perhaps deserves fresh consideration. In addition, we have been moved by the author's passion and feel it deserves recognition. Thus we present this Letter to the Editors as an article in its own right. Not every philosopher hails from academia. Spinoza himself, readers will remember, refused the offer of a prestigious academic position, preferring independence, grinding lenses for a living.

4 September 1955

To the Editors:

I write in response to R. G. Bosanquet's "Remarks on Spinoza's *Ethics*" (*Mind*, July 1945, Vol. 54). With apologies I come, a decade late, having just discovered—

I with my paucity: a high school education, an inclination toward Thought. I have been for many years immersed in *The Ethics*. Immersed, grateful, carried, puzzled. I bow my head in gratitude to the young soldier, his life given, his thoughts unfinished, necessary, who calls me out from my private notebooks.

I rode the rails, a young man myself. Homeless. Seeking. Another boxcar rider, perceiving my need, pulled from his sack: *philosophy*. The sack soiled, the book inside. The book: clean and offered. I accepted the bound pages, the geometry of thought, the work of the God-intoxicated Spinoza. No atheist he, I insist. Deep in the discipline of philosophy, happily unfettered by synagogue, church, or mosque, he nevertheless studied fervently the traditions, gleaning essence. Spirit enveloped him.

In a short time he—my Baruch, my Benedict—replaced Madame Blavatsky. You, editors of a philosophical journal of highest standing, will be glad of that, though perhaps appalled by the mere mention of the esoteric. I do understand a thing or two.

Let us turn to the thought of young Mr. Bosanquet. He has discovered that Spinoza—interpreted variously, condemned and acclaimed by the contradictory knowledgeable ones from the beginning —is best understood if we approach differently: backwards, sideways, upside down. Forgive my colloquialisms. I urge to the surface what I have heard breathing beneath.

If we want to imbibe the thought of our philosopher, allow it to mix with our own mind's substance—

If we want to benefit—

If this is our intention—and what other might we have?—we will come, says Mr. Bosanquet, with abundant intellectual forgiveness, brushing aside logic. With self-effacement, forgetting what we know. With love. This I understand to be only reasonable. How else are we to read any worthy work?

The soldier goes further. Do we want to understand the difficult *Ethics*? Begin, says he, with the single question: "What was Spinoza trying to express?"

Not: "What argument did Spinoza make?"

Not: "Did he demonstrate truths about existence and essence, cause and effect, freedom and contingency, good and evil?"

None of that. Only this: *What was the philosopher trying to express?*

As if a man—a philosopher, a Spinoza—had a certain experience. As if he felt compelled year after year to spend himself in an effort to *express his experience.*

And what does Mr. Bosanquet believe Spinoza was trying to express? "First, there were his mystical experiences." Start there, advises the young soldier philosopher.

I must stop. I must allow entrance. The desk at which I write tilts.

The height and depth and breadth of Unity—the Extremity of All—Existence Itself—how it runs through the Thought, how it hides inside every sentence, how it dances through every clause. And then bursts. Bursts into and out of.

Into and out of: the particulars! Each leaf! Each lonely rock! The very eye of the grasshopper! The first thought of the infant! The child in red dress, running, falling, raised up, comforted, laughing! The One and the Many! An implosion that is also an explosion!

Simultaneously. Eternally. Infinitely.

The mystical. The ineffable. That which cannot be—and demands to be—expressed.

I pause. I breathe. I ponder, searching for—

Do we want to understand Spinoza? His words come from elsewhere. We must hear each in relation to all, *inside the work*, says the young soldier.

As if this were new language. As if Thought Itself were new.

As I have striven to read—each word, definition, axiom, proposition, proof, corollary, scholium—into and out of each other. As I have striven, but—

The young soldier gives sudden frame: "First, there were his mystical experiences."

(Others will see another Spinoza. I care not. My desk tilts.)

Let us look at a single moment early in Mr. Bosanquet's article. We are asked to consider Proposition 35 of Part V of *The Ethics*: "*Deus se ipsum Amore intellectuali inifinito amat.*" I would translate: "God loves himself with infinite intellectual Love." (I have learned my scraps of Latin, even I.) But the young soldier translates: "The World worships itself with an infinite mystical worship."

The World!

The student philosopher has taken into his own hand Spinoza's bedrock phrase, has held it, has felt its hard unbreakable substance: *Deus, sive Natura.* "God, or Nature."

We would say: "God loves himself with infinite intellectual Love." Yes. But Mr. Bosanquet dares to assert, to offer, transformation: "The World worships itself with an infinite mystical worship."

The fountain of astonishments that *Nature* is: honored. *God*: honored. *Spinoza*: honored.

I open my *Ethics*. Here is Spinoza himself, in simple—mystical—declaration: "The more we understand particular things, the more we understand God."

Astonishment rises up. It overflows.

Imagine. Spinoza, in the grip of the mystical, the ineffable, that for which there exists no language. Dare to enter his mind. Make the effort, difficult as it might be. Be the young thinker in the seventeenth century, Baruch who became Benedict. Write strange things about your "God, or Nature." Write that your *Deus, sive Natura* possesses "attributes." Write that we who are merely human are able to know—to *know*—two of these attributes: Thought and Extension; Mind and Matter. Say that this is enough, for "The human mind has an adequate idea of the eternal and infinite essence of God." And then, bursting, declare that your "God, or Nature" has "infinite attributes, each of which expresses eternal and infinite essence."

And infinity of attributes beyond Mind and Matter! An infinity!

And yet we are sufficient. The human mind has an adequate idea…

Advise then—

Advise every seeking human to dare to desire *intuitive intellectual love of God*—and thereby to experience spiritual depths of—philosophical heights of—*joy*.

I bow my head in gratitude to Spinoza. And to Mr R. G. Bosanquet. The young soldier's thought was worthy and has perhaps been forgotten. Let us not forget.

Yours respectfully,
Henry Schuh

P. S. I wish to express gratitude to my library for access to your respected journal. The Bangor Public Library. Bangor, Maine. You will notice that I write from the outskirts. This is perhaps appropriate.

~ ~ ~

It is four in the morning when Wilma lies down and sinks to sleep. She dreams of stone houses in flat fields. Each stone is solid but it is possible to discern, by a tilt of the head, corresponding ghost stones. These glow. Substance is not thereby reduced. Realities are permanent, along with erasures. The dreaming brain is in love with itself.

She sleeps for five hours. It is enough. She rises, she showers, she turns on the radio. *Boléro*. She opens the living room window and lets in the day with its bright sun and abundant heat and spends some minutes observing the sharp shadows. These faithfully adhere to their respective objects, one of which is the neighbor's Volkswagen bug, painted to match a robin's breast. She does appreciate a bit of Ravel from time to time. *Boléro* is a phenomenon with its steady beat and steadily expanding sound—a miracle of discipline for the musicians, one assumes, and they must want to laugh out loud with pride and relief when they complete the performance yet another time.

The piece ends. She laughs and applauds. Apparently she is unharmed by late hours spent eating pizza, conversing with friends, and reading her father's published philosophical thought. That poor mind—so drawn to intellectual work, and to *mysticism*—how it tangled in the end. But there he was in her own nighttime—Pa—pouring forth thought, pouring himself forth, his innards, onto the page, in precious drafts of ecstatic humility.

And there in the studio was Marlene, her innards also, thrust out into paint.

Wilma must ponder. She will do so, but not right this minute. Everything calls to her now. She stands breathing at the open window. Here is the world. These shadows—another of which belongs to a rocking chair resting at the edge of its lawn, *For Sale, $25*—will expand

127

and contract in accord with the sun's trajectory and the passage of time, an indication of the order of things.

A further indication might be the sale of the old rocking chair. Or it might sit there, unsold and contented, failed efforts being useful in unforeseen ways. One must not presume.

Place the folded blanket on the floor now and stretch the interested muscles, neglected yesterday. But did they complain? They did not. Was the night sky observed last night or was it forgotten? Never mind, it was a day off.

Chopin from the radio.

Fauré.

Clementi.

Finished with her routine, Wilma sits on the floor, listening. Beethoven now. *Seventh Symphony, Second Movement, Allegretto.* The original audience in Vienna—Beethoven himself conducting—went wild, demanded an encore. So said the program's host, introducing. The music is propulsive, compelling, invisible lines slipping back and forth, in and around, the design increasingly complex, more and more daring. Times intersect, Beethoven's Vienna, her very own Bangor. The soul is roused to the essential dance of existence itself and Wilma herself is conducting, arms raised, eyes closed, still sitting, aware that a bomb, a simple bomb made by a child, could shatter this. An explosive device could go off any minute now and reconfigure the design, as is happening in a multitude of locations around the globe, while the *Allegretto* continues, while Robin, singer with a crow's voice, wrestles with her next song, while she, Wilma Schuh, still inside the weave and rhythm of the music, gets to her feet, starts coffee water, and puts bread into the toaster.

Marlene is to arrive late this afternoon. "Just us two, Wilma. No Henry. All right?" Henry mimed shock at the idea—two women! alone! —then twirled on his toes with dignity, waved a friendly goodbye, and let himself into his father's apartment. The apartment is directly across the street from the gas station, one Wilma has patronized from time to time. Everything has a story. Most are unknown to those who pass through and soon leave. This is not a flaw in the design, this tucked away quantity of stories. It is not even sad. Or is it? A strain of sorrow does run through the fabric. It seems necessary, joy's shadow. But Marlene *will* come this afternoon. Perhaps she will stay the night.

128

The Beethoven ends. She turns the radio off. Here she is with her coffee, her toast, and a single sheet of paper whose creases reveal much folding and unfolding. Might she like to put peanut butter on the toast? Yes, she might, but she will not. She has been called back to the track of the god. She looks at Stage One of her Plan. She certainly did take the day off yesterday. Self-care? Barely any. Meditation? Certainly not. Reading from the works of Spinoza, Rilke, Henry, Alma? Not before midnight. In the wee hours, though, there was Henry, father, glowing. She stops, thinks of her dream's ghost stones, echo of a glowing father. They will remain with her.

4. Leave apartment at least once a day.

She was pulled out by friends. Did that count?

5. Speak at least minimally to another human every day.

Well, yes. Oh, my, yes, she did do that. She wonders how she managed her part of the conversation. All that talk of art and its intention to skew common realities. She quoted Rilke, she remembers that. "We are the bees of the invisible." The poet conjures the invisible into words. Francis Bacon did the same, using paint. Not distant, this, from what Henry Schuh said Spinoza did with his *Ethics*. Is that accurate? It is, decides Wilma, daughter of Henry Schuh, published writer in the field of philosophy.

At some point in the long late-night conversation, knowledgable Young Henry tried to explain Spinoza's use of "the geometric method" by comparing it with Bacon's painterly use of "the diagram," something about order and chaos which she hadn't actually followed, but a mysterious greathearted sense of things came through to her.

Marlene was bewildered by the idea of geometry, a bit cranky in fact, but then she burst out. "Maybe that's a metaphor, too! Whoever thought of geometry as a metaphor?" They had gotten to metaphor by way of the bees.

Henry was stunned. "Wait," he said. "Wait."

So they sat in silence.

"That's it," he said quietly, nodding. He was serious, his eyes shining. "Maybe all of philosophy is a metaphor—it might be our way— our human way—how we think about anything at all." He smiled. It was a new idea. His. Wilma had seen him holding it inside himself and now he'd released it, an idea entirely his own and not his own, both. They

129

talked about that, how a thought is held within a single mind, yet shared. This came close for her: eight years old, her cone of sun, a piece of it entering her like a new thought all her own. It still felt private, an experience exclusive to herself. She said nothing.

She looks down at her much-read page. *It is permitted to throw everything over in favor of a gust inside the god.* Might there have been a gust or two by the time yesterday, which certainly extended past midnight, had completed itself? A gust inside the god at Pizza Hut! And didn't something resembling an entire storm buffet her as she sat in bed and read her father's writing, paragraph by paragraph, sentence by sentence, once, twice, thrice? A force did seem to fill the room, a force like wind and water—powerful and penetrating, but also gentle, or perhaps *merciful*—as her father's words gathered and poured themselves over her.

And then she slept. Gift from the god, that sleep. Or from Spinoza. Or from her father. Are they distinguishable?

She can say this: she feels refreshed.

After staying out much of the night.

At her age.

It occurs to her that the unexpected might thread itself through her days and weeks henceforth.

Difference: this morning there is Difference.

Difference, she now knows, is a term favored by Young Henry's beloved difficult thinker, Gilles Deleuze. Marlene's art was connected last night to Henry's passion for difficult thinkers by way of Francis Bacon's paintings and Deleuze's book. Lines—invisible—were pulled— by *thought*—to geometric visibility. Difference was somehow at the center. She feels it as she looks at her own single page, not a particular difference among particular things, but Difference itself—a profusion—a suffusion—an upspringing—a something-or-other that enters the crevices.

Crevices?

Maybe capillaries would be better.

No, not quite.

How *do* the poets find their metaphors? And the philosophers!

But this Plan. What happens to it now, if there is Difference? And what, really, *is* Difference? She notices that, unlike the god, this aspect of

130

reality—this Difference—seems at least at the moment to call for capitalization. Its voice is clarion.

But doesn't she require a second piece of toast? She will add peanut butter this time, a generous amount, for she is apparently having brunch, two meals in one.

While waiting for her toast and deciding even to indulge in a second cup of coffee, she remembers: Lyle. She intended to take Henry's article to him. The morning is passing. She must meditate, that is of the essence. And she has an abundance of pondering to do. Art, philosophy, mysticism; Henry Schuh, father unfurling; Young Henry Whitsun, the phenomenon, the fact, the brightness of him; Marlene O'Connor, conundrum.

Everything interweaves, is that it? The *Allegretto* replays for a moment in her mind, in her body. She taps the table to the percussive repetitions, feels the weave as strings, winds, and brass enter and leave, enter and leave.

Plenitude.

And she must read something by Iris Murdoch, perhaps many somethings. She cannot ignore this need—propulsive, compelling—to know Lorraine as if from the beginning. She will dare to enter the woman's reading life, that private and intimate route to revelation. Only Murdoch can show her the way. A sense of inspired certainty rises within Wilma.

But Marlene will come.

Well, not until late afternoon. She did say, and even emphasize, *late* afternoon.

Now. If gusts inside the god have come—

And if there is Difference—

She really ought to consider Stage One. Is it still in effect? If not, what follows?

She considers. She wonders. She waits. She strives, reaches, strains. She waits again, shakes her head, smiles ruefully, and concludes: she does not know.

And bursts into laughter. Defeated by the god. Well, then, she'll crawl along in blind serenity. Nothing wrong with crawling, whyever did humans decide to pull upright? Such an unstable method for negotiating the world which her father's young soldier philosopher said *worships itself with an infinite mystical worship.* Or was it Spinoza himself who said that? Never mind, she'll crawl until she can walk or she'll crawl forever. Either seems perfectly acceptable on this fine morning. She stands in her kitchen and breathes and feels the day. Soon she'll meditate and learn what that enigmatic practice has turned itself into.

Turned itself into.

As if, Stage One or not, meditation itself might have metamorphosed.

Which is possible, for today there is Difference.

She looks forward to this next meditation and, of course, to this next bit of food. Here it is, in the toaster. How long has it been ready while she wandered in thought? Her appetite is suddenly fierce.

She is savoring the first bite of her second piece of toast with its welcome addition of peanut butter and wondering how Lorraine's toothbrush is faring, poor discarded thing, when Marlene arrives.

"I know, I know. Earlier than I said. I just had to. At least you're dressed, your hair is even combed. I couldn't sleep, I was so stimulated by our talk, talk, talking—wasn't it great?—it's special, the three of us— and then my curiosity—did you read your father's article?—and you did say something about a *god*, didn't you?—and, all right, my insecurity or maybe it's uncertainty. Wilma Schuh, we just plain have to *talk*."

And thus the shape of a day shifts, thinks adaptable Wilma Schuh, shaking her head, offering food.

"Peanut butter? Yes, definitely. Plenty of butter first, though, thanks. And you'd better make more coffee because I really didn't sleep and I don't want to fall face down on the table like you did last night."

That said, Marlene waits for food and drink in silence, as if spent. Then, toast in hand, she fumbles and stumbles and bumbles—Wilma thus frivolously characterizes the production of Marlene's opening paragraphs, all of which are quite extended—until she is able to focus on the central question, or at least what appears to be the central question, defined as "the two of us, or maybe it's the three of us."

"Young Henry, you mean," said Wilma.

"But leave him out for a minute."

"Let him depart, then. I assume we shall summon him back in due time."

132

Wilma is experiencing an exceedingly pleasant tolerance. She finds her visitor a welcome, even delightful, presence. Or distraction. She wonders if she might be accused of playing hooky. Again. From the god.

"So here's one thing," Marlene says. "Are you just too *innocent* for me? If we are going to—"

Long pause. Wilma smiles indulgently. Either the god will have to wait or this woman *is* the god.

"If we are going to what, Marlene?"

"You know damn well what."

"Oh, my."

Marlene sighs, then works on her toast for a while and drinks most of her coffee. Neither woman speaks. Time passes.

"More toast?"

"Yes, please. And coffee."

At the toaster, with her back to Marlene, Wilma says, "I could make an educated guess."

"You'd just guess that I'm talking about being cuddle buddies."

Cuddle buddies, thinks Wilma. Not lovers. Not even casually sexual old lesbians. She looks at the cliff over which she nearly catapulted. She is down on her hands and knees, gripping some tough little piece of vegetation that keeps her in place. Layered over this reality is the fiction of standing and waiting for the toaster to do its work. The scene is encased in silence. Thought has stopped.

"Butter it," says Marlene who seems to have gotten up and placed herself in the hugging position, an attack from the rear.

Wilma butters the toast. "Peanut butter?"

"No, just butter this time. Lots of it, though."

Wilma adds more butter. Marlene is pouring more coffee now for both of them.

"Sit down, Wilma."

"Yes," says Wilma, and manages this.

"I'm sorry," Marlene says.

"What happened?"

"We fell into a hole."

"I thought it was a cliff."

"We didn't go over a cliff. It was just a little hole. We're all right."

"Are we?"

133

"Yes, Wilma, we're all right. I'm sorry."

"I doubt an apology is in order."

"What order?'

Wilma ponders the question. She decides it might do to look directly at Marlene who is smiling, or trying to. "Were you crying, Marlene?"

"A little."

"You have the strangest effect on me."

"Ditto, my dear Wilma."

"I've never been certain what that meant."

"I suppose your parents didn't say ditto."

"I suppose not."

"Nor Lorraine."

"Not that I recall."

"You've seen it in books."

"Have I?"

"Maybe not the word. The sign, under something, used as a shortcut, instead of writing out that entire something. It looks like a quotation mark. In this case, I was trying to lighten things while expressing a thought similar to your own. Identical to your own, actually."

"I can't remember what I said that you were, um, ditto-ing."

"Well, think."

Wilma thinks. She feels difference, which has lost its need for capitalization, floating through the air like smoke, lovely strands of it. She wonders what on earth. Then she remembers the thing she is being asked to remember.

"We have a strange effect on each other," she says.

"Apparently," says Marlene.

They sit with that. There really was no cliff. But there was a hole.

"I suppose I ought to inquire. Were you meaning to go in the direction of more or less? In relation to being cuddle buddies, I mean. Which endearing phrase was, you indicated, not what you began to speak of."

"You don't fit the definition."

"I'm not appropriate for cuddle buddy status."

"You're not *appropriate* for any word or phrase, Wilma."

"But you're here."

"With bells on."

134

"I believe I was enjoying the fact of your being here."

"I have no words to sum up the fact of my being here."

"You have, or had, when you arrived, a mountain of words."

"Oh, that."

"Marlene, Marlene, Marlene."

"I suppose I'm confused."

"It's in the air."

"What are we doing?"

"Taking turns clutching at a modicum of sanity?"

"Well, yes. But beyond that, Wilma. What are we *doing*?"

They sit looking at each other. Wilma reaches across first. Marlene responds. They squeeze hands and let go. They smile their rueful smiles. Wilma realizes she has the answer.

"I have the answer."

"Well, tell me."

"We don't know."

"We don't know?"

"We don't know. The answer is: we don't know. Isn't that—well, let's see—isn't that—"

"Appropriate?" says Marlene.

"Precisely."

Slow smiles are exchanged. The smiles broaden and spill to laughter. Wilma is quite pleased with herself. In the ensuing hours many topics are introduced. Some are even discussed. The next day they will go to Lyle's bookstore They will not have spent the night together. This fact will not distress either woman. After all, now there is that strange thing: difference.

Three: Wilma

Nude by Way of Hammer on Glass

Let us consider difference. Let us assume with Gilles Deleuze that this unruly element constitutes the wild red beating heart of all that is. Let us imagine that Wilma has, step by unpredictable and somewhat blind step, come upon an invisible (but open) door into the structure of difference-infused essential existence. There are many such doors, but this one is hers.

She has stumbled in the dark. We do know this.

The door, remember, is open. Tripping on the slightly raised threshold, Wilma Schuh, approaching the age of seventy, appears to have fallen—according to the order of Accident or Fate or Something Else—into the unexpected but ever-present though generally unperceived realm of pure difference. It does seem possible.

She is falling, or floating. She has not landed.

Her god might be waiting in this realm. Perhaps her god is whirling in mirth here. Dancing. These things remain to be seen.

A few weeks have gone by since we last saw Wilma. She has had some profoundly satisfying times in the interval. Her level of functioning has been well within the normal range. Her Plan, Stage One, is in place: her social life, her reading life, her self-care, her meditations—

Her meditations. We do want to know if her mantra is serving her well. Has she, in her falling and floating and tumbling and (daily) meditating, been having a good time? Wedge, wedge, wedge. Beat, beat, beat. Ravel's *Bolero* and Beethoven's *Allegretto* have entered in. Pulsating expansion. Profusions and plenitudes. Yes, she has been having a good time. She has found herself returning to the experience of Charles Arrowby, protagonist of Iris Murdoch's *The Sea, the Sea*. Young Henry, you will remember, read the passage aloud as he sat on Wilma's living room floor amid novels and philosophy texts by Murdoch before the trio sought food and communion at Pizza Hut. Night comes upon Charles and upon meditating Wilma and they are looking at, or into, or beyond the sky and there they see "lost utterly silent falling stars, falling from nowhere to nowhere…as if the universe were quietly turning itself inside out." This could be terrifying, but for neither Charles nor Wilma (floating in difference) is it the least bit frightening. Instead, it is deeply, rhythmically satisfying. As is the presence of the meditator's father who appears at times and offers his hand. He walks with her for a few rhythmical steps (but she is only sitting, sitting) and then departs. He offers no instruction. She knows his mind is a clear glass bell now, vibrating in a paradox of silent sound at the heart of his joyful, tumbling, unique after-death existence. She suspects he has met Spinoza and the two have taken to each other nicely.

Ah, whimsy.

In this realm of difference, where times can be expected to intersect, we might now step into the moment when Young Henry Whitsun will again quote Gilles Deleuze, informing Wilma and Marlene that difference is assumed to be "light, aerial and affirmative." The description brings smiles to the open faces of both women. This pleases the young man who finds himself somehow more at home with these aging women than with his contemporaries. Neither Wilma nor Marlene seems ever to have been constrained by academia, yet they are far from uneducated. He can run with them. Here he is, sitting in a booth, eating pizza, and running ecstatically. The wind is in his hair. Might he one day try to mime this?

Back to the actual present, the normal earthly plane where time passes in a somewhat orderly fashion and where, in general, those who sit do not simultaneously walk or run but do metaphorically or metaphysically fall or float. Wilma is still falling or floating. She does not know—nor do we—if she will encounter any semblance of ground in the near future. Perhaps this does not matter. If what she falls or floats through has such pleasant qualities—if pure difference is light, aerial, and affirmative as the optimistic Monsieur Deleuze asserts—might she fall or float safely for as long as it takes, whatever "it" might be? Let us hope so.

While we are engaged in hope, which is admittedly a stopgap measure (the great Spinoza was not a fan, considering hope twin to fear which is a sad passion indeed) let us comfort ourselves with those words from Gilles Deleuze presented to Wilma and Marlene for memorization by the young mime not so very long ago. "A single and same Ocean for all the drops, a single clamor of Being for all beings." We can almost feel the great puzzle of the One and the Many solving itself again and again as these phrases ring out across time and space. Granted, there is a Deleuzian caveat in the text itself (a text forthrightly titled *Difference and Repetition*)—something about each drop being required to reach a state of excess, and then difference entering in and messing things up a bit, and a turn on a mobile cusp, and—

Well, never mind. The words as Young Henry offered them are a wonder. Wilma thinks exactly this as she lets them roll over her again and again, convinced they are inhabited by the god. She has only to learn to slip inside, yes? "A single clamor of Being—wedge, wedge, wedge—a single and same Ocean—"

And here is more from Deleuze, duly memorized by Wilma and Marlene: "Individuation is mobile, strangely supple, fortuitous and endowed with fringes and margins." Surely this has something appealing to tell us about difference.

Individuation is mobile—wedge, wedge, wedge—

Wilma conjures a mobile, work of Alexander Calder as seen in a poster Lorraine framed and gave to Alma one Christmas, which poster Alma insisted on moving from its place of honor in the living room to the bedroom wall Lorraine faced—literally and metaphorically—as her illness progressed. One must have a bit of cheer, said Alma. There were times when Wilma wondered if Alma understood Lorraine better than she herself did. Lorraine could be caught gazing at the poster, a human soul distant as a lost star, possibly turning herself inside out.

But Lorraine is gone. Somewhat. The poster remains, hung now on Wilma's bedroom wall in the Bangor apartment. Its floating elements are pure pulsating red, bits of the red beating heart of existence itself. *Individuation is mobile.*

This bit about the poster is a simple linguistic echo-response, *mobile* calling forth *mobile*, as Wilma perfectly well knows. Still, it seems fortuitous.

Fortuitous or not, no single image can be expected to encompass—

Certainly not.

She repeats the sentence. *Individuation is mobile, strangely supple, fortuitous and endowed with fringes and margins.*

That suppleness—

Those fringes and margins—

Infinite permutations fluttering through—

Tumbling within—

This fluttering and tumbling can be located, truth be told, in Wilma's belly, as if she were a child again with a round and happy belly. The words tumble and flutter—mobile, supple, endowed with feathery fringes and comforting margins. They tickle her.

Wedge, wedge, wedge. Ravel, Beethoven, her father's hand. *Wedge, wedge.* Red bits of a mobile, fragments of Deleuzian wisdom. *Wedge.* Stars lost in the sky. *Wedge, wedge.* The universe quietly turning itself inside out.

A species of awe, then. Gentle so far. Utterly natural. As our heroine floats through difference.

~ ~ ~

Sunday, deep into July. Summer has materialized. Time tends to slip from Wilma lately, or she slips from it. Her moments separate, one from another. She sees them. Solid little bars of time. If a body were to slip between, what might be found? Amused, she watches. Slipping becomes swinging. She is swinging by her hands, letting go of one bar, somersaulting in the air, catching the next. From time-bar to time-bar she goes. Is there a safety net? None visible. Does she need one? Certainly not, she is in no danger.

In fact, the image is inappropriate. The ground is firm beneath her feet now. She feels her feet inside her socks inside her shoes against the grassy ground. Sweating, she bends to chain her bicycle to the wrought iron railing. She stands and pulls a handkerchief from her pocket, wipes perspiration from her forehead, from her neck.

These concrete steps will take her into the old red brick building where Marlene O'Connor lives and works, third floor, number nine. This is her second visit. The first one is with her—that formidable painted hand, her near-collapse—but this will be different because difference, that essential element, has made itself known.

Seven steps up, open the building's door, traverse the hall, proceed upward: to lunch, to art, to whatever comes next between women who have spent a good number of hours together and who harbor, she is convinced, mutual affection. It is possible decisions will be made. She has her intentions.

The day is fully planned. In the late afternoon she and Marlene (and Lyle who has agreed to join them) will watch Young Henry perform at the Bangor Opera House. Something to do with Winnie-the-Pooh. Young children in the audience, many young children. Not the usual thing for her. An adventure, as this entire period of life seems to be. Afterward she and Marlene and Henry (without Lyle who has already respectfully declined the invitation) will proceed to Pizza Hut, which appears to be the necessary setting for their necessary conversations.

Winnie-the-Pooh. She found the book this morning, slightly musty, neatly mended, in one of the bookcases. She opened it, read the familiar sentences, heard her father's voice. "And the only reason for being a bee that I know of is making honey. And the only reason for making honey is so as I can eat it." Dear old Pooh, fervently, innocently, delightfully self-centered as ever. Times intersected, as they are wont to do these days. She was four years old and she was nearing seventy. She sat in the old farmhouse and she sat in her Bangor apartment.

Time and space. Anchors, both of them. Anchors that sprout difference.

Anchors do not sprout.

Lorraine?

'Tis I.

But metaphors must be allowed to sprout, must they not?

Good point, Wilma. I'll give you that one, though it's not a lovely example. Now proceed with your ascent. I leave, but I shall return.

This has been happening. Has Lorraine replaced Alma?

Of course, it's pure fantasy, this recurring presence of the dead.

Or is it?

No elevator here, not that kind of building. Let the body work, let the sweat pour, let the mind open, let thoughts come forth. Her legs and back are strong today, her hips willing, her feet supple and firm. And her mind? Her mind is mulling many things for she is in a new stage of that Deleuzian phenomenon, difference. She is no longer falling or floating. She landed gently, almost without noticing. It's been a few days now. She walks on the ground of difference—or, as the case may be, ascends a staircase. But still on the ground of difference.

Up she goes, slowly. Humans, dead and alive, surround and reshape her in this era of grounded difference. Nothing is quite what she expected as she set out to experience the divine.

Now there is Marlene.

Now there is Young Henry.

Now there are the dearly departed, newly known. Alma had a twin, and visions. Pa was in love with a man. His writing was published—respectably published, for Young Henry says *Mind* survives to this very day.

And Lorraine. Lorraine was in love with a philosopher novelist. Platonically, of course, and the whole thing was a bit one-sided, but that would hardly matter to the ardent reader. And now they have met, they have eternity. What might they be doing? If Pa and Spinoza are having a *tête-à-tête*, then Lorraine and Iris are sharing a nice swim. There does seem to be an abundance of swimming in Murdochian fiction and Lorraine was not averse.

Or is Murdoch still alive? Never mind. Times intersect. Surely, then, eternity—

All quite accurate, Wilma.

Back so soon, Lorraine?

Here and gone, here and gone. It's rather easy. You'll see.

Truly?

Well—

But now she knows she's playing.

She stops, breathes, closes her eyes. She is approaching the final flight of stairs. Too soon she will be at the landing, take a few steps to the right, knock on Marlene's door. She wants to gather it all—the abundance of particulars, past and present—put her arms around it, contain it, before Marlene opens the door.

She wants to do the same with difference itself—that light, aerial, affirmative (wild, red, beating) heart of existence—which comes naked to her at times, a multi-armed god, whirling in mirth. Embrace it, contain it. Before Marlene opens the door.

She never understood Lorraine's attraction to Kali, the fierce many-armed goddess. Lorraine would open a book, point to the images, try to explain. It made no sense. This was sacred? She did not speak the language. Then yesterday, for one moment—

Not that Kali is her god. Certainly not.

But as a metaphor of considerable power—rooted—reaching—

She knows now. The god has been waiting—almost palpable—inside this deeper difference, this difference she will never be able to explain to another, cannot truly explain to herself, and does not even

144

want to try. She has caught the gleam at the core, that tiny local fountain of a vast eternity, the one she imagined when she began to meditate. She has known the gust inside the god. In the brief time since she stopped falling or floating and gently landed her meditations have changed. It is as if she has felt existence itself, the depth and the reach of it, how it is seated in her, and in the god, and in all. From time to time she has almost gone to the heart of the paradox, the fecundity at the core—the core that *is* the fecundity. This has not been dramatic unless it is dramatic to sit on a worn brown couch and experience the calm clarity of her own radical existence inside the circle of the larger—much larger and supremely companionable—reality, the reality of existence itself.

Here is the landing.

She stops, gathers it all, the particulars, the essentials, in a sweep of her arms. This is literal. No one to see her, so why not? Open the arms, take it to the heart, all of it, including the moment when she and Marlene understood with some hilarity that they knew nothing at all about the nature of their relationship. They have cherished their liberating ignorance, but now, having touched the ground of difference, Wilma knows. Marlene is simply going to have to hear about this particular bit of knowledge.

Third floor, number nine, here we are.

She knocks gently on the door.

No answer.

She knocks firmly.

No answer.

She knocks very firmly.

"I'm coming, really I am, just a minute. Damn, damn, *damn*." The door opens. Marlene is struggling with the zipper of a pair of jeans stiff from newness.

So she yielded, thinks Wilma, amused.

"Jeans, please," Henry said, "or a reasonable equivalent. I want two dykes there, dykes who look the part, old style. You both know what I mean." Marlene protested. She was too fat and too old for jeans. She had no jeans. What was the vehemence about anyway? The vehemence, said Young Henry, was about terror. He was going to perform for *children*. He was a *faggot*. He needed unassailable dyke protection, which they are to

145

provide through the magical power of jeans. "You are neither too old nor too fat, Marlene O'Connor. Get some jeans."

Wilma, luckily, almost always wears jeans, has done so since childhood. She never felt the need to make a change. Lorraine liked this about her. Marlene also likes this about her. Her best pair, which she is wearing, is broken in, comfortable, and still decent enough for the circumstance.

"Sorry about that," says Marlene. "Bathroom emergency." The recalcitrant zipper is up, the stubborn button is buttoned. Wilma has the unseemly urge to approach, unbutton, and unzip.

"I am taken by this new look."

"What?"

"You look good in jeans, Marlene. Attractive shirt, too."

"Oh, Wilma. I'm a mess. You shouldn't be here."

"Shouldn't be here."

"I have to return to the bathroom."

"Go, then."

Moaning and holding herself, Marlene rushes away. From the bathroom she shouts, "Stay away from the art. Please."

But Wilma has already glimpsed the most astonishing thing: a full-body portrait of Henry. It took a moment to see, but there can be no doubt, it is the young mime. He has been pulled apart, stretched and twisted, reassembled strangely, and become himself. He is lovely, a nude human set into a background of compelling unidentifiable forms that might have spun off from him. The effect is of plenitude rather than crowding. Distortions pushed and jerked across the canvas have emerged as pure rhythms. Colors created to war with each other have instead fallen in love. Wilma is hypnotized. The painting is alive with its own becoming and she has witnessed this, the process itself, how the paint still vibrates with it. She, with her radical ignorance of art, has seen.

She is sitting cross-legged on the floor, adoring, when Marlene, struggling again with her zipper, arrives.

"I asked you not to."

"Too late. I had already seen it."

"I wanted to be here, to introduce you—the two of you—to each other. I didn't want you to faint. Did you start to faint? Is that why you're sitting on the floor? Is it ugly?"

146

"As you can see, I have not fainted. I am entranced. It is not ugly. When did you do this? Why didn't I know? Are you in love with him?"

"Of course I'm in love with him. Every painter is in love with the last thing she did. Until a week or so passes, that is. Rilke says it's best not to let it show, how you're in love with your own creations. It's in the notes. I almost love the notes more than the poems. I'm talking about Alma's Rilke collection. So many excerpts from his letters, what a letter writer. So I suppose it's a flaw, that you saw it. The love."

Wilma is staring, still waiting for an answer.

"Oh, you mean am I in love with *that* Henry, the actual person. What a question. I'm only in love with him the way you are. We've talked about this."

"We have. We are—in love with him, with the bright being he is— both of us. Exceedingly fortunate to have him. He enriches. I had to ask, though, in case I'd misunderstood. Especially today. One does fall in love with the painting. Almost with paint itself. Sitting here, looking, I have the most unexpected sense of knowing everything I need to know about art. I believe Henry—this Henry, your painted Henry—has shown me. We had a nice bit of time together. From that perspective, it's rather good that you had bathroom problems. But are you ill?"

She puts her arm around Marlene who has sat down beside her on the floor.

"I'm not sick unless it's sick to be this nervous about having you here."

"Maybe we should eat. That's a good normal activity. Are you in condition to eat? Or would you rather give me a tour first? I see that changes have been made since my memorable visit when, yes, I did almost faint. You overwhelmed me, or the art did. But witness the progress. Today I am intelligent about art, captured by your painting, unlikely to faint, and ready to eat. Or ready to look further, whichever you, as hostess and artist in residence, might desire. Are those terrible heads over there by your Francis Bacon?"

"I can eat. We'll eat first and tour, as you put it, later. The heads are by Bacon and aren't you smart. Why especially today, Wilma?'

"What?"

"You said you had to ask whether I was in love with Henry especially today."

147

"Did I?"

"You did. And then produced quite a flow of language."

"Well, it was careless of me."

"What did you mean?"

"I hadn't planned—so suddenly—yes, it's a bit abrupt to—"

"What did you *mean*?

"What did I mean."

"Yes. I'm asking."

"I'm not quite—I might have to rush to the bathroom myself."

"I doubt it. Here." Marlene is standing and putting out her hand.

Wilma is being pulled to her feet, she is being led to the table, directed to sit. No food is brought. Marlene is sitting, hands folded under her chin, waiting for words.

"Speak, Wilma. Why did you have to ask especially today?"

"I thought a conversation might develop more naturally. Organically, as you might say. There's a great deal of the organic in your portrait of our Henry, despite how broken to pieces it once was."

"You think you can avoid saying what you mean to say by getting me onto art. I'll remember that you seem to know a lot about the history of a painting you never saw in process but I shall not be deterred. What are you afraid to say to me?"

"I don't know that fear is exactly—"

"Wilma."

"Yes. Well."

Silence. They are evenly matched. Wilma believes the term for this would be standoff. Two women in a standoff, facing each other across a table, trying not to yield, trying mightily not to reveal by facial expression what their eyes, traitors, are already communicating. Marlene is waiting. It is obvious there will be no food until the thing is said.

"I don't suppose you'll help me."

"I don't think so."

"No. Well. Hmm. Perhaps if I offered a gesture?"

"Try it."

Wilma gets down on one knee, thankful for the hours she has spent stretching her body. She feels quite graceful and very nearly appropriate. And inspired. This was not part of the plan. She reaches one hand toward Marlene who laughs and takes the proffered body part.

148

"Wilma, Wilma. Is this a proposal? Shall we go to the courthouse? Or maybe a church? I'm not sure I could find a priest—"

"Yes. A proposal. I hereby propose, well, sex. Marriage for those of our kind being not quite legal. Though maybe some day. I hear there are those who hope for that."

"Not quite legal indeed. Would you want it?"

"Marriage? Premature and beside the point, Marlene."

"How did you know?"

"Know you would be ready?"

"Yes."

"I am discreetly psychic. I believe that's the term."

"You are not."

"Or simply perceptive?"

"Maybe that. But different, too. From how you've been."

"All right. Different. Will you?"

"Agree to try a bit of sex?"

"Agree to try being sexual even if the first bit isn't entirely—"

"Ah. What a precise approach you have, Ms. Schuh."

Marlene bends to kiss. This is a tender kiss on the lips, tenderly responded to. "Shall we eat, my dear Wilma?"

"Is that a yes?'

"That's a yes."

"Good. Help me up. I'm very hungry. Are your insides better?"

"My insides are amazed."

"I'll assume that's an improvement."

"Your assumption is correct."

Wilma is up. They are embracing, ventral to ventral, gently, firmly, erotically.

"Tonight?" Marlene asks.

"Tonight," agrees Wilma.

Broad smiles. Happy women. Light, aerial, affirmative.

"I made soup. Hot soup. I believe in it. Eat hot on a hot day, sweat it out, feel better."

"Did you learn that from your mother?"

"Philomena, actually."

"How is she?"

149

"Dying. I suppose the meal is in honor of her in some way. Her recipe. Lentil with veggies and lemon juice. A good hearty bread. I'll slice some cheese."

"Is she ready?"

"She is. The question is whether I am."

Marlene is holding the knife to the block of cheddar, looking at Wilma, tears rising in her eyes. "I'm happy," she says. "Happy with you, that is. But Philomena—death—"

"Come here. Food will wait." She leads Marlene to the couch. She has been given the history. Philomena was married and older, a patron of the arts. Now she is a widow and older still and very ill. Dying. And a patron of this artist. Yes, they had sex for a while, but it made Marlene feel guilty: the hurt to the husband, who knew and tolerated; and the unequal feelings. She wasn't attracted to Philomena, not intensely, though the sex was quite sweet. Philomena thought she was wildly in love with Marlene but her real desire, it became clear, was to be part of an artist's life, to follow the development, to make a difference. She had no talent, she had passionate interest, intelligence, appreciation, and she had money —her own, not her husband's—and the frank desire to use it to support this one woman, this young lesbian artist. The trio became friends, Philomena, Marlene, and the husband. When the husband was diagnosed with pancreatic cancer, Marlene and Philomena took care of him, a team. His death, the loss, was terrible for both of them. They comforted each other. Yes, in bed. No, not sexually. The sex had been over for a long time. They had been cuddle buddies, then just very good friends, and patron and artist. It might have only been for a few nights after the husband's death that they slept together, it's blurry now.

"Philomena took me seriously. She paid spectacular attention."

Marlene, at ease about the physical aspect of that relationship, was a tad defensive about the money. But Wilma just listened, fascinated.

Now, on the couch, Marlene cries, talks, cries, while Wilma holds her.

"Has Philomena seen our Henry? The painted splendor of him?"

"Yesterday. She said she wouldn't die until I agreed to bring her here. It wasn't easy—the steps, there are so many of them—but we managed."

"Did she appreciate what you did with him?"

150

"She said it was the top of the mountain, that she'd been watching me climb, she'd been waiting, hoping to live long enough, and this was it, I'd reached it, she could die." Marlene breaks into sobs.

Wilma surrounds her, loves her, whispers, "She was right."

"I don't know."

"You know. Not that it's the end, some final pinnacle, there will be others, but she saw—"

"Maybe." Marlene wipes her eyes, takes a deep breath. "I used Alma," she says.

"What?"

"To get her out of here, back down the steps. I remembered what you told me about Alma going down on her butt. On her bottom."

"Well, it's practical."

"It was. It took a long time. She said it was worth it."

"Of course it was."

"Now she'll die."

"You'll miss her."

"I'll have you."

"Yes. And you'll miss her."

They sit. Marlene blows her nose. Wilma's stomach growls. Marlene giggles. Wilma says, "Let's eat Philomena's soup."

~ ~ ~

Wilma is descending the stairs, smiling to herself. Marlene, most likely also smiling, is doing the post-lunch cleanup. A plan—workable, if awkward—has been made. They will spend the night at Wilma's, for the familiarity. Also, as Wilma was pleased to announce, clean sheets await them.

"What confidence, my dear Wilma," said Marlene.

"Warranted, you must admit," said Wilma.

"I admit," said Marlene, bowing deeply, rising up, grinning, flirting. And laughing at herself, laughing at both of them, for engaging in such a silly, splendid thing as flirting—old ladies that they are.

The problem, now solved, was the bicycle. It cannot be left overnight. The chain is flimsy, the landlord would object, *et cetera*. Wilma will therefore cycle home. Marlene will come soon, having

151

stopped to pick up Lyle. The three will go to witness Henry as he performs, no doubt beautifully. The women will allow Lyle to sit between them if need be, but if they can manage to sit side by side, legs brushing from time to

time—

They said that: legs brushing. They agreed to be kind to Lyle, but not too kind.

"We shall see what we shall see," said they, in unison.

My, my, thinks Wilma. She feels each solid step, down, down, down. She opens the door to to the street, descends the seven concrete steps to the sidewalk. She bends to unlock the chain, mounts, pedals, hopes to arrive home before the rain starts. Or perhaps she ought to welcome a downpour? Her first afternoon with Marlene was marked by hard rain, thunder, and lightning, so why not this singular moment?

Because these are her best jeans, that's why. Henry deserves her best jeans and she's too old to wear them wet through an entire performance, she'd end up chilled and stiff no matter how hot the day. Adventure enough to go down on bended knee and propose sex to another human being. May the rain wait.

The sweat pours. Wilma pedals. The rain waits.

Lunch was superb in the realms of the gustative and the conversational. The tour of the studio was intriguing and very nearly comprehensible. Marlene has indeed been climbing a mountain, striving, persisting. Gilles Deleuze's difficult book on Francis Bacon has been both spur and aid. Bacon himself, the same. More posters have been added to the studio walls. Henry donated a somewhat tattered one, a self-portrait by Antonin Artaud who seems linked in his mind to Bacon. He's ready to relinquish Artaud, an early influence on his work as a mime. The poster was offered as inspiration, Marlene must begin to produce her own self-portraits. No, no, no, said Marlene. Yes, yes, yes, said Henry. It was obvious to Wilma, listening, that Marlene was tempted and terrified, in equal proportion. Meanwhile, she is determined to paint Wilma, in the nude. Wilma is determined to avoid being painted, nude or clothed.

And by the way, she asked her artist lover-to-be, what was the procedure, with Young Henry? Was he naked in the studio day after day, week after week? Marlene replied that it was only two weeks, she was in a frenzy of creativity, and no, he was not naked in her studio. She

152

requested a photo and received one. She was following the example of Bacon, who preferred photos to live subjects. She'd be calmer with a photo, more alone, more *real* while she worked. A live model would be disconcerting, especially if the model were Henry. Especially if he were naked, "though we do prefer, as artists, to say 'nude,' so much more respectable."

"Why especially?"

"Oh, you know. He's exuding all the time. And moving. Even when he's still as a statue he's almost visibly growing, like a plant caught on camera. I'm thinking of how he was when he showed us that Noh theater exercise, absolutely still and yet somehow in motion. But mostly it's his eyes. Or maybe not. Do you remember Rilke's sonnet about the archaic torso?"

"'Eyes like ripening fruit.' Alma wasn't fond of that image."

"Well, it's a bit weird. Especially since the head of the god is broken off and there are no eyes, ripening or not."

"Alma kept turning the missing eyes from ripening into rotten. But she forgave. She loved the basic idea, how the gaze of Apollo comes to the poet from every part of the torso, the head being gone."

"The gaze and then the command: 'You must change your life.'"

"An interesting command, in our current context. But back to the photograph. You needed to make your own movement out of what stayed still long enough for you to see it. Is that it?"

"Wilma, Wilma. You do know something about the process. How is that?"

"It's there in the painting, especially in those parts where things get denser and stranger, more chaotic and more precise at the same time. That might be a way to put it."

"You see it."

"It's there, my dear Marlene."

Wilma smiles as she cycles along in cooperative mild traffic under skies which politely continue to refrain from pouring down rain. She had things to say about art. How had those words come to her? She cherishes the mystery of this, the fun.

In her maturity, these suddenly materializing bits of fun.

And tonight, sex.

153

Lorraine had fun with sex, pulled Wilma into that. Her fun was secondary to Lorraine's. Still, it was quite—

This will be different, Wilma.

Lorraine?

Just riding along. It's an interesting development, after all. All these years of celibacy and now, old lady that you've become—

Lorraine Benedict, you are a figment.

Of course I am. Just wanted to wish you well as the day progresses.

And she's gone.

While they were eating, Marlene said, "Philomena has been so innocent with me all these years. She's a little like you that way, Wilma. Did we ever talk about your innocence?"

"I remember you used that bewildering word."

"When you almost fainted at the sight of the art that first time—I suppose it was mostly Bacon's triptychs that upset you, but you were standing at my *Hand in Slow Motion Grasping*—"

"And I had to sit."

"You had to be helped to sit."

"I remember, Marlene."

"Eyes determinedly closed."

"Yes. But note that today—"

"You might be less innocent today."

"Or more prepared."

"Certainly bolder."

"Now you're thinking of my proposal."

"I am."

They talked a bit about innocence, Marlene's sense of it in Bacon's art, how his subject matter hardly seems innocent and yet she feels something—hard to put into words—and then here comes Wilma Schuh and she's certainly more innocent than most and maybe she ought not to be meddled with.

"Meddled with. My dear Marlene. Are we speaking of innocence as opposed to experience or to guilt?"

"Both? It's not a honed assessment, just a feeling. Or was. I'm not sure it fits, now that I know you better."

"I'd say we're both a bit old for innocence. But I confess I almost understand. I shouldn't tell you this, but I will. Remember our first set of hours together? How you sat in my apartment wrapped in a blanket, not a stitch of clothing on?"

"I would hardly forget such a thing. Besides, it was only a few months ago."

"Not quite two months, actually."

"Really?"

"Really. You were reading Rilke's unicorn poem."

"I read it out loud."

"You did. I think of that, rather often."

"You connect the unicorn and innocence?"

"And you, Marlene."

"What?"

"Rather like your deciding I might be too innocent to meddle with, isn't it?"

"Yes, but—"

The things she and Marlene say to each other!

Three Moirae, age twelve, come suddenly into view. They wave their young arms wildly as she approaches. "Hey, Old Lady!" Friendly.

"Hello, girls!" She waves and pedals on.

Innocence.

Her wave was brief. She needs both hands on these handlebars. A few minutes and she'll be home. The rain held off. She hopes Young Henry isn't one iota more nervous than might be necessary for his task.

~ ~ ~

"The Penobscot Theater Company's summer programs at the Bangor Opera House always draw a good crowd of children and their attached adults, but even unattended adults are warmly welcomed."

This Wilma hears from Lyle who apparently knows more about the world around him than she assumed. Or did he simply absorb what the program states? He does sound as if he's quoting, while she, over-stimulated, has been unable to make meaning of a single word on the folded page in her hand. Lyle did not, poor man, know enough to dress comfortably. She is seated between him and Marlene and the experience is somewhat surreal as he sits in his serge suit with the musty tinge, last worn to memorialize Alma, and Marlene sits in her stiff new jeans.

155

Wilma's physical awareness of both humans intensifies by the minute. There is nothing erotic in her sense of the serge and the man within, but his dear presence is almost as potent as Marlene's sexy nearness.

Lyle, having spoken his piece, sits quietly, eyes on the stage curtain. It will be at least ten minutes before the performance begins. Marlene turns and cranes, scanning the audience. This, she says, is normal pre-performance behavior: "Don't you want to see if you know anyone here?"

"Unlikely," says Wilma.

"*There's* someone," says Marlene. "Three rows back, on the aisle."

"I don't think…"

"*Look*."

"I refuse to stare, Marlene."

"Don't you recognize him? Lyle, isn't that Wilma's poet?"

Lyle responds with vagueness.

Marlene reaches for Alma's backpack and pulls out the little book. All three look at the author photograph, casting surreptitious glances at the man three rows back.

Lyle nods. "That's the fellow. Shy when he brought his books to the store. Three still on the shelf, been there a long time. I believe you're the sole purchaser, Wilma."

Marlene grabs Wilma's hand and pulls. Wilma resists. Marlene pulls. Wilma yields, a scene will ensue if she doesn't.

So here they are, standing in the aisle, interrupting a private citizen as he waits for a bit of entertainment. The private citizen appears to be in his late fifties. Slightest bit paunchy. Thin crinkly hair, mostly black but the graying has begun. Face pleasant and intelligent, but worn or fatigued beyond what it ought to be. The quality is there, thinks Wilma, but something is not quite right. She's remembering the poetry. Parents who committed suicide. Lover who left him. But all of that was years ago, wasn't it?

"Michael Solomon?" says Marlene.

"That's me." He looks directly at Marlene.

Not offended, a bit curious, thinks Wilma. Well, all right.

Marlene plunges on. "This is my friend Wilma Schuh and she would like you to sign this, if you don't mind. We're sorry to bother you, but it's not every day—"

156

"Sign?"

Marlene hands him the book he appears to have forgotten. Surely a writer doesn't forget his own book, but they took this one by surprise. Did Pa forget his article, the fact of its publication? That mind, and then its disintegration—did she ever truly comprehend—?

Michael Solomon turns the book over and over, looks at a few pages, says, "Well, well."

Marlene comments that it is apparently not every day for him, either —that he gets asked to autograph his work, she means—and does he have a pen?

The woman next to Michael offers him a pen. "Isn't it good I dragged you out, Michael dear?"

"Right, as ever, Petra. But you could have told me this was a children's event."

The girl sitting next to Petra—Wilma wonders if she is perhaps twelve years of age—tells him that Winnie-the-Pooh has many levels of sophistication.

"As do you, Sephie, but am I really about to see a production based on Winnie-the-Pooh?"

"Sign the book, Michael, and then after you've been courteous to your readers you might want look at the program, show a hint of interest," says Petra, who can't be his wife, can she, because isn't he gay?

Wilma is trying to sort the situation—and think of something, anything, to say—while also experiencing an eerie vestigial need to hold her father's hand. Why would that be? But here is Michael Solomon, poet. She has read the poems again and again, as if searching for something written in code.

The author signs the book and returns it to Marlene who gives it to Wilma who says, "Thank you, Michael. I've read *Keep This Deep and Velvet Night: A Self-Portrait* more than once in the midst of my own acquaintance with family death." Which is awkward, but at least honest.

"She likes it that you're gay, too," says helpful Marlene.

Wilma tells Marlene to behave herself, looks Michael in the eye, and quotes, "'The hands of the mother, the hands of the father—'"

He's paying close attention now.

"I do appreciate the hands. And Billy, your very own mime, offering his heart—right out in the open—there you were—and the little audience

157

—'We all breathed in, breathed out, breathed in'—I do hope, despite how he left you in the end—'Paper crying in the rain'— Yes. Well. We can credit Lyle Franklin. I required a book. My mother's death was the occasion. I slipped into confusion, but found my way past."

"Thank you. Wilma, is it? Thank you very much. You certainly did read the book," says Michael Solomon, breathing deeply. "My condolences on your mother's death. I hope it was—"

"She was quite complete, thank you. One hundred years, you know. Your parents, too. Complete, I believe."

"I think you must be right, Wilma. But your mother, a century of life. Amazing. This is a gift, Wilma—your approaching me. A rather unique and—um—stunning gift."

"A gift returned, then. All credit to Marlene, for the approaching." The poet and his reader shake hands. They take a long silent moment. Something rises in the air between them—something gentle and comforting—waves of it, rising from the theater floor between a stranger and herself. Wilma gives an internal nod to her hidden god who is perhaps gusting again.

Marlene says, "We'd better—"

Wilma says, "Enjoy our Young Henry and his friends, Michael."

Michael nods to both women, smiles with his eyes, picks up his program.

As they walk back to their seats, Wilma hears him say, with a decided change of tone, "You brought me to a performance by *Henry Whitsun*?"

To which Petra replies, "Henry Whitsun means something?"—while Sephie, sophisticated child, says, "Henry Whitsun is a *good mime*, Michael."

Marlene looks back and whispers, "Your poet appears to have seen a ghost."

But the performance is about to begin. The stage is bare except for three straight-backed chairs. The backdrop is plain and muted, sky-blue. The performers are Frank the narrator, Milo the musician, and of course Henry. Frank's voice is a rich intelligent mix of tenderness, irony, humor, and pathos. He reads passages from *Winnie-the-Pooh*, leaves generous spaces, and creates a sense of perfect pacing. His narration anchors the entire hour. Milo's subtle, flexible guitar accents the events of the story, humbly enters the silences, and altogether beguiles. Henry himself is bewitching. He is the spirit, the essence, the energy, becoming by turns each of the characters—Christopher Robin, Pooh, Piglet, Kanga, Baby Roo, and dear old narcissistic, depressed Eeyore—echoing the story and creating layers of physical poetry beyond the words, weaving an entirely fresh thing. Never has he seemed more of a bright presence.

Half-way into the performance Wilma assembles the pieces: poet, gay, mime, distress. Henry must be "Billy," the mime of Michael's poetry, the lover who refused to speak, the lover who left.

But the performance is so compelling that everything else recedes. The audience is offering frequent giggling, little bursts of applause, and, above all, attention. She herself is now entirely attentive, the perfect audience. She is also for a moment onstage with Henry, being Henry, enveloped by the attention of others. Waves of energy invade and overflow the stage. How much of this can a body absorb without toppling over? Is this why he fainted the day she first saw him? When Christopher Robin finally takes Pooh by the leg and drags him up the stairs—*bump, bump, bump*—she finds herself with tears in her eyes, gripping Lyle's arm and reaching for Marlene's hand. Young and old are on their feet, the applause is full and prolonged, this has to be perfect for Henry and his friends. But how is it for her poet?

She turns in time to see him leave his seat and hurry down the aisle.

Oh, Michael. Dear Michael.

Petra and Sephie get up and follow.

Good, he's not going to be alone. Unless of course that would be his preference—

"Let's go see our star," Marlene says, and once again Wilma is being pulled along—rather like Pooh Bear—and she herself is pulling Lyle along, gently, but also quite firmly, because, yes, of course, they must go to see their star.

The happy performers are much in demand as they sign programs and bend to shake small hands. Wilma and Marlene and Lyle wait, smiling, absorbing the amazements of the afternoon. Finally the theater clears. Six remaining humans stand in a loose circle. Young Henry makes the introductions.

Frank, narrator and choreographer, appears to be about Henry's age, maybe a little older: "He gave me *so* many ideas and isn't his voice a *wonder*? Backbone of the show."

Milo is much younger, perhaps still in his teens: "Up from Cambridge just for the adventure. Musical *genius*, which you no doubt noticed. Couldn't have done it without him."

Lyle is friend and proprietor: "Best bookstore in town."

Marlene and Wilma are old friends: "Re-found, currently indispensable."

Energies run every which way as the six stand and beam at each other. Lines cross and bend and recross, creating intriguing designs, entertaining Wilma so thoroughly she wonders how she'll manage to consume and digest the rest of the day. She tells herself she'll simply have to expand her being, hoping she's able, watching lines of energy run hither and thither.

Frank and Milo depart. Henry's gaze follows them.

Love, thinks Wilma, hardly knowing what she means.

Lyle declares himself ready to return to his quiet life, not that he hasn't enjoyed himself, indeed he has, an unusual and most fascinating, *et cetera*. They watch him limp away down the street, a cherished human.

Henry and Wilma and Marlene get into Marlene's car and drive to Pizza Hut.

~ ~ ~

Mary, their preferred waitress, approaches. "Ah, my old friends. Welcome once again. The usual? Good. I expect to hear some of that talk I can't get a speck of sense from. Don't disappoint me now, dears." This last is thrown over her shoulder as she goes to place their order.

Marlene leaps in. "So, Henry, who are Frank and Milo? I mean who are they *really*. And don't leave out the erotic elements."

"Why, Marlene O'Connor, whatever leads you to imagine—"

"Oh, I imagine, darlin'. And can't I read a vibe or two? 'Fess up."

"Frank *is* rather enchanting, isn't he?"

"Oh my God. Are you—"

"Early stages, nothing serious, don't panic." Wilma thinks of Michael and sends a quick good wish his way.

160

"And little Milo? I trust you know he's in love with you," says unrelenting Marlene.

Henry sighs. "I know. It's complicated."

"You haven't—"

"No, I have not. I'm not even sure he knows what's got him stirred up. Maybe he thinks it's the artistic connection. Maybe he's right. I do think he's a genius. He can slip right into anything I do."

"Just don't let him slip right into your behind."

"*Marlene*. What's got into you?" Grinning and shaking his head.

Marlene blushes. Wilma's head spins. Perhaps it's hunger. Or are they all intoxicated from the wonders of the afternoon? Is this what people call a natural high? Mary would be perfectly capable of understanding the conversation and isn't it fortunate she's out of earshot?

A young man approaches the booth.

"I'm sorry to interrupt, but I was at your performance just now—"

"A fan!" says Marlene.

"Well, I suppose I am. But I confess I'm also—that is—I should tell you—I'm a reporter—um—John Stone, reporter—I—"

"Hello, John Stone, reporter," says Henry Whitsun, mime, moderating his grin, extending his hand.

How utterly gracious, thinks Wilma, filling with love.

"I wondered if—such good luck—I was just sitting down with friends—at that booth over there—and here you are—and—well—I thought you might—um—"

"Out with it, John," says Marlene.

Wilma smiles encouragingly at the reporter.

"I'm new at this, I suppose you can tell. But would you—if it's not too inconvenient—maybe you'd be willing to—um—give me an interview some time?"

"I'd be honored, John."

"Really?"

"Really."

"Oh. Well. I was thinking of something in-depth—not that I can promise—I mean—maybe the *Republican Journal* down in Belfast would—or even the *Bangor Daily*, if we're lucky—once they saw what —well—you're so talented, I—"

"Sounds good. Do you have a card?"

161

The card—John Stone, Freelance Reporter—is clumsily and happily produced. Henry promises to call tomorrow. Off goes the novice reporter.

Marlene is trying to control her slide into hilarity as she says "How much do you suppose the poor guy heard? I can see it now: *Our newest local entertainer, mime Henry Whitsun, appears to have anal penetration much on the mind. Or at least his friends do, on his behalf. However, Mr. Whitsun was courteous and friendly when approached by this freelance reporter at the Pizza Hut restaurant on Broadway in Bangor last Sunday after a stunning performance—*"

The hilarity is contagious. They are still in the grip of it when Mary arrives. "This is new," she comments wryly, setting pizza and sodas on the table, the order exactly right as always. She stands there a moment, shaking her head. "At least three steps past anything I've seen from this bunch. What'm I gonna do with you?"

"Go away, Mary," says Marlene, wiping her eyes and breathing heavily, still laughing. She blows a kiss. Mary catches and pockets it. They all breathe deeply and gain basic control over themselves.

"Where were we?" says Marlene.

"We are not returning to where we were," says Henry. "Mind your manners or you will find yourself suitably punished."

"Propose a topic, then, oh thou master of ceremonies."

"That's easy, and thank you for asking. Tell me what you thought of the performance. The audience was perfect, I am a human surfeited with praise, but I am also an artist in need of discriminating and intelligent and of course supremely objective feedback. Please."

"I suppose, then, we are not allowed simply to gush," says Marlene.

Henry gives her the expected look and waits.

There is a change of mood, an interval of thoughtful silence. Wilma closes her eyes. Calm familiarity rules this group. What a quantity of experience the three of them have compressed into their short time together, as if they were compelled to plant seeds, grow the crop, and gather their harvest as rapidly as possible. Can she speak of what she saw on that stage?

She opens her eyes. Her companions seem to be waiting, for her.

She finds herself speaking.

"I'm trying to catch a thought—or maybe it's an image—it's not very clear—something about the elements—mime and music and narration—

162

braided and unbraided—so effectively, Henry—but something else, too —I might be referring to levels—the details would be one level—Pooh so full of honey he can't get out of Rabbit's hole, Owl pontificating and misspelling, Eeyore bemoaning his missing tail—that's one very satisfying level, you did it so creatively—but there was another—maybe it's not so much levels as layers—overlapping layers—I remembered the word palimpsest the other day—layers of rhythms drawn back and forth and above and below and around and about—which sounds like weaving, doesn't it? Yes, that might be best—weaving—and then, at the center, it now occurs to me, sitting like a spider in her web—what an inappropriate creature to introduce here—or perhaps not inappropriate at all—because—"

But her thought won't quite—

"Don't stop," her listeners say in chorus.

She takes a breath. "All right. I think I have it. At the center—let's say it's the center of a web since we seem to have a web now—" Her listeners are patient, and beautiful. She's distracted by their beauty.

But she can almost say this next thing. "At the center of the web is some sort of—innocence—I can't quite—but, yes, innocence—"

Marlene is smiling. It's that word again.

The completion of Wilma's thought seems to slide away—the slippery core of what she's trying to get to—but she catches it. "I felt the innocence—I do think that's the word—and then the parallels—it was astonishing, actually, how this happened—I believe I somehow *experienced* the parallels—physically—in my body, I mean—the parallels with the portrait, which I saw for the first time today, Henry— and when this happened—I—well—I was so very pleased—so very pleased about the three of us—"

She cannot quite believe she is saying exactly this, but why should she not? After all, just a few hours ago she proposed sex on bended knee. The faint image of a many-armed goddess flits past and is gone. Kali.

"Yes," she says, finishing. "So pleased. About the three of us."

"Portrait?" says Henry

"Of you, of course. I did so appreciate the experience, Henry."

Henry addresses Marlene. "It's finished?"

"Well—"

"You showed it to Wilma before—"

163

"I forgot to tell you, Wilma. Henry hasn't seen it."

"Oh," says Wilma. "I see." Part of what she sees is that there is to be a change of topic. These two have something other than the slippery workings of the mind of Wilma Schuh to talk about. Very well, then. But what did she just do? She spoke of love, without quite meaning to. She stumbled along until she got to love. How interesting. And now their road has taken a sudden sharp turn. Perhaps Kali will hold the thought which seems a bit octopus-like—the layers, the parallels, the performance, the portrait, this threesome, love—hold it in her many arms.

She looks at poor Marlene and says, "I suppose this failure to show Henry his own portrait was due to—"

"Embarrassment, yes. Mountains of insecurity. I thought if *you* seemed to think it was all right, then—"

"Oh, Marlene." She puts an arm around Marlene and squeezes.

"Tomorrow, Henry," says Marlene. "Will you have time tomorrow? One viewer per day. Think about your own work, how it is before anyone sees a new thing, how you're—"

Henry sighs, looks long and hard at Marlene. He tells her he supposes she is forgiven. "Tomorrow's good, actually. Nothing else on the schedule. I do understand. But Wilma was talking about innocence and parallels—your art and our performance—"

Innocence and parallels and love, thinks Wilma. There was a scene in Murdoch's *The Unicorn*, if she can just—

"The idea of parallels is tantalizing," Henry is saying. "I *have* to see the painting. Still, do you think Wilma's caught hold of something?"

"Oh, yes, Wilma has caught hold of a great deal. She does that lately," says Marlene, her eyes sliding sideways, full of implication. Which implication Wilma is perfectly able to make sense of. She kicks to the side, catching Marlene's ankle.

"Ouch!" says Marlene.

"What?" says Young Henry. "Are you two—"

"Forbidden topic," says Marlene. "Apparently."

Wilma chuckles. Life has changed. However, enough is enough. "Address the issue, Marlene. Henry asked a real question."

"I don't know if I—"

"Well, maybe if you just try to tell us what happened for *you* in the theater."

"You're asking for it, Wilma Schuh."

"I'm asking, as you well know, about your response to the performance, as per request of the performer himself."

Henry looks at them. "My dear ladies," says he. "Blessings upon you. But, Marlene, you *must* give me one good sentence. Take pity on an artist in need."

Marlene nods, ponders, speaks. "I confess I also thought about my painting, self-centered artist that I am. You were stunning today, Henry, so of course I wondered if I had caught the tiniest fraction of you. But I wasn't distracted, I was with you every minute, you and Frank and Milo, and I couldn't help noticing how you were working together—it was so beautiful, Henry, and, well, *erotic*."

"Erotic," says Henry.

"Erotic. I don't think this was just my personal response, related to my—um—current personal experience. There *was* something erotic. You know it, too—don't you?"

"Hmm," says Henry.

"So I wondered how this was coming across to an audience full of kids. Of course it was all in perfect taste. There was nothing the least bit risqué. It was sweet, really. A sweet eroticism. Even a chaste eroticism. I wonder if that's an oxymoron. Let's say it isn't. So, yes, at the center, as Wilma says, a very interesting and complicated—and *effective*—innocence. We entered another world, the innocent world of Pooh—and you made it sweetly, innocently erotic. As for the parallels to my painting, I can only say how delightful, how flattering, how possibly nuts my dear Wilma is being."

Marlene takes Wilma's hand, squeezes, lets go. Which gesture is itself sweetly erotic, or so thinks Wilma as she listens and nods and cherishes the company she is keeping.

"And, Henry," continues Marlene, "I don't think I ever saw you quite that—well—*good*."

Henry is silent. Silent and nodding. Finally he says, "Well. I feel I've been attended to. Thank you. I knew you were the ones I wanted to be with. But enough of that. Almost too much. We shall now speak of our

165

reading lives. I'm starved for a reading conversation. Wilma? Oh, wait, I wanted to know, did Lyle ever say anything about your father's article?"

Wilma smiles. "He did. He handed the article back to me today when we picked him up. He said, 'I believe your father was a scholar, then, Wilma. Your mother wondered, but I believe he was.' End of discussion. Man of few words, as ever."

"I forget that Lyle and your mother were friends," says Marlene. "I wonder if the erotic was ever—"

Wilma places a cautionary finger over Marlene's lips. Truly, enough is enough.

"OK, I'll shut up," says compliant Marlene, but not before she has caught and kissed the finger.

"Books, ladies," says Henry. "The reading life. Remember? Well, maybe I'll start, since there's a link to what has apparently and rather mysteriously become our current word. I'm reading Deleuze on Nietzsche and I just came to a section titled 'Existence and Innocence.' Nice serendipity, don't you think? I can't offer anything developed about this, but I find myself returning again and again to the words, existence and innocence, existence and innocence—as if existence itself is innocent—which is actually what I think Deleuze is saying Nietzsche meant."

Existence itself is innocent. With this, Wilma remembers. Effie, in *The Unicorn*, is lost in a bog. It is deep night, he is caught, he is sinking, he might not be able to free himself from the suck of the mud. Already he can't move his legs. He could die. Effie is no saint, but the near prospect of death works a momentary miracle. He looks into the depth of the blackness that surrounds him, focuses his attention on what he cannot see, experiences his "self" as gone, almost wonders if he has already died. What is left? Everything. Everything that is not Effie. He looks into the darkness which is everything other than himself, everything Real, and the Real is full of being, full of light, the darkness has become light, and this light, this Reality—here is the revelation—is automatically lovable. Effie, habitually full of himself, experiences love in the face of his death —a death which does not come that night, he is rescued, but of course it will come someday. He realizes—temporarily, but still, he does realize— that he could have known this all along, this automatically lovable Reality, because, as Murdoch puts it, "the fact of death stretches the

166

length of life." Wilma is so delighted when the words come to her that, without meaning to, she says them out loud: "The fact of death stretches the length of life."

Marlene and Henry lean forward, ask her to repeat. She repeats, then comments that this might appear to be a *non sequitur*. But there are links, if she can explain—

Which she is of course urged to do.

She tells about Effie, his vision, his moment of seeing into Reality. She tells how love rises up in him—because Reality is automatically lovable. "And we could know this constantly if we grasped that death stretches the length of life. Maybe this is the web *I'm* sitting in. I do keep returning to it: Reality, automatically lovable. Death, stretching the length of life."

Marlene has been holding her thought. Now it bursts from her. "That's *it*. That's what I'm doing with Francis Bacon. Those 'terrible heads' of his that you commented on today, Wilma. I know they're ugly. But the ugliness turns to beauty if you really *see*. Maybe this is like Effie. Look and look until the darkness turns into light. Bacon paints horror and violence and weirdness and ugliness and yet, with him too, somehow at the heart of it all is an *innocence*—I know we've talked about this but suddenly I see innocence from a new angle—as if anything at all— everything—is in some way as innocent and as lovable as a puppy— especially if the puppy has not just had an accident on the living room floor. Well, I guess it's more that the little pile on the floor is innocent, too—and it gets stepped on in the night—the owner steps and slips and dislocates her back and *still*—" Marlene is laughing at her own thought's progress. "OK, you get it," she says. "Anything, anything at all is worth looking at so closely that you come to see the beauty—which is always innocent—true beauty is always innocent—and, seeing the beauty, you want to paint it—or you want to paint it to get *to* the beauty—and beauty is the same as reality—automatically lovable reality. This might be what I'm working on now. *My* web. Deleuze would say we're talking about affirmation, wouldn't he, Henry?" Henry nods, but absent-mindedly. "Henry?"

Henry looks at Marlene. He looks at Wilma. He takes a breath. "I believe I want to tell you both something."

167

~ ~ ~

"It happened when he started to tell," Marlene says. She sits on Wilma's bed, legs crossed, arms stiff, hands pressing against the mattress as if something threatens to emerge from below. Rigid and shivering and trying valiantly to "explain," this precious human is in danger of becoming a set of unmanageable words that need to be pressed back to flatness. Wilma is holding her own hands tightly clasped to each other for two contrary reasons: to refrain from reaching out to sooth what cannot be soothed, and to prevent the violence of pressing to flatness what is not and never will agree to be flat. Marlene O'Connor is a fully rounded and entirely vulnerable human being, alive and suffering—a being who has spun an alarming and brittle casing around her own insides.

"No, I'm wrong," Marlene says. "It was before, just before he said he had something to tell. I was going on and on. I must not have been paying attention—to how *he* wasn't paying attention. He's never absent, he's always *there*. That's part of what we— I'm sorry, Wilma, I really can't be touched. I know I'm here on your bed, and any other woman— you're so beautiful—do you know you look like Lorraine's writer, that Iris Murdoch?—such a dear and warm face you have—don't let me hurt you—I don't ever want to hurt you—but don't touch me."

"I can refrain from touching, Marlene. Something happened to you when Henry—"

"I did see—suddenly—that he wasn't with us. That's when it happened. *Before* he said he had something to tell. Then he said he had something to tell. Then he told. But it was before. What happened to me. It was before."

"Can you say what the thing was, that happened to you?"

"I think I'm be afraid."

"Afraid."

"Of destroying you."

Such drama. Wilma has a rather strong urge to chide. The young man has a heart condition. There is no indication he will die from it and certainly no indication he will die soon. And if he did die—

Well, human beings die.

Swiftly, briefly, Kali flits through.

168

Kali: goddess of death and destruction, always a few skulls hanging on her somewhere, a necklace of them, if Wilma is recalling correctly. But this fierce goddess of the force of time is also the goddess of creativity and of preservation, is this not true? Still. Poor Marlene. Of course if they lost Young Henry, if he did die, so young, it would be—

"But I know that's silly. I haven't destroyed you yet, Wilma. You're probably sturdier than you seem. I do understand I'm being impossible. I'll just say it, I think I can just say it."

Wilma waits, afraid to speak.

"I felt it," Marlene says. "I felt it rush through me. Death. I felt death." She takes a large gulp of air and goes silent.

Wilma loosens her hands, one from the other. She breathes very carefully. She waits, unsure of what's needed here.

"I felt his death," Marlene says finally. "I felt us losing him. I felt the *world* losing him. I don't know how to find my way out of this. No, don't touch me."

"I can refrain, Marlene."

In fact, the impulse to reach and touch is frightening, as if touching Marlene in her current state might shatter her. Where is the woman who moaned and dissolved into tears and thrived on being held when distressed? Further, where is the version of Wilma who "knows things"? —who fell or floated with equanimity through a strangeness labeled "difference" and landed softly and found herself walking on some ground that appears to have been illusory. Or, no, the ground is still in place, but with each passing minute it seems to move toward its own silent splintering. The ground she walks on. The ground within the self. Is the self, the very self, again ungrounded?

The self again ungrounded. She finds the sound of this quite interesting. *Again ungrounded.* She likes the alliteration. *The self again ungrounded.* She is entertaining herself while waiting for Marlene to produce more tight words. Yes, that must be what she's doing.

The self again ungrounded. The phrase becomes a chant, hypnotic, lulling.

Then, quite suddenly, the words break away from each other, fly off.

Self. What can that have meant?

Again. Surely repetition could occur only inside the structure of Time which appears to have disintegrated.

169

Ungrounded. Ridiculous concept. One would have to know what its opposite meant before one could begin to—

Wilma can feel her hands, white with the pressure of holding something. Each other. Holding each other. Again. Under pressure. It is a stark white sensation.

Vision blurs. Dizziness threatens.

But Kali comes, not lightly flitting by, but swooping through in a rush: a force, a wind, a gust of the god.

The blurred world clarifies.

Wilma's hands relax, she can feel them, watch them, as they loosen and let go of each other and her mind loosens and relaxes and knows how to follow the impulse, the impulse that rises within, definite and beckoning, while Marlene can be seen looking at her own right hand, still pressed against the mattress, from which mattress some terrible thing *must* be threatening to emerge. Poor woman, still in the grip, but perhaps she can be freed.

"Marlene."

"Wilma?"

"I have a proposal."

"A proposal. Oh, Wilma. I'm so sorry. I can't. I know I said yes, but I can't."

"I didn't mean—no, of course not—I shouldn't have used the word —proposal—an insensitive choice—but I didn't mean—"

"Well, what then?"

If only the dear woman would not stiffen herself so. Still, doesn't her voice already seem just a tad more Marlene-like? Wilma instructs herself to say what the terrible paradoxical Kali wants her to say.

So she says it: "I think we should get off this bed, leave this bedroom, and go to your apartment. Not to your bedroom, to your studio. And you may do whatever it is you do when you begin a painting. Of me. Nude, if you prefer. As you requested."

Marlene glances up. She looks back down at her tensed right hand. She starts to nod, takes a breath, another, and another.

"Well, that is certainly unexpected, Wilma Schuh. I don't know. First our Henry, now you. I never knew how poorly I respond to surprises."

How irritating this cherished woman can make herself.

170

"One might think, my dear Marlene, that this would be a little different from the surprise of Henry's news."

"Oh, it's different, I just mean—"

"I thought perhaps—but, of course—I understand. I can't expect to lure you away from—"

"LQTS."

"Yes. Do you remember what the letters stand for?"

"Death."

"No, really, Marlene. I know it's useless, but I am driven to object. Death is such a remote possibility."

"I know what the letters stand for. LQTS, Long QT Syndrome. I know his heart might simply decide to take its time getting to the next beat, get there, and get itself back to normal. But it could go the other way. If he faints when he's with us and we don't get help soon enough—"

"If that happens he might very well spontaneously regain consciousness. I saw him faint. I think he came to quickly enough. And he's obviously fine now."

"No guarantee that next time—"

"I know, but—"

"I felt it—death—*before* he told us. I *felt* it, Wilma."

"All right. He might die. He might even die when he's with us."

Marlene's eyes fill and overflow, her entire face melts.

Well, finally, thinks Wilma, as she reaches out. "Come here."

Marlene complies, sobbing, seeking sturdy arms.

Time passes. Marlene quiets. The ground solidifies. Two woman rest on it.

Then the shaking begins.

So there is more, the poor stubborn woman will not be so easily comforted.

But Marlene, woman of the unexpected presentation, is shaking not from distress but from something quite other. Marlene is in fact: giggling. "If we were heterosexual we'd be into hot sex by now," says Marlene O'Connor.

"Is that a fact," says Wilma Schuh.

"Fact," says Marlene.

"Well, the erotic element of this situation escapes me."

"Ditto, I'm afraid."

171

So this is how it will be, thinks Wilma. One thing, and then another. How very interesting. Comfortable now, and knowing a thing or two, she says to Marlene, simply, wisely, "We have time."

"I hope so, Wilma."

"Oh my dear Marlene. Well, I hope so, too. I made an offer, in the realm of art, not sex. What do you think?"

"I don't know. I don't know if it's in me. At the same time, I hate to pass up—"

"The offer will remain on the table. Even the nudity part. It's one of those oddly inspired things, I suspect you're familiar with the phenomenon."

"Rock-solid as soon as it arrives."

"Yes."

"I think I'm hungry," says Marlene.

Thus passes the storm, thinks Wilma. Or the worst of it. For the moment. "I believe I neglected the category of food," she says. "I haven't shopped. I was focused on clean sheets."

"You thought pizza would be sufficient."

"True. I didn't anticipate developments. Was there any soup left?"

"Philomena's lentil soup is never finished in a single meal. But going to my place wouldn't mean I'd have to—"

"I'm not exactly panting to be painted."

"Who knows, maybe we'll both be panting in some other way—"

But the statement has none of Marlene's sassy sexy energy. She's only making her effort.

"I'm in no hurry, Marlene. About anything. Please don't put me in that position."

"No. I'm sorry. I'm a little off tonight."

"And you're hungry. As am I. We should change our venue and allow good Philomena to feed us. I'm so sorry about Philomena. Death is looming everywhere for you, isn't it?"

Wilma cannot believe she said this. Equanimity is restored and she goes and—

But Marlene just looks at her and nods and says, "Yes, it is."

So there she is, resilient Marlene, grounded, real, automatically lovable. Who wouldn't fall for such a woman?

Telling herself to make no further references to death for at least fifteen minutes because why take chances, Wilma says, "Let us proceed in the direction of food." Marlene smiles and begins to dress for the journey. Wilma does likewise, breathing the air of her own difference. Will she ever tell Marlene about this "difference"? Is telling even possible?

~ ~ ~

They sit at the table. Here is Philomena's lentil soup. Here is good substantial bread. Here is silence. It ought to be bedtime, but that oasis is far into the distance. Now this strange interval of nourishment and silence and uncertainty.

Abruptly, Marlene speaks. "I want you to stay, Wilma. I also want to be alone. Would it be OK if I disappeared into the bedroom after we eat? Just for a little while, I mean. Inhospitable as that sounds."

Wilma knows immediately what a relief this would be, and what she would do with the time. "There is nothing inhospitable about such a plan, my dear Marlene. I'll do up the dishes and then I believe I might meditate." Meditate. The word slips out as if it's at home here. Wilma looks at it, sitting jauntily on the table, proud of itself.

"Well, well," says Marlene.

"I don't suppose I mentioned that part of things before."

"You made reference to taking a day off from—I believe you said it was 'the god'—the night Henry and I brought your father's article over."

"And you have not pried."

"I have not dared. Also, I have not forgotten. It seemed private."

"I suppose it was."

"And now?"

"I surprise myself."

"Well, it feels like a gift."

"Good. I hereby give you the gift. Now get thee to thy room."

"All right, but the gift appears to be wrapped up tight. You might have to unwrap it for me."

"I could make the attempt. Not this moment."

"No. Not this moment." Marlene gets up from the table, starts to leave, turns and says, "Maybe it's like Russian nesting dolls—open one, another is inside—and another, another—"

"To your room, Marlene O'Connor."

Marlene goes to her bedroom. Wilma finds the dish washing liquid, makes hot sudsy water, thinks of their first day together, how they shouted at the thundering, drenching sky gods, shopped together, had baths. One woman in the tub, the other in a separate room, reading. Companionable solitude from the beginning. It will be possible to meditate here in the near-presence of Marlene.

But when she finishes the dishes and sits on the couch, intending to begin, a sense of prohibition overtakes her. *To meditate is to transgress.* What a peculiar thought. Does it mean anything at all? She feels restless, unable to stay seated. She gets up and enters the studio. Is this, too, a transgression? She feels overly large as she moves from one piece of art to the next, pausing, absorbing, moving on. Overly large and suddenly buoyant. Might she expand to fill the entire space if she were to meditate? Might Marlene, who could come in at any moment, be engulfed? She sees herself, meditator and art afficianado, large as a sky —a sky full of gods—gods playing like wild children, hurling lightning bolts, roaring thunder, pouring down sheets of rain.

She's a bit alarmed by her own sense of well-being. Marlene is currently distressed by death. Be cautious, she warns herself.

But caution eludes her. When the impulse arises, she is obedient to it, shedding her clothing piece by piece, slowly, almost reverently, as if performing a ritual. Kali appears, nearly hidden, somehow seen. Lorraine steps from behind Kali and bows to the goddess, mocking the sacred while bringing more of it into the studio. Both of them approve the nude state.

She will simply ask Marlene what the best pose is. She will be painted. That, after all, is what Marlene wants, is it not? And that, truly, is the only thing that will even out the energies here. If Marlene is the artist she cannot be engulfed. What fine thinking.

"What the hell—" This is Marlene, arriving in concert with the shedding of the final garment, a comfortable and fairly new pair of white cotton underpants. Why "pair"? Such an unfathomable phenomenon, the English language. Wilma stands and faces the artist.

174

"How do you want me?"

"Jesus, Wilma."

"I've never been a painter's model before."

"Oh. Painter's model. You're rushing things a bit."

"It seemed the only way."

"Well, give me one second. Put something on. Please."

Wilma picks up the underpants.

"No, wait. I'll get you a bathrobe."

Wilma waits. It should not be a surprise that a little interim is required.

Here is Marlene, handing over the piece of apparel that will cover nakedness. It's rather large.

"It's rather large."

"That's because I'm larger than you are."

"You were floating and supremely large one day."

"Damn, but you can be annoying. Explain yourself."

Two women stand facing each other. Such a lot of facing to do. Face the goddess. Face Lorraine. Face Marlene. She takes a breath and tries to gather her normal mind. "I see. Yes. I caught you by surprise. You did tell me that surprises are not welcome. I was following my own—that is, I neglected to consider—I mean—"

Marlene frowns.

"I apologize, Marlene."

Marlene is not mollified. She stands, breathing audibly.

Wilma continues. "As for explaining your floating and supremely expanded appearance—well, yes, I can do that. It was during a meditation. I believe it might have been shortly after the day of the downpour. We shouted at the sky when it stormed. We shopped and ate and—"

"I remember, Wilma. I hardly need—"

"No, of course you don't."

"I visited your meditation after that, did I?"

"You did."

"Floating."

"Yes."

"And large."

"That, too."

175

"I see."

Marlene softens the tiniest bit. Or perhaps more than a bit. She seems in fact to have difficulty keeping good humor at bay. Wilma allows herself a smidgen of relief. She ties the bathrobe she has been holding closed and lowers herself onto the couch. It occurs to her that when an expanded Marlene entered her meditation she, Wilma, might have become the one engulfed. Might have, but didn't.

"Sit, Marlene."

Marlene takes her time, a pondering human. Slowly she sits.

Two women on a couch. The distance between, Wilma decides, is not prohibitive. She stretches out her hand and says, "Peace?" Marlene shakes her head in defeat and allows the smile she's been holding in check. A bit crooked, this smile. A mixed state of affairs, thinks Wilma. But they are shaking hands. This is a formal handshake, a parody of high-level political detente.

Where there is humor there is hope, thinks Wilma, feeling almost wise.

Marlene speaks. "You thought if we just started the portrait—"

"I might have been indulging in something other than thought."

"You understand this might not be the time."

"Yes."

"I might not be able, at the moment."

"Yes."

"Do you *want* me to do the portrait?"

This stops things.

"Wilma?"

Wilma is now the one pondering. Her pondering takes the form of a flight. She is flying with many-armed terrible Kali. *Observe thyself,* says the stern goddess. Down upon the scene she peers. Through layers—high sky, thick cloud, opaque rooftop, dense air of the room itself, concentrated flesh of two women, even more concentrated psyches—she peers. One sees from this height quite completely—sees through every barrier—if sight is demanded by such as Kali. A woman in a bathrobe is the self she is, stirred within. The woman with her is also stirred within. Two stirred women look into each other. From the Kali-inspired vantage point it is clear: the portrait is feared and desired by both women.

"Yes," says Wilma.

176

"What?"

"Yes, I want you to paint my portrait."

"You do?"

"I also fear it."

"Well, that makes two of us."

Plunk. Wilma is dropped back to rather puzzling mundane reality. "I *believe* I want it," she says. "I do *think* I want it."

"You *think* you want it."

"Yes."

"You are uncertain."

"So it seems."

"I shall murder you soon," says Marlene.

"I suppose so," says Wilma. "And why not?"

After which, they embrace.

And Marlene says, "Well, damn."

All this vigorous language from dear Marlene.

They make the attempt. Marlene takes a long time to gather her materials. Wilma observes from the couch as she sits inside the artist's large robe. It is a colorless comfortable old garment, soft and faded from wear and washing. She finds herself pulling the cloth belt tight, loosening it, pulling it tight. She doesn't look at the art in the studio, though the view through the wide opening between rooms would make this possible. She doesn't think about the fact that wanting and fearing this portrait is what she now shares with Marlene—is perhaps the whole of what they now, this moment, are able to share.

"Disrobe," says Marlene.

Wilma, nude, is directed to sit on the chair she was once lowered onto by two near-strangers who prevented a fall. Marlene is pondering again, wondering, no doubt, what to do with an old female body sitting on a straight-backed chair. Wilma suppresses a chuckle. What a sight she must make. Marlene fusses with artist things, putting items here, there; moving them; replacing them. Nervous Marlene.

But Wilma, bare bottomed on a bare wooden chair, finds herself not the least bit nervous. She feels calm now, curious, and quite blissfully steady. She is determined to be responsive to direction, a mere object, something an artist is about to turn into art. Let come what comes, thinks the artist's model. Bits of difference bounce around the studio.

177

Marlene speaks. "I don't want you to be uncomfortable. We'll have short sessions. After I get the sketch you'll be released for a while." Very business-like. How different this must be from working on the portrait of Young Henry. A live model, for one thing. And the question of sex—shoved aside, but lurking.

The artist appears to be gathering her strength. Again, she speaks. "I like your legs a little apart, just like that. And your feet are planted firmly. Good. But I don't want you just *sitting* there. Try leaning forward, elbows on your knees. Good. Can you clasp your hands loosely, just let them fall together in front of you? Good. Is that comfortable enough? Now look up, mostly with your eyes, I don't want you straining your neck. Great. I adore the hint of skepticism. I can't ask you to hold an expression, but let's try to remember—"

Marlene steps back. Her hand covers her mouth. "Oh my God, you're—"

"Marlene?"

Marlene looks bewildered, overcome, as if she's seen something beyond her capacity.

"We have to stop, Wilma."

"What?"

Marlene is gathering Wilma's clothing, handing the bundle to her, leaving the room.

Wilma does not follow, does not call out. She gets dressed. She sits on the couch, waiting for instructions.

Time passes. Marlene is missing. Missing in action. What must Wilma Schuh therefore do?

Perhaps if she approaches the art—

She stands looking. She sees. She enters. She moves from piece to piece to piece, becomes paint, becomes color, thickness, line, shape. Here, after all the rest, is the portrait of Young Henry. She faces him, and understands. She is nodding, accepting, when Marlene comes to stand beside her, tentatively taking her hand. They stand together, unspeaking, looking at their boy.

Wilma asks, "Was his death with you while you were painting?"

Silence. Two women hold hands before a painting.

Finally, Marlene says, "How do you *know* these things?"

178

"Well, yes. One does wonder. But look—it's in the rhythms—a falling into and out of form—as if the shine of death—oh, dear—"

"All right. So you do see. But it was only the universal reality. All flesh. Every living thing. Death comes. It was only a part of things. Not horrible. Not *soon*. Look at him. He's *living*."

"Then when he told us about his heart—"

"Before he told us. Remember, it was *before*. A premonition—death is coming—not far off. A real knowing—accurate, solid. I don't want it."

"Death was compelling and not horrible when you were painting—but as a thing far off, the universal fate, part of his vitality."

Marlene nods. Wilma can feel the nodding. Perhaps it's peripheral vision, evidence of the senses, nothing strange. But as they stand facing the portrait, still holding hands, a sense of the uncanny rises up—as if she's been here before—*déjà vu* is the phrase—

"And then I was about to do the same thing to you. I would paint you and you would die." Marlene says this in the flattest tones possible. "And you were real." Flat-toned. Distant. She lets go of Wilma's hand. She sits on the couch. "And automatically, horribly, dangerously—"

Wilma is sorting through. Things seem to have piled into a commotion—is that the word? Marlene might want to paint this commotion some day when she needs to get away from flesh and its tendency to go mortal on her. This, right now, is not about flesh. It is more like a little collection of unstrung balls of yarn, tangled. It could be a series. It hangs in a gallery on one wall, the tame spool series is on the opposite wall. White walls. A plain and simple gallery. The artist in her loose and colorful clothing and her uncanny confidence, happy at the opening, confidently silent. Every visitor has wine and a little napkin of goodies but they are all ignoring the wine and the goodies, they are entranced by the art. They make no facile interpretations. This is the perfect opening, silent, except for human breathing and the hum of attention.

This wish for the artist rushes through her as she tries to sort. Art and mortality have gotten confused for Marlene. This has to be feeling, not faith. She doesn't *believe* she will kill anyone with brush, paint, canvas, and thought, does she? Also, Marlene has seen the Real—the automatically lovable—it matters not where, or in whom—and it frightens her.

179

Lorraine offers a quick thought. *This is existential anguish.*
Thank you, Lorraine.

So Marlene is feeling existential anguish as she perceives the reality of another human with whom she is becoming entangled. Young Henry has unwittingly caused this. He lives with death as near neighbor.

Meanwhile Wilma herself goes flying through time with a foreign goddess and a philosopher's concept and several other bits of unreality, having her own private good time of it all. Except that a sense of *déjà vu* hovers at the edge. Inside this flashing moment of sorting, while Marlene holds her head in her hands and breathes heavily, she finds herself almost grasping what's behind the *déjà vu*—

Something about standing together, hand-holding, two women, looking. Looking not at each other but at what is there in front of them, what must be seen and known and—

Stop.

The woman sitting here, head in her hands, needs to be thanked— thanked for the effort to communicate, which cost her a great deal. She takes Marlene's hands gently from around her poor head and holds them in her own. "Thank you," she says.

"For not going ahead with the portrait?"

"No. No, no, no. Oh, my dear Marlene." She tries to embrace. Marlene twists away.

~ ~ ~

Marlene, silent throughout the drive from her house, pulls up in front of Wilma's building and sets the emergency brake. She keeps the engine running. She stares straight ahead, as Wilma can see from a quick glance. It is nearing midnight, still Sunday, still the day Young Henry triumphed with Winnie-the-Pooh.

And talked about his potentially fatal heart condition.
Only potentially.

Wilma doesn't send her thought into the tense unyielding air, there would be no point. She opens the car door, gets out, turns back to the car, leans in.

"Please take care of yourself, Marlene." Marlene nods but does not turn her head. Her profile is endearing. Tense and stubborn and endearing. "Thank you for the ride." Marlene nods again.

Wilma says good night.

Marlene says good night.

Wilma shuts the car door and walks toward her building. She doesn't get far before Marlene is beside her. The hug is a stiff one, and brief. Marlene says she's sorry. Wilma says she knows. She wishes she could brush her hand against the side of the troubled face, venture into the mussed hair. She lets the wish die. They part this way.

She climbs the stairs, enters her apartment, heads toward the bedroom, changes her mind, and goes to the kitchen. She runs a full glass of cold water and stands drinking. Nothing catastrophic has taken place. Marlene simply needs a break, a hiatus. Marlene is somehow unable at this moment to see more of her, it might be only a few days, there is no reason to think beyond. Not that a timeline, short or long, has been spoken of.

And of course the portrait was not begun.

Of course not it wasn't.

She gets ready for bed, folds back the tan bedspread and the pale green Warm Feelings blanket. In the night she can pull the blanket up, should warmth be needed. It was Lorraine who saw the ad, felt drawn to the name, said they deserved such an item. One Warm Feelings blanket for them, one for Alma. Lorraine could produce comfort when she had a mind to.

Wilma stands now, looking at the opened bed.

There are the clean sheets.

She takes a deep breath, feels the futility. There will be no sleep tonight.

Very well, she has a great deal to do. It has not been her way to work in the night but lately her ways seem to shift themselves. A list might help. She gets paper and pen, places them on the kitchen table, and stands there, waiting to learn what comes next. Impulse, direction, inspiration. Follow, follow, follow. Surely this is the current way. She finds herself moving from room to room, light switch to light switch, lamp to lamp. Never within memory has every light source in the apartment been called upon at once. The result is a solidification of the dark outdoors and a firmer barrier between outside and inside. Good. She lives in the light in the middle of the night. A fine state of affairs, complete with alliteration, assonance, and a dash of rhyme.

And now to the list.

1) Determine the déjà vu. (She means: catch it, hold it, comprehend it, no matter the difficulty.)

2) Think about food. Shop. (For how many days? What sort of food? To be decided. Or discovered.)

3) Review Stage One of The Plan. (She sees the piece of paper in her mind's eye, another list, but the details blur. Where is that piece of paper? Never mind, it's somewhere.)

4) Surely one must meditate.

5) A project for the hands. (But what?)

She puts pen and paper aside. Elbows on table, head in hands. *Determine the déjà vu.* She can do this.

It came over her twice.

She and Marlene stood looking at Young Henry's portrait, holding hands, talking about art, and about Henry, and about death. That was the first time.

It came again, more eerily, later. Marlene had twisted away, but they got past that, somewhat. They stood at the foot of the bed, again holding hands. The bed was neatly made, it was not the rumpled site of chaos she had irreverently expected.

And then the *déjà vu.* It took her breath away.

Marlene said, "What?"

She would have explained. In that moment, she would have, but it was gone.

"I don't know."

"Something, though."

"Yes."

Marlene nodded, did not insist, seemed almost not to attend.

They focused in their parallel way on the bed, silent.

Marlene gathered herself and spoke. "OK. So here we are. The sheets aren't fresh, but I'm almost sure I changed them about a week ago, they can't be bad. I shower every morning. I'm the only one who's slept on them, in case you were wondering."

"I wasn't wondering. I suppose it's a good thing to know."

They stood there. It was strange, how they continued to hold hands. Too strange. Wilma gave a squeeze and let go. "Perhaps it's best if I go home."

There was a pause. Not a long pause.

Marlene nodded. "Thank you."

Marlene waited patiently while Wilma took time to look around the room she might never again enter.

Bare finished wood floor, two small bright rugs, one each side of the bed.

Bedspread with soothing geometry of overlapping blues and greens.

Dresser, all drawers closed, the surface holding hair brush, photos, neatly stacked papers, a few odds and ends.

Dull green upholstered chair, old, with a single dark green shirt draped over it.

Straight-backed chair next to the open door of the closet.

Closet, clothes hanging comfortably, one might almost say cozily.

Shoes on the closet floor, three pairs, all sensible.

Next to the shoes, a wicker laundry basket half-full.

Series of sketches on one wall, shirts and pants pinned to a laundry line, flapping in a playful wind. Wide clear sky behind, ocean in the distance, tiny island visible at the horizon. Light shifting with each sketch, hours of the day passing by. The tender, quirky spool series in the other room comes to mind.

Books. No bookcase, just books on the floor all along one wall, spines out, as if shelved in a library.

She bent to read titles. Art, fiction, poetry, letters. Letters of artists, letters of poets. Van Gogh, Gaugin, Mallarmé, Marianne Moore. She wanted to stay and peruse. She almost asked permission, it might be a way to grasp—

But Marlene was ready to take her home.

Glancing backward, she saw what lay on the bedside table. *The Complete Prose and Poetry of William Blake. Francis Bacon: the Logic of Sensation. Letters of Rainer Maria Rilke.* There was a bookmark in that last. Marlene had read deep into Rilke's letters, never mentioning the fact. A secret? A clue? Or had it simply never come up? Most likely the last. Marlene was not devious.

Alone at the kitchen table in her thoroughly lighted apartment, Wilma mentally measures the space. Plenty of room for a bookcase. She knows how to build a bookcase.

~~5) A project for the hands. But what? Decide.~~

5) *Bookcase for Marlene.*

She moves to the living room, lies down on the couch. *Déjà vu*, she remembers, means "already seen." Lorraine must have told her.

Already seen? Already lived, is the feeling.

She closes her eyes. It comes.

Another hot humid Sunday, a quarter-century ago. Lorraine, propped on pillows, very sick, still fierce, has removed her reading glasses but holds them in one hand. It is a new aid: glasses to magnify, to lessen the effort it takes to churn print into sense. *I churn and churn and if I keep at it I get something. It slides away, but I've had it, if only for a minute.* The day she was able to say that was a good one. There have not been many of those lately. The book rests on her lap. Murdoch, *The Philosopher's Pupil.* Her hand rests on the book, the hand holding the reading glasses.

Alma and Wilma stand at the foot of the bed, holding hands. Their hand-holding was spontaneous, and their shared sharp intake of breath. Neither expected what Lorraine just asked. She had told them, opening the book for the first time, that when she finished reading *The Philosopher's Pupil* she would die, but—

A bookmark shows her progress. She is not far from the end now.

Another book lies on the bookstand. *Gravity and Grace.* Wilma stares at it. The title rises up and hovers. *Arrogant*, she thinks. She means *threatening.* She has the strongest urge to let go of Alma's hand and reach to press the words back to flatness, deny them their imperturbability, their power. Gravity. Grace.

She resists the urge. A question is hanging in the air. Lorraine has placed it there. What is the answer? What exactly was the question? It seems to be blurring.

"I need an answer," says fierce Lorraine.

"Yes," says Alma.

"Yes you know I need an answer, or yes you'll do it?"

"Yes, we will do it."

184

Gravity. The situation is subject to gravity. And grace. A certain grace is being exhibited at this moment by Alma. Again Wilma resists the urge to press the words back into the book's cover. They are not evil words. She is amazed at her mother's prompt assumption of responsibility, her certitude. She focuses on this compelling, almost mesmerizing aspect of the scene.

But a new question emerges from the background, repetitive, like the wheels of a train—*What are we doing? What are we doing?*—rolling and sounding—*What are we doing?*—the train, a monstrous machine, unstoppable—*What are we doing?*—the tracks, impossibly long, polished, slippery—*What are we doing?*—the glare of the tracks, blinding, the wheels, rolling and sounding, steadily, ceaselessly, unspeakably repeating, repeating—

While Alma and Lorraine discuss specifics.

As soon as the prognosis was clear Lorraine acquired, rather easily as it turned out, a supply of heroin. She couldn't count on collecting enough pain medication, such things are watched over by the medical people. Syringe and drug and directions are waiting at the back of the closet shelf, wrapped in the winter scarf she will never again need.

"Yes, the green and black plaid one, I appreciate your clear head, Alma. Wilma?"

But Wilma is now living at a skewed distance from everything real, enveloped in a sense of expansion, of floating, into which comes the seductive sensation of possible imminent crumpling. Might she find herself simply dropping to the floor? It seems a solution, she thinks from her place of floating distance. Also, she is worshipping Lorraine and her crisp, clear plan. To achieve such a thing while a relentless tumor is shoving her brain this way and that—or is it gluttonous, eating away at the brain—or both, relentless and gluttonous—inside the dear well-shaped firm skull. But is the skull firm? Might the bones themselves yield to the force from inside? Might there be an explosion any minute now? Or an oozing? The precious, necessary, intelligent matter oozing out—

"Wilma," says Alma, strict-toned, kind.

This is new Alma. Alma of presence, compassionate and firm. A mother. A mother with a right to command.

Wilma, daughter, pulls her own brain back to shape.

185

"Yes," she says. "We will do it."

So she and her mother, a fine team, will murder this dear sick woman, but not until the reading of *The Philosopher's Pupil* is completed, which completion will come "very soon," assuming the reading brain will agree to hold itself reasonably steady, maintain the current rate of travel along the impossible, irreversible set of shining metal tracks. They—or one of them—will inject heroin into dear appalling Lorraine who feels the need for, and why should she not have it, control over her own death. Lorraine wishes to be accompanied, companioned, helped. The act of injecting heroin in solitude, she tells them, while possible, is "not preferred." Wry Lorraine, still functioning.

Wilma opens her eyes, sits up. The *déjà vu* has been determined. She gets off the couch, goes to the list, draws a line through item number one.

Item number two: food.

Of course.

Very well, then. Next meal: breakfast. Does she have oatmeal, raisins, *et cetera*? She checks. She looks into the containers, one by one. Is there a sufficiency in each? There is.

What next?

Another list might be useful.

1) Breakfast, Monday. Oatmeal with the customary additions. Quantity: sufficient.

2) Lunch, Monday—

But she breaks off, returns to the living room, sits on the couch, closes her eyes. She will meditate. *Wedge, wedge, wedge.* Ah, yes. Wedges. Here is one, hanging in the air before her closed eyes. It is large. It is black. It has been put between herself and Marlene. It is called Wait. That is its name, a wedge called Wait.

Breathe and continue. *Wedge, wedge, wedge.* Now comes another, a wedge labeled Death. It is huge, a divider of Space from Infinity, Time from Eternity. All of Reality is subject to segmentation by way of wedges. Lorraine, physical Lorraine, is thus kept at some distance from this room in this moment.

Wedge, wedge, wedge.

Segment, segment, segment.

Between the segments, tiny gaps.

In slips the god. The slippery god. Hello, god.

Wedge, wedge, wedge.

The god can slip out, any time. One must expect this.

W*edge, wedge.*

Out slips the god. Goodbye, god.

At this moment, as if finally permitted, Wilma leans to the side and crumples onto the couch. Her legs come up, fold themselves. She is fetal. She is inside fetal-ness. Inside fetality. Or fatality. Inside, where it is dark. And actually quite comfortable.

But the room is here, lit profligately. Eyes closed, she knows this. She is in a lighted room inside a determinedly lit apartment. There are barriers, inside is separated from outside.

Think of the apartment. Outside is dark, inside is light.

Think of the body. Outside is light, inside is dark.

This is a dance!

All of reality, she sees it, is a dance. Death is a dance.

She killed her lover.

Her lover wanted to be killed, it was a kindness.

But she did not kill with kindness, she killed with heroin. How did they get away with that? Because death was expected.

Not that soon, not that soon, not that soon.

But, yes, truly: the train was on the track.

It was difficult, this act of murder. But worthy of respect. Alma said so.

Alma, mother: "This is an act worthy of respect, Wilma." This statement came as they were filling the syringe. Who filled the syringe?

They.

They were a team.

"We are doing this as a team," said Alma. "Together. The three of us." Lorraine nodded. Lorraine was watching them fill the syringe. But who filled the syringe?

The injection she remembers. She, Wilma, injected the heroin. It was an act. An act of love.

Or an act on a stage. She watched herself perform the act of lovingly killing dear fierce Lorraine, who died rather peacefully. They, the team, achieved this, a rather peaceful death. An act, on a stage, with a cast of three. So it seemed.

Lorraine thanked them. Before she closed her eyes, she thanked them. Were there tears in those eyes? Were there tears in the room anywhere?

I am the only person in the world who knows about this, she thinks, lying fetal on her familiar and comfortable brown couch. Now that Alma is gone, I am the only one.

She might have told Marlene, but Marlene is also gone.

No, Marlene just needs a break.

Well, but we know, do we not, that Marlene is gone?

Would she have told Young Henry? While they, the threesome, ate pizza and accomplished extraordinary conversation, would she have told them both?

Oh.

She sits up.

Young Henry. He belongs to Marlene. Or to Marlene-and-Wilma. But not, surely not, to Wilma as her single self. She closes her eyes. She is alone. Alone in the world with her imaginary god, and a stray ghost or two, all of whom appear to be absent just now.

Alone.

Well, there is Lyle.

Yes, that might be the case.

Yes, there is Lyle.

After Lorraine died, but not long after, she began to have a terrible repetitive dream. Lorraine had thoughtfully predicted this. "It's possible, Wilma, that you and Alma will have unwanted thoughts—afterwards—or images you can't shake, or bad dreams. All of that will fade. I wish my death could be made simple but I'm afraid it can't. Wilma, beautiful Wilma, I am eternally, *eternally*, grateful. I feel such a need to *do* my death—actively—with you, and with Alma, too. I know—I do know what I'm asking. I know, too, a little of what I'm sparing—sparing all of us . . . . spare . . . . bare . . . . barren . . . . big black bear . . . . fur . . . . down . . . . oh . . . . oh, no . . . . I . . . . feel . . . . so . . . . sorry."

The ability to speak coherently, the little miracle, dissolved. A week later Lorraine finished *The Philosopher's Pupil*. She could barely (*bare, barren*) follow the story, but she persisted to the end of the final page. There was wild triumph in her eyes when she slammed the book shut. Wilma had just entered the room with medication. It was a terrible sound,

188

that book slammed shut, and those eyes were terrible but also wonderful and Wilma at that moment felt nothing but gratitude, that she could witness such *reality*. Gratitude and a surge of pure love.

Iris Murdoch is right. What is real is automatically lovable.

Death is real. Time is real. Separation is real.

The terrible repetitive dream, when it came, was real.

In the weeks before she died, Lorraine turned restless, almost violent, in her sleep. Wilma left the bed, slept in the living room on the couch. This couch. After Lorraine was gone she continued the practice, avoiding the bed they had shared. It was not until she and Alma sold the old farmhouse and moved to Bangor, to this apartment, that she felt able to return to sleeping in the bed.

The bed which at this moment has clean sheets and which once again cannot be slept in.

She is lying down again, closing her eyes, waiting for the dream. On the couch. She never called it a nightmare. She wonders why.

It comes.

The grandfather clock they do not own in daylight strikes the hour. The hour is midnight. Of course it is midnight, it is the hour of horror. She sleepwalks in the dream in her long white nightgown, an eerie light around her eerily walking sleeping self which she observes from a distance, appalled. She is approaching the bedroom where Lorraine is waiting for her, she, a woman named Wilma, a pillow in her hands, a pillow held in front of her in her two hands, the pillow and her hands as white and glowing as the nightgown she does not own in reality but wears in the dream. She, the woman named Wilma, enters the bedroom. Lorraine is lying there, smiling and ready. Lorraine's eyes gleam readiness and with her mouth she says gleefully, "Let's go!" She, Wilma, brings the pillow down and the suffocation game is begun. She holds the pillow and Lorraine struggles, her body writhing in anguished choreographed contortions as the death game goes on and on and she, Wilma, is not permitted to stop, it is fated, and Lorraine fights like a doomed mythic figure, which she is, and she, Wilma, presses and presses until finally little by little the scene diminishes like a pin-pricked balloon, a slow collapse, and there is Lorraine, dead as she demanded to be, a sly smile on the face of her cold corpse which will have to be washed and

189

otherwise dealt with, but at this point she, Wilma, invariably wakes up, shuddering, and tells herself it was not like that, not like that at all.

Wilma—the real Wilma, twenty-five years past the real death of her real first lover and will there ever be a second?—sits up and breathes.

And where was Alma in that dream? Alma was nowhere at all.

Kali flits by. Hello, Kali. Goodbye, Kali.

Wilma gets up, empties her bladder, and takes another drink of very cold water. She returns to the living room. Cautiously, as if it is a precious fragile burden, she lays her body lengthwise on the couch.

It was no nightmare.

It was wonder, horror-laced wonder, mystery.

Through which shone beauty.

She falls asleep. Her dreams are stars, turning themselves inside out.

~ ~ ~

Wilma wakes to bright sunlight. On the couch, stiff of body, strange of mind, far from rested, aware of needing some undetermined something—distraction, perhaps, but from which of the various?—she hauls her body to sitting position, places her feet flat on the floor.

Rise up, steady the body, steady the self, stretch a bit, yawn loudly. Solitude is a privileged state. The woman yawns in freedom, hurries to the toilet, no witness. Ah, release.

The bathroom clock says nine. A fine time to begin.

Brush teeth. Floss. Shower. Don clean clothes top to bottom.

Starting over. Good.

Next, breakfast.

While eating, she looks at her lists. Didn't get far with the food list, did she? All in due time. She glances at the other list. *Déjà vu* determined? Well, yes, and then some. What else? Groceries. And supplies for building a bookcase. Both seem possible. What else? Locate the Plan. She sets her coffee down. It must be in the bedroom. Did she hide it away when she put those unnecessary and apparently inappropriate clean sheets on the bed? Marlene reads Rilke's letters, says not a word. They keep things from each other. Why?

Marlene. Gone.

Never mind.

190

The Plan—

She is about to search in drawers, but sees it, folded, blank side out, neither hidden nor displayed, resting beside Alma's bones. Just where she put it, how nice. Hello Alma, where are you?

Silence from the realm beyond.

No matter. Solitude is a privileged state.

She takes the Plan, Stage One to the kitchen, sits and sips coffee, reviews. Self-care. This is to include exercises, she seems to remember— blanket on floor, stretch those muscles, *et cetera*. She'll get to that. Reading: Spinoza, Rilke, Alma, dear Henry the father. She seems to have veered off in the direction of Lorraine by way of Murdoch. Must she rewrite the Plan? Not this minute. Meditate, says the page. Does the attempt in the wee hours, the one that ended with crumpling, suffice? Perhaps not quite. Try again, but later. Leave the apartment once a day. Yes, as soon as she produces her shopping lists, for cooking and carpentry, she will step out into the world. A word or two with an actual human will ensue with no effort at all. Perfect.

It is 10:00 when she closes the door, descends the steps, unlocks her bicycle, and pedals away. She observes the morning sky as she rides, feeling efficient. She has gone only a few blocks when she realizes it is not possible to carry lumber for a bookcase while bicycling. She chuckles to herself, returns home, gets the car. Will the lumber fit? It will. What alternative does it have?

It does fit. The young man looks at her plan for the bookcase and most likely also at her gray hair and offers to cut to size. He cheerfully loads the pieces into the car, utilizing the passenger seat with open window as well as the entire back seat, and why not, for she has no passenger, no companion.

No companion—

She sighs and reminds herself to pay attention to her driving.

She does so. Her mind is judged to be in exquisite control.

Here we are, home again. The boards that jut out the passenger window have fine red flags attached. The young man knew what was mandated, what was prohibited. As does she. She has her Plan, Stage One. Also, she is to give Marlene O'Connor a modicum of "space." As to Young Henry Whitsun, the situation is less clear. Never mind. She has groceries to put away, lumber to carry piece by piece up these steps, lunch to make and consume. Such a busy human. How would she squeeze a woman or even a young man into her life?

There are angles, she notices. Angles from which to view the current state of things. This idea, appropriate for a human who is about the engage once again in carpentry, a thing not done for decades, occurs to her as she goes up and down the recently cleaned back steps, again and again, carrying the bounty of her shopping efforts. She makes these trips a tad more slowly each time, but the thought of angles occupies her mind and she keeps going, up and down, up and down.

Angles of carpentry, angles of vision.

For example, there is the angle from which she observes that despite all efficiency she is perhaps the tiniest bit concerned about herself. Is she quite all right these days? From another angle, possibly accompanied by Kali and other entities at home in the realm of difference, she observes that she is *amused* much of the time. What days—and nights!—she has. The unexpected arrives again and again. It is entertaining, truth be told, from a certain angle. She intends to learn more about that many-armed fierce and ancient goddess. A library trip one of these days. Raymond will be a help and never blink an eye. He was kind to Alma, he will be kind to her daughter.

Final trip up the steps. A wee bit out of breath. To be expected.

Yes, she would like to see Raymond. Such a polite and friendly librarian with that quiet Native American manner of his. Intelligent eyes. Contented with his lot, or so Alma believed.

~ ~ ~

She does see Raymond. It is now Tuesday, two days beyond the Sunday of Winnie-the-Pooh, LQTS, and the ensuing events with dear absent Marlene. The bookcase project is well begun. The Plan has been followed meticulously. The library will close soon, she is later than she planned to be, but here she is, about to speak at least minimally to another human. As The Plan wishes.

He is at the desk. Others have engaged him. She will wait.

Those others, something familiar—

Isn't that—

192

Yes. Sunday. The poet Michael Solomon, who seemed to have forgotten his own book, whose handshake evoked an intensity. And the girl, Sephie, who knew all about mime. Another man is with the poet and the girl today, a tall plump pleasant creature of the modest sort, or so Wilma decides. All three of Raymond's current interlocutors: pleasant people. Bright lines connect the trio to Raymond. A quartet, then. Smiles, gentleness, warmth. "Did you shop, Danny?" says Raymond. Danny grins and says he did indeed. "Shop for what?" Michael the poet asks. But there is a secret in the shopping. Michael is pointedly not answered. Sephie giggles. Raymond says, "Give me half an hour, I'll be finished." Danny says, "We'll be back." Wilma, who has stepped a bit out of sight, not wanting to intrude, sees the river of love that follows as the trio leaves. Raymond is smiling at their backs, the river comes from him. Now he is craning forward, smiling at her, she is receiving an invitation, the river is for her, too. Wouldn't it be nice if Marlene, former cuddle buddy, would produce such a—

"What can I do for you, Wilma?"

And where is Alma?

"Is there something I can do for you, Wilma?"

"Yes. I believe I need—"

The pause is longer than even Raymond can endure. He has come around the desk, he is beside her, he is guiding her to the bench nearby. Now they sit side by side.

"Better?"

"Oh, I was fine, Raymond. You know, though, I've been just the slightest bit—"

They sit in silence for a few minutes. This is companionable.

"I was thinking about your mother just the other day, Wilma. How's she doing?"

"Well, that might be it. The reason for the plethora of sitting incidents. I didn't expect another just now. It seems that since she passed away—"

"Oh, I didn't know. I'm sorry—"

"Oh, no, Raymond. She was complete. But I wonder if you could help me learn something about a goddess called Kali. Hindu, I think Lorraine said."

"Interesting question. Sit here and let me see what I can do. Will that work?"

"Quite nicely. I was happy to learn that your circle includes my Michael."

"Michael Solomon? You know Michael?"

"Through his poetry, yes, which might be the best way, wouldn't you say? And his fine handshake."

Raymond is smiling broadly. He is happy about connections, just as she is. He leaves to see what he can do about Kali. She closes her eyes. *Wedge, wedge, wedge.* The river of love lifts the entire library, the floating away has begun. *Wedge, wedge.* "All shall be well and all manner of thing shall be well." Julian of Norwich, as quoted by dear Lorraine. *Wedge, wedge, wedge.* Sit and breathe. Sit and breathe. A library is a place to rest.

And here is Raymond, books in hand. "Try these, Wilma. We're closing in a few minutes. Will you be all right?"

"I have recovered equanimity, Raymond. These will be fine."

As he finishes checking the two books out for her, Raymond smiles to himself, the tiniest private smile, but she sees it.

"I didn't know Michael was a poet," he says.

"Oh, my. I hope it wasn't a secret."

"I suspect it just didn't come up. Gives a new view. Michael's a good person."

"Yes. Yes, I believe he is."

"Let me know how the books work out, Wilma. I appreciate your telling me about your mother. I liked her."

When bedtime arrives Wilma finds herself settling between the clean sheets. Life without Marlene is perfectly possible. Also, the bookcase is coming along nicely. If Pa were to appear, he would be pleased to see that the skills carried forward. Use of the mind, use of the hands.

Pa, however, seems disinclined to visit.

She opens one of the books. *Kali: The Black Goddess of Dakshineswar.*

She reads until she can read no longer, then spends the night dreaming of violence so bizarre it is cartoonish and wakes up laughing at the workings of the human mind. That book, that book! Kali is indeed a

194

fierce goddess, so murderous she kills demons a second time when there are none living left to kill. And bloodthirsty! The goddess is the absolute exemplar. There she is, lifting Raktabija high above herself and letting his demon blood pour into her—swallowing, swallowing, not daring to let a single drop spill, for spilled drops sprout new demons—and dancing and laughing like a crazy woman, rageful and brutal, and what a time the gods had trying to stop her. And here is Wilma Schuh, laughing right along and, when she can get herself up out of bed, she just might join in the dance.

Well, probably not. Better get going on the day. She supposes it's all very serious and symbolic. No doubt a great deal of religious philosophy undergirds the whole thing—the book is actually quite reverent—but the goddess: what a wild, strange mystery of a woman.

And welcome!

And who is Wilma Schuh that she has such a response? She is the latest version, schooled by Young Henry Whitsun and dear Marlene and thrust into the realm of difference. She has looked at the art of Francis Bacon and seen violence wedded to something so vivid, so real, so compelling, it is—what?—*lovable*—and beautiful. All of that and now Kali.

Angles, she thinks. It takes a particular angle of vision. Because from many angles the violence braided into human experience is abominable, absolutely unacceptable. Suffering is suffering. She has not abandoned all normal values. Still, there is something compelling about the idea of eating it *all*.

Eating?

Well, yes.

And perhaps the normal morning routine had better begin because she is ravenous.

She reads while consuming a particularly delicious bowl of oatmeal. *Hindu Goddesses: Visions of the Divine Feminine in the Hindu Religious Tradition*. Possibly there is a way to comprehend Kali if her sister goddesses are added in. She meets a handful. Usas, Prithvi, Sarasvati, Vac, Lakshmi, Parvati, Radha, Durga. Their stories shift, their relationships are a tangle, their associations to the cosmos, to the earth, to humanity make up a bundle of complexities and inconsistencies impossible to retain as the author takes her through a long wild venerable

195

history. All of this is somehow at home inside her own recently discovered difference.

Or is it that her own small portion is hidden somewhere inside the large holdings of these goddesses?

Ah, the ins and the outs. What surrounds is suddenly born out of the innards of—

Enough, enough, enough.

Perhaps a bit of stretching of the single human body on the firm and sturdy floor would do.

~ ~ ~

After stretching her body, Wilma spent the rest of Wednesday morning in a slightly frenzied pattern, veering from carpentry to reading to carpentry to meditation and back around again and again. It was almost a whirl. It was certainly not a settling. She has read bits and pieces of the writings of her mother, her father, and her first lover, as well as random passages by Alma's Rilke, Henry's Spinoza, and Lorraine's Murdoch. Also Michael Chaim Solomon's poetry. A ragged pile of books and papers threatens to topple from the kitchen table. She has not returned to the world of Hindu goddesses nor has Kali flitted through. No gust from the god has come. No ghost, either. Absent, absent, absent: all. As are Marlene and Young Henry. Present now is her Michael. He understands. He sits on his couch. His parents have killed themselves. "Tears shed, breath taken, face dried." Alone, alone, alone.

Lunchtime arrived. Attempting to eat a tuna fish sandwich, she found herself unable. She has now been sitting at this kitchen table for quite some time. The sandwich is on its plate, not far from her, going stale and dry. It ought to be wrapped, refrigerated. The day grows late. She has not spoken, minimally or otherwise, to another human. The Plan, Stage One, is next to the plate that holds the sandwich. The Plan accuses her, but what is she to do? Might Lyle know?

This seems an inspired thought. She has a phone. She rarely uses it but this might be its moment. If she phones Lyle, if he says hello, if she responds, she will have fulfilled item number five of this domineering Plan. The phone and phone book are not of course on this kitchen table, why would they be? She rises. She creaks. She stands tall, stretches. The body still works though something is definitely out of kilter, as is commonly said though not by her. When did she ever use the phrase? What *is* kilter? On the way to the phone she feels herself drawn to the bookcase. A second volume by Rilke caught her attention earlier. She ignored it. That might have been an error. She was never invited to read from this book during the time when Alma, sliding toward death, was unable to do her own reading. Why was that? From what was she being kept? She bends to reach for *The Notebooks of Malte Laurids Brigge*, and manages, book in hand, to phone Lyle.

"Lyle's Bookstore," says her old friend.

"Hello, Lyle."

"Hello?"

"Hello, Lyle."

"Oh. Wilma. Hello, Wilma."

She hangs up. Mission accomplished, as they say on the radio. She has spoken, quite minimally, to another human. Was there another reason she called Lyle? Not that she can recall.

She is lying on the couch, holding Rilke's *Malte*, feeling estranged from her surroundings—which surroundings appear to include a feverish body—her own—and yet perhaps not her own at all—when Lyle arrives. He must have knocked.

"You failed to answer, Wilma. I knocked. "

"Hello, Lyle."

Lyle stands over her for a while. No words are needed. With Lyle Franklin a person can be alone. Quote, unquote. Alma.

"It's getting dark. May I turn on a light?"

"I'd appreciate that. I have a passage to read to you. It's Alma's poet."

"Rilke, that would be. Are you ill, Wilma?

"Why, yes, I believe I am."

"Do you need a doctor?"

"Oh, no. That would be excessive. The poet produced a novel, of which I knew nothing. Sit and listen, if you would be so kind."

Lyle sits. Wilma reads.

The fever dug into me and out of the depths it pulled experiences, images, facts, which I had known nothing about; I

197

lay there, overloaded with myself, and waited for the moment when I would be told to pile all this back into myself, neatly and in the right order. I began, but it grew in my hands, it resisted, it was much too much. Then rage took hold of me, and I threw everything into myself pell-mell and squeezed it together; but I couldn't close myself back over it. And then I screamed, half open as I was, I screamed and screamed.

Having read the passage, Wilma feels strong, even happy. Perhaps she is not ill after all, or it might be ending. What might be ending? The illness. Yes, she must mean the illness. But here is Lyle.

"You will notice, Lyle, that I do not scream. Poor Malte was taken over but here I lie, reading in a normal tone from a worthy writer and conversing—with a worthy friend, I might add. I believe I'm feeling better. I'm able to sleep in my own bed now. I had a most interesting night and am curious what tonight might bring. The angles are all in place. Amusement, for example, still rises in me. But I find it fortuitous that you have arrived. I pondered the passage and felt akin. Except for the screaming. I'm quite sure rage is not my way though it seems the way of many. Kali, for example, enjoys a good deal of it. The goddess. For a variety of reasons, no screams. Neighbors, for example. But you are welcome here, Lyle Franklin. There are others who would be also, but they are unlikely—"

She falls to silence. How was she going to end the sentence that dangles, waiting for completion? She can see it there in the air, about three feet away. Now it separates to lovely fragments. Now the gliding down, feathers falling, no breeze. On the ground beneath, dear little feathers.

"Wilma, I find myself concerned."

"Well, yes. I imagine that explains your presence here."

"It does."

"And then the brevity."

"Of your phone call. Yes. Might you be able to sit up?"

Wilma sits, feet flat on floor. "Do I look a sight?"

Lyle peers with his one good eye. "Not sure," he says. "I brought your mail up."

"Anything beyond bills and advertisements?"

198

"Didn't look. Your mail, not mine."

"Well, let's see then."

The envelope with Marlene's return address is directly under the phone bill.

"Something important?"

"I don't know, Lyle. I just don't know." She presses a firm thumb over the return address. Keep it in place, she thinks. At least until Lyle leaves, hold it down.

"Would you rather I left?"

"That might be best. I do appreciate—"

"Yes. Well. If you need me—"

"This is a new era, isn't it?"

"For us, I suppose you mean."

"For us, yes. How did you even know the address?"

"I found it in the rolodex. I suppose Alma ordered a book. I take the information when there's an order. I have a phone book, too. You're not hidden. But there it was, in the rolodex. Will you be—"

"Best alone now, yes. But I'll come by soon. I have library books to return. I'll stop in, an exchange."

"And there's the phone. A little more information next time, Wilma."

They nod, a hint of grin on both faces.

"Maybe we really are friends now, Lyle."

"Maybe we are, Wilma."

~ ~ ~

Dear Wilma,

I will try to explain. You know the basics, but I owe you something more explicit. Maybe I mean more expansive. I've come up with a linkage: art/love/death. The strength of the linkage exceeds the strength of the individual links. You and Henry sit inside the spaces. Can you see it? A chain, the links of a chain. Inside the iron ovals are the spaces. Actually, you both hop around, one space to the next, I can't keep you settled. I shouldn't have said "sit." Both of you, hopping: art to love to death, art to love to death, round and round. A disturbing, reeling vision. Therefore, for the moment, I do what I can. I exile you, Wilma, from the art. By this I mean my inability which is also a choice—that I will not

199

again attempt to paint your portrait. I have already gone too far with Henry, there is no going back. As for love, that is a slippery thing, I'm unsure of choice with love. Whether choice is possible, I mean. And then there's death. We're all inside that one, but now it's real. You know what I mean. And I won't do that to you. Thus the banishment from art.

I'm repeating myself.

I suppose you wonder how long? How long does irritating Marlene need for this "break"? Or is it permanent? All I can say is that for now we must not see each other. I can't know how far the separation stretches, whether it might stretch to unworkable thinness. I must mean the connection, it might—

Oh, hell.

It would be better if I knew what I'm talking about.

Can you tell I've been drinking? Maybe the damn piece of paper smells of the stuff. An exception to the customary practice, I don't even like alcohol. I won't keep it up, don't worry. It's only in order to write this letter which I will take to the post office before I turn sober or I'll never send it.

Thins to cessation is what I mean. Cessation of being. Ceases to be any real thing. Our relationship. A sad thought.

How could I know how long? Or the outcome? I'm doing my best.

Let's take art. All my life, it was the core, the need. But as for talent, I doubted it. So there was passion (about art) and doubt (about me). Difficult braid. Every woman I somewhat-loved had to put up with coming second. Stand in line behind the ragged scrap of art I'm working with, my dears. Cuddle buddy turned out to be a handy concept. Philomena was and is (she continues to live, barely) the exception. I have loved her, plain and simple. But she's safe. She put herself second to the art from Day One.

You'll say you'd do the same. Maybe you'll say that. But there's only one Philomena. Don't ask me to be rational. At any rate, it's not up to you, I have to—

Never mind. On to the next.

Reality. I think I explained this. Saw you as real, quite suddenly. Real in the way you said Murdoch thought it: automatically lovable. What is real becomes necessarily, unavoidably lovable. Get thee behind

200

me, Wilma Schuh. Do you see? A temptation: something that might wrestle with the art and win. Not allowed.

Real: a thing (human, superbly human) I might fall into; a long dangerous fall; an existential threat. I don't know what existential means. I thought I did, but I've stopped and looked at the word and I haven't the faintest. Ought to cross it out, but so far the page looks good, as if I had some control, so I hate to think of deletions.

I'm no philosopher. It wrenches my mind to read and reread the paragraphs in Deleuze's book on Bacon. Except for how it came to me, it would have sat unread. I understand a sentence here, a sentence there. Some of them touch the core. Henry runs around inside the mysteries and I keep trying to catch him. I wonder at times if your suspicion was warranted: <u>am</u> I in love with him? I think I answered that not only cleverly but accurately the day the topic rose up, a minor monster in the room. Trouble is, at the moment the answer escapes. Let that be.

I think I'll have another beer.

OK. Back again, dose of liquid courage having been guzzled.

So I've been reading Rilke's letters. Love that collection you have. Alma's Rilke. The poems—stunning. Of course they are. But for me it was those notes. Stephen Mitchell, what an editor. And inside the notes: excerpts from the letters of the poet who loved to attempt his own explanations. Very likely while sober. Oh, well. So I got Lyle to order his collected letters, hundreds. They pump up my old need: it's the art, it's the art, it's the art. People, well—

The poet's letters have come to me. Poet, painter, it doesn't matter. A new intensity.

In this time.

As if fated.

This time: it began before you and Henry entered. I'm trying to keep that fact in mind. Chronology might matter. I stumbled into the weird part of art. You see it in the room you generously call my studio. Blake's monstrous flea, Saville's fat woman readied for fat surgery, Bacon's blood-marked sex scenes, distorted bodies. The dance of the abhorrent and the beautiful. A few attempts of my own—that hand, for example. Beauty: not different from ugliness. Rilke got that, he's explicit—rise above the distinction: the beautiful, the ugly, no difference between the two. From a certain perspective. The perspective of sheer existence. The awe—the awe-full-ness —of existing. And can he ever write a letter. Well, he's a writer.

So now I have to add another link. It's there, the fourth in the chain, a confession. Art/love/death/god. Do you capitalize it? God? I put all that aside, the Catholicism, et cetera. Just stepped out of it, like an outfit whose style I no longer liked. Shed it. An old skin maybe. Choose your metaphor. Anyway, I ditched God. Took no substitutes, either, unless maybe art.

No. Art is a need, not a god.

That's right. A need.

But I heard you. You. Wilma. You mentioned "the god" once as if you had one. We never really talked about it, did we? And then on Sunday, I think it was still Sunday, you said you thought you'd "meditate." Do you see what happened? I had to reconsider. Reconsider God. Already I had Rilke, but then there was <u>you</u>. Rilke believes and doesn't, has his own version, something—

Never mind all of that. What I'm getting to is this. I thought, as I set out to write this epistle, that if you read all the way through—it was a plan from the beginning, I'm not too drunk to plan and follow through, in fact you must see that I've done better than we expected here—if you read through this whole damn letter, step by step, you would deserve a little gift. So here it is, my dear Wilma. It's a quote from one of Rilke's letters. I thought of you. You basically leapt alive inside me. When I read it, I mean. You'll like it.

Here it is. "I cannot comprehend religious natures who accept and follow God as given and sense him with their feeling without trying their hand at him creatively."

Trying their hand at him creatively! What a concept. And I thought to myself, I'll bet anything Wilma's right in sync with that. This is, you should understand, a major compliment.

Of course I might be wrong.

To sum up: My sexual history is one of protecting myself for the sake of my art which seemed tiny but necessary. I was never even sure I wasn't a pure fake—until this recent turn to the unbeautiful beautiful, the unwanted, the repulsive, where beauty must be worked for against the grain, <u>and I could do that</u>. Also, I am very near to confessing I'm in the first religious crisis of my life, precipitated by you and Rilke and the fact

202

—I know it in my bones, though you doubt me—of Henry's coming death. Death inevitably links to religion, doesn't it?

An incomplete summary. I think I left out the real. Murdoch's real. Enough, enough. I'm almost sober again, a dangerous state.

Forget me for a while, dear Wilma.

No, I don't suppose you can. Shouldn't have said that, it demeans you. Demeans us. I'm still not inclined to resort to crossing-out, though. The words came. Let them be.

Would that you could—forget me, that is.

And then if I want you back, remember me. (There. The honest drunk speaks.)

Oh my god, what if you walked away and never give me a second thought? How humiliating this letter then is. I don't believe it. But dump the suffering, Wilma. Move on. And come back if I want you. I know, I can be a selfish bitch. Also, a good judge of quality. You have a lot of quality. May you know it forever. I hope your god is a comfort now, if he/she/it happens to be the type.

Good place to end.

Sincerely, very—
Marlene

And now to the post office. Fast.

~ ~ ~

Wilma read the letter twice, sat breathing, rose from the couch, prepared for bed, placed herself between still-clean sheets, and slept. It was a bit like dying. Nothing was gone from her, she was gone from everything. But she came back, woke at a reasonable hour, and decided she was hungry. Now, Thursday morning—it seems advisable to keep track of the days—she sits and eats and watches the rain pour. Oatmeal with almonds and walnuts and raisins and blueberries and cinnamon and honey and milk. A good hot breakfast, hearty, a concoction she got from the radio and produced for Alma and Lorraine and herself—and then Alma and herself minus Lorraine because Lorraine was missing, dead— until Alma refrained. For months before she died, no breakfast for Alma.

Then death. For quite some time it has been breakfast for one. A body ought to be accustomed. The rain is thick, loud, heavy. It must be unreasonably wet. A person could drown, at least a very, very tiny person could, a thimble person, a Tom Thumb.

She did try. Marlene did. To explain.

She rises from the table—leaving the unwashed bowl and half-cup of cooling coffee—and follows the magnetic pull to the letter resting on the couch, handwritten pages folded and tucked back into their envelope, a slightly bulging neat little bundle obedient to the laws of nature, gravity in particular. Where she placed it, there it waited. She sits beside it, looks at it. She picks it up and puts it on her lap and lays her hands over it and waits.

Nothing.

But she stays.

Nothing.

Perhaps a bit of meditation?

Wedge, wedge, wedge. The weather is having an energetic moment. Wind-driven rain is attacking the windows. Attacking? A war, then. *Wedge, wedge, wedge.* Or the rain is dancing with the wind. *Wedge, wedge.* Or it's a drumbeat against the windows. Will they crack? *Wedge, wedge, wedge.* Inside, no rain, no wind. *Wedge, wedge.* Inside the apartment, inside the woman, no rain, no wind. *Wedge.* The storm, the dance, the drumming, the celebration, the war: the external world. *Wedge, wedge.* Go inside. *Wedge, wedge, wedge.* A pool. *Wedge.* The pool within is clear and calm. *Wedge, wedge.* Inviting. *Wedge.* Enter. *Wedge.* Down into difference dives the mind. *Wedge.* Wait now. The commotion, external, will hush itself. *Wedge, wedge, wedge.* Wait. *Wedge.* The cone of sun. *Wedge.* The cone of sun comes walking down the woods path. *Wedge. Wedge.* Wait. *Wedge.* Wait near the pine. *Wedge, wedge, wedge.* That was long ago. The path of innocence, and long ago. *Wedge.* Child's time, child's vision. *Wedge.* Now she is a woman. *Wedge, wedge.* Grown. *Wedge, wedge, wedge.* With a pool. *Wedge, wedge.* Out of the pool rises a sword. *Wedge.* Excalibur?

She stops, opens her eyes.

Excalibur? She smiles. Pa made sure she had her books.

All right, then. Enough.

She takes Marlene's letter to the kitchen, places it on the table, sits, looks at it, does not read it. Waits. The next hunger reveals itself. Rising like a sword out of the waters of Marlene's letter, the radical impulse returns, the eagerness, almost a craving, to have her portrait painted. The painter being of necessity one Marlene O'Connor. From whom she is exiled.

A hunger. A craving. A sword.

A sword of desire, inexplicable, dangerous.

Or a boa constrictor, for it squeezes the breathing mechanism as it circles the thoracic region.

Hunger. Sword. Snake. The metaphors do not match.

Choose your metaphor, advised drunken Marlene.

Or choose your angle of perception, thinks perfectly sober Wilma who is firmly held in the unmerciful grip of the force of desire and simultaneously flitting around, viewing the phenomenon from all sides and even from above. For it is a phenomenon, this longing for what she cannot have. It is the next hunger. It arrived on Sunday when she took off her clothes and waited for Marlene to emerge from her bedroom and begin painting. Five days old, then, this hunger. But it's been refrigerated. Wrapped and refrigerated. As the tuna fish sandwich ought to have been. Ended up in the garbage, sad little sandwich, but this hunger has been kept fresh.

An unwieldy metaphor if ever there was one.

Think. The letter asserts that there will be no portrait painted by Marlene the artist. As for the woman herself, surely more than an artist, a reappearance is possible. But no portrait.

However, even Marlene O'Connor cannot penetrate the veil of Time, see the future. There is, after all, a bookcase-in-progress of which she knows nothing. Which bookcase hacks into the unknown and clears a path for all possible alternatives. It will have to be delivered. To Marlene.

Still: no portrait by the artist any time soon and the felt need is urgent.

You, Wilma Schuh, are on your own.

She is staring at the cover of Michael Solomon's book of poems. *Keep This Deep and Velvet Night: A Self-Portrait.*

A self-portrait.

A portrait done by the self.

205

A project for which no other human would be needed.

Kali flits through, laughing her violent laugh. Kali, goddess of Time, Creation, and Destruction. Wilma finds herself in the living room, picking up her father's hammer. She stands contemplating the bookcase-in-progress, but the hammer is not currently a carpenter's tool, it is an artist's tool. A bit violent, but just the thing if used with an artist's focus.

At this moment, astonished at the workings of difference, Wilma knows herself to be an artist. She shakes her head, amused, perplexed, accepting. The unexpected has not ceased to emerge.

There is a full-length mirror in the hall that leads to the bedroom. Framed in oak, it is the one possession Alma retained from her childhood. Between bedroom and living room, between the territories of Day and Night, hangs the mirror.

Wilma walks to the bedroom, removes every stitch of clothing piece by piece, folding carefully, laying the items one by one on the bed, the bed with recently washed currently invisible sheets. Invisible because the bed was made earlier this morning when Little Wilma was perhaps ordering the world.

Little Wilma? Lorraine's designation? Here this morning? She did hold the days to a shape. Perhaps in fact she's been around. Possibly she has been needed.

Another Wilma, naked, is now walking hammer in hand into the hall, turning on the overhead light for there is of course no window in the hall and furthermore the daylight available this morning is dark, the wild rain is still tearing around the world outside like an out-of-control child, but inside there is another drama, the drama of the unborn artist, the little chick, pecking its way out of the egg, peck, peck, peck. This is Wilma, making the first tentative blows, hammer to mirror. A series of cracks, her first drawn lines as an artist, have appeared. She can barely breathe. Will the frame hold? She has no vision of pieces falling away, none whatsoever. Cautiously, with intense focus, she works. Glass is an unforgiving medium, there will be no alteration. Kali flits through, stomps the floor. Kali! Careful! Kali laughs and departs. But hasn't she left a new set of cracks in the lower left corner? Caution be damned, then. And the artist proceeds, breathing heavily, daring.

It is complete before lunchtime. She takes a bathroom break, drinks a cold glass of water, puts the breakfast dishes in the sink, makes a fresh tuna sandwich, eats at the table with the stacks of books and papers which constitute a wild welcome presence. None of them have fallen to the floor.

She is still naked.

Of course she is. She has not yet stood looking.

She does the dishes, takes many deep breaths, walks to the hall where the light is still on—she was hesitant to turn it off lest the work disappear—and stands, and looks. *Wilma Schuh, Nude by Way of Hammer on Glass*. This is herself, taken piece by piece. A slice of shoulder, a bit of breast. There is her left foot, created by Kali. One long crack shoots upward at a slant from foot to crotch, the longest and most dramatic line in the portrait. The face is lightly tapped, a little spray against the left cheek with a thin line emerging from the spray, breaking the nose. A break in the jawbone, right side. A cauliflower right ear. Perhaps her essence is that of a pugilist, a fascinating interpretation.

Or this is a body subject to accident.

Well, certainly that. Hammer against glass: the accidental element would be assumed.

She lowers herself, sits cross-legged on the floor. An entirely new self-portrait. *Difference: the Sitter.* While working, utterly focused on making lines, she had paid no attention to the shifts in the image, the mutability of mirror art. But Marlene said it herself on Sunday. "The artist fails to comprehend the work until it is finished." Her tone was one of wonder, sorrow, and deep strange fear. In Marlene's poor mind her own painting in conjunction with Long QT Syndrome put Henry's dear heart in mortal danger.

Not a sliver of the mirror has fallen to the floor. The frame is holding. The floor is therefore safe to walk on, or sit on, assuming no earthquake. But the work itself: how safe? And what might she mean by such a question? Surely she has not predicted her death? Or, as Marlene would have it, caused it? Well, at least it would be her own. But she is not inclined toward such nonsense.

Still, might there be danger lurking in the work? In any self-portrait?

What does poet Michael Solomon mean by his incomprehensible title? The poems are about his deceased parents and his departed lover.

207

Still, he calls the collection a self-portrait. An artist's term. Marlene would be the one to ask, but Marlene is unavailable. Lyle, then.

Yes, Lyle.

She gets up from the floor, goes to the bedroom, dresses quickly, returns to the hall. Broken and wild is the woman in the mirror. Her hair is a mess, her features are fractured, her clothing is ripped and pulled from its form. *Wilma Schuh in Cubist Dishevelment.* Her hair really is a mess. It's the undressing and re-dressing. She would rather be naked just now, but to walk down the street with no clothing would be a breach. She'll settle for these old jeans, an apparently untucked and wrongly buttoned shirt, and disheveled hair. The day needs its due.

She glances out the living room window. A miracle. The storm is gone, the sun is out, the sky is pure sudden blue. Well, then. She looks around. What does she need? Alma's little backpack will do. She gets it and quickly fills it. Spinoza, Rilke, Murdoch's *Unicorn.* One of her father's notebooks. His published article. Her mother's writing. Marlene's letter. And of course Michael's book. As she leaves the apartment, she calls to Kali. "Coming?"

But Kali is not one to answer a summons.

I'm here, dear.

Alma?

Yes, dear. You are wise to think of walking. I'm not certain a bicycle would be prudent. And certainly no car. But a walk will do us good. Lorraine is here, too. We'll find our way. But whyever did you break my mirror, Wilma Marie?

She has not been called Wilma Marie since the day she filled the syringe—it was she, Wilma Marie Schuh, who did that, filled the syringe and injected Lorraine. Alma is the only person who ever called her Wilma Marie. Three times now. The day Pa died, the day Lorraine died, and today. This is serious. And Alma's question is unanswerable. Wilma shakes it away and proceeds down the steps out into a clear bright world.

~ ~ ~

The walk to the bookstore is lovely. Alma and Lorraine and blue sky and puddles and even little streams. The streets are bit flooded, water runs cheerfully along its appointed path beside the curbs. The day is hot,

208

her feet in thin old tennis shoes are soaked and cool, the passersby are smiling. Strange smiles, as if catching sight of a peculiarity, but welcome nevertheless. Well, my goodness, here is one of the Moirae, the one who will be a quiet beauty in a few years. Must be Clotho, who spins life. Look how innocent she is, Pa. Never one to cut the thread, is she?

Of course Pa isn't actually present, he relishes only eternity, but one does like to acknowledge one's debts and who but Pa introduced her to the Moirae?

"How nice to see you, dear," says Wilma to the girl who is looking unaccountably concerned.

"Hi." A greeting with threads of hesitation woven in. So young, this one.

"We appreciate the sun in such a moment, don't we?"

"Are you OK?" says the girl, having gathered courage from the sun. Do we not, all of us, gather such courage?

"Are you OK?" says the girl again. She has put herself together in a taller fashion now, hesitation banished.

She deserves a response, Wilma.

Of course she does, I was getting to that, Lorraine. You might modify your tone, I need no chiding.

Right. Just tell the girl whether or not you're OK, if you happen to know.

"Oh, perfectly. And you, Clotho?"

"Um. Fine, thank you. My name is Mary."

"Of course it is, dear. A good name, though with bitterness mixed in. I have a version of it myself. For the middle one, you know. I must be on my way now."

"OK. If you're gonna be OK."

"I'm going to see my friend. The order of things is sure to prevail. Have a good afternoon. But why aren't you in school, dear?"

"Oh. Well. I'm supposed to be." With a giggle.

"A fine day to play hooky. I'm doing a bit of that also. Not to the point of chaos, we must not go that far."

"You're playing hooky?"

"Even the old lady must have her times, Mary. Be a good girl now."

"I will. I'm going tomorrow. I just wasn't ready for the test."

"Ah, yes. That appears to be a common condition. Goodbye now."

"Goodbye, Old Lady." With a very nearly conspiratorial smile.

Well done, Wilma.

Thank you, Lorraine. I do appreciate the company, I don't mean otherwise. Is Alma still here?

Right behind us, pretending to be out of breath from walking.

Not true, Lorraine. I stopped to commune with this patch of sidewalk grass. Look how it very nearly drowned this morning. It has told me of its inhabitants, the tiny ones who are even happier to see the sun than Wilma is. Their little lives depend on it.

Wilma remembers her morning musings, Tom Thumb in danger of drowning, but she herself was inside then, in different weather, and in another era. She does not speak of Mr. Thumb with Alma who exists incurably in the present moment, which is a blessing because she hasn't repeated her question. But why *did* she break Alma's mirror? It seems quite some time ago, and a mystery.

When they arrive at the bookstore she asks her ghosts to wait outside.

Very wise, Wilma. Please say hello to Lyle for me. I do think of him. He'll tend to you nicely. Lorraine and I will be right here, should you need us.

Wilma has been inside the store for ten full minutes when Lyle, customer-less, appears.

"Oh. Wilma. I heard the door but I was tied up—er—call of nature —not feeling too well. What about yourself, though? Has the illness passed? Tell me this unwanted condition passes quickly."

He holds his belly and bends forward just a tad. Poor man. What illness, though?

"Sit, Lyle. I'm sure you'll feel better soon. Is there anything I can do for you?"

Lyle sits on the chair at the end of one of the stacks, the chair she herself sat on shortly after Alma's death. She stands and waits for him to take his breaths and gather his resources. There were some tears that day, were there not? And he gave her Michael's book. How did he know? But then he always knew. Alma appreciated that.

"So, Wilma."

"Yes, Lyle."

"Well."

"Yes."

There is another rather long break. She goes and sits behind the desk. They have exchanged roles. The dance of life proceeds.

"I'll be able soon, Wilma. Just a little—"

"I'm in my hurry."

"What?"

"Oh. No, that wasn't right. No hurry, I must have meant. I can't see why I'd be in a hurry."

"Good." He is doing his breathing, finding himself. A valuable man. Got a bit old, didn't he?

From the desk she can see what she'd been pondering during the ten minutes she waited for him to appear. Mud. Muddy footprints. So Lyle has had an abundance of customers already today. And now the sun pours in. An ecstasy comes over her as she observes this conjunction. Many customers. Much sun.

"You sold some books today, Lyle. I'm so glad. "

"What makes you think that?"

"Footprints."

"Oh. People were here, yes. No sales. They were escaping the rain. Came down with a vengeance, I suppose you noticed. I believe I'm better now. I appreciate the patience. What can I do for you, Wilma?"

"You just sit there. I have an urge for the floor. And for the door. The long glass, you know, and the sun. It occurs to me that the sun is the essence. There might be a cone."

"There are times I can't make head nor tail of you, Wilma."

"I'm only saying I'm about to sit on your floor, here at the door. If a customer approaches I'll yield."

"Fine, Wilma. Though unusual."

"Well, yes. These are unusual times. Marlene and Henry are gone, but the sun is back, a more than adequate—"

"Gone, are they? A trip?"

Wilma has seated herself. The sun is agreeing with her. It is almost time. "Time for what, though, Lyle? What do you suppose it means?"

"Wilma?"

"I suppose it relates to the beginning—"

"What?"

"In the beginning—"

211

Lyle waits.

"In the—"

"Wilma?"

"—beginning—"

Lyle waits.

"I could use help, Lyle Franklin."

"Yes, I can see that, but—"

"In the beginning, Lyle, in the beginning—"

"Was the Word?"

"Yes. Thank you. I have it now. In the beginning was the Word and the Word was with God. And the mirror. There was also the mirror."

"Mirror."

"Yes. This relates to Alma's question. She says to say hello, by the way."

"What?"

"I've become, quite unexpectedly, an artist. That might be it. The correct response. To why I did it. Or something entirely other perhaps. Alma has raised a question, you see, and I'm unsure of the answer. I suppose you ought to call him." She holds Michael's book out.

"Call this author?"

"Oh, look, it's the missing Marlene. As well as Henry the mime. It might be necessary to rise and provide a welcome. They're friends, though, aren't they? We needn't stand on ceremony. I'll just scootch over —"

Wilma, still sitting amid the footprints where she feels properly placed, moves just enough to allow Marlene and Henry to squeeze in, should they so desire. It seems there is some question. A pause, therefore, as she observes Marlene's uncertainty, her quick consultation with Henry, and the halos that surround this pair of beautiful humans. Whole body halos though at least one of them, Marlene, is hardly a saint. The sun is indiscriminate, a fine thing to be.

The pause extends. It occurs to her that her two former friends might be hallucinations. Reality does seem a tad shaky. But, no, reality is only opening itself, which can be a blurring operation. Yes, that's right, opening itself, as the door opens, as her friends enter. Pa might be getting his first glimpse, he really ought to show up some time. Meet Marlene, Pa. And we call this one Young Henry, though not to his face.

212

How contented she feels. Blissful, were the truth known.

"Wilma?" says Marlene.

She stares, absorbing the phenomenon of Marlene O'Connor. No saint, but an expression of the god nevertheless. Isn't that what Spinoza would say, Pa?

"What is this, Wilma?"

"Hello, Marlene."

"What are you *doing*, Wilma?"

"Hello, Henry."

Henry nods and smiles.

"Wilma," says Marlene. She is becoming exasperated. Not a good supply of patience in this woman, is there? Shucks a person off at the first twinge of fear, for example. Lyle is patient, though. Look how he stands there. A good man. He has Michael's book. It will be safe with him. And from another perspective, Marlene is of course a shining individual soul, unique in all the world, as in *The Little Prince* which Lorraine loved. Look within and there it is, the shining soul.

"Wilma suggests I might call this fellow," Lyle comments. "I suppose he's in the book."

"Call the poet?" says Marlene. Young Henry stands quietly, a calm young specimen.

Henry, Lyle, Marlene. Her friends. A body could burst from expansion of the heart.

"She might mean in his capacity as a therapist. A bit of confusion maybe this morning. Last night, too. I can attest to that."

"You spent the *night* with her?"

Lyle looks at Marlene with his one good eye. He seems to be feeling considerably better. No more holding of the belly. These facts comfort Wilma who notices that the conversation is now in his hands, which have aged. Time does pass.

"Doesn't he have fine hands, Marlene?"

"What?"

"Lyle. He'll manage quite nicely. I seem to have—"

"Wilma, will you *please* get up off this floor?"

"Oh. Well. Yes, I think it might be time."

"High time, I'd say."

213

"I'm trying your patience. It's exceedingly pleasant to see you, Marlene. I got the letter."

"Oh, God."

"Yes, I'd say that."

"Lyle, is she asking for a *therapist*?"

"I think so. Want this fellow for a therapist, Wilma?"

"He's been having a time of it, Lyle. I think it might be mutual. The benefit, I mean."

"Look him up, Lyle," says Marlene.

Lyle leaves the customer's chair, he's going to make the phone call from behind the desk, a sign of order. Perhaps she should have gotten Alma's permission, about the mirror. It was a presumption, is that it? Marlene is treating her like an invalid, helping her to the chair Lyle recently occupied. She can feel his warmth. A good man and a friend to Alma in addition. This was the place to take herself to. Now the next stage will begin. The Plan, Stage Two. Soon she will find a way to write it. The word comes to her. God. Didn't Marlene just pronounce it?

God, she says to herself, taking care lest it spill out into the air as some other words appear to have done recently. God. One syllable, tiny as Tom Thumb. Easy to slip into the pocket like a stone polished over time through fond absent-minded rubbing. She had one as a child, always in her pocket. A smooth irregularity was its condition. Where did it come from? Where did it go?

God. A single unassuming syllable. Like a ghost stone. Didn't she have a dream—?

Somehow they've gotten into Marlene's car. It's the three of them. Goodbye, Lyle, take care of yourself. He's waving from the sidewalk.

They drive through the streets of Bangor.

"Remember that young journalist, Wilma? The one who approached Henry in Pizza Hut after Winnie-the-Pooh, remarkably for a toy bear, thrust him into the limelight?" The news is being delivered to her. Also, Marlene is demonstrating the thinnest shadow of a sense of humor with her remarkably adept toy bear, though possibly with a tinge of hysteria. But no worry, she's one who will recover whether she herself, Wilma Marie Schuh, returns to the status of cuddle buddy or lover or old neighbor briefly taken up or—

214

"The young journalist—are you listening, Wilma?—John Stone. He interviewed Henry yesterday. It went well, didn't it Henry?"

Henry, who is not currently demonstrating a sense of humor—rather somber is this Young Henry—confirms that yes, it went just fine.

Oh, dear. He's worried. I've caused worry in the young.

"Are you worried, Henry?"

"I suppose I am. Just a little, Wilma. But Michael will help."

He has Michael's book in his hands, did Lyle give it to him? His hands are trembling. Two hands for one small book, and they tremble. What if he really is the mime in the poems?

Well, then, the workings of the gods—

She experiences a powerful surge of fondness and takes a deep satisfying breath as Marlene pulls over to the low flooding curb. What a fine day this has turned out to be, and we'll add Michael in. She smiles to herself. Yes, Michael will be a find addition.

Four: Michael's Poetry

We all breathed in, breathed out, breathed in.

KEEP THIS DEEP AND VELVET NIGHT: A SELF-PORTRAIT

by Michael Chaim Solomon

I: MOTHER AND FATHER

Ashes, Ashes

The child grows.
The parent pair goes.
All fall down.

Poison

Note of the father, found on a table.
Note of the mother, pinned to a pillow.

Into the meadow dry went he.
Down to the rock at the stream went she.

Death is a solitary act.
Death is a matter of fact.

It Was the Camps

It was the tangle of bodies,
the raw, the starved, the hollow of eye.
It was the gray and grainy photos, it was the relatives.
It was their own emigration, early and lucky and haunted.
It was the American plan, precise and determined,
a plan to pin death to the mat.

They got his shoulders down without a hitch.
They sat on his thin bony middle.
They spat at his fleshless grin.
It was hardly a match. Hardly a match at all.

The Refrain

They on the rose-colored couch,
I on the floor with Raggedy Andy,
rain at the tall cold window.
First telling, plain-spoken and calm, not understood.
But remembered.

~

They on the rose-colored couch,
I, cross-legged and stubborn, tending my stamp collection.
They explained. I sorted.
The pink one came from Germany.
Not damaged. Not even canceled.

~

They on the couch in their worn-out robes.
I in my best-man tux, perched on the rickety rocker
after my best friend's wedding, age twenty-four.
"I'm gay, Mom and Dad. I'm a queer."
"We're Jews, dear boy. Life is hard."
And added their unchanged intention, plan in place.

~

They on the rose-colored couch, Stanley and I holding hands.
"We plan to live together."
"And we, my son? We die together."
Mother with a hiccup, whispering.
Father with a book of poems, nodding like a sage.
Stanley blond and blanching as the script played out.

~

They sat on the old rose couch.
Mother held her long-sober head. Father held his old fountain pen.
Stanley was gone. I was bereft. They had listened.
We stared at the rug on the room's hard floor.
Someone took a breath and said, "Well."
Someone looked up. We all looked up.
It came to me to ask: "Still?"
They nodded. I nodded, too.
Together we stared at the old worn rug.

220

Fundamentals

Death was
the mother tongue.
Death was
the family language.
Death bound
Mother and Father, a unit.
Death bound
us all.
We were
Jews.
Life was
hard.
The end would
come.

There Came a Fearful Naked Dream, Blood-Red

The hands of the mother, the hands of the father,
the embarrassed hearts held in those hands—
pulsing hearts in the piteous hands
and the shy offering they made.

Eager and piteous, the hands of the son,
the terrified hands of the terrified son,
receiving the blood-red hearts
of the humans who made him.

And the dream ends.

After

Tears shed,
breath taken,
face dried,
details seen to,

day become dusk.

I am the son
on the rose-colored couch.

I am the son on the couch.

II: BILLY

The Party Mime

He climbed the stair
with a swish and a glow
and a mask unwilling to tell.

He pushed the air
where he wished it to go
and into his eyes I fell.

Into his steel-blue eyes fell I,
as into a well with the water high
and the moon like a god far in the sky,
a cold white god with a steel-blue eye.

Apparition

Here is my shining boy Billy, my silly.
Some days divine is young Bill.
Some days frustration vexatious.
Arresting angel. Wrong-headed imp.
Foolishly furnished with wings is my love—
improbable, undeniable, white-hot wings.

But His Hands Say No

How brave to be a mime,
how brave to be a man who is a mime—
Billy on the street and a wiggle to his ass,
a wiggle to his ass inside the box his bare hands make,
a wiggle to his ass inside the glass,
but his hands say no.

Never a Word

Never a word gives the mime to the fag.

Never a word
unless written on paper,
with the breath removed,
and the heart cut out.

The red beating heart cut out.

Paper Crying in the Rain

Scissor me into the street, young Bill,
drop me in sections when you walk away.
I am but paper you once cared to write on,
old news from a old yesterday.

Cut me in columns and leave me in gutters,
the rain for to wash me along.
Someone will wonder and pick up and read me.
Someone will take me home.

Glass Box Lacking Door

A door would let a body in.
A door would let a Billy out.

Billy lived inside a box.
He lived beneath a mask.

He disappeared the box
but didn't disappear the mask
the day he walked away.

Coda: Keep This Night

One night in the square Billy halted.
He wasn't wearing white.
He wasn't entirely sober.
Stand there, Old Man, said he. Be audience.

He took off his jeans and the rest of his clothes,
folded and stacked them with care,
stood in the street-lit night,
commenced to turn in the air.

Three boys stopped.
Billy worked his turns, thickened the currents he caused—
he was a woman, churning, and the butter would all be hers.
The boys sat down.
Around Billy new butter, smooth.

He changed the scene and cast a line, a wrist-flicking fisherman now.
Hooked me, but I fought. Played me. Let me go.
Rewound the line, laid down the careful pole.
Closed quietly his body, made a pause.

Sprang open next, leapt high,
molded with his mouth a silent shout.
Landed. Stiffened.
Stood and saw the far pale stars
and held his breath.
The boys and I held back our breathing too,
then cautiously expelled the hard-held air.
We all breathed in, breathed out, breathed in.

Billy pulled a knife from the warm night sky and sharpened it.
Against a firm and willing finger he tested his mime's cool knife,
thrust it into his breast,
in triumph extracted his heart.
In his hand then, his heart.
He offered it to me.
The night was deep and velvet now. His touch was velvet, kind.

Billy dressed, blowing kisses to the tender audience.
They gave a gentle round of young applause.
He skipped away, a child.
I followed, running,
holding in both hands
his heart.

Five: Michael

You have a wonderful mind but it's your heart—

Almost midnight. Michael closes the chapbook and holds it quietly in one hand. His poems. Long time since he's read them. Long time since he's had a day like this one. Old client, Bob Smith, boring old Bob, comes in transformed, and for the better. New client, Wilma Schuh, presents as pure mystery, unlike anything he's seen before, and he loves her already. Furthermore, standing with Wilma in the waiting room is none other than Henry Whitsun, the bewitching Billy of these poems, and what the hell was he doing there?

To top it all off, after work he found himself at a surprise birthday party, his own.

And it was surprisingly bearable.

He sits on the old rose couch. After his parents died, before he moved to Maine, he had it reupholstered. It's sturdier now. It holds its shape, doesn't sink when he sits, or when, for reasons unknown, he sleeps on it. The fabric is an altogether different texture, he insisted on that, but it had to be rose—dusty rose—as it had always been. He insisted on that, too.

He's been sitting here since he got home from Danny and Raymond and Sephie's—reading, staring, reading, staring. Staring into blank space or across the room at the wall that holds the painting. *Der Kramer. The Chandler*, the candlemaker, seller of candles, seller of soap, seller of any little thing a village might need. The painting, like the couch, is from his childhood home, as is *Der Lumpen-sammler—The Rag-and-Bone Man—* which hangs behind him, out of his sight line, if he has a sight line. Both are by Marianne Werefkin, Expressionist, his mother's favorite artist. He hasn't paid attention to either in forever. Nor has he paid real attention this evening. Staring does not engender attention.

But now he focuses. Attends. Allows. He loves this old man—he assumes he's a Russian Jew—when he remembers to know him at all. The old candlemaker walks through a scene of deeply saturated red, blue, green, and black, a mythic figure in a dreamscape. Whatever might be dull in the whole of existence has been banned. If his day has been a difficult one, he has lived through the difficulty. His entire being, his very soul, is alive and well. What would it be like to join him, not really talking, just walking side by side, mostly silent, for an hour or so?

Salvation is the word that comes to mind.

Salvation?

229

Well, all right.

Michael looks at the chapbook in his hand. As soon as he got home he went to the bookcase. Would it be there? It had been so long since—

There it was, between *As a Driven Leaf* and *Giovanni's Room*. He had to chuckle. Had he really placed his own poems between two classic novels, one Jewish, the other gay? What chutzpah. He sat down on the couch, turned to the first poem, kept going, quickly, skimming surfaces, all the way through.

So, all right, he did that.

The painting, the poems. What next?

He puts the chapbook down, picks up Robert Walser's little gem, *The Assistant*. Bob Smith, bland depressed sixty-five year old who threatens as no other client to put his therapist to sleep week after week after week, entered the office this morning holding this book in his hands as if it were a sacred object and looking himself like a human spirit aglow. Bob Smith, vivid, vital, first surprise of the day. It was this novel Michael lent him last week, said Bob, and proceeded to tell about the cascade of shifting revelations he had experienced as he read. It was important that the book was physically small, not some tome. "Look how it fits in the hand, Michael." Michael came awake himself, pulled to a level of alertness he hadn't experienced in some time.

The Assistant took his own heart years ago. Opening it at random now, he finds one of his favorite scenes. Protagonist Joseph Marti swims, immersed in the "wet, clean, benevolent element...fluid, green, firm, unfathomable." After the swim, the text exclaims: "How splendid that was!" Michael, whose undergraduate work was in English, loves this daring exclamation point. Next he comes to Joseph's nightmare. Poor Joseph, so vulnerable. "Everywhere there were eyes that took a malevolent pleasure in his peculiar nakedness." But the character is buoyant, more the ecstatic swimmer than the victim of malevolent eyes. And he is brilliant. Eccentrically brilliant. Or at least Walser was.

How had he known to lend this book to bland Bob Smith? It was as if the gods of therapy had declared, "Enough already. No more boredom required on the part of client or therapist." It was inspiration. It won't last, Bob Smith will no doubt return to dullness, homeostasis is a powerful force, but they had a moment.

230

Closing *The Assistant*, he turns back to his chapbook. This time he reads the poems slowly, thoughtfully, allowing them the bring what they will. His parents. This couch. Their telling, again and again. His coming out. The naked fearful dream. The deaths. And "Billy," now suddenly strangely present as Henry Whitsun, muteness apparently abandoned. There were so many ways the mime protected himself when they were together, held off the world, held off Michael Solomon, his besotted older lover. But then came the night with the three boys, the stripping naked, the churning of the butter, the knife, the heart.

Reading. Remembering. Allowing.

Not drinking. (Well, one beer.)

Not watching television.

Not losing himself in *The Spy Who Came in from the Cold* with depressed, aging, cynical, very nearly unsalvageable Alec Leamas. Or seeing himself therein. He's planning to reread the Smiley-and-Karla triad, nothing quite like those. Le Carré: an indulgence, almost an addiction lately. Also, an echo of another bad period. After Henry left, he read le Carré compulsively, six or seven books in a row. So, yes, almost an addiction, then and now, along with the four or five beers he's been drinking every night, and the hours of television. How long has it been this time? Six months? A year? What happened? Did the move to Maine, the change, the refreshment of it, simply wear itself out?

Could be. As if a tire had a very, very slow leak.

But today was different.

Well, today was an island. Or an oasis. Or a mirage.

No, not a mirage. Today was real. And *interesting*. It's been a while, a long dry stretch.

Except for Sunday, but Sunday was more startling than interesting. There was Henry, up on the stage. His Henry. In Bangor. It was startling, disconcerting, overwhelming. And heart-stoppingly wonderful.

And then again today in the waiting room. Henry, intense, contained, unreadable, and to Michael's eye more beautiful than ever. But he had not come to see Michael, he made that immediately clear. He had simply come with—given a ride to, it seemed—this new client, Wilma, a story in herself, and her friend Marlene. Or Henry had ridden along for support, having by chance ended up in the bookstore at the moment of a

231

stranger's decidedly unusual need. That might have been it. She sat on the muddy floor, they said. And asked for him, Michael Solomon.

So there was Henry, but ancillary. It was Wilma who mattered, had to matter if Michael were to be the professional he did try to be. Still, there stood Henry, causing the knees to weaken. Two feet away. Intoxicating. And with a copy of this chapbook in his hand.

When Michael entered the waiting room, Wilma, woman in search of a therapist with "the right kind of handshake," and Henry, former mute lover, were looking together at the back cover of *Keep This Deep and Velvet Night: A Self-Portrait*. At the last minute, in a moment of whimsy, he had added the perhaps unjustifiable subtitle and sent it to the folks who promised to turn it into a book, twenty-five copies for a very reasonable fee. And they did that. Truth: it was a thrill the day the little books arrived. Five years ago. Seems longer.

The two—Wilma-the-intriguing and Henry-the-mime—were bent together over what was probably the very copy he had autographed on Sunday. Marlene-friend-of-Wilma stood looking on with a tender, irritated, worried, rebellious countenance. Maybe it's Marlene who needs treatment, he thought—he found he could think, despite all—because Wilma seemed to him a model of pleased relaxation, not the least bit in need. When she turned to greet him she exuded something so intuitively intelligent and benign that he wanted to inhale her very being right then and there. A most unusual response to a new client.

Had Henry seen what was inside the chapbook? Had he read the poems? These questions have haunted the hours.

Will he see Henry again? Another haunting question.

These questions will be with him as he accompanies the old candlemaker, soothed by the slow, regular rhythm of two men walking with no need for talk unless to mention a few details from the day, as if the day had been an ordinary one. *Herr Kramer* had had a fine one, yes, his days were generally fine. And you, Michael? Well, Michael had turned sixty today. Ah, then I must wish you many happy returns. Sixty is a fine age, I remember it clearly. And they move along in silence on the blue-white road between high red hills and low green houses, two calm men in a dreamscape, one now sixty, the other surely past eighty.

But of course it was not an ordinary day. In the morning Bob arrived all aglow. In the afternoon Wilma, who might elude all diagnostic

232

categories and more power to her, began treatment. Henry stood in the waiting room, near and real enough to touch, though of course there had been no touching. And then the day's finale: his friends surprising him with a small, warm, pleasant "party" consisting cautiously of a simple supper, a few presents, and a prudently early ending. It was only Raymond and Danny and young Sephie (who produced the decorations with all of her twelve-year-old artist's sensibility in evidence) and Petra and her partner Nat (who had recently had some sort of female surgery but seemed to be doing well though she handled her body in a careful and most un-Nat-like manner). Just those five familiar, comfortable humans. They took a chance. Would Michael turn glum? Poor friends of his, he's been a trial lately, and will no doubt be again, but their stars were with them, or his were. He did not turn glum, the day was not one for glumness.

He stopped to ponder Danny's old posters on his way to the bathroom. Sephie had demanded that they be framed—framed properly, under glass—since the last time Michael visited. They still showed their age, faded and frayed at the edges, but they looked good. Protected. He filled with tenderness at the thought of such protection. These old blues guys with their harmonicas and their guitars and their old misshapen hats, dead though they all must be, seemed in need of protection. Not a drop of alcohol at this little party, so it wasn't that. It was the day, the whole day, ending with this sweet undemanding variously focused celebration—celebration of his birthday and of the five years he's been in Bangor and, since Petra happened to know about it, of the five-year anniversary of the publication of his chapbook. Michael himself hadn't remembered that the publishing date coincided with his birthday. He hadn't planned such a thing, could not have planned it. The date would depend on recondite elements known only to the scruffy crew who were turning the poems into a book. It was serendipity that he became a published author on his fifty-fifth birthday.

They were sitting around the table, the main meal finished. Petra stood up, taking charge. "Happy birthday, Michael. Happy birthday, little book." She had her copy in hand as she stood tall—tall for Petra, that is —and held it up for all to see, proud possessor of a precious artifact, autographed "by the poet himself." Everyone applauded. Danny stood up next, stared at the cake with its uncountable candles, matches in hand.

233

"Looks like a real cake," he said. It was his first, made from scratch, as everyone had been told a number of times. Sephie asked quickly, before a match could be struck, "Can I light the candles?" She had been in mature mode until this irresistible moment when the lurking five-year-old popped out. Michael feels fond of Sephie, but a little wary. She's impressive—bright, creative, confident—a fine specimen of a child, being raised by Raymond and Danny with abundant assistance from Petra. Michael knew the history. Sephie's mother was Raymond's white half-sister. She called herself Bright Star though she was Raymona in her youth. An artist, and quite strange, from all accounts. She killed herself when Sephie was an infant. So far there's no sign of disturbance in young Persephone, known as Chippie to her soon-to-be-dead mother. The father, Chip, only possible source of her Wabanaki appearance, probably never knew of her existence. Just passing through, seduced by Bright Star, a stranger with obviously strong genes. Sephie was of course permitted to light the candles, her grown-ups watching closely, their collective breath held, though each knew perfectly well the girl was capable of the task.

Raymond had been grinning to himself, shaking his head. Finally he spoke. "Didn't know you were a poet, Michael. Until a couple days ago, that is. Patron came into the library needing some help and referred to the fact. She seemed to know you, but then it was just through your book, or that's how it seemed. So you've kept your true calling in the closet, eh?"

Michael smiled. "Not much of a closet, Raymond, since Lyle, at the bookstore, is selling the poems."

"Ah, that must be how Wilma came to find out about you. I know she knows Lyle. Her mother was the connection. Interesting lady, her mother. I was always happy to see the two of them—"

"Wilma?"

"Schuh. No reason you should know her. It just amused me when she happened to mention—"

Michael steered the conversation elsewhere. Being a therapist has its weird edges, the strictures of confidentiality among them. He'll be glad to see Gertrude in the morning, glad for the relief and release of supervision. He can tell her about Wilma who might require some creative moves on his part, and about boring Bob who is suddenly anything but boring. Life itself is suddenly anything but boring. He'll

234

have to tell her about Henry, too, at least give a sketch of the few minutes in the waiting room. But let that be for now. Best not to get obsessed with Henry. Gertrude Benstein, superb woman, is part of what has made his life in Bangor work, at least until whenever the tire began its slow leak. She's still his anchor, keeps him as steady as possible.

Mixing metaphors here, thinks Michael. Let's say she's the hand pump that puts a little air in the tire at regular intervals. He likes that: elegant Gertrude, refined of intellect, cultured and well-read beyond anyone he knows, as hand pump. But he'd better get some sleep. His appointment with her is an early one.

~ ~ ~

"Good morning, Gertrude."

"Good morning to *you*, Michael."

The woman is alert, interested, centered, impeccably dressed, tall, thin, perfect, and ready for whatever he might bring. As usual. Also, right now she is just slightly, annoyingly, amused. Less than one minute, three measly words from him, and she sees. Can't hide a thing.

But what does she see? The anticipation, the bewilderment, the rumble of excitement, the signs of a sleepless night, or something he himself is entirely unaware of? All of the above, no doubt. He hasn't come to supervision this alive with contradiction—this alive, period—in a long time.

"All right, so you get it, oh thou most perceptive of humans. Something has happened. A number of somethings about which you will hear in due time. What are you reading?"

"So I am to delay gratification. Hmm. Being mature in addition to perceptive, I think I can do that. This is Lucretius, *On the Nature of Things*. Have you read it?"

"I have not, as you could have assumed."

"I refrain from assuming."

"Virtuous of you. Tell me about Lucretius."

"Roman poet and philosopher, first century B.C.E. I'll read this passage where—let me see—he's just told us the first bit about what his argument will be and—"

"Argument?"

235

"This is a philosophical text. Philosophers argue."

"Of course."

"He starts with the idea that reality has two aspects, or elements, or forces, or—never mind—the two things are void and matter. Void is, well, a void. Matter starts with these wonderfully active seeds, 'seeds of matter,' that become everything—constantly becoming, becoming—it's all very dynamic. So there's this necessary void and all this lively matter but we don't know yet how this is going to explain the nature of everything. In this passage, which I will read in my most mature and perceptive voice, he says that the first glimpse of his very large system of thought is itself a seed, or a trace, of the substance—"

"Void. Matter. Trace. Substance. Gertrude, Gertrude."

"Well, yes. But it's not all abstractions. It's poetry. Plus abstractions. It *is* a book on the nature of everything. Just listen, Michael. This is about learning. Or, really, about thinking.

For even as hounds, roaming a mountain side,
When once they catch the traces of the trail,
Ofttimes with nostrils keen scent out the lair,
Deep hid in leafy dell, of savage game,
So thou thyself from facts new facts shalt know,
And in such arguments shalt learn to creep
Into the secret lairs of hidden things
And thence drag forth the truth.

"So I'll be creeping into the secret lairs of hidden things and dragging forth the truth. Rather nice, don't you think?"

"You're stretching me, dear literary supervisor. It's been decades since I tackled anything that dense, and in language that archaic."

"But you followed."

"Basically, yes. Enough to comment that in my experience you already creep into the secret lairs and drag forth truth."

"Only if you let me. I've been tempted to give up on Lucretius, but if I take him slowly the beauty comes through. It's like watching a photograph in developing fluid. I'm also deep into Charlotte Brontë's *Villette*. Quite another thing. Emotion, emotion, emotion. My reading life

236

is thus nicely balanced. What about you? Still sunk in the cynical world of hopeless spies whose era has passed?"

"How unkind. I do intend to finish *The Spy Who Came in from the Cold*. I'm almost there and I sort of remember the finale from the first time I read it. It isn't pretty but it's probably one version of redemption. The cynical spy's version. But last night I went back to my chapbook, as you've been advising for months. Not because you advised it, mind you. More about that later. I've also returned to Robert Walser. Remember him?"

"I remember. You loved *The Assistant*."

"As usual, your memory amazes. Walser links to a client."

"Wonderful."

"The client is Bob Smith."

"Really?"

"I know. He's is my chronic complaint. But yesterday he was a vital human being. Seemed to be because of the Walser, which I lent to him last week in a moment of divinely inspired perspicacity."

Michael has noticed over the years that his vocabulary tends to sharpen in Gertrude's presence. He talks briefly now about the session with Bob who continued almost literally to vibrate with presence as he talked about *The Assistant*, about Joseph Marti's innocent boldness, his endearing humility, the sweetness possible in an alienated protagonist. The book bristled with strips of paper. He took them out one by one as he read passages aloud. He handed the book to Michael at the end of the session, the sacred object returned. Michael said he could keep it for a while but he said no, he needed to move forward, he'd already gotten *The Robber* from the library and ordered Walser's other books. Michael saw a man on a mission.

Gertrude smiled and nodded and said, "You liked Bob yesterday."

"I did, and I'm thinking now of his first session. He's an art historian, you might remember."

"I do, though you hardly mention it any more. He had that intelligent, even passionate, response to your art. You expected to like working with him."

"You do remember. Well, of course you do, being you. That was two years ago."

"Tell me the story again. I don't remember the details."

"When I went out to the waiting room he seemed absorbed in the Kandinsky, but he made no comment. Then we went into the office and he stood looking from wall to wall, back and forth, back and forth. Not a word. Finally he said, 'You have Marianne Werefkin on your walls.' He told me *Large Moon* was one of his favorites and every time he sees *City in Lithuania* he wants to follow the old woman to be sure she makes it all the way to the lit-up distant city. He's sure that city was Werefkin's image of a spiritual haven. He seemed sophisticated, but not academic, not alienating. All this before he sat down. Then he sat, sort of absent-mindedly, and kept talking, talking. His 'area' is the Expressionists. I got a quick lesson in their theories and methods, the significance of the vivid colors, Kandinsky's leap to abstract art, the connection to Schoenberg's experiments with twelve-tone composition, all that energy at the beginning of the twentieth century."

"And at the beginning of his therapy with you."

"Yes."

"Your mother loved Werefkin, didn't she? I do, too. Such color. My Ruskins seem a little tame by comparison, almost washed-out. But of course they're also just what I want."

"I love your Ruskins, especially *In the Pass of Killiecrankie.* But Werefkin is certainly vivid. Bob said she's known for refusing to follow the other Expressionists into abstraction. He also said she's the best of the bunch. When she was young, someone called her the Russian Rembrandt. Critics say Kandinsky built his thought on her ideas—not that she got credit. But enough of that. You're right about Bob, I did think I'd have a good time with him. He'd get what he wanted, his life would begin to satisfy him. He was bored with himself. All that energy for the paintings, and then he tells me he's bored with himself. He came every week after that, on time, check in hand, but I never saw the passionate version again. And then yesterday—I didn't make the connection until now—first session Bob was back. Where this will lead, though— "

"Won't it be fun to watch?"

"We'll see."

"You feel cautious."

"Of course I feel cautious. Maybe a little less so, sitting here with you. As usual. But we'd better move along. I have a new client, and a personal complication."

238

"Sounds like a lot."

"Right. So I'll do my best to avoid rushing."

"Very wise."

It's one of their shared nuggets. When there's too much to do, slow down. Sometimes the art helps. What would Bob Smith see in Gertrude's art? She uses *Study of Gneiss Rock* as a Rorschach. She stands there with a client and with the lines and shadows, the soft evocative gray-white-black complexity, always seeing something new herself, while the client talks about what comes to mind, or what does not. When Gertrude loves something it is with total tender intelligence, or so he firmly believes. Will this positive transference ever tarnish? Once in a while humans must get to keep what they have, right? Especially if they keep it contained in a pleasant defined space, such a this office.

He looks from one Ruskin to the next. *Gneiss Rock* is fine, but not what he needs right now. He chooses the most severe of the four, a pure cold view of a lake and its surrounding mountains, all icy blue and white with black accents and shades of gray, delicately drawn. Tiny figures make their way up a mountain trail. What catches his eye, what he failed to notice in the past, is the glow of pure white on a distant peak. Sun on cold snow. A shiver runs through him. There it is, a mountain top. Glowing. Seen. Seen by him. While he breathes.

Gertrude's silence matches his own. Her breathing matches his. Perfect Gertrude.

"I can't remember the title of that one."

"*Bay of Uri, Lake of Lucerne.*"

"I never noticed the white mountain top in the distance. It must be at the perfect angle to catch the sun."

Gertrude looks and nods and waits.

Sun, then. He'll start with Wilma, leave Henry for later.

"The new client—her name is Wilma Schuh, S-c-h-u-h—kept making references to the sun, most of which sounded perfectly clear but failed to communicate. Something very important about the sun. I assume I'll learn what some day. She was delighted the sun was 'back,' as if she hadn't seen it for decades, not since she was a child. I can't remember how she conveyed such a timeline. Picture this woman, about seventy, sitting on the muddy floor in Lyle Franklin's bookstore. He called me, I had an opening, so now I have this interesting client."

239

"Interesting indeed."

"Doesn't sound quite normal, does she? Poor Lyle. But she was happy, I could tell it had been a happy moment. She does seem to know Lyle, not that that makes her behavior—um—ordinary. The sun was a theme, it came up several times, and there was a mirror. She said she broke a mirror, apparently it was deliberate. Not your usual client-breaking-a-mirror. No anger, no self-hatred, no sense of acting out at all. More like an art project, an attempt at a self-portrait, or that's what I thought she meant."

"More and more interesting."

"Yes. I asked if she generally works with mirrors. She looked confused and said, 'Oh, no, Michael.' I wasn't sure by the end whether she was saying she was an artist or not. Maybe it's her friend Marlene who's the artist. She said someone named Alma questioned the breaking of the mirror—'Why did you break my mirror, Wilma?'—she quoted this Alma several times during the session, so she's probably important. Apparently the mirror, now broken, belongs, or maybe belonged in the past, to Alma. Later in the session I got the impression Alma had died, but I couldn't be sure."

"Interesting and confusing."

"I suppose it's possible the entire mirror incident took place in childhood, but that didn't occur to me when I was with her. It had the flavor of a recent event. It also seemed that Kali, the Hindu goddess, participated in the breaking of the mirror."

"Oh, my."

"All of that came in a rush and then she asked why the subtitle of my chapbook is A Self-portrait. I should tell you I fell in love with this woman."

"Love at first sight. How very pleasant, Michael. Go on."

"This falling in love was of course not erotic."

"Of course not."

"It was at some humming level."

"Humming level."

"It's the word that comes to me. As if a state of mind, or heart, or being—something—expresses itself in the body."

Gertrude nods wisely, obviously enjoying herself.

"Again, not erotic. But just do it—" She hums. He joins her. They laugh. He says, "I really think that's it. A new category. We should write a paper. The Phenomenon of the Humming Relationship and Its Implications for Treatment. But I might want to see Wilma another time or two before we do that."

"Well, well," says Gertrude. She's sitting back now, arms folded comfortably, shaking her head, smiling fondly.

"I know. You haven't seen me like this in a while. Shades of the newly enlivened Bob Smith."

"Hardly. You are never boring. Sometimes unhappy, but never boring. You really like this woman."

"I do really like this woman. She's a complete mystery. I have no diagnosis in mind, the very idea of diagnosis seems irrelevant. I'm not sure there's anything wrong with her."

"Of course not. You're in love with her."

"I'm glad you understand. An old fag like me has to have a moment or two—"

"Yes, I do appreciate it when my supervisees are in love with their clients. It makes for such astonishing objectivity."

"Right. And supervision with you is sometimes such fun. But before I go further I have to tell you what happened in the waiting room. We have come to the personal complication."

He stops. His gut aches.

Gertrude waits.

He takes a few breaths and says, "Do you remember who Henry Whitsun is?"

"Oh, Michael. I do, but I'd forgotten. I heard something on the radio just the other day, an announcement about a performance, and I knew the name rang a bell, but I couldn't—is he your Henry?—the 'Billy' of your poems?—is he in town?"

"That's him. In town and, yesterday, in my waiting room."

"Unexpected, I gather."

"Yes. With Wilma. I don't think he knows her. I got the idea she was sitting on the floor at the bookstore and he was there and offered to— well, I don't know exactly how it—"

"Wonderful image—this older woman sitting on the muddy floor, happy about the sun's return—it's one I'll remember—

241

"You really do remember everything."

"Hardly. But tell me about Henry. You had no idea he would show up like that."

"None. I accidentally went to his performance on Sunday, but I didn't know he was still around.'

"'Accidentally went to his performance.'"

"Petra and Sephie dragged me to it. I didn't bother to find out what they were dragging me to. I was just being compliant with their ongoing goodhearted attempts to make a real human being out of me again. They had no idea I knew Henry."

"So you were caught by surprise on Sunday and then again yesterday. And—?"

"And. Well, yes. So this is where the chapbook comes in. Henry and Wilma were looking at it together when I came into the waiting room—at the back cover."

"Had Henry known about the poetry?"

"I doubt it."

"Do you think he saw enough to—?"

"The question of the hour."

"And the other question is whether you'll see him again?"

"That is the other question."

"This shakes you."

"This shakes me to the goddamn core."

"Oh, Michael."

They sit with his shaken core. He sees them looking together into the deep crevice where it's quivering, trying to hide. He's on the verge of tears, but pulls himself back. This is supervision, not therapy. Also, he wants to talk more about Wilma. She might shake him too. He'd like to be prepared.

"So you need to know that that's going on with me—Henry and his showing up—because I might not be at my most centered, or sane. But let's go back to Wilma."

Gertrude has been leaning forward, joining his Henry intensity. She sits up straighter now, shifting her energies as he shifts his. He will never see the flaws in this woman.

"So. Wilma. She's wearing a backpack, a little old frayed thing, packed full. She sits down and takes it off and empties it, telling me while she's doing this that it is—or was—her mother's. What comes out are books and papers, books and papers. You will agree this is an unusual opening move on the part of a client."

Gertrude smiles and nods.

"Once she has all this stuff arranged on either side of her—she's sitting on the couch and commenting that she's quite partial to brown though my brown couch is darker than hers at home and it's possible she prefers hers but that might be simple custom—she said that, 'simple custom'—once she gets everything arranged, my chapbook settled along with all else, she expresses condolences for the death of my parents and the loss of my lover. This is a repetition. She was at Henry's performance on Sunday and her friend, the same friend who brought her to the office, Marlene, dragged her to me so I could sign her copy of my chapbook and she expressed — "

"Wonderful. You have a fan."

"Or at least a reader."

"Who is now your client."

"Yes."

"With whom you are in love."

"Hummingly. I promise never to sleep with her."

"Good."

"As I was saying, this was a repetition. She expressed the same condolences on Sunday. But yesterday as soon as she said how sorry she was she stopped herself, looked a little flummoxed, and said, 'Well, that's not quite right, is it, Michael?' I'm sure I looked confused because she didn't wait for my response, just went on to 'explain.' Her explanation had something to do with a thing she called 'difference' and how she fell through it and thought she landed but perhaps not. I gathered she has a philosophy that makes room for death and loss being fine ingredients in a radically affirmed totality. How's that for matching your Lucretius?"

"I'm starting to see why you might resist the idea of diagnosis. It would be difficult to find a category. And that affirming impulse—"

"Exactly. She did a little show-and-tell at one point. She had Spinoza, two volumes of Rilke, Iris Murdoch's *The Unicorn*—I remember you were reading Murdoch a couple years ago—and handwritten materials by both of her parents. Also, a xeroxed copy of an article *on* Spinoza by her father, which seemed to be quite precious, and

243

a handwritten letter from her friend Marlene who seems to have refused to do a portrait of Wilma though Wilma came around to wanting just that very thing and she would certainly like to grasp why such a desire might present itself."

"Bit of a self-portrait right there in her backpack maybe."

"Oh, very nice, Gertrude. I like it."

"So do I. What happened next?"

"She opened one of the books by Rilke. *The Notebooks of*—somebody. "

"His only novel. I can't remember the name either—Malte something— "

"You know it. Of course."

"Only the title, and not even that."

"Ah, a gap in your education."

"She opened it and…?"

"She read a quote, said it was the reason she thought to come and see me, in addition to hoping I'd benefit."

"Hoping you'd benefit. She's wonderful! What was the quote?"

"It was about being ill and everything inside gets pulled out. I think it gets pulled out by a fever—thoughts and feelings and experiences—and the character, Malte, is supposed to sort all of this but that's impossible so in the end he just stuffs it back in, creating disorder in the mind. He screams with considerable energy afterward. Wilma was at pains to tell me she did not scream, one has to be concerned about the neighbors."

"So she has some things to sort and you will help and be helped in the process."

"I guess it's pretty simple, isn't it?"

"I'd wait a bit before committing to that view."

"Speaking of views, I think it was the session with Wilma that led me to see the glowing peak in Ruskin's *Bay of Uri*. There's definitely a spiritual element to what's going on with her and the energy of it is contagious. Was contagious for me. She kept referring to a god, not just Kali, but something she called 'the god' and I suspect her god connects to how important the sun is. It's all a bit tangled, but not psychotic. I really don't think she's psychotic. Her ability to make non-verbal contact is stunning. Also, she makes me feel good."

"So of course you fell in love, as anyone would."

"Right."

"Humming love."

"Right.

"I wish we didn't have to stop."

"I think I got the essentials in. You'll have to be on the alert, making sure my multi-pronged countertransference as evoked by yesterday's events doesn't go excessively wild. By the way, Raymond and Danny and Sephie gave me a birthday party yesterday—the finale to an unusual day —Petra and Nat were there—and it was so mild and brief that I had a very nice time, didn't mind at all."

"Your birthday! How old?"

"Sixty."

"Oh, right, we're the same age, as I'm sure we've noted in the past. Notice that I do forget things. How is Nat? Petra mentioned she'd be having surgery."

"A bit tender, I thought, from watching her move, but looking substantial and basically very fine despite."

"Sounds like Petra's Nat. In all the years I've known Petra I haven't met her, but I like her long distance. I will certainly keep my eyes open for wild countertransference, but you're an old hand at this game and you'll no doubt tame it before you bring it to me."

"If I perceive it at all."

"Well, there is that."

"Thank you, Gertrude. I think I'm steadier."

"Thank *you*, Michael. I look forward to our next meeting."

~ ~ ~

It is noon, Thursday, one week since Michael's slow leak was patched by events external to his sorry self which no longer seems sorry at all, in fact he's rather partial to himself today. Petra, good friend, good colleague, once showed him a brochure advertising a professional workshop. She pointed to the phrase "warm self-love." Therapists would be taught to nurture this in clients and in themselves. Techniques would be offered, always there are techniques. Petra, who did not attend the overpriced workshop, said the idea itself had been useful to her.

245

"Personally and professionally, Michael. It's a handy encapsulation. Odd, that I saved the brochure. Here, take it." The implication was obvious. This was around the time he began his vague descent in mood and manner. He threw the ad away, but he didn't forget the phrase.

All right, Petra, warm self-love, why not?

One week since the shift, the shake, the quake, the helpful rearrangement of the ground beneath his feet. Bob Smith. Wilma Schuh. Henry Whitsun. His first birthday party ever. And then, the very next day, Ruskin's mountain top, glowing with sun-struck snow for him, Michael Chaim Solomon, whose parents, possibly because of a certain obsession with death, tried to pour an extra measure of life into him by way of his middle name.

Chaim. Which means life.

And now, this morning, Bob returns. Not boring Bob but Bob the Passionate, Bob the Interesting, Bob the Suddenly Somewhat Mysterious. And what might Wilma the Intriguing, with whom he fell in love last week, bring to her second session?

He is eating lunch at his desk, a ham sandwich from the corner store. His first rebellious act as a Jew was to buy himself a ham sandwich the day after he turned eighteen. He still chooses ham unless he's in the mood for sharp cheese. *Tinker, Tailor, Soldier, Spy* is propped open, but he's not reading. He's been enjoying George Smiley, the short frumpy introverted bookish old spy, and this is one of le Carré's best, but he's also enjoying his work life which has been so lively that his sorry old lover's soul, roused by Henry's being in Bangor—he's probably already left—has somehow found a way to settle back into its customary humble position on his personal scale of things that matter for a man of his age.

All week, little sparks, right here in the office. This morning two couples sessions went exceptionally well and then along came Bob Smith, Walser's *The Robber* in hand. Again there were strips of paper marking passages that must be read to the therapist, but this time only about a third of the way into the book. Bob found *The Robber* more difficult than *The Assistant.* Same author with the same mind and the same heart, he could assure Michael of that, but not a straightforward story with a normal protagonist. "We're going deeper with this one, Michael. Walser, or it could be his character—it's not easy to tell them apart—advises healthy people not to limit their reading to healthy books,

246

says we need to explore pathological literature, take a few risks, what else is health for, after all? I find the concept intriguing, don't you, Michael?"

Michael listened.

"A cornucopia of intriguing concepts in this one," said Bob, "like a classic still life, the excess spilling out onto a table covered by a pure white cloth. You have to ask, is the fruit a little rotted here and there, or is that just shadow?"

Michael takes another bite of his sandwich. He has a hard time imagining the author of *The Assistant* veering toward the pathological. He thinks of the gay literature he read when he was coming out. There wasn't a cornucopia. Gide's *Immoralist*. What did he make of that? What would he make of it now? And Baldwin's *Giovanni's Room*. Would that hold up? *The Well of Loneliness* was presented forcefully to him by a lesbian client just last year. "It's not over, Michael, the pain isn't, and how it twists us, just because these young dykes have fantasies of legalized gay marriage which of course will never happen. It's absolutely not over. The pain. The twisting. You know that." She was arguing with him, though he'd taken no stand. "It's a sin and a shame, as my mother used to say, that you haven't read Radclyffe Hall. Well, Ma wouldn't say it in this instance, but you know what I mean. Anyway, it's a lesbian classic. Read it."

So he read *The Well of Loneliness* and tried not to slip back through the years and down into the well of his own worst times. He was only twenty, confused and lonely and studying English literature at City College—taking a summer course, getting his first taste of William Blake, which was the good part—when news of the Stonewall riots broke. He was a late developer, unsure if he belonged with the rioters or with the good citizens who were righteously appalled by sexual freaks who had no respect for law, order, and essential conventionality. It took most of college for him to understand he was gay, and a year past that unwanted insight for him to walk trembling into his first gay bar. Bold he was not. Things changed, of course—inside him, in the culture, in literature. In Allan Gurganus' *Plays Well with Others* the pathology is centered not in gay behavior or being, but in the virus. For example.

The virus.

Which he escaped.

247

For which inexplicable piece of luck he feels daily grateful, though to whom he knows not.

He met Gurganus once at a party, liked him very much. He went to a lot of parties for a while, thought he wanted to be a writer himself. So many young gay writers and artists in the City. So many gay suicides, too. Things were changing, but that didn't mean being gay was easy. He decided to do graduate school, not in English literature but in psychology. And here he was, a therapist, but not entirely sure how to be that to Bob who continued to talk Walser, Walser, Walser. "He broadens the palette in *The Robber*, he's adding darker tints. Still, right away he lightens things. Master of the quick turnaround, that's Mr. Walser. I find Joseph, our little assistant, more to my taste than the Robber, I want you to know that, Michael, but I feel compelled to know *all* of Walser. No one is single-sided. It's like the need I sometimes have to sit with Soutine's *Carcass of Beef* or Rembrandt's *Flayed Ox*. Are you familiar with either?"

Michael had to confess to ignorance of carcass art, but at least he knew of Chaim Soutine whose *Mad Woman* he says good-night to every night. She hangs on his bedroom wall along with a portrait of Soutine himself. He found both prints in an old shop in the Village the day after a particularly awkward early sexual encounter with an "older" man who was probably all of thirty. Wandering, not knowing what to do with himself, he walked into the shop, and there she was, framed and propped unceremoniously against a battered chiffonier, sitting hunched in her vivid red dress with her crazy green elf's hat, looking right into him with her big eyes. He stayed there, hypnotized, until the shop keeper, an old Jewish guy, led him further into the bowels of the place and left him to ponder Modigliani's *Chaim Soutine* while he tended to another customer. Michael stood and looked, trying to see into the innards of the mad woman's creator, feeling acutely conscious of his own middle name and an uncanny meant-to-be sensation. The old man came up behind him and started to talk, both of them captured by the portrait of Soutine. Modigliani and Soutine, two Jews they were, trying new things with paint, the man said. Soutine was from a poor family in Belarus, tenth of eleven children, maybe not the most stable fellow in the world, but determined. It was against the practice in his synagogue, sinful, to make an image, but the boy had to paint. He ran off on his own, ended up in

248

Paris with Modigliani and a crew of others. These were inexpensive prints but pretty good for all that, and the frames were good enough, perhaps the young man could afford to buy both, the Soutine and the Modigliani? The young man could. The old guy beamed when he saw the name on the check: "Solomon. Just as I suspected, a young Jew walks into my shop and knows good art." Michael left with a modicum of restored confidence and two large pictures to manage as he made his way home. He had purchased art, what an adult thing to do. "Come back another day, we'll find more for you," the old man had said. He never went back, though he meant to. He was otherwise occupied. It was the mid-70s, life was becoming full beyond belief. *Chaim* and *The Mad Woman* have hung in every bedroom he's had since then. He can't imagine going to sleep without them.

"That's expected, Michael. Your field is not art. That you have the two Werefkins, that you've even heard of Soutine, these things are beyond expectation."

Michael caught up. He wasn't expected to know carcass art. Strange how Bob was evoking the past today.

"My mother loved the Expressionists, Bob. It rubbed off a bit."

"Well, good for her. I think I'll put *The Robber* down now." He set the book down carefully, almost as a ritual.

Michael waited. It was one of those moments. The therapist holds his breath, then remembers to breathe. Something is coming.

"Meeting Joseph, or meeting Walser himself—a writer is met in his work as is any artist, don't you agree, Michael—?

Michael nodded.

"Meeting a human of this particular kind—well—it brought forth—perhaps I should say it revealed to me—"

In the end it was almost as if Bob was saying he had discovered Walser, or maybe Joseph, inside his own being, and that the dear person had been there all along. He shimmered with insight as he talked, though he wasn't ready to know what to make of this Robber character, maybe he was inside, too. But as for Joseph, innocent humble Joseph, it was as if he, Bob Smith, saw—"saw inside my own constellation"—something he had thought necessary, but lacking. He was awed by the sight.

Warm self-love, thinks Michael, taking the last bite of his sandwich. Or was this Bob's pathology? But his own mood is too pleasant to engage such a question. Call it mystery, so much more congenial a concept than pathology. There's definitely something still hidden, some strangeness around the edges of the man.

He tidies his desk, puts *Tinker, Tailor, Soldier, Spy* inside his satchel, and decides he'd better empty his bladder before Wilma comes.

He's returning from the rest room down the hall when she arrives with her frayed and stuffed little backpack. She shakes his hand in the waiting room, offers formal good wishes and intense eye contact, enters the office, hands him the check for her co-pay, sits on the couch, and attends to her unpacking, carefully arranging books and papers. When she has settled herself and folded her hands in her lap, she looks up and smiles at him.

Perfect. If the session had begun in some other way he would have felt deprived.

She starts right in, all business. The woman is not shy. "I'm happy to find myself able to report progress, Michael. I have resumed obedience to my plan." She turns to her books and papers and locates, without much delay at all, a piece of paper which she hands to him. He has to get his reading glasses from the desk, apologizes, is forgiven, returns to his chair, and reads.

Stage One
1. Maintain self-care routines.
2. Meditate daily.
3. Read daily from Spinoza and/or Rilke; and from Henry and/or Alma.
4. Leave apartment at least once a day.
5. Speak at least minimally to another human every day.
6. Observe the progress of the season.
7. Know the look of the night sky before getting into bed.
Note: it is permitted to throw everything over in favor of a gust inside the god.

"You are my human today," she says. "To speak to, I mean. Point number five. I had thought perhaps Stage Two by now, but that has not come to mind. As for the gusts, I find they generally don't interfere. My body is pleased with the regular stretching. I place the blanket on the

250

floor and attend and if one occurs I pause until the passing. Or with the reading. I'm able to move back and forth quite readily. Marlene has not seen fit to call, nor does she appear with bagels, though I thought after last week she just might, but as for today I think my parents, and then if there's time Lorraine will enter in. Might I have mentioned the twin the last time we met?"

Michael is lost but it's a pleasant state and he feels no need to get his bearings. He glances down at the paper. No Lorraine. Are her parents here? The name Henry stops him but Wilma's Henry would have nothing to do with his former lover.

"I don't remember a twin, Wilma, though my memory isn't always —"

She is again turning to her books and papers.

"The first page will be helpful. I'm told I don't always make myself clear."

She hands him another piece of paper and opens one of the books by Rilke and seems instantly involved. Parallel play, of a sort, then. He smiles to himself.

He reads, never losing awareness of her, though it seems she's lost awareness of him.

It is five years since I participated in the death of my daughter's lesbian lover, Lorraine. It is autumn and I will soon achieve eighty years of life. Death and endurance meet in my mind. I think to write. But writing was Henry's sphere. With some trepidation I enter his sphere.

"I think to write." Did Henry once say the reverse, that a human writes to think? Will matters here become a bit topsy-turvy? Never mind. I proceed despite.

On this anniversary of Lorraine's death, Adam comes to my dream. Death is the link. I discover myself at his small grave with the little marble marker, a place much visited throughout my childhood. Each blade of grass is carved to clarity. The green stuns my sight and I fall back in time. I am floating to the house, floating up the steps of the wide porch with its columns. It is the Hour Between. Adam is not alive, nor

251

is he buried. He is dead in the house. I stand at the foot of the tiny coffin in the Great Parlor of the house I am to grow up in.

Surely I cannot remember the dimensions of my twin's coffin, nor would it have seemed tiny to me. I was a child of eighteen months.

But the dream insists. I see the gray shine of the tiny coffin, how it stands on its thin metal legs in the parlor, how the adults sit on the straight chairs that line the walls, watching and silently weeping. I toddle and reach out to touch the black-clad knees one by one by one. Adam is there, over in the corner. He wants a drink. No one else can hear him, only I. Dink, dink. Dink, dink.

So Wilma has a daughter and somehow Wilma participated in the death of her daughter's lover and Wilma had a twin and, furthermore, she's quite a writer—but, wait— *I will soon achieve eighty years of life—* this woman can't be eighty years old. Seventy, at most.

He looks up. Wilma closes her book at the same instant. More aware of her surroundings than she seems to be. Better keep that in mind.

"How old are you, Wilma?"

"I'll soon turn seventy. I do like the round numbers. I believe I find them a comfort. Or an achievement, that might be it."

"You didn't write this then? Or is it a piece of fiction? Are you a writer?"

"Oh, no. I found the pages tucked into my father's notebooks. My mother's contribution, you see."

"Ah. That clarifies things. The handwriting is so similar to—"

"Similar?"

"You did write this other page you gave me?"

"Oh, yes. Stage One of my plan. In relation to the god, Michael." She takes both pages back and looks at them. "Alma and I do have similar handwriting. All these years and I hadn't noticed! I find it rather gratifying."

"So Alma is—?"

"The owner of the mirror, yes, cracked beyond repair. At times it satisfies but then I discover a desire within, an incompletion, as if only Marlene could have—you do remember the mirror?"

252

He nods.

"Alma has come to terms. She understands my effort now."

"I remember she questioned—"

"It was an understandable response."

"I suppose it was."

He's putting the pieces together as quickly as he can. Alma is her mother, writer of the page he just read, owner of the broken mirror, and dead. He does remember, he's sure he remembers, that Wilma referred to her mother's death at the theater. So, yes, dead, and speaking to her daughter.

"I was unaware of the twin."

"You didn't know your mother had a twin?"

"Not that it was any concern of mine. The pouring forth might be what unsettles, a great contrast. In life Alma told no stories, but the pen brought forth. Since death she's been rather talkative, but not about matters previously hidden. I try to keep in mind that the ghosts are whimsy, but that might be an infringement. Do I fail to respect the degree of reality? The writing mentions other items I hadn't known. Visions, for example, and lines of attraction that passed among the three when they were young. Alma, Henry, and Steven Builder. I believe I met Steven once, the priest, if I have assembled the pieces correctly, who arrived one afternoon at Pooler Pavilion where my father lived inside his poor diminished mind. Unto death, inside that mind, inside that brick container. Bangor Mental Health Institute, but the Pavilion was separated off. For the demented, you know. Alma summoned Steven, a gracious act, or possibly it was for herself, seeking comfort. He was a tall man, quite real. I gave them their privacy. A Pepsi from the machine, a short walk down the hall, and wandering away for a while. And now, after her death, a light thrown, by way of the writing. Hurled down you might say, that light, onto a variety of things. The sky, for example. Or that my father was in love with Steven. That they both were. She looked at the sky a great deal. When I was a child I thought she wanted to be there, away from us. She sat in the garden and gazed. The twin, his secret existence, explains the sky, or would if the generations were neatly separated. Her mother, you see, enters in, which is the cause of some confusion. Though perhaps Steven Builder also—" She stops. He waits.

She picks up Rilke's novel. "I feel a need just now, Michael. Would you mind a bit of repetition?"

"Not at all. Would this be the quote about illness and what it can do to a mind?"

She nods, smiles, and reads thoughtfully, more to herself it seems than to him. "'The fever dug into me and out of the depths it pulled experiences, images, facts, which I had known nothing about; I lay there, overloaded with myself, and waited for the moment when I would be told to pile all this back into myself, neatly and in the right order. I began, but it grew in my hands, it resisted, it was much too much.'" She lays the book on her lap, still open. One hand hovers over the passage. She shakes her head gently—as if reminding a child of a little rule, a slight prohibition—then lifts her hand, and closes the book. She looks up at him and smiles. "Rilke has been an aid when the intensities threaten to surge. I believe he had some of his own. I think of the effort, how he drew the words out of himself and set them on the page one by one, and then the sense of order. Order, despite disquieting experience. I do hope you can follow, Michael."

"You and I will be sorting through some of what's gotten pulled out of your depths, is that it, Wilma?"

"I'd take it as a kindness. It appears I require conversation after all. More than in the grocery aisle, I mean."

"Most of us do."

"Yes. I should not have gotten accustomed to Pizza Hut. Lorraine does push in. The death Alma refers to, our mutual participation. Lorraine had cancer, you see. Of the brain. A parallel to my father, two exceptional brains set awry. Death would come. Mother and I stood together at the foot of the bed. We held hands and listened to Lorraine who had her desires. Attention, but also generosity, both were called for. Do you know, Michael, I have never complained, not once, about Lorraine's tendencies? I believe one is allowed, in therapy. Is that correct?"

"It is."

"There were times I would have liked to have my say."

"Lorraine prevented that?"

"She had a certain need. My own was lesser. It seemed right, at the time, to allow her. But I see that in her notes—she left notes in the books —"

Wilma turns to her books and chooses *The Unicorn* by Iris Murdoch. She shows him a handwritten set of notes pasted inside the back cover.

"Lorraine's notes?"

"Yes. I have learned a great deal from them. My own effect is an aspect of what I learned. Perhaps if you read this—"

Michael once again puts his reading glasses on.

Gothic. Hannah at the center. Victim. (Or is she?) Imprisoned. (Or is she?) Three times I chose to read The Unicorn—*while still in the convent. Why? I remember talking to others about it. What did I say? How did I use it? I myself must have felt imprisoned: the strictures, the structures, early 1960s religious life. Hannah is unicorn: strange; mythical; figment of everyone's imagination; figure around whom all others spin their fantasies. Our dear Hannah is far from innocent when reality breaks through at the end. Perhaps I was imprisoned by my own fantasies. Which I, the human animal, tried year by year to brush aside. They were like gauzy curtains, those fantasies, one behind the other. Brushed aside, they fell back into place again and again. How to see clearly? Who was I? Scene in the bog: Effingham lost, alone in the dense dark night, sinking, sinking. Reaches the very verge of death, receives for a moment the blessing, gift of the Real. When Reality comes upon Effie he learns about actual love, which trumps any fantasy he ever concocted about Hannah; learns love is the automatic human response to the Real. Automatic! Gave me a kernel I kept. I take it out and roll it around in my hand today. My own death coming near. When? I have striven to see the real Wilma, the real Alma. At least those two. With limited, fractured success. Do they know? I have experienced—I do believe I have—the ecstasy—the dangerous white water ride into the Real. Moments. And then one climbs back onto shore. Classes to teach, after all. Only two more classes now, though. And then I yield. To death? To illness at least. (Headaches severe today.) Wilma, my Unicorn. Her innocence. (Or is it?). Her uncanny, even mythical Reality. How she controls my every breath. Does she know? But her innocence. Yes, I insist on that. It is my salvation.*

"So you see, Michael, I was not innocent, or possibly I was. I have read through to the end and Hannah kills also, but of me it was *asked*. Required, I might say. Alma has been reassuring on that particular point and then there is the beauty."

He's listening, aware of spikes in the flow he ought to catch hold of. The word *kills*, for example. An abortion? Wilma glances at the clock. He silently thanks her. He'd forgotten the time entirely.

"I believe I have only one more topic. I want to be certain my meaning is clear in relation to the god. 'Twice and twice and yet again, until the bright logic is won.' I believe that would be the way Hart Crane put it. A persistence is required. He was a part of my parents' youth—the poet was—by way of the priest, Steven. Though he wasn't a priest then, was he?"

Wilma pauses, seems to need to reorient herself.

He almost remembers the quote. If she doesn't have it word for word, she's very close. He wrote a paper—"Crane and Blake: the Visionary Impulse and the Refusal to Repent"—something like that. Crane was gay—that was the fascination—gay and brilliant. Also, difficult. And disturbed. Ended his life by diving off a ship. Did the bright logic elude him or was he diving into it?

Wilma is peering at him.

"I studied Hart Crane when I was in college. That phrase, bright logic—"

"Yes. I have every intention, and the results are coming, as I said, working themselves in with the rest of Stage One and daily life in general. The gusts. I appreciate that you have read my Stage One. I find the written word such an aid, and here, also, with you. 'One word is enough to lift up and purify the entire world.'" She looks at him and smiles, obviously pleased with herself, and somehow sure she's pleasing him.

"That's beautiful, Wilma."

"I decided I'd learn a bit about the Jewish version—of mysticism, you know—in honor of you and your parents. I do keep their death in mind. I believe death is too large a topic for the time remaining, but the simplicity, Michael. Yes, the simplicity. Such a comfort, if comfort is still needed. My plan is to gain as much experience of the god as I'm able to before my own death. Do you know the quote?"

"Quote?"

"Yes. One word, you know. Lifting and purifying."

Ah, so she was quoting. "I don't think I know it. Wait. Do you mean you've learned something about Hasidism?"

"An introduction only, but the essence, yes."

"The mysterious power in a single word…yes…I seem to remember —"

"Of course you do. A memorable statement."

"I'd have to go back some decades—"

"I am familiar with the way words rise up. I'm teaching myself to tolerate the phenomenon. Perhaps I'm kin to the Hasidim. A whimsical thought. I must remember whimsy. With Marlene's current absence I might have lost track of it. I see that our time is up. My father failed to enter in significantly, though there was Steven."

"Another time perhaps."

"Yes, unless a little more clarity about Lorraine. Or the self-portrait, which remains a troubling mystery. Or the god, there are still things I might—"

She's putting her books and papers into the backpack, standing up, shaking his hand, looking him in the eye, telling him she's gratified to see that his happiness has increased, and then she's gone. He sits down and breathes, exhausted and exhilarated in equal parts. An entire week between now and her next appointment. It seems excessively long.

He hears his next client enter the waiting room. The phone rings and it is Henry.

"Yes, Henry, I'd be willing to meet at Pizza Hut. The one on Broadway, good. Saturday, 5:00. Yes, I'll look forward to it. Sorry, I have to go, I have a client."

Still in town, then. Wanting to get together.

…experiences, images, facts…to pile all this back into myself…it was much too much…

257

Deep breath. Two. Three. Stand up. Greet Sarah. Sarah looks terrible.

Michael becomes a therapist again.

~ ~ ~

He stands near the doorway at Pizza Hut as customers pass by, entering, exiting. He spots Henry, who is reading a book, soda half gone. Reality beyond the book is no doubt non-existent. Seven years disappear. His heart leaps.

Damn.

He walks forward, slides into the booth, waits. Nothing. He clears his throat. Henry looks up, smiles, index finger holding his place in the book.

"Michael." No tension apparent. No wariness. Nothing but simple welcoming fondness and perhaps a good part of his mind still in the book.

In the book, where he buried himself again and again when they were together. He'd be so far away from the world of the living that burial would be the right image. He emerged, or resurrected, pressing the book to his heart. Never seemed to read what failed to thrill him. He'd scribble a sentence, a paragraph, explaining, exclaiming, with insight, with awe, with delighted bewilderment. Was ever another human so delighted by what bewildered? All the while the enticing, frustrating fence of silence.

No wonder I fell in love.

No wonder he drove me crazy.

"Good to see you, Henry. What are you reading?" Trembling inside, but only slightly.

"This? Oh. Deleuze on Nietzsche." He looks at the page number and closes the book.

"Still at it, then."

"Keeps my mind alive. I was in a section on the guilt-sin-innocence gestalt."

"A philosophical gestalt."

Henry nods, smiles.

258

Unnerving how self-possessed he seems, how mature. But youthfully mature. The shine is not gone.

"Gestalt is such a perfect word, isn't it? I love knowing you'll recognize it, dear old Michael. Not everyone would, as you know. I learned it from you, or I think I did. Still doing Gestalt Therapy?"

He hasn't been asked to categorize his work in a long time. Not that Henry means to confine him to some box, that wouldn't be Henry. In fact, the question is interesting, as were most questions he posed back then, writing them out, handing them over, listening attentively as he, Michael, fumbled for an answer, free-associated, did some real thinking, or avoided the question altogether, possibly by jumping the mime's lovely buns. They laughed a lot. They played a lot. And, in their strange way, they conversed often. It suddenly occurs to Michael for the very first time—and why has he not thought of this before?—that it was a lot like being in therapy, the bulk of speech being provided by Michael while Henry raised questions and shaped the dialogue through the power of silent attention. The questions ranged wide, but many were personal. Very personal. So, yes: a lot like therapy. Or Henry would be the student trying to pry answers from the older man, the professor; or he'd be the teacher, pointing to a paragraph and expecting his dear old Michael to understand, or at least bow down in awe-stricken appreciation of the mystery. Or he'd be the curious lover, probing the mind and heart of the beloved. Yes, he was that too. But all queries came with silence. Now he speaks. And asks a question.

"Interesting question, Henry. *Am* I still doing Gestalt Therapy? I have no idea. Everything seems to have melded into something quite basic. A lot of silent listening. But 'guilt, sin, innocence'…?"

"Preparation for seeing you. I wanted to get myself clear about the uselessness of contrition. Nietzsche's good on that. Deleuze, too. Or do you think it would help?"

So this is what it's like when the man talks. Dive right in. Oddly relaxing, really, or almost so, since he has an answer. "Contrition is not necessary. I got more than hurt, Henry. It really is good to see you."

"I don't think I realized how going mute affected others. Affected you. I know you tried to tell me."

"I suppose I tried but took back every word as soon as it got out. You know I was besotted."

He's watching himself slip into the old familiarity, amused at his confession. But it's hardly a confession. He couldn't be more transparent than he was in the past.

"I know. And then after I left, you wrote poems."

Henry produces *Keep This Deep and Velvet Night*. Michael groans. Henry laughs. Mary the waitress appears.

"Henry, love, who's your new friend?"

"Mary, Michael. Michael, Mary. Michael's an old friend. A good one."

"Not too old for me, hon'." She slides her eyes, a parody of flirting. "What can I get for you boys?"

"Pizza for two," Henry says. "Deep dish, mushrooms, black olives, Canadian bacon, Pepsi. Right, Michael?"

"Perfect, except ginger ale for me, Mary. I'm too old for caffeine after noon these days."

"Ain't we all, sweetie," says Mary, winking at her new friend and turning to fill the order.

"Sign it," Henry says, pushing the chapbook across the table.

"I don't have a pen."

"Ah, Michael. A poet without a pen?"

Henry produces a pen. So be it. But what to write? He looks at Henry, helpless.

"Tell me what to write."

"Write, 'To Henry, whom I forgive and still delight in.'"

"Damn. Maybe you were better mute."

But it comes to him and he writes. *To Henry. As Gertrude Stein would say, 'I forgive you everything and there is nothing to forgive.' Love from the old days, Michael.*

"Not sure about current delight, eh?"

"Not sure of anything. You show up—"

"That was weird, wasn't it? I certainly didn't plan it, didn't even realize. I hope Wilma's OK. I know you can't tell me."

"Right. I suppose it would have been beyond even your powers to engineer a situation like that."

"It was an unusual way for us to run into each other."

"Yes, possibly unique. So are you just passing through? What brings you to Bangor? Was it Winnie-the-Pooh?"

"You heard about that?"

"I was there."

"You were there? You were there and didn't even—?"

"I didn't know it was your show until I was seated. I was brought there by a well-meaning friend who knew not what she wrought. I ran away, but not until the very end. You were of course stunning, in more ways than one. I wasn't prepared. So, again I ask: are you just passing through?"

"No."

"Oh. Well. Does that mean you *live* here?" And what answer does he want, he asks himself as Mary appears with their order, serves them, and quietly leaves. Tactful waitress.

"I live here now. I didn't know you were in Bangor, Michael, I swear I didn't. You've been here a while, I gather. The office looks lived in. Nice off-kilter stacks of magazines. I like the selection, by the way. *Smithsonian*, *New Yorker*, *Saturday Evening Post*, *Jack and Jill*. Emblematic of your vast range as a human being. And I see you put Kandinsky's *Composition IV* in the waiting room this time. A piece to contemplate. So how long have you been in—?"

"Five years. I needed a change. Until the last couple of weeks I was wondering if I needed another, but life has perked up. Why would you decide to live here? I never expected—"

"Nor I. Something pulled. I don't know. I couldn't feel firmly planted anywhere else and I was ready to try for that. Roots, planting, something like that."

"You talk as if you grew up here."

"I did grow up here. Maybe I never said."

"One of the many things you never said. You're *from* Bangor? Unbelievable."

"Born and raised here. Right now I sleep on Dad's couch in the living room, pump gas at the station when not otherwise occupied. I expect these things to change."

So he's here. He's *here*. And that means—?

"Your dad. Hmm. I hope he isn't—"

"Drinking? Not right now. Up and down with that, but I think he likes my being back, no matter how strangely I turned out. I think it helps, at least for the moment."

261

"Well, good. I can't believe you're really here. You know, the day you gave me those pages, your 'autobiography'—well, I hope I communicated how much I—how much it—"

"You communicated."

"It was a bit sketchy, though. It told me your father was an alcoholic and your mother ran off with some guy from the circus, but failed to mention Bangor. For example."

"Well, if you knew I came from Bangor you might not be here."

"That might be right."

"So how is it that you ended up here, big city boy that you are? Or were. I certainly didn't expect—"

"Crazy, isn't it? I mean, both of us—"

"Certainly strange. What brought you here, Michael?"

"Apparently it was Fate. I thought it was Petra, though. Petra Kalinowski, friend and colleague. We ended up at professional trainings together and got to know each other—two gay therapists, which was part of the bond. Just part of it, though. At some point she started saying I needed a change and Bangor needed me. Hardly a faggot therapist in the area, said she."

"Fate in the form of Petra then. And here we are."

"Yes, here we are."

They fall silent. A bit awkward. What next?

Henry shakes his head and says, "I can't believe you were at the performance."

Good. A safe topic.

"I saw the review in the Bangor Daily. Nice, Henry. Very nice."

"It was. It's already bearing a little fruit. A couple of kids' birthdays. Bits of cash and some sweet experiences. I'm at the square across from the Grasshopper Shop most noon hours, too. Catch those pedestrians, you know. They've been kind to me. And we're working up a new show. We'll do it at Bass Park near the statue."

"In the shadow of Paul Bunyan. Very Bangor."

"Right."

"Also, a young freelance reporter happened to catch me after the performance—right here, actually—and asked if he could interview me, so we did that. He's trying to get the BDN to print it. I might be having my fifteen minutes of fame."

262

"That's great, Henry. I'll watch for the interview."

Another silence, but Henry breaks it quickly.

"So, Michael, you're reading Gertrude Stein these days."

"God, no. I'm reading John le Carré. Petra, who is also the well-meaning dunce responsible for my presence at your performance, gave me the Stein quote a few years ago. She belongs to a group called, believe it or not, Dykes Who Love Literature. They call it DWELL."

"Ooh, scrumptious. I want to join.

"I know. They've read Stein. Pretty ambitious. I find the forgiveness idea useful, personally and professionally. Apparently it's good for book-signing too."

"It's a great quote. Reminds me of Deleuze: 'Paradox is the pathos or passion of philosophy.'"

"I like that. Makes more sense than a lot of the quotes from Monsieur Deleuze you wanted me to swoon over."

"Finally, success with Deleuze. I'll try not to ruin it by quoting him again, at least not in the next ten minutes."

"Oh, quote away. I'll feel free to look blank."

"A blank look will be perfectly acceptable. You'll see. I have matured."

"Or maybe I'll understand, it's always possible. I don't remember specifics but I remember a sense of almost catching at the hem of your philosopher's trailing garments."

"You make him sound like a guru."

"He wasn't?"

"He'd throw a spitball at you for such a comment."

They look at each other, shake their heads. Here they are, after their hiatus.

"Well, Henry."

"Yes," says Henry, nodding, taking a breath.

They've done a little of the intimate and a little of the catching up. Michael looks at the younger man. He knows him so well, and knows him not at all. He feels utterly at home with him, pleased to be with him as they converse, pleased *that* they converse, but there's definitely some agitation in his own sorry innards. Not sexual agitation, just plain old nervous agitation. Does Henry feel anything similar? If so, he's a master at masking it. As ever.

263

"I'm sorry about your parents, Michael. When did they die?"

"It was about a year after you—"

"After I left you."

"I was going to say moved back to Cambridge, which we both knew was likely from the start. I was lucky to have you for three years. I hope it worked out for you there."

Henry opens the chapbook and looks again at the quote, closes the cover, puts it aside. "I loved the group, loved performing in Harvard Square, the energy, the challenge. It worked until it was time to come home. So I guess I was hard on you, Michael."

It's too sudden. Michael is not ready. He dodges, grabs at the first thing that comes to mind, watches himself do it.

"Did you know 'dunce' comes from what the followers of John Duns Scotus were called? That's another thing I learned from Petra. Apparently Duns Scotus was not everywhere adored."

"I did not know that. I gather Petra is in fact no dunce at all. So, as I was saying, I was hard on you, harder than I realized. I'm trying to start a new level of conversation here, Michael."

"I'm trying to rise to it. Give me a minute."

We know each other so well. We know each other not at all.

He reaches for *Keep This Deep and Velvet Night*. "I actually reread this, after being at your performance." He opens to the "Billy" section, while Henry, who will understand, waits.

He pushed the air
where he wished it to go
and into his eyes I fell....

Foolishly furnished with wings is he—
improbable, undeniable, white-hot wings.

---

never a word unless written on paper
with the breathing removed
and the heart cut out,
the red beating heart cut out....

He skipped away, a child.

264

I followed, running,
holding in both hands
his heart.

He looks up. *Henry.* Unbelievable.

"I've been thinking about how slanted these poems are, Henry. As I said, you brought more than hurt into my life, much more, as did my parents whose death I was apparently obsessed by when I wrote these poems. I know I focused on your being mute—and not staying with me forever—the pain—all of which was real. Your brightness is here too. I hope you noticed."

"I noticed."

"You *were* hard on me. Also, worth it. I must say this is pretty damn weird, how we're sitting here using actual spoken words."

"I know. I've been talking like a normal human, or as close as possible to that, for some years now. When did we separate? And why didn't we keep in touch?"

"It's been seven years. Why do *you* think we didn't stay in touch?"

"I'm not sure."

"Maybe we just couldn't. Or maybe I just couldn't. And you were busy, Henry.

"Maybe. That's as good an answer as any, I suppose. You've been counting the years."

"I figured it out last night. I had stopped counting. And I expect nothing."

"Liar."

"All right, I *try* to expect nothing. Or maybe I really . . . hell, I don't even know if I'd want anything now. It's a moot point. I saw you on that stage. With your narrator. With Frank."

"Well, yes."

"So that's that."

"It's new, but yes, there's Frank."

Henry looks him right in the eye. Always did know how to make good eye contact. But there was a wall, too. The muteness made a wall, but not only that. Maybe it was the charisma, maybe that was a wall, too. Which is a new thought.

"So there's Frank. Well, good luck with that."

"It's very good to see you, Michael. Exceedingly good. Stabilizing, really."

"Stabilizing. The older man, solid career, *et cetera*."

"No. The man who was so damn good to me, way beyond what I deserved. So tolerant, accepting, loving. Also sexy, generous, excellent mind—"

"Damn it, Henry."

"So I'd like to try being friends. Seven years, after all, Michael."

"What?"

"You heard me."

"I heard you. Friends? Ongoing? I don't know. I thought this would be a nice little one-time chat."

"You thought no such thing."

"Well, I prepared myself. Damn. I don't know, Henry. Talk to me about something else. Talk about being mute, and then not being mute."

"You need a change of topic."

"I need a change of topic."

"I caught you off guard."

"Yes, you did. But talking about muteness is hardly just a delaying tactic. What was that, really? Not that it wasn't fascinating, it was. But a hell of a challenge to live with."

"I know that now."

"Good. So."

"I'm not sure how to—not sure I can—"

Silence.

His old theory might be a place to start. "I used to think maybe you were doing something like Method actors, living the role 24/7."

"Only some Method actors do that, but, yes, I suppose that's not too far off."

"But an actor's role ends, Henry. The play ends, the movie gets finished, the actor goes back to real life."

"Right. So I was doing something different."

"Care to share?"

"Will you listen?"

"And not scoff, you mean."

"That, and try not to bristle."

"I'm already bristling."

266

"I can see that. And I'm already cautious."

"I know, Henry. My fault. But we can do this. I need to hear something."

Henry reaches across the table and puts both hands around Michael's right hand which has been just sitting there. Like a sitting duck. Did he want this? Out of the corner of his eye he sees Mary the excellent waitress decide not to turn abruptly away. She was on her way to their table and it would have been worse to pretend otherwise. This entire dynamic he perceives instantly, and he loves her for it, but, damn, here he is with his hand being held by a man.

"She's cool, Michael."

"I'm cool, Michael. My son's a sweet little gay boy. Just moved in with his first boyfriend, or the first I know of. Anything more I can get you two?"

"We're good, Mary, thanks," Henry says.

"Nothing wrong with the pizza?"

Which question leads them to look at their untouched pizza.

"Always did prefer it cold, Mary," Michael says, straight-faced.

"Ah, a man of discriminating taste," says Mary with matching expression. "Good. We like our customers to come in at a cut above the common. Let me know if—"

And she's gone.

Henry Magic. That's what he used to call it. Wherever Henry goes, whatever he does, he gets away with it.

"So, Henry, what was being mute all about for you?"

Their hands separate as they both lean back. Henry nods, looks as if he will speak. Then, to their apparently mutual surprise, they both reach for the pizza. And laugh. And declare that they can do it, they will do it, they certainly will get to the heart of Henry's prolonged and extreme experiment with muteness, but they really must have some nourishment.

~ ~ ~

Michael is standing in his living room looking out the window at the spreading pink drama of sunset and the two small children—they are Suzy and Joshua—who are running in circles on their front lawn across the street. They run and giggle until they hold their bellies and fall into

267

happy aching balls of small humanity while their mother, Janie Sue, sits on the step and smokes a cigarette. Her brand is Winston. He hopes it tastes good like a cigarette should, though how a cigarette can taste good he knows not. He never smoked. Matter of luck, not virtue. The man in the family is Richard and he too sometimes sits on the front step and smokes and watches the kids go wild at sunset, but he's away on a long run. Truck driver, good man. Janie Sue knows she can call on Michael if she needs something. She doesn't do it, but she was grateful when he made the offer. He knows he can call on her and Richard. He doesn't do it, but he could. He's not alone on this little patch of earth.

He and Henry made a plan to meet again at Pizza Hut in a couple of weeks. More cold pizza most likely. They weren't finished.

"We'll just have to do this again," said Henry.

"I suppose Frank knows we're meeting, and who I am," said Michael.

"He knows and he's fine with it. Stop fussing. I'm a free man, I get to spend time with my old lovers."

"Old lovers? How many are there in Bangor?"

"Well, just the one."

And once again Henry captured his hand and squeezed it. They paid, leaving generous tips for Mary who saluted them as they walked out. Frank was waiting beside his car. Michael, with laudable sincerity, wished them a good evening and headed home.

His own evening looms. He doesn't feel like watching television. He doesn't feel like reading, not even le Carré. He wanders, pours a beer, sips, turns on some lights, wanders some more, and finds himself standing at the couch looking at Werefkin's *Rag-and-Bone Man*. He stays there, letting art do its mute work as it enters his slightly bewildered wide-open psyche.

Flat calm dark lake, sunset-tinted. Tame dark hills at the lake's edge. Wind-driven waves beyond the hills, huge elemental uprisings from an unseen body of water. Clouds that threaten like dark claws.

A swath of gold in the sky—energetic gold between waves and clouds—insists there will be no storm, at least not yet.

There are humans in this painting, sketched-in, almost incidentally present: the rag-and-bone man; his skeletal customer; and a lone, nearly

268

invisible figure of no discernible gender in a tiny boat out on the lake, oars in motion.

Michael stands looking for a long time. Stirred-up bits of his own most elemental self co-exist these days with something so undisturbed he hardly recognizes it. On a calm lake a barely-known part of himself quietly rows along in a small steady boat, wondering at the forces around. Henry is first among those forces.

Going mute was an experiment, Henry said, an experiment inspired by theorists of the theater, theorists of language. Antonin Artaud, Jacques Derrida, Gilles Deleuze. It was all about language, really. Henry was this poor kid from Bangor and his guidance counselor managed to get him into college on scholarship in the great city of Boston because he was good with words. "Full scholarship—a *miracle*, Michael, such a *privilege*." Henry loved language, it was the most deeply human awe-inspiring mystery, but the theorists said it was over-used, worn-out. He found mime, which meant gesture. Gesture, said Artaud, could become the materialization of speech. He had felt called—it had the force of vocation, almost religious, though of course he wasn't religious, Michael knew that—called to this work that wanted to restore the force of language by limiting speech. Had Michael ever thought about the speech of silent dreams? The power of silence? He believed being mute made him more present in relationship. "*More* present, not less. With you, Michael. With everyone." But, yes, he could see it now, he *had* been living inside a box of ideas, a glass box, yes, living apart from normal connection, there *was* that. "Still, Michael, look at your own last poem."

Together they looked at the poem. The night in the square. Henry stripping naked, inserting the knife, extracting his heart.

"My *heart*. And I gave it to you."

"Yes, but by then you knew you were leaving."

"I know, Michael, I know."

It was shortly after the night in the square that Henry left to join the mime collective in Cambridge. No, the others weren't delighted with his experiment, they talked when not performing and wanted him to talk. But he kept it up when he could for a few years. It had somehow separated the deepest layers in him from the busy mind, kept them lively.

Michael looks at Werefkin's painting where the wildest parts of the scene are separated from the deep calm lake with its little boat and its

269

nearly invisible human. Separated, but composing one scene. He sips his beer and shakes his head and smiles, tenderness welling.

They will see if they can manage as friends—friends who were once lovers, one of whom was crazily in love with a younger man, the other of whom was also crazily in love, but with ideas. Henry's mind, his entire being had been filled to bursting with Deleuze, Derrida, Artaud, others. He adored the sex, Michael was such a sweet lover, he *liked* Michael so much, Michael was wonderful, and so generous, financially as well as in *all* other ways. "But falling in love with a human being, Michael, it just wasn't…"

When they were together there were lines of force going every which way, they agreed—love and creativity and thought and power—conjunctions and collisions—balances and imbalances. Sitting in the booth with their pizza finally eaten, they put it all into language.

It was good, very good, but also just a tad over-stimulating. It will take a while put it all in place. It seems the art might help. He salutes the rag-and-bone man and his customer and the solitary figure out in the boat and sits down on the couch and slowly drinks his beer, giving a nod to the old candlemaker.

Beer finished, he gets up and goes to the kitchen where there is yet another Werefkin. This one is titled *Anthill*. Bright, cheerful, windy scene, rural folk at work, harvesting. There might be a storm coming, but not soon, and it will not devastate. Red-orange dominates. Even the horses in the distance are red-orange, as is the load of hay in the cart. The horses wait. The humans work. They are not overwhelmed with thoughts and feelings, they are living in their bodies, aiming to accomplish all they can before the sun finally sets. He loves this painting.

Yes, the art will help, but a friend will, too. He goes to the phone and calls Petra. Might she be able to meet for coffee some time tomorrow? He's fine, it's just that he has a load of life to spill and she's the best catcher of such. Good, good. Thanks, Petra.

He sits back down on the couch, second beer in hand, eyes on *Der Kramer*.

He drinks the beer, slowly.

He gets a third beer, then a fourth.

So, Herr Candlemaker, let us converse. I must say you are one beautiful old man. A face like that, you've had your loves. No longer,

270

though, right? So here we are, you and I, after the fact. The fact of the falling. The falling and the flying. Let me enumerate. One, two. That's my total: two loves. Only one for you? Life-long, you say? Good for you. She's passed on but you still communicate in your own way? Good, good. Well, I had my two. Ken, Henry. One, two. When Henry—you know about Henry, I've been pondering him in your presence with some regularity—when Henry asked today if I'd heard from Ken the air wavered and there he was, Ken, long gone but resurrected, as if back from the dead, though as far as I know he's not dead. Oddest thing. I had both of them right there with me. Cozy, it was, the three of us chomping our pizza. Or maybe Ken abstained. Being nonmaterial, he must have. Called him Stanley in the poem. Used to write poems. Not any more. Why not? Petra read the chapbook, said I progressed in it from defended heart to available heart. Progressed beautifully, said Petra. Inserts praise as needed, does my friend Petra. I had my own assessment when I was in the middle of the project, less praiseful. Went like this: *Too many poems with a bitter twist hung on the edge of the glass. Drink the drink down and move on.* Didn't put it in the book. Good thing.

Which has zilch to do with now.

I was telling you about Ken. First love. Six years, off and on. Dear Ken. Nurse by profession, saint by character. I lost him to AIDS. No, not that way. Lost him to the work. He nursed the dying and they consumed him. Escaped the virus himself, at least as far as I know. Three of us, Ken, Henry, Michael, escapees all, small miracle. Nurse Ken had a predilection for those *in extremis*, kept falling in love with them, then off they went to another realm and back to me he came. Periodic departures didn't mean he wasn't still in love with me, the man simply had an expansive organ. By which I mean his heart. It beat strong. Or strongly. I heard it, felt it.

My besotted head
I laid upon on his chest.
To strongly beating heart
I can thus now attest.

Michael Chaim Solomon, acclaimed poet. What? You're right. Sorry. I am indeed speaking of serious matters. Yes, my own heart, a serious lump of matter indeed. Tends toward the besotted state. That's the

271

topic. My heart, not Ken's, not Henry's. But back to Ken for a moment, a story begun begs for an end. His heart wore out from overuse, or at least felt the need to shift gears. Automotive metaphors lately. Did you notice my tire leaking? Slow leak, long time at it. I think maybe it's patched.

But Ken. Six years he slaved, and the epidemic still going strong. *I can't go on, Michael, I just can't.* Disappointed in himself. Sense of failed sainthood, I suppose. Right then his own first love called. I mean that exact moment. I can't go on, Michael, says Ken, and the phone rings. First love, name of Ernest, whose wife had died. Could Ken come to Sioux Falls? Big house, plenty of room. Poor old Ernie was too, too dreadfully alone. Maybe Ken could stay for a week or two? Ken went and stayed. Still there, as far as I know.

"No, Henry," said I today, "Ken and I haven't been in touch, not for years."

Hear that? Clock striking midnight, new day coming. I shall see Petra, pour a load of life upon her head. But back to the automotive metaphor. The leak of the tire, which is the heart, has apparently been patched. Furthermore, the tire, which is the heart, has apparently been pumped up again, because, look at me, old man, am I not doing just fine? Henry's heart, however, I learn today, is vulnerable. Nothing a repair person can fix. My dear Henry has, as they say, a heart condition, which could kill him. But that is statistically unlikely, and I shall therefore refrain from dwelling on the matter.

If possible.

Henry himself thinks about death quite a bit.

"Yes, quite a bit, Michael," said he, smiling apologetically.

Death seems so *interesting* to him. The exact word he used, interesting. So now I have Wilma and I have Henry and neither will admit to trepidation about death. What about you, Herr Candlemaker? Ah, same thing, natural phenomenon, to be expected, *et cetera.* Well, then, I'm surrounded.

Wilma, by the way, tugs at my mind. Or Henry's tone when speaking of Wilma tugs. Not that he said much, just that he feels remiss, dropping her off at the office like that and leaving her, and he hopes she's all right. Something in his tone, as if he knew her. I didn't attend at the time. He might have meant he knows her and feels responsible for her, regrets how busy he's been, hasn't checked in on her. Well, I might be going beyond. He didn't say all of that. Would it make a difference? Clinically, I mean. If he knew Wilma? My old lover and my new client? But I'll save that for Gertrude.

On marches time. Entering the wee hours soon. Must stop. You see, dear old man, how I'm letting them run through my mind, all the little matters of the heart, a bit like Suzy and Joshua running wild in the sunset, asleep now, I hope, so that Janie Sue can have her final cigarette, or maybe she's sleeping herself, phone nearby in case Richard calls. Sometimes he does that in the middle of the night, needing her. Matters of the heart. Mine and those of others. No conclusions necessary. You and I, we've had the privilege. Of having loved. That was my point. And you're right, I really ought to go to bed. Thanks, old man.

~ ~ ~

He didn't exactly go to bed. He slept on the couch, couldn't leave his confidante. The candlemaker would have been fine on his own, but he, Michael, needed the company, the equanimity, the fellow unafraid of death, of loneliness. Sometimes four beers will turn on a person. Sometimes life will.

So he slept on the couch under the kind eye of *Der Kramer*. Slept like the dead, as they say, though it's doubtful the dead get much sleep. Waking now, he contemplates his murky head and stiff body. Might take a while to become human. Or perhaps he's all too human already.

Human, All Too Human. He's read his bits of Nietzsche. Nowhere near the *Übermensch* this morning. He yawns and stretches. Nice long comfortable couch.

Couch, Albion.

Chains of association. Fine way to start the day.

Albion, William Blake's quintessential human. Poor guy dreams his nine-night dream on a "rocky" couch—couldn't have been comfortable.

Couch around which beat "the seas of time and space." Different scale from here and now.

Or is it?

Ah, that poem! *The Four Zoas*. Impossibly long, muscular, slippery, ever-shifting, heart-wrenching, mind-stretching, dream poem. Wrote his thesis on it. Senior in college, big Blake expert. Bold, and so young. Bold

273

because so young. Hubris. Sort of sweet, though. Been years since he's read the old visionary. So glad he studied literature before turning to psychology. Good for the soul. Any kind of art is. Would Blake and Herr Kramer get along? Interesting conversation, that. Maybe they're having it right now. Fiery poet and calm candlemaker, two bright souls.

Brightness of soul. Appealing concept. Henry has it. Does Wilma? Indeed she does.

Did I dream about Wilma? Maybe. What's that woman doing in therapy? A bit quirky, but no quirkier than Blake. Of course many thought him mad. I didn't. Feels wrong, taking Wilma's copay. Haven't submitted the paperwork for Medicare. Usually so prompt, get it done, get paid a bit sooner. Can't diagnose her, is the problem. No problem is the problem. Must talk to Gertrude about her again. And to Petra about Henry.

And to myself about—

What?

Blake painted a portrait of Albion. Not the frozen couch-caught disastrously divided fellow sleeping and dreaming his monumental dream. No, this was the luminous version, naked, lovely, youthful, arms flung, sweetness embodied, displaying himself before all creation. Must have been before the fall, the division, self against self. Before he got stuck on his couch. Or after. Dreamed himself back to sweet unity, didn't he? Came through. Good for you, Albion. Kudos!

Enough. Up, Michael.

He gets up, stretches, arms reaching wide as sweet Albion's, performs his morning ablutions, feels pretty good, makes coffee and toast, wanders into the bedroom, sipping and chewing, and stands before Soutine's *Mad Woman*.

So, my mad dear, how are you this morning? Same as always, eh? Shall I tell you about Wilma? My suspicion: you're no madder than she is. The two of you would get along charmingly. Think she's diagnosable? And what about my being in love with her? Crazy, but after flippantly telling Gertrude I fell in love with Wilma, I've been wondering what truth there might be in it, and not just for me. In love, we say, as if it's a place to occupy. A boat, for example. Are the two of us in the same boat? Wilma and Michael, floating in a boat of love? Or rowing along. That would be it. Nothing to do with sex. Not on her part, not on mine.

274

Nothing erotic at all unless eros means life energy. Good thing, life energy. I have more lately. You noticed? Well, maybe you didn't. I do think she came in a dream last night. Don't ask for details. Wait. Yes. She came, she sat, she looked at me. That's all. No words. There she was. So pleasant, just to sit with her, be seen by her. What thinkest thou, sitting in your red dress, with your green elf hat, and with those eyes?

I quite sincerely do not believe we're talking transference and countertransference when we speak of Wilma. Never mind the professional language, just listen for a minute. Feels like some *transparent* version of love. Pure water. Stream under sunlight, deep cold well, that sort of thing.

But what is love? Such a question. Still, what is it?

Life energies roused?

Passionate well-wishing?

Joy in the sheer existence of the other?

No opinions this morning? I blame you not. I suspect Petra will have some. Not about Wilma, though, we won't talk about her. Technically, I could. Professionals consulting, it's allowed. But, no. Save Wilma for Gertrude. And for you, of course. One of these days you might speak. I don't for a minute think you're mad. Peculiar, my dear, but not mad. You might actually grok Wilma's brain. Yes, you might indeed. Grok. Word from the past. Would I enjoy *Stranger in a Strange Land* now? Odd, how the old writers are coming back to me. But there might be something in that: Wilma as stranger in a strange land. Think ye so? Could be. Farewell for now, my dear. Time to go and pour my load of life upon the head of friend Petra.

~ ~ ~

Sitting with Petra and coffee and a doughnut, Michael feels content. No, more than that. He feels happy. Sunday morning murmur all around, nothing bothersome. They avoided the Bagel Shop where they often meet. Too popular on Sundays. They need a booth they can inhabit indefinitely with no qualm of conscience and an atmosphere quiet enough for real conversation. That's what a decent mediocre chain is for and that's where they are. The place is busy, but not overly so. They can sit here forever.

275

"So, Michael, a load of life to spill."

"Right. But tell me how you are first."

"I'm fine. My whole life is fine. Nat's feeling better, recovering right on schedule. Sephie and I have good times. Danny and Raymond are steady and wonderful. My clients are humdrum, surprising, stubborn, creative, infuriating, inspiring, as always. My writing is strange and intriguing. Dykes Who Love Literature still has vital meetings after all these years. I'm a lucky woman. Speak, Michael."

"What a fine and complete report. As for me, hmm, where to start? I've already had some conversations with my painted people."

"Your painted people."

"The old candlemaker and the mad woman."

"Ah, yes. Good confidantes."

"A little on the quiet side, though."

"I suppose."

"You might have noticed a shift in my energies."

"I've noticed. You were different at the party. Lack of the huddled-in syndrome. You look good today, too. Beautiful, I'd almost say. So, yes, I'm noticing. What's up?"

"I am, I guess. Up in mood, but more than that. I hadn't thought about it this way, but *I* am up. The I. The self. Right up front, can't be ignored, topic of the hour. Really, I hadn't thought about it this way. Things have happened, I'll tell you about them, but I do believe there's something about myself, almost separate from events. You're right about what you saw at the party. You exceed the usefulness of the painted ones already."

"How nice. Keep going."

"At some point within the past year or two, as you know, I started to lose energy—gradually, like a tire with a slow leak—that's how I've been thinking of it."

"Good image. Accurate."

"On my birthday several things happened. A habitually boring client turned fascinating, a new client intrigued, an old lover showed up, and I was given a surprise birthday party. Also, to top it all off, the party failed to annoy me."

"Nice list. I notice you tucked the old lover in as if he—I assume it was a he—was just one item along with the others."

276

"He, yes. He's major, and we'll get to him. But about the leaky tire you've been putting up with—"

"Yes, I have. All of us have. Not easy to watch."

"I know. I think that day, my birthday as it happened, the tire got patched."

"And somehow got itself inflated?"

"Yes."

"And it's a strong patch?"

"Seems to be holding."

"And the pounds of pressure are at a good level?"

"Well, they're not decreasing. There have been moments when I've felt them increase, almost too much."

"Danger of bursting."

"Not quite, but—"

"That's when you called me."

"That's when I called you."

"To release a bit, get back to proper poundage."

"I love you, Petra."

"I love you, too, Michael. Are you going to tell me about this lover —whose identity I think I know, of course, based on how strange you were at the mime show—and tell me also about your upsurge in selfhood?"

"I am. I think I am."

"Start with the lover, please."

"You're right. The mime was my lover. Henry. We were together in New York for three years. He left me, moved to Cambridge to join a mime troupe. That was seven years ago. I know I shut down after the performance and probably squirmed or shrank or otherwise turned strange during it. I know you saw. I should have talked then. I wasn't ready."

"It's OK, Michael. I knew the time would come."

"Later in the week Henry ended up in my office, standing with the intriguing new client."

"I love it that you have an intriguing new client."

"Yes. That's a whole story on its own, but we're not here for clinical consultation."

"No, we're here for personal disclosure, gossip, and friendship."

277

"Right. So Henry shows up in my office. Totally unexpected state of affairs for both of us. He was doing a good deed, the woman seemed to need help and he entered in. I think that's how it went."

"Good person, then. Well, I could tell. Good mime, too. Not that I know mime, but Sephie tells me he's amazing."

"He is. A very good person. And a very good mime. And amazing."

"And you still love him."

"In some way, yes."

"And we might try to figure out what that way is?"

"We might, but time and life will probably have to do most of that. *Time. Life.* Makes me think of the magazines. I sold subscriptions to my parents and their friends every year, raising money for the school. Did you do that?"

"Girl Scout cookies is what I remember."

"Those magazines. Always there on the coffee table, windows to the world. What a reader I was, even as a kid. I've been doing a lot of free associating. And thinking about things I read in the past. Reading might matter, part of this current gestalt. Art, too. But back to Henry. He grew up in Bangor. I didn't know that until yesterday."

"You were with him for three years and didn't know where he grew up?"

"It was an unusual relationship."

"Well, right. The mute mime, as portrayed in the poems."

"Yes. The point is that he's back to stay and he wants us to be friends. Just friends. He has a new lover, Frank, the narrator at Sunday's performance."

"Oh, Michael. After seven years, out of the blue. But you didn't learn about a new lover in the waiting room with a prospective client standing there—"

"Henry and I had pizza yesterday."

"And conversation?"

"He talks now. Beautifully."

"Of course."

"I look back and it seems far weirder than it felt, how he didn't talk. You know how it is when you're inside something."

"Did *you* talk?"

"I talked. He's a great listener."

278

"Could be considered a luxury, I suppose. Listen for a living and then come home to silence. You did live together?"

"We did."

"Sounds sort of restful when not infuriating. Do you like him, talking? Well, of course you do. I can see it. Stupid question."

"I like him, talking or not. But I don't know what to do with him. Or with me."

"Right. That's part of why we're here."

"Part of it. He and I are having pizza again in a couple of weeks."

"So you're in the middle of a process."

"Yes. And I'll have tolerate not knowing where it will lead for a while."

"Which is life."

"Which is life. In fact, I might not have a lot to say right now about him."

"OK."

"I needed you to know."

"Good. But is it related to everything else? This matter of your self? And there's the reading from the past, and something about art. I'd better have more coffee."

The waitress comes, both cups are filled, and Michael talks. As he talks, as Petra listens, as they laugh and squabble and concur and add to and subtract from each other's thought, things start to clarify. It all has to do with time, how the past is surging into the present, how the future is impatient for its assignment since there will be no forever, at least not in this, Michael's one short life. And it has to do with self, what Petra describes as a glowing coal at the center and then says is his heart.

"That's you, Michael. Heart at the center. Basic. You have a wonderful mind but it's your heart—"

Which baffles him. Isn't it everyone's basic—?

"No, Michael. Listen. For some people it's more mind, for some it's body. For you it's heart. Your chi, your essential life energy, is all about heart. It's powerful, nothing soppy about it. You have a huge capacity to be moved to love. Nothing to do with needing to hop into bed with Henry or anyone else, though that might be side effect, and a sweet one."

"Sweet."

"Yes."

"Henry said I was a sweet lover."

"How good of him to say it."

"Yes."

"You want to be friends with him."

"I do?"

"You do."

"You're right. I do."

"Well, good. That's settled. What else do you want?"

"Do you work this quickly with your clients?"

"Would that I could. I'm bolder with my friends. And pushier. As you will be with me, please, when my own existential questions raise their interesting heads. What else do you want?"

"It's the right question, isn't it? What do I want?"

"I'm thinking about your reading, what you said about reading from the past—"

"This morning, for the first time in decades, I thought about Blake."

"Wonderful. Tell me about Blake. Should I read him? I haven't, not since college. Little lambs and fearsome tigers—"

"But when you really get into him—I did a study, for my thesis in college—when you really get into him, there's so much. Do you know about his prophetic works?"

"Rings the vaguest bell. I know I never read them. I seem to remember one professor who dared us to. I didn't take her up on it. Long time ago, Michael."

"Just as long for me, but suddenly vivid."

"Along with your suddenly vivid self."

"You are *much* better than my painted people. So I did this study, even got a grant."

"As an undergraduate?"

"Impressive, isn't it? Enough money to pay ten students a hundred dollars each to read *The Four Zoas*. I wanted avid readers, up for a challenge. Wanted their entire beings, really—as experienced through reading. I was asking for a lot. All of them grew up poor, the money meant something—a hundred dollars was more back then. Still, they must have made about ten cents an hour. They were amazing. They kept journals. Faithfully, though not without complaining. And I interviewed them. The whole focus was on the reading experience. What would it be like for students from different disciplines—there were a couple of budding scientists, even one business major—to read this insanely long, wonderfully difficult *poem*. So much happened to me when I read Blake —so much—you're right, I suppose, when you say I have that capacity— how did you put it?"

"The capacity to be moved to love."

"Right. I was moved to love when I read Blake. I wanted to know what happened to other readers, was it anything like what happened to me? Reading was *real* for me—"

He has to stop.

"Oh, Michael. I don't think I've ever seen you—"

"Do you have a tissue?"

"Oh. Sorry. Yes. Here—"

"I'm crying over reading?"

"Must go deep for you."

He wipes his eyes.

"I used to play the harmonica."

"Same thing?"

"It's all connected. I lost—"

"You're finding."

He blows his nose. Petra hands him another tissue. He blows more, takes a breath. "I've been loving my painted people, too. Really loving them. Henry loves his life as a mime, he's very intense about it. Philosophy, too. This morning I was thinking about brightness of soul."

"Nice phrase."

"I like it. I was thinking about Blake, and then Henry. You should hear him. He reads this guy, Deleuze—"

"Deleuze?"

"Twentieth century French philosopher. He was reading something by Deleuze on Nietzsche at Pizza Hut—sitting there reading, waiting for me. Later he pulled out another Deleuze, something about Spinoza as Expressionist. We must have been talking about art. He carries these books around. My new client brought a book by Spinoza to her session. She brought a backpack full of books."

"Synchronicity—"

"Right. Who carries books around like that? And then Spinoza, both of them. It's a bit much to ignore. Have you read Spinoza?"

"My father was devoted to him, said I had to read him. I tried. Every once in a while a sentence, even a whole paragraph would light up, but —"

"Takes a mind like Henry's."

"His heart is in his mind?"

"Yes, maybe so. But in his body, too. Do I have your permission to dare to want him in my life again?"

"Absolutely. Would you like that in writing?"

"Oh, that won't be necessary. Thanks anyway."

"Most welcome."

"This is helping, Petra."

"Good. I didn't know you played the harmonica."

"Long ago."

"Should you—?"

"Now? I was never as good as Danny."

"Danny never abandoned it. Wasn't he wonderful on your birthday? I loved how proud he was of his cake."

"Me, too. He might give me some tips, if I—"

"Do you still have a harmonica?"

"Somewhere. I think if it's not played for a long time there's some process for bringing it back to life."

"Like you."

"Like me.

"Danny would know. Ask him."

"I'm no musician."

"There's something about art in here, though. Do you still write at all? Secret poems?"

"I haven't done anything since I published the chapbook. I think I was so astonished to have this little book—it was beyond what I expected of myself—and I'd satisfied the current need, what I needed to write about, with those poems—"

"You just stopped?"

"I just stopped. Same with the harmonica. And now—you're making me think—I might need to start again—music, writing, something— might want to—"

"You have it, Michael. Brightness of soul."

"I don't know. Tarnished over the years."

282

"Well, all of us—"

"I know, but this—whatever's happening—is forcing me to—you were right, I suppose, about existential questions."

"I have to go soon, but tell me more about Blake, about his *Four Zoas*. Seems important."

"It feels important, though I can't quite see how. I remember I had to read parts of it over and over. Well, I wanted to. Every time I'd reread a passage it would be new, different. The whole poem kept shifting and shifting. And the thing itself—the plot, if there is such a thing, and the characters, if that's what they are—a bundle of metamorphoses. There's this primeval man, this Eternal Man, Albion, and the story is essentially about his cataclysmic Fall. Before the story starts he's been living in blissful harmony with himself, but he breaks into warring parts—because of sexual Jealousy, actually—Jealousy with a capital J—intellect against emotions against sensation, *et cetera*—but that makes it sound simple—as the struggle goes on and on the parts emanate more parts—and the emanated parts themselves divide—you end up with this massive cast of characters. Some of them seem like real human characters and some are anything but—shadows and specters and a humongous serpent—and all these pieces of the former whole keep changing into each other, doing and suffering violence in the most impressive ways, then seeking each other out again—it's crazy. And glorious. The whole thing is a dream, Albion's dream. I remember the moment I got that—that it's a *dream*. It's obvious, Blake *says* it, but it's impossible to remember because the characters are so active and real and the drama is so intense. Time goes back and forth and sideways.Things appear and reappear, overlapping and mirroring each other. There will be a slight movement, like a torque, and the whole pattern shifts, as if Blake gave a little twist to his wrist—"

"Like a kaleidoscope—"

"*Yes*. All these pieces, and the design changes, and if you can hold it up to the light—good image, Petra—you see all these different patterns, or versions—beautiful, different, and yet made of the same—"

"Sounds wonderful."

"And then in the end it—the poem, the dream, the story—it all comes down to a lovely, innocent, rural scene of redemption—seed planting, plowing, harvesting, the wonders of nature, everybody getting along—"

283

"Reminds me of my work with multiple personality clients."

"Really? How interesting. I've never happened to—at least not that I know of—"

"Not only the sense of multiplicity, the shifting, the overlapping, the inconsistencies, but also the intensity—you exude such intensity, such energy, as you talk—"

"That's Blake."

"And you, today, Michael."

"Well, yes. You said you have to go. I hope I haven't kept you—"

"No, no, it's fine. Nat said she'd like to go for a walk later—part of her recovery plan—but we have time—"

"This is enough—plenty—a cornucopia which I shall take home and dump on the table and see what it's all been, which image my suddenly vital formerly boring client used, giving it his own twist—which I must think about. Thank you, Petra—very, very much."

"Of course. It's been great. I hereby welcome you back, Michael."

When he gets home he looks for his harmonica. It takes more than an hour, but he locates it. Wonderful, how it feels in his hand. He blows a tentative note, then a few more. He remembers: needs to be soaked in water, he'll have to ask Danny about the exact procedure. And he'll have to take it bit by bit, get his lips into shape.

He thinks of Wilma. A humming relationship. Yes.

~ ~ ~

Michael wakes up, stretches, sits on the edge of his bed. It is Thursday, suddenly his favorite day of the week.

Who will Bob Smith be? What will Wilma do?

He actually has two Wilmas: client Wilma and dream Wilma. Again last night she came and sat down and looked at him for a long time. Minutes, hours, days. Such knowing fondness. His heart expanded and soared and was dancing in the sky. Two hearts, his and hers, hearts that were also minds and souls, dancing in the sky. Dancing turned to swimming. They were swimming, like innocent Joseph Marti, but in soft air instead of Joseph's wet, clean, benevolent element. Wilma and Michael, two hearts, two souls, two bodies, swimming through the ether, farther, farther, farther, all the way to Zarathustra. Zarathustra singing

284

and dancing in space. Zarathustra welcoming them with arms wide-spread like Albion's. Embrace of eros. Eros beyond body, eros of the spirit. Strange to themselves and familiar, two passionate beings, embodied, buoyant. Wilma and Michael. Then: bump, bump, bump—like Winnie-the-Pooh being pulled down a soft set of stairs behind Christopher Robin—two humans with hearts in place.

Bump.

And they were back on earth. Happy, unhurt.

He sits on the edge of the bed and calls it all back and laughs out loud and and gives a nod to Modigliani's *Chaim Soutine* at the head of his bed and a nod and a wink to Soutine's *Mad Woman* beyond the foot of the bed. He gets up and starts his day, rubbing his hands together, anticipating Bob and Wilma and today's other clients—for the others have also become magically more vital. First, though, Bob, early this morning, some urgency upon him. Michael feels a great need, a swelling-of-the-heart need, to see what's up with Bob.

~ ~ ~

Bob arrives. Excessive courtesy, stiff manner. The art critic speaks, seems determined to fill the session with theory, the move from Impressionism—"painted the world as seen through the human lens, the fleeting incompleteness, but still it was a world"—to Expressionism —"and the world barely matters, it is the soul, the human soul with its surges of emotion, its hidden powers, expressed through the world…"

Professional passion, that paradox: bubbling, boiling passion, with the lid locked down. Michael is fascinated and disturbed in equal parts.

The art critic continues, quoting Wassily Kandinsky: "Color is a power which directly influences the soul."

He stops.

Silence.

Michael waits, reminds himself to breathe.

Another quote from Kandinsky, but delivered differently, almost shyly. "'Everything starts from a dot.'"

Bob closes his eyes, seems on the verge of revealing his own dot, his own everything.

But, no.

285

"I let the Expressionists do my expressing for me," says Bob, suddenly sardonic, cynical, distanced, challenging.

More silence.

The man holds Robert Walser's *The Robber* in one tense hand, bookmarks bristling, while a briefcase—there has never been a briefcase before today—sits in front of his feet, as if blocking his exit.

The silence extends. Michael watches and waits.

"Werefkin, for instance." This is unassuming Bob, familiar Bob, voice muffled, almost whispering. Michael has to call back the last thing he said. He lets the Expressionists do his expressing. Werefkin, for instance.

Well, good. Use it.

"Would you come and stand with me before one of hers, Bob?"

His client eyes him, changed again: suspicious, sophisticated.

"Which one?"

"Either one," Michael says, barely breathing.

"Can't do *The Large Moon*. Death in the offing there. Not today. Some day."

"No problem. I see what you mean."

"No, you don't."

"You're right. I don't. I can see death hovering over the scene, an interpretation I can go with, but what you see is yours. I can't know what you see, what it might mean to you.

"Correct."

They are almost sparring. Who is this man?

Bob bends and moves the briefcase and gets up and walks across the room. Michael follows. They stand together before *Stadt in Litauen*, *City in Lithuania*, two men entering the work of a woman painter. An old peasant woman clothed in black from head to toe makes her way along a blue-white road toward a distant city. Night is coming on but the city is lit, beckoning, almost insisting. The woman's journey is uphill. The blue-white road is probably only snow-covered but it has the look of a river rushing downward, a force moving against the direction she travels. The bare, bent roadside trees, though, lean toward the city, uphill. They are joining the traveler as she takes step after difficult step, living beings, forces, assisting an old woman in her long journey—her long physical journey, which is *also spiritual*. Michael is gripped by an eerie intuition:

286

that he is entering Bob's experience, that this is possible, that this is happening. Neither man speaks.

Michael feels something touch his cheek, the whisper of a kiss, a mere peck.

What?

He glances sideways. A kiss? He feels almost hypnotized. Could he have imagined such a thing? But Bob is unchanged. Bob is sunk into the painting. He is the woman walking, walking, walking. He has been walking for years up this road to the shining city in the distance.

Bob turns away from the painting, walks back to the couch, sits. He places his briefcase again in front of his shoes. The shoes are set firmly on the floor in tight parallel with each other. Bob is good schoolboy, sitting with his schoolboy briefcase, looking up as Michael takes his place. Bob is a child, waiting for direction.

"Powerful," Michael says.

"Always," whispers Bob.

"I suppose we all have our distant cities, our roads to walk."

Bob seems to nod. Or he is paralyzed and could not possibly have nodded.

They sit together, two men. Or a man and a child.

Time passes.

They continue to sit, both of them, waiting to see what happens next. Two men, definitely two men now. Michael takes some deep breaths. He feels peaceful. He is just a therapist sitting with a client. This is his work.

"I had a dream last night," says Bob Smith.

Michael nods, ready.

"It goes back to my first Walser, the one you leant to me. I have my own copy now. When *The Robber* is too much for me, I return to Joseph Marti. I might have spoken of this dream already. I suppose it's a nightmare. I'm not sure of that."

Bob pauses. Michael doesn't think Bob has ever before mentioned a dream.

"Joseph's worst dream, pages fifty-six through fifty-eight, seems to have become my own. Recurring. Three times, I believe. One ought to pay attention. Our time today is almost up, I see that, but another day we might take a closer look. You and I. As part of the treatment. 'He tried to

287

get up to escape from the locus of shame but he was stuck fast in it.' At that point Joseph wakes up. We both do. I am to give you this, Michael."

Business-like Bob, picks up the briefcase, opens it, hands Michael a manila envelope along with his check, and leaves.

Michael closes the office door behind him and stands, hand on the knob, oddly shaken. It's the same dream, or nightmare, the one he opened *The Assistant* to himself the other day. "Everywhere there were eyes that took a malevolent pleasure in his peculiar nakedness."

Three more sessions are somehow accomplished.

Noon. Messages to check. Gertrude not feeling well, she's sorry but she's calling to cancel tomorrow's supervision.

Not great timing, Gertrude.

He calls to wish her a speedy return to health.

Two client phone calls to return, both blessedly brief.

Lunch to get. As he hurries along it occurs to him that of course *The Assistant* opened readily to that dream/nightmare when he was perusing it. Bob had probably opened the book again and again to that very dream, read and reread those pages. Fifty-six to fifty-eight. He'll have to take another look, but he's sure he has the sentence about the eyes right.

Back in the office, he unwraps his sandwich, draws the typed pages out of Bob's manila envelope, eats and skims.

Stops eating, stops skimming, starts over, reads rapidly, but reads every word, then dials Petra at her office. *Be there*, he prays.

"Hello, this is Petra."

"Thank God."

"Michael?"

"I need a very brief consult—one minute—and if you have any time at all tomorrow—I could use—Gertrude is sick—hell of week for her to get sick on me—"

"Slow down. One minute on what topic, Michael?"

"Multiple Personality Disorder."

"I see. Well, interesting. Take some deep breaths. "

"What?"

"You heard me."

She's right. This is all there is time for. He takes several deep breaths.

"You are an experienced and excellent therapist, Michael. You know all you need to know. I'll convince you of that tomorrow. Can you be at your office early? 8:00? I have a meeting at 9:00 in your building. Fortuitous. The rest of the day is packed."

"I'll be here. I bow down in gratitude."

"I get up early, Michael. No problem."

"I'll pay you."

"You won't. You'll do the same for me some day."

"Thank you. Thank you very much."

Next, Wilma. A quick trip to the bathroom first.

~ ~ ~

Here she is, backpack in place, handshake as usual. Ah, stability.

While she is setting her books and papers on the couch she tells him this will be her final session.

Final session? He must have misheard.

She locates her check for the co-pay and hands it to him.

She has folded her hands in her lap and is looking at him, just as she did in the dreams. The intriguing client and the dream woman are the same person.

"Wilma, did you say—I might have misunderstood—did you say this would be—"

"My final session, Michael. Yes. So there will be a good deal to fit into the hour. A small container, but we'll manage. I see that a bit of solidity has been lost since our last meeting. I am speaking of you, dear. A few cracks, but superficial. Possibly a difficult morning? The essential is intact, we mustn't worry. As for me, it has sorted itself. I have a list."

She turns and picks up a piece of paper neatly positioned on top of Murdoch's *The Unicorn*. She looks at it, seems to be reading and rereading it. She folds it and tucks it into the book. She holds the book in her hands.

"I think not, after all. The topics do not reach out to me just now. I had better read the words of Gerald. He is not likable but I imagine an author sometimes places wisdom into the unexpected mouth. Gerald is, you see, asserting his control. Marian is quite vulnerable, her attempt to rescue the unicorn—that would be Hannah—having just failed. Neither

289

you nor I quite understands just yet, but we must follow." She opens the book to where her bookmark is. She searches the page, very serious. "Yes, here is the sentence. 'There are great patterns in which we are all involved, and destinies which belong to us and which we love even in the moment when they destroy us.' Now, Michael, what do you suppose that means in the present circumstance?"

They look at each other. Michael has been challenged by clients many times over the years in many ways, but—

Is that a bit of a grin, just a tug at the corner of her mouth?

No, of course not. Such a serious quote.

The eye contact then: intense, almost unbearable. They are peering, striving to see into each other's minds. How ridiculous. They both see it, the absurdity. They slide into laughter.

"Wilma, I don't know what the hell we're doing."

"We're saying goodbye, Michael. But it's only temporary."

"So the upsurges—the multitude of things—what you found yourself having to—"

"'The fever dug into me and out of the depths it pulled experiences, images, facts...' I do value Rilke who is able to express the intensities. Alma would be pleased he has become an aid. Her favorite writer, you know."

"Was he? A good one. So the sorting—"

"Is sufficient for now, Michael."

"And the need for conversation beyond the grocery aisle?"

"Yes. Well. I make my efforts. I believe a bit more patience—"

"Patience?"

"Marlene has been silent. I work on the bookcase. Have I told you about the bookcase?"

"I don't believe you have."

"I've undertaken to construct a bookcase. Without Pa it goes a bit slowly but Marlene is not yet ready. I am too real for her at the moment. Patience is called for while her books wait—bookcase-less, we might say —but patience comes to them more easily than to me. Pa and I worked together when I was a girl—quite a number of bookcases over the years —the two of us. That was long ago. And then Lorraine, also gone for quite some time. And Alma. Dear Alma. I am alone now, though never entirely. I ought to clarify that I have a streak of whimsy when I am not

290

mistakenly distressed. Distress is a mistaken state, I have come to see that. Lately whimsy has linked itself to my dearly departed. Strange phrase, dearly departed. Is the manner of departure dear? The adverb seems incorrect. Alma is perhaps primary among mine, but Pa and Lorraine have their importance. Of these three I am concocted. And the god of course. My own flavor persists. I do have that."

"You certainly do. How long is it since your mother died, Wilma?"

"I must say Lorraine could have chosen a dearer way."

She falls silent.

He waits, trying to do his own sorting.

"Did you have a question, Michael?"

"How long has it been—?"

"Oh. Yes. How long since Alma died."

She falls silent.

He was tempted by the reference to Lorraine. Fork in the road? But let the client choose. Is this really her last session? Was their dream flight to Zarathustra preview to a termination? What about their humming relationship?

"It was springtime, I'm quite certain of that," she says finally. "That Alma died. May, it must have been. Yes, early May. And here we are in August. Just three months, then. It seems longer. Or like no time at all. That also. A great deal has come and gone in the period. It filled me just now."

"Three months. A short time, really. After a death, I mean. Or so it would seem to me, Wilma."

"Yes, I suppose so. She comes and goes. I enjoy the ghosts for the most part, whether they are mere whimsy or firm reality. I'm never entirely convinced, in either direction. Alma, and also Lorraine, coming and going. Lorraine less often, which might be understandable since we killed her. Alma and I. Though it was I who injected. At her request, Michael, be assured of that. She appreciated it at the time and has offered no complaints since. Do you suppose the earthly is the only realm? Time and space? The constraints? Such an unlikely vision, to my mind. I understand the physicists might open the matter. Differences. Infinities. Eternities. Quite compelling, at times, these hints. But we are only at the beginning, as a species. Still, perhaps we have always—"

291

She stops in midstream and smiles at him, tenderly. As if he's her child.

"You do leap into the mysteries, Wilma."

"Yes, I suppose I do. Now, Michael, I believe we ought to discuss Young Henry."

"Young Henry?"

"I think you know who I mean."

"Well, it's another leap. Let me land and catch my breath. I suppose you mean Henry Whitsun."

"Our mime. Yes. We have skirted the topic."

"Have we?"

"Yes. He is your young man, isn't he? Your Billy, as the poems would have it?"

Michael takes a deep breath. He shakes his head. What is he to do with her? They look at each other. She knows exactly what she's doing.

But what exactly *is* she doing?

"Yes, Wilma, he is my Billy. We are friends now. Just friends, as they say. And this is somehow important to you?"

"Because of the threesome, in case it should be reconstituted. Marlene and Young Henry and I. Conversations of considerable vitality, generally at Pizza Hut. He is Marlene's, first and foremost, and since she is unready I hold myself in abeyance. Or perhaps his time with us is finished. A busy young man, as you might know. Bass Park, a week from Sunday, for instance, as I learned from the announcement on the radio just this morning. I have it in mind to attend, perhaps under a veil of invisibility. I wouldn't want to create obligation. Will you be there, Michael?"

A week from Sunday. And Saturday, the day before, he and Henry will meet at Pizza Hut which seems to be where Henry conducts his social life. And now Wilma is woven in. The quote she read—something about patterns—great patterns—

"Michael?"

"Sorry, Wilma. Yes, I think I'll plan to be there."

"Good. Love takes its forms. You do know that."

She falls silent again. Is it right, that she end the therapy today? *Has* she put her disparate pieces into order that is "sufficient for now"? She seems to have, for herself. And, actually, even for him. Somehow it all

292

makes sense. He has the strongest feeling of coming to land, very gently. Bump, bump, bump, and then the gentle landing. The two of them, from Zarathustra in the sky to Christopher Robin's steps, two old toy bears. Despite gaps and obscurities and strange fringes flying here and there, there is a sense of rightness, as if it's a work of art—all she has offered of herself—complete now, though a challenge to interpret—as if he's watched an artist at work—abstract, and yet not at all abstract—

"I am compelled to speak of the painting, Michael, before I go."

Painting? The woman reads his mind.

Ah, but she means an actual painting. He follows her eyes. At least she's not choosing the same one Bob chose.

"Do you know it, Wilma?"

"Only from being in this room. Does it have a title?"

"*The Large Moon.* The painter was a Russian woman, Marianne Werefkin."

"How nice. It brings in the topic of death, you see. When they have gotten their little boats out on the water under the large moon they will search but they will not find the man they are looking for, though they will find his boat floating, quietly. There are mysteries. Death will draw them all together. As you can see, this has already begun to happen. The women will wait at the edge of the dark water. The men will go out and they will return. A strong story. I don't judge the artistry, I'm not equipped, but strong is the word I want. Death comes, Michael."

He nods.

"I do mean that, Michael."

"You think I need to hear it."

She nods.

There is a substantial pause. He waits for more. Or he waits to be cut off, left—

"Not that you fail to know, but that you still, as happens for so many, can be disconcerted. It is possible to move beyond—"

She stops. She is the one waiting now, for him.

"Is this about Henry?"

He cannot believe he said that. He has no reason to think Henry told her—told her and Marlene, apparently they are a threesome—about his heart condition. She's read the poems. She's suggesting he ought to come to terms with—mother and father—their deaths. Of course.

"Yes. This is about Henry."

He takes a deep breath. He nods. "All right."

"Good," she says and finally places *The Unicorn* back on its pile.

There seems to be nothing more to say. They look at the painting.

"I agree, Wilma. It's strong."

"And the other one. The woman will complete her journey to the city of light. It's a matter of taking the next step, and then the next. She knows that. You needn't worry."

He smiles. "I can quite easily agree not to worry about her, Wilma."

"Good. I ought to inform you, a little matter I almost forgot, that I have visited Lyle. I've assured him that I am less unusual now and will refrain from sitting down as I did."

"On the floor."

"Yes. It was the return of the sun. I am more accustomed to it now, how it enters while being entered, the lines crossing and forming, multitudes, splintering so beautifully, quite similar to a new thought. And claiming it, as one's own. Perhaps I can be explicit now. As a child I experienced it that way as I sat on the path. The sun entering me, like a new thought all my own. I believe I said those very words to myself at the time."

She looks at him.

"I'll remember, Wilma. Like a new thought all your own. It's lovely."

"Yes—resolving—and yet impossible—though the words, rising up —we make our attempts—yes, well—"

She stops. He waits. She has turned to her books. "We will say goodbye now," she says. She is filling her backpack. Is this difficult for her? It's certainly difficult for him. He's on the verge of tears. She stands and offers her hand and her entire being is in the handshake and in the glow of her very serious eyes. And then she smiles, tenderly, as if to comfort him. "But this is not the end, dear."

Not the end. All right, this is not the end.

"Thank you, Wilma Schuh." He doesn't really know what he's saying. He's lost inside something—or found—inside—something—

"You are most welcome, Michael Solomon."

And she's gone.

~ ~ ~

294

When Michael looks back, beer in hand, sitting on his couch under the eye of the old candlemaker, the rest of the afternoon is a blur. He's quite sure he did adequate work—perhaps barely adequate—with the remaining clients. Between Bob and Wilma his mind was stretched thin. What a strange and somehow appropriate reversal of roles Wilma pulled off at the end. The end which is not an end. He'll look for her at Bass Park, try to find her under the intended veil of invisibility. Will they run into each other once in a while as the days and weeks and months follow, say hello and feel at ease with each other? He sips his beer and smiles at Herr Candlemaker who would nod and smile back politely, knowingly, if he were able. If he were not mere paint. Then he pulls the pages from Bob's manila envelop and reads slowly, entering the sentences, thinking of William Blake, of Blake's Zoas, how they fall to separateness after their time of blissful unity, how they are and are not part of each other, how they shift and shift, in anguish and in tenderness, into and out of each other. He thinks of the slight turn of the wrist, the kaleidoscope with its mirrors and colors and pieces and patterns. He thinks of Petra, who has been doing this strange work with the radically divided psyche for a long time, decades, and who will very generously appear in his office to educate and steady him first thing in the morning.

He gets up from the couch. He'll read a bit of Blake before he goes to bed.

And no more beer. One was enough.

~ ~ ~

Bob Smith's Pages

Dear Michael,

The one among us whom you have generally seen, our Bob, is the one least cognizant of The Reality. There is also the Art Critic. His name is Robert Quentin Smith and you have met him, but not often. He reads fiction with Bob in addition to knowing ALL about art and making our living through that means.

I write on behalf of The Others. We share the body and watch from within.

Those who are capable of such watching, that is, watch from within.

Bob forgets. He can remember, with help. Help him, please. We will do our best from within. Some of us are fading. Sixty-three years for the body. Less for the individuals, but it has been decades. Decades of difficulty. You will appreciate the alliteration. (We have located and read your book of poems. Lyle Franklin's bookstore. Just yesterday.) When possible, we will write these notes to you with care. Not always possible, as you will understand. Horror in the background.

Robert Quentin Smith knows nothing of distressing matters unless by way of the pleasures of vicarious experience gained through art and literature, kept vivid and harmless. Though perhaps this technique is not holding so well now. I learn this only as I write. A bit distressing.

I know, but do not feel, most of it. I will be an aid. I have been an aid all along, but how would you discern that?

The Robert Walser book: excellent timing. We wonder how you knew. For this alone we would try to trust you. As Bob has told you, he resonated with Joseph Marti, mild hero of The Assistant. *In contrast,* The Robber *has disconcerted him, increasingly so, but what a gift to the rest of us—divisions, leaps, uncertainties, contradictions, sudden ecstasies, sudden agonies, much in the way of missing connections and disguised or pervasively invisible information. What a book!*

(You will excuse the exclamation point. Such excess. I would erase it but we do not erase each other's insertions as a rule and why not let it stand, you will see worse.)

When you consult professionally it will be appropriate to mention Multiple Personality Disorder. Or Dissociative Identity Disorder, that bland and obfuscating substitute. (Perhaps we are mistaken in this response.) Years—decades—we lived without official, recognized language. Now we have a surfeit. The way of it, isn't that right, dear, dear Michael? You will understand. We see your intelligence, and how you have responded to our initial revelatory energies, our little hints as to the Entirety, so tentative as of yet—

(I would not bother you with that "dear, dear"—another example of excess—but you will come to see that such expressions sometimes slip through, no matter the attempt at constraint.)

We must do this slowly. You have brightened as we have allowed our little steps ahead. We are encouraged.

In reference to the rhythm of things, pacing you might call it: it is possible, even probable, that Bob will disappear for a while. None of the rest of us are ready to enter the office naked, without the veil of him. Therefore, sessions might, or will, be missed. We intend to pay for any session we do not attend. Please hold our spot in your schedule, no matter what. You will see talk of suicide. We will prevent it, as we have always done. We have honed the capacity. To paraphrase Douglas MacArthur, "We shall return." It is not the Japanese who surround and endanger us but merely our own outdated terrors. This we (some of us) have come to understand. You have been of assistance. In your presence we have achieved a modicum of clarity. Some have. Not all. As indicated, Bob knows almost nothing.

Though his discomfort increases of late.

Since Walser's The Robber, *his discomfort increases.*

We believe you would speak of unconditional positive regard. We cannot go that far since we have deliberately and of necessity limited the scope of your regard, but you have tolerated Bob with admirable equanimity. That has been an enormous and unprecedented help. And you have responded with humanity to the recent and livelier version of him, the one Robert Walser has produced for you. Perhaps this not precisely a livelier version of Bob, our old familiar Bob, but something other. In this matter we are stirred to confusion.

Confusion is terrifying. I make my attempts. Containment!

You are beginning to understand. You will find professional consultation, learn what is necessary for your equanimity, and accept us. That is our hope. That is our only hope.

The documents enclosed are the totality of we can provide at this moment. I am fading. Please forgive. We have determined to give you the worst first. Marble Man. Please remember that "marble" comes from the Greek for "crystalline rock, shining stone" and has therefore positive associations which might not be expressed in the writing. You will see from internal evidence that there has been nothing in the way of what your profession seems determined to call "acting out." You may, with justification, be at ease.

Sincerely,
The Container

297

*

Marble Man

unfinished piece of fiction by Robert Quentin Smith

(FICTION, Michael)

He was marble. Made of marble. Not smoothed to a shine. Not that kind. Hard, rough, original. Still: when his cock hardened the proof was there: his marble essence, visible. And they had to feel it. I'm made of marble, he'd say, and they had to say Yes. That was all he required, that Yes. Then pull out, let them go. He wasn't one who needed to hurt, needed them to cry, needed their resistance. Nor did he wish to impregnate. But he required that assent, that brief moment of agreement.

He chose only the lucky and it helped them too. If not for him, their own material would be a bore, all smoothness, nothing unique. Whereas his needed smoothing, having an excess of the ugly irregularities resulting from his difficult fate. It was communism and he was its most daring practitioner.

But only in his mind. He never touched them, never even let them see he saw them. Still, after he watched, after he took one in, after he possessed her as a sketch artist does—

a sketch artist who is a genius—

after he possessed her as such a sketch artist possesses his subject—

after this, clear in his genius, he entered her. In his mind. Alone. Always in the bathtub, he'd never think of making them unclean.

Smooth and velvety, they were. No resistance. A welcoming.

One time out of three they refused the Yes. At first.

It's a lonely life, the life of a scholar. To stretch thought is difficult, muscle-building work. Thus and only thus does one become marble. Without study, nothing is solid.

He had done it. He had discovered that without which nothing holds its shape, that which lies beyond good and evil, beyond beauty and ugliness, the force that catapults man and mind beyond all limit. Already at thirty, his own genius: firm.

Now, however, he has come upon a crack in thought. This very night.

*

Note to Michael: this is the totality of the "Marble Man" writing. We can tell you that the writing, though written in the third person as if it is fiction, though labeled forcefully as fiction, is closer to fact than fiction. Is fact. It is expected that the author will communicate with you in some way at some point in the future. Please be patient.

*

About the Unfinished Piece of FICTION Titled Marble Man

It began with the Art Critic. He was in the ascendancy. Robert Quentin Smith.

Work pressure was high, several brochures were coming due, art exhibits all over the place, his research was not finished and he was blocked, unable to produce. Unable as writer, as historian, as critic, as appreciator, as promoter, as designer. Unable. Unable to complete even a single brochure.

He walked away from his desk, from his apartment. He'd never had a family, always been a single guy, was now a long-time bachelor. He lived alone. This was in New York City. Before Maine. He walked around Central Park for hours and got the idea that he would try his hand at fiction, to hell with work for today. (He was frustrated. He was angry.) By then it was evening. He hadn't eaten all day. He went back to his desk, cleared it quickly into piles he put on the floor, sat down at the computer and began to type, hardly knowing what was coming out. He stopped dead, went to bed and slept soundly. Which never happened (sleeping soundly, that is) but it did that night. When he got up in the morning he found the writing, Marble Man's, on his desk. He was still Robert Quentin Smith, Art Critic, with deadlines ahead. He remembered (though the memory left him quickly). He remembered the day, the evening, the writing. He was terribly excited and appalled.

299

It never went further but since that day he's known, not consciously, about this aspect of himself. He has dreams. Now we are talking about Marble Man, he has the dreams. He has always known the location of the writing, what book it is tucked into, hidden; where he can find it. He takes a bath, only occasionally does he do this, and reads the writing and masturbates. After which he is in an agony of excitement and confusion and contrition. The contrition might belong elsewhere, it is possibly not his.

Marble Man has never before been revealed. You, Michael, have been interested in what Walser has evoked. Now is the time. There will be trembling as someone types out the copy of this writing for you. Also, excitement. (We are composing in longhand, but wouldn't ask you to decipher.) The typist will feel quite dramatic. Or, wait, maybe not— maybe she is alternating between looking like a scared loser and seeming sort of thrilled that she can be so interesting; that, finally, she can be interesting.

*

Marble Man is the worst, Michael—the worst that we have for you. Of our writing, that is. At the moment, that is. What follows are messages from within, one after another. You will understand.

Sincerely (again),
The Container

*

Notes from The Crew

Enclosed are a few of my brochures, Michael. My passion is with Art. To know me, you must know this. How I love your Werefkins. They have kept me coming to your office though I've been behind a strange barrier a good deal of the time. (Robert Quentin Smith, Art Critic)

~

Hi Michael I Love You!! (Signed, Bobbie Socks)

~

300

I have some concerns about gender identity and/or sexual orientation. Probably unwarranted but let us clear the air. (Robert)

~

There will be a surge toward death. We must all beware. (Guardian Angel)

~

May we suggest you read Mary Shelley's Frankenstein: Or the Modern Prometheus? Pity the monster! (The Group Inside)

~

Hey, Michael, be prepared for a bit of nastiness. Some of these guys! And that one who isn't really a guy, if you know what I mean. (Your Pal, Sonny)

~

You just keep your hands off my boy, Doctor Solomon. I have lawyer friends. (Mom)

~

Hey, Mike, not to worry. She's just a bit uptight. Know what I mean, sweetie? (Robbie Lou)

~

We have just learned that Bob intends to reveal his growing, and to him mysterious, interest in the painter Francis Bacon. I had better, therefore, add a comment or two. Bacon was an innocent who felt it was his soul's way to live at the extremities, in a cultural underworld, we might say, a world in which he located ascendant naked violent beauty stretching toward the sublime. Sadomasochism. Men and men. Forms and energies. Forces. See Gilles Deleuze who grasps the essence of such. Deep into the virtual, out into the material. (Francis Bacon: The Logic of Sensation.) If you were privileged to witness the Bacon interview at the time of the Tate exhibition you will have intuited the innocence, the gentleness, the devotion to Art. Our Bob is a mirroring innocent. Identical and reversed. He has never engaged in carnal relations though others inside have, in the forgotten past. Please respect that "forgotten" and ignore the "past" which, after sliding out, slides back to oblivion. I know not what I write. Let us move on. That particular triptych by Bacon, the one Bob intends to speak of in session—Studies from the Human Body, 1970—is lacking the reds that evoke blood. Bob would have more difficulty with red, which associates to carnage. Stay with orange and green, mirrors and

301

witnesses, an interested photographer. The bodies engaged (center panel) are pure violent creative forms, circular, complex, almost liquid. Liquids pouring into each other. Boundaries surpassed. Please focus on the aesthetics. All is acceptable. (The Container, in concert with Robert Quentin Smith, Art Critic. Note the cooperation, Michael. An achievement.)

~

I still love you, Michael. Kisses and hugs!!!! (Your Best Friend, Bobbie Socks, age nine and three-quarters)

~

I'm the one that typed this for you, Doctor Solomon. Some terrible handwriting, hard to read, but I tried to make it perfect. Please forgive typos, if any. (The Secretary.)

*

Michael: the following are lines from Robert Walser's The Robber
—lines of considerable importance to us as individuals and as a group. Interruptions in the form of comments were unavoidable. (I'm still typing, Michael. The Secretary)

"...when we laugh, we are good..."

"One should make an effort not to see just the wickedness in what is wicked, but its beauty as well..." (Yeah!)

"...the Robber stood once more before an art gallery and resolved never to read anything again, but all the same he did read this and that on occasion." (This made Robert Quentin Smith laugh out loud. How happy we were!)

"...No one knows who you really are..." (Someone says this to the Robber, accusing him. That was cruel.)

"...all the people moved silently back and forth, as though a song were resounding from all humanity, and everything good and tender

302

appeared strolling harmlessly past..." (We can see this. Really see it. Not consistently, but we can. We want you to know that, Michael.)

"...he was enraptured, for a time, by a blue-trousered little boy." (DAMMIT. WHO PUT THAT IN?) (As explained above, we do not erase or delete what has been written.)

"I'll say it straight out: from time to time I feel as if I were a girl." (The Robber was very brave when he talked to his doctor!)

"But of course I'm not a real girl." (I SHOULD SAY NOT.)

"....the question of whether I might possibly be a girl has never, never, not for a single moment, troubled me..." (Ha!)

"I'm sure you understand the difficulties of explaining oneself in such inexplicable matters." (Take heed, Michael.)

"'Let yourself remain as you are, go on living the way you live. You seem to know yourself, and to have come to terms with yourself, exceedingly well,' the doctor said and rose from his seat." (You are just as good as that doctor, Michael.) (We hope!) (He IS.) (We'll see.) (STOP.)

*

*The following are lines
from Robert Walser's short story, "Kleist in Thun"
with which we resonate.
We offer them bare.*

"The world around is like one vast embrace. What rapture this is, but what agony it can also be."

"He is too sensitive to be unhappy, too haunted by all his irresolute, cautious, mistrusted feelings. He would like to scream aloud, to weep. God in heaven, what is wrong with me, and he rushes down the darkening hill."

"He would like to shed his life; but first he wants to shatter the shells of his life."

"Something hurts him, yes, really, quite correct, but not in the chest, not in the lungs either, or in the head, what? Nowhere at all? Well, not quite, a little, somewhere so that one cannot quite precisely tell where it is. Which means: nothing to speak of."

*

We are very tired, Michael. Also, excited. Almost hopeful. But tired. It should probably be noted that the German writer Heinrich von Kleist committed suicide.

REMEMBER: WE SHALL RETURN.

THIS IS THE END OF OUR WRITINGS FOR NOW.

I hope I did a good enough job, Michael! (The Secretary)

Six: Bass Park

a plain raised wooden platform

As Gracie Bicker would tell it, she was produced and raised by two bright crazy parents with enough money to forego the working life. Educated, both of them: college and beyond. Lots of church-going, very respectable that way. Episcopalians. Odd, though. Stayed to themselves other than church, swimming around in their creativities. Father: sculptor. Mother: potter. No kids after Gracie, she was enough. You could take *that* two ways.

They probably meant well, her parents. George and Cassie. Dead now, due to a single efficient car crash. Icy slide, not their fault. Long time ago so don't worry about it.

Gracie herself is educated. Graduated college with an enriching but useless degree in English Literature. Made it as far as marriage and a baby of her own (little Milo, *not a bastard*) before she went off the rails.

Or fell off the horse, as they say.

Got *right back on*, Gracie did, leaving the husband who was so normal he frightened her. She joined a twelve-member Christian church composed of peculiar and interesting plain folks of the poor variety who helped her with Milo. She began to feel at home in the world and before long she was their minister, a position she still occupies. The members appreciate her. She reads the Bible a minimum of one hour per day and prays to relax herself in addition to praying up a storm in church but that's only Sundays and Wednesday afternoons. She took a yoga class once right after college—such strange people she found there, not her type—and has retained vestiges to decorate her lonely evenings. That and country music, of which her parents would not approve but they are gone to Heaven for the Eccentric.

Gracie likes to think she has a first-class sense of humor.

At times anyway.

Heaven for the Eccentric is a nice example of that quality.

All right, so she's lonely, who wouldn't be? Especially since Milo left home. How could he have?

Milo: only nineteen years old at the present date. Had a devil's need to exit his mother's home at the age of sixteen.

Which need he gave in to.

Milo is a worry, truth be told.

307

Milo is a very good son, don't think otherwise. Calls weekly, writes to give his address when he has one, would come running in an instant if Gracie had a need, yes he would.

Milo has a sweet soul and a sweet disposition and a sweet face and all of these are part of the problem, which is that he played with dolls, *et cetera*. He lacked the natural bent toward maleness. You know what I mean. Beating him was singularly ineffective. The world had entered the poor boy.

The world: every year more and more inclined to countenance such sin. Dear Milo. What could he do?

What can *she* do?

There are things, things a mother can do. Has to do. *Wants* to do.

She has her instructions. The Guides have been annoying at times—well, terrifying—but today they are a comfort.

Ever since Milo sent the clipping, that interview in the Bangor Daily News (when did it arrive? must have been Friday) she has been in the hands of the Guides. She's on her way up to Bangor now. A mother can do no less.

Henry Whitsun, mime, is the interviewee. *The Unicorn and the Minotaur and Argus of the Many Eyes* is the name of today's performance by this Henry Whitsun and two others, one of which is her own son, Milo. She's done her homework. A Unicorn is a mythical beast though some have thought it real, humans being unable to tell the difference at times.

Between real and unreal, that is.

Clarity is precisely the thing humans have difficulty locating, but her little church knows the answer to *that*.

Unicorns symbolize Innocence. Or Unicorns symbolize everything from Christ to Death. Depends on who's saying. Sounds like a stretch, Christ to Death, but Christ and Death *do* go together. Think about it. Thanks to Jesus on the Cross, Death in other words, some of us are saved. Like a pure cool drink is being saved. Thank you, Jesus.

Gracie takes a substantial grateful breath and passes three tractor-trailers. Clear stretch ahead for a bit now. Her own art is mental. Daughter of artists has to do *something* in the realm of same. Family trait, after all.

Mental. Meaning having to do with books, *et cetera*. She reads and turns the words—turns them like a potter, faster and faster, finding the inner shape, seeing what they'll hold. Bible passages, mostly. Anything printed, really. This newspaper article in her pocket, for example.

Or sculpts them. The words, the sentences, even whole paragraphs. All sorts of shapes can be discovered, pushed here and there, made into more. This is something she tries not to do while driving. Best done with the page right there anyway. Still, she *can* see print—

Jesus wept.

The words bend, they are turning inside themselves, reaching, seeking—

Stop it, says Gracie to herself.

Which works.

There are those who claim the Unicorn is in the Bible. Something about the steps of translation, language to language to language, the one-horned beast ending up a wild ox which means the ox is really a Unicorn. But translation can be a bitch, so said Arianna once, having made the mistake of entering into dialogue with a non-believer and arriving at Wednesday service in a snit. The non-believer was an atheistic expert in languages, especially those related to the Bible. Poor Arianna, she was bested. So *possibly* the wild ox is a cover for the mythical beast with one horn who is not so mythical after all unless the entire Bible is a "fascinating myth" as the language expert has concluded. Such scholarship is a bit beyond Gracie. Besides, a myth can be as strong as reality so why quibble?

And then there's Faith.

These days Unicorns are invisible except to the Chosen among the Innocent. Into the virgin's lap falls the relieved head of the Unicorn. And then the hunters arrive, with their spears. And then Death.

Or you can sugar the whole thing, paint little horses pink with long single horns and call them Unicorns and let them prance around and you'll enjoy your false good feeling, but that's Error. So Gracie has concluded, at least for now. The real Unicorn is the Invisible seen only by the Innocent. Like all ordained symbols, this one is unsafe in the hands of the unworthy.

The Minotaur, for example. Another symbol mistreated by unworthy readers. Part bull, not at all what a real human ought to be. Monstrous, in

309

fact. All right. But that is *not his fault*. If a Queen lies with a Bull, what can you expect? Why twist a boy's mind inside a maze and and trap his body there along with it when the whole thing is *not his fault*?

Then there's that story by Jorge Luis Borges she read back in college. Her favorite professor's favorite author. Gracie has a good memory, a blessing. Now that was a minotaur story, but with salvation stirred in, a genuine comfort. Borges's Minotaur *knew the Way Out*. Just as Milo will. Professor and writer both did show evidence of being pagan, a concern. Maybe one or the other had a religion not obvious to her. She's made mistakes before.

Never mind, her Guides will tell her if it's her task.

To bring them to Jesus, that is. The professor and his favorite writer.

Anyone might find themselves in the arms of Jesus in the end. Milo, too.

And then there's Argus Panoptes.

She really did do her homework. Today required preparation.

Many eyes has Argus. Hundreds. "And the goddess stirred in him unwearying strength: sleep never fell upon his eyes; but he kept sure watch always." Of course everyone has to sleep some time, even Argus. If he has to sleep, a few of those eyes do close. Only a few. Until Goddess-guided Hermes arrives, that is. Then every eye closes. Oh, oh.

Well, Death comes to all.

Gracie has many eyes herself. She's not captured inside her church, you can see that already.

Traffic not too bad for a Sunday in August. Look over there, though. Leaving Maine, that's where the crowd is. *She* was never one to follow a crowd. Look at them: have to get back to work after their weekend in Paradise. Milo wrote that word on the postcard tucked safely into her skirt pocket along with the article. "Maine is Paradise for me, Mom. Your son, Milo."

Paradise.

Is this blasphemy?

No, he's just happy. That's a blessing, a happy child. Learning to recognize a blessing is a lifelong task. One blessing today: she is not alone. She's packed her parents into the back seat for the trip. George and Cassie, more useful since they've been dead, easier for them to see what's

310

what, attend, offer parental wisdom. Along with the Guides come the parents today.

So she's not lonely, not the least bit, not right now.

A purpose is a good thing. And she'll see Milo.

She has the article from the Bangor Daily News almost memorized. "Milo Bicker, guitarist, forms the third point of the triangle." She likes that, it reminds her of the Trinity which she has secretly pondered. An intriguing Mystery, that Trinity, though not in the Bible and therefore not brought within the walls of the church which is actually just Arianna's house, but the House of God when they Gather.

Also in the article are the crucial bits of information. These she has memorized word for word. "The performance of *The Unicorn and the Minotaur and Argus of the Many Eyes*, with mime Henry Whitsun, narrator Frank Griveau, and guitarist Milo Bicker is scheduled for 2:00 Sunday afternoon, August 17, at Bass Park in Bangor."

John Stone was the writer of that article which is the record of a long interview. Mr. Stone got Henry Whitsun to spill the details and now she knows the hidden places of that man, every cranny. Lower class, for one thing. Mother runs off with a circus fellow, father runs a gas station. A running family. Ha! Run, run, run. A gas station, who'd want that? Think of the smell. And the grime. Cleanliness is next to Godliness.

Henry the son must have a mind, though, because he went to Harvard. Didn't graduate, no staying power. Well, what might you expect with such a family? No real job, she can tell, though it's not exactly stated in the article. Devotes himself to this business of being a mime. Strange to choose such a way to perform. No words. *Hubris*. Even God needs a Word.

The Unicorn and the Minotaur and Argus of the Many Eyes. An opportunity for Milo, despite drawbacks. That Henry, though. Wrong kind of influence over her son. Devil's tool. Dares to say right out that he's a homosexual. "I'm gay," he says to John Stone, the interviewer, and so close to the beginning, doesn't even wait to work it in later when a person might not notice, which does bring on an urge to vomit.

A strong urge.

Swallowing hard, forcing her stomach back to where it belongs, Gracie takes the exit. She's got her directions. Bass Park is on Main Street, not far off the exit. Watch for a big statue of Paul Bunyan.

311

Should be soon.

There it is, no problem.

An hour early, but she'll look around, choose her spot. She takes her bag with its substantial contents, a bit heavy but she's never been a weakling, locks the car, and starts walking toward the statue which is even bigger than she expected, and very colorful.

Nice day. Eighty degrees was the prediction. Cooler than Cambridge, that's for sure. She's in the right place, she can feel it. Preordained. She looks at the sky. Overcast, no rain until tomorrow, the radio promised. She's glad of that, for Milo's sake. How proud she is of him. Only nineteen and his name in the paper!

~ ~ ~

Michael, all unknowing, pulls in directly behind Gracie Bicker. He feels for his harmonica (left breast pocket) and turns off the ignition.

Way too early for the performance, but he couldn't keep pacing the floors at home.

Pointless, that pacing. As if he could suffer pre-performance jitters on Henry's behalf. Does Henry even experience such?

Well, probably. Don't they all?

He'll just sit here for a while, nice enough day.

The early bird gets the good parking space.

Two early birds maybe. He watches the woman get out of the car just ahead, big old Pontiac, cream-colored, Massachusetts license plate. In her fifties is his guess. Wild dark hair, the thick springy kind, just visible under a seriously-brimmed straw sun hat. Long peasant-type skirt with an energetic print—red blue green black swirls—plain white tee-shirt, not tucked in, over-sized. The woman herself is just a tad over-sized. Looks like a person in charge. Confident. Maybe she has a role in the production. Would Henry hire someone to organize this? She's headed into the park.

Ah, she stops to consult with Paul Bunyan.

Out loud, it seems.

And the consultation continues.

Hmm. Maybe not the one to make sure this event is a logistical success.

312

Michael Solomon, diagnostician extraordinaire, thinks he's observing someone supremely on top of things and it turns out she's a bit off her rocker. Probably homeless, all worldly belongings in the big old car. He chuckles to himself. So be it.

Or maybe she has a big house and a rich husband in Massachusetts and she's just having a bit of fun with herself, a whimsical woman.

Like Wilma.

He already misses Wilma, hopes she'll be here. Maybe he'll get a handshake.

Getting that phone call from Henry yesterday morning canceling their Pizza Hut date wasn't easy. Understandable, though. Day before the performance, too busy, silly to have thought he could manage it, they'll reschedule soon, not to worry.

And in fact there's no need for worry. They'll find their way. He, Michael Chaim Solomon, imprudent prophet, predicts delightful platonic intensity, their history pulled to new shapes, his own life significantly altered, and for the better.

He knows things might turn mundane, he hasn't lost all grip on reality. In fact, mundane would be fine.

Will the article in the Bangor Daily bring a crowd? What a sweetheart that John Stone was. Such a full and compelling portrait of Henry, and then the free publicity for today. Michael has read and reread the article, filling up with love. Love for Henry and love for young Mr. Stone and love for the world itself.

There's quite a conversation in progress over there. The woman speaks, she pauses, she nods, she speaks again. Nice rhythms. The whole thing is so persuasive he almost expects big old Paul to climb down from his pedestal, lay his tools on the ground, and walk off with his new friend.

Diagnostician extraordinaire. Yeah, right. *Two years* he's been seeing Bob Smith and not once in all that time did he suspect Multiple Personality Disorder. Or Dissociative Identity Disorder as they're dubbing it now, a fact that Bob Smith, well-informed client, acknowledged in his writing. Petra was, as usual, impeccably supportive. "It's often like that, Michael. These folks can be very good at covering and it takes a long time for them to trust anyone. He trusts you now, pat yourself on the back."

313

Gertrude, back to health on Friday, was amazing. She took the elements of his life and turned them into wonder. "A new time of life for you, Michael. Petra's right. Working with MPD, or I should say DID, will be a fresh challenge. Stimulating. Good for you. And Wilma who declines all diagnostic categories gets what she wants from seeing you— including a therapist who's in better condition than before he saw her— and comes and goes so quickly her therapist hardly knows what happened, but she knows. I can't think of a single move you could have made that would have been better. Falling in love, hummingly, appears to have worked just fine. In this case, mind you. And then there's your Henry, the beginning of a new kind of intimacy, a special friend with whom you have a special history. All perfect for a man who was in a slump and needed to be pushed and pulled and maybe even needed his sixtieth birthday, and then, look, he finds himself un-slumped. A perfect neologism, my very own. Don't laugh." She went on for a bit, riding her own energy. Maybe it was the convalescence. Was she on medication? He sat back and let her go, smiling and shaking his head over her performance and finally saying "Enough, enough" and agreeing not to disagree.

Something is in fact happening. It's not just Bob and Wilma and Henry, though each has been crucial. His reading life has been taken over by Blake whose intensity is addictive. He has decided this is a perfectly fine addiction, it makes him happy. Add in the paintings, Marianne Werefkin in her various modes and moods, Chaim Soutine's crazy lady, Amedeo Modigliani's loving portrayal of his friend Chaim Soutine. He stands and looks and lets them overtake him, one by one by one, and loves them all.

Gertrude is deeper into Lucretius. How did she know to copy out that particular passage for him? He pulls the piece of paper from his pocket, unfolds it.

...in numbers vast
Shifting now here, now there, the primal seeds,
Harried by blows relentless through the course
Of endless time, where'er their tiny weights
Might speed them on, have gone their wonted ways,
Meeting at random, groping sightlessly

314

For whatsoe'er they haply might create
By meeting...

This is about the beginnings of the Universe, but what a metaphor for the psyche in the midst of change. His psyche, the psyches of his clients. Or any relationship in the midst of change. He does hope he can be adequate for Bob Smith who, as expected, failed to show up on Thursday. Petra, when he called her for reassurance, simply said, "Take a deep breath, Michael. Good. Now try not to worry. He'll be back." At least he doesn't worry about Wilma who somehow convinced him she'll be fine, and more than fine. Gertrude laughed, delighted at the surprise of Wilma's suddenly stopping treatment, if "treatment" it ever was. They agreed: Wilma was essentially a gift from the gods, a thing fallen from the sky. Michael's task had been to open his hands and catch her, and be graceful when she hopped down out of his grasp. When he told Gertrude he had let Wilma go without a single cautionary gesture, she just said, "Perfect." It was as if she believed everything he did now would be perfect. What had come over her? Was she in fact on some medication?

Not that he's complaining.

The woman from the Pontiac has completed her *tête-à-tête* with Paul Bunyan. Off she goes, carrying her over-sized purse, or whatever it is. Looks heavy. She seems fine, really. As if she has a purpose, knows what she's about. Determined. He decides he likes her.

He takes out his harmonica. Thanks to Danny, it's in good working order. Cleaned and soaked, and something else Danny did to it, he isn't clear what. He's been fooling around with it, trying this 'n' that, getting his lips and tongue into condition. Had to pull back after overdoing a few days ago, so he's taking it slow, slow, slow. What an experience, though, even at his level. He loves this sound, how physical it is, how it reverberates through him. Hums.

So he has another humming relationship. He'll be watching for Wilma. Will she have her little backpack? Pretty soon he'll get out of this car, get himself moving, see where the woman who converses with statues has gone. Maybe he'll offer a few words, see if she wants contact. They might have things in common. After all, he converses with painted people.

But first a bit of *Oh, Susanna.*

315

~ ~ ~

Wilma is walking, solitary and companioned, best of both. No actual living human walks with her, but her ghosts are along for the journey. Alma and Lorraine have been good company lately. It's almost as if the three of them are living together again, but without the irritations of actuality. Whimsy is a talented ghost-maker, if whimsy this is. She is pleasantly aware of her little burden, Alma's frayed backpack, the literary and philosophical contents of which are: Michael's poems, Murdoch's *Unicorn*, Spinoza's *Ethics*, Stephen Mitchell's Rilke collection with a bookmark at the sonnet about the unicorn, Alma's pages, and Pa's article on Spinoza. A light load, just enough to give the sensation of physical presence beyond her own body, which is feeling fine today, and intellectual presence beyond her own mind, which is also doing well, thank you very much. It would have been impractical to bring Pa's notebooks though she had an urge to do just that. They did want to come but reality was recognized. They stayed home, as did the water bottle, filled and waiting on the kitchen counter. A forgotten bottle. Thirst is already a part of this walk. Never mind. When she needs water, she'll find it.

Dear Pa. At least his article is with her. Imagine: Henry Schuh, published writer. She still shakes her head in wonderment over the fact.

He sends his greetings, Wilma.

Thank you, Alma. Send mine back.

He and Spinoza are having one of their talks, dear. I'll speak to him later. My, how happy they look.

Wilma smiles and thinks about the notebooks. Pa's Folly, they could have been, but are not. What if she'd brought them? She can see her body bent at the hips, her back a horizontal surface holding the two-foot-high pile of notebooks. She hobbles along, earnest daughter of earnest father.

But she topples with her tower. Smash! All fall down.

In the real world she walks on, laughing but sturdily upright, anticipating. She's on her way to Bass Park and the next stage of her life. There are scenes ahead, scenes of difference, layers of reality. The park, the people, the performance: a complex prospect.

The complexity breaks to separate melodies, played simultaneously. Counterpoint?

316

Polyphony?

She ought to call on Bach, for consonance amid the complexity.

Dissonance will no doubt enter in. It might even become the Tone of the Day, who can predict? Off into dissonance, then! And adventure!

But harmony in the end, courtesy of Bach.

Aren't we in a good mood today?

Yes we are, Lorraine.

I understand you intend to make a thing or two happen before evening comes along.

That I do.

I'm reminded of the last time you attempted—

I shall again ascend the stairs.

I can only wish you luck, and add that outcomes are unpredictable.

Wilma knows very well that outcomes are unpredictable, but if she's not invited to go up the stairs to Marlene's apartment, if Marlene perchance is not even present at the Bass Park event, she will nevertheless walk to the building, take the steps one by one, and knock purposefully on the door behind which strange art and a beloved though irritating artist reside. She regrets having left the bookcase half-painted, but she's had so much to do. The Plan is being followed, the god is gusting frequently, her reading hours have expanded, and she has become a walker. *Become a walker*, she wrote, adding to The Plan after her last meeting with Michael. She left the man to his own devices and began to walk daily, several miles. Increased strength and a habit of action have been her goals. The bookcase has been patient.

What if she'd manage to finish it? Assembled, it wouldn't go into the Volkswagen. Onto the back then, in place of Pa's notebooks. Bent forward, burdened by her own project, she takes the final steps. She sees herself entering Bass Park. Marlene of course runs to her immediately, knows the beautiful thing is for her, is unable to contain her pleasure, hops around and around in circles. Leaving Wilma, by the way, bent and burdened with bookcase.

Oh, my. Unrealistic on more than one front. For one thing, some man would be sure to come along and insist on lifting the thing from her back. Also, she happens to be seventy years of age. There are limits.

In fact, today is her birthday.

Happy Birthday To You.

317

Why, Lorraine, you can hold to a tune now.

There are some benefits to the afterlife, Wilma.

In addition to books and papers, a few other things rest inside backpack. Toothbrush, pajamas, underpants, clean shirt, socks. She has her intentions. It's been long enough.

What is not in the backpack is that abandoned water bottle, lonely on the kitchen counter. How thirsty she is.

On she walks.

And on.

Finally, Bass Park. She can see that she's in plenty of time. Small crowd milling around, some folks involved in setting things up. She takes her backpack off and sits on the grass beside another early woman, this one in a large sun hat and a long colorful skirt. The woman looks at her for a moment, a quick and careful assessment. Wilma passes inspection, she can see that. She must appear harmless.

"We're early," Wilma says.

"I've been here a while already. I drove up from Massachusetts."

"What an effort you made."

"A man came by. Why would he do that? No one else was here at that point. I couldn't be sure what sort he was, so I sent him away."

"That might be best. Have you by any chance located a drinking fountain? I find myself with a thirst."

"He was here for the performance."

"Well, he might have been all right then."

The woman reaches carefully into her large bag without really opening it, feels around for a moment, then pulls out a bottle of water.

"Oh, I couldn't—"

"I have extra, dear. It's only Christian charity."

Wilma drinks.

"Thank you so much. I must be getting forgetful. I have a bottle sitting on the kitchen counter all ready to go but it didn't come along. My name is Wilma. Wilma Schuh."

"Gracie. Pleased to meet you. I'm the mother."

"Oh! Of our young Henry?"

There is a stiff pause.

"My son is Milo. He's musical."

"Of course. Now that I look I can almost see the resemblance. I met Milo at the Winnie-the-Pooh performance. He is indeed musical, a brilliant guitarist. Inventive, I'd say. Not that I'm a judge, but sometimes a body knows. Were you present at that performance?"

"I was not."

Gracie's jaw clenches.

This could be going better, thinks Wilma. Gracie of no last name is a contradiction on first meeting, open-faced and cautious, generous and secretive. What's in that bag, for example? But she gave a stranger a whole bottle of water.

The two sit in silence. Wilma turns her attention to the little stage, a plain raised wooden platform, a backdrop with artwork. The mythical characters of the day seem to be represented, the Unicorn, the Minotaur, Argus of the Many Eyes. She's almost certain she's looking at the work of Marlene O'Connor.

So this is what the woman has been doing with herself.

She takes a deep breath, closes her eyes, tries to feel the god gusting, entering everyone, including her.

No gusting, at least not in a way perceptible to her.

In fact, she's plain nervous. She turns to Gracie.

"How long has Milo been playing the guitar?"

"What? Oh. I don't know. Young. He was young. I can't—"

"I find memory a bit slippery myself. I studied up on these topics."

"What?"

"The unicorn and the others. I went to the library. I have a friend there. Raymond. He doesn't know if he's Penobscot or another sort of Wabanaki."

Words are coming out without intention or comfort but she seems to be paddling the same stream Gracie is, two women not quite themselves.

"It's not an Indian creature," Gracie says, "Wabanaki or otherwise. I have a Wabanaki in my church. We like to welcome anyone decent. It's not from the Indians, I know that much."

"The unicorn? No, I don't suppose so. Maybe you know more about it than I do."

Perhaps the god *is* gusting, but with unaccustomed rapidity—or it's Kali—wasn't she whizzing past just now, burdened with the implements of violence?

319

"It goes back to the Bible," Gracie is saying, "or some claim it does. My version says wild ox. The issue is translation. Maybe your librarian told you about the lap of a virgin."

"That's what Raymond led me to, a write-up of the myth."

"Lays his head in the lap of a virgin and the hunters come."

"And kill him. Yes. Death enters in."

Gracie smiles. "Yes, death enters in," she says.

Wilma relaxes. They have communicated, nothing more needs saying. A comfortable silence ensues. She drinks more of Gracie's water and closes her eyes, grateful. She has sat herself down beside the right woman.

~ ~ ~

If we were physicists we might find the bright logic of this Bass Park scene, the kind that digs down under common rational energies and gets to the red beating heart. If we were intuitive physicists, that is, gifted and inclined toward such an exercise, we might reach into the field and pull out just the right thing, the perfect metaphor; the atom, for example, with its unclear boundaries. They say it's difficult to predict the behavior of an atom precisely because of those wobbly edges. Where might it go? What might it do? No normal measuring device can manage it. And then *inside* that smallest unit of ordinary matter: up, down, charmed, strange, top, bottom, all that whirling and bouncing!

Kandinsky's abstracts come to mind. Lines, energies, colors, colors, colors.

And Lucretius's seeds of matter, how they swerve.

And Deleuze's creatively exploding ongoing difference.

Also bombs. Hiroshima. Nagasaki.

And the silent electrical substrate of contemporary civilized life. On good days we don't even think of the terrifying potential. We have the lamps in our living rooms, and the poems they enable us to read on quiet winter evenings. Rilke. Blake. And hot showers. Cold lemonade for summer. Streetlights. How could any of that hold a kernel of violence?

~ ~ ~

It will be hours before streetlights are called for. A subtle sun, modest behind clouds, illuminates the park and the people who have gathered. Henry Whitsun is moving around the park, briefly greeting those he loves—including his father, sober today—and greeting also those he barely knows and cannot yet love but probably likes well enough and is certainly happy to see. It is not only Michael and Wilma and Marlene and lover-narrator Frank and sweet young guitarist Milo, but also a decent number of Bangor area gays he met not long ago and those he has yet to meet who populate the park; and scatterings of children along with their parents; and adults who fit no known category. And Gracie, of course. And John Stone. Thanks to him and the Bangor Daily News, Henry is suddenly, in a local, minor (but certainly exciting) way, known. Known as mime and known as gay man.

It isn't all *that* many people, we mustn't exaggerate. Twenty-five? Thirty? A good crowd, considering. Overwhelmingly, these people gather because of love, or at least real interest, and even a sort of joy. Today's performers have already declared the day a success. If they fall flat, surely they'll be caught by loving arms. And they won't fall flat, they can feel it, it's going to *work*!

This is faith; and hope; and large-hearted far-spreading charity.

Milo, excited and confident and nervous—a roiling mix—and definitely feeling his youth, has been in conversation with John Stone who, assigned to write an article about the afternoon's happenings, and feeling his own youth and the wonder of his success (his interview article was *published*, and with barely a word cut!) wants very much to be introduced to the mother of the guitarist. He doesn't know that the father of the mime is present or he'd be getting himself introduced there, too. In fact, as events unwind, he never will quite grasp that the mime's father was in the park. Gracie will be his focus, the center of a longer article than he meant to write.

My mother *came*, she *came*, Milo says under his breath as he and John Stone walk toward Gracie and, he suddenly realizes, toward Wilma Schuh whom he met briefly after the last performance. Wilma has not, of course, moved from her place beside the right woman. As soon as he arrived at the park, Milo saw his mother. She was sitting alone then. Very much alone. He had time only for a hug—sorry, he had things to do, he'd

321

see her later. He could feel her pride as she smiled and spoke of the Will of God and held on. She could hardly let him go.

She *came*, my mother *came*.

He hopes she won't mind meeting a reporter.

Michael has joined Petra and Nat, Raymond and Danny, and an enthusiastic young Sephie. They make a comfortable little circle. He is, on a dare from Petra, blowing and drawing on his harmonica, his hands cupping the instrument, producing note by careful note the opening bars of *Swing Low, Sweet Chariot*. A few bars only, that was the deal. There is enthusiastic applause from the little circle. Danny, as agreed, takes over. The tune's full potential comes pouring out. Everyone sings the chorus as it comes around again and again—*Comin' for to carry me home*—good words, sweeter and deeper and more saturated with pain and longing at every repetition.

Milo has gone to do last minute things up near the stage, leaving John Stone to interview Gracie. Wilma is feeling happily superfluous. She listens in a vague way to John and Gracie but her mind is free to wander over to the singing circle. She does not, therefore, miss the moment when Marlene joins and starts singing along, standing beside Michael as if she's his best friend, her voice more robust than any other. *Swing low, sweet chariot—*

Suddenly, as Wilma can clearly see, her dear friend breaks into sobs.

She keeps herself where she is. Michael will take care of Marlene. This is not the time for her to—

Count to ten, dear, says Alma.

Better make it twenty-five, says Lorraine, *and don't look.*

Wilma counts, she waits, she doesn't look. She tries to listen to the story of Milo's life as told to the reporter by his mother Gracie who at this moment seems not the least bit suspicious or secretive as she lets loose a flight of words, obviously pleased to have a listener who takes notes.

Enough. Wilma lets herself look. She was right to stay put. It couldn't have been three minutes ago that Marlene started sobbing but she's laughing now, probably at her own disintegration, and urging Danny to take them back into the tune. The chorus is gently sung a few more times and silence falls. Wilma can feel the solemnity of the moment in the group she would like to be part of.

322

Michael seems to be playing host now, introducing Marlene.

The conversation grows lively over there but cannot be heard in detail. Should she—?

Not yet.

Gracie talks on. John Stone takes more notes.

The performance will start soon. Before it starts, shouldn't she—?

But, no. Marlene has left the circle. She's coming this way. Here she is. Introductions, then. "Marlene, this is Gracie. Gracie is Milo's mother." "Oh, Milo's mother, such a sweet kid." Marlene and John remember each other from Pizza Hut the day of the Winnie-the-Pooh performance. "Great article." "Thanks."

Time gets a little choppy for Wilma. Marlene has her by the hand and is taking her in the direction of Michael's circle and telling her that this woman, Petra, has invited them to join Dykes Who Love Literature and isn't it just what they both need? A rush of words, unstoppable. "One of DWELL's members—they call the group DWELL—her name is Ricki, is moving downeast to be closer to her Indian friend, Ann Marie Redfeather, isn't that a wonderful name, though they aren't lovers any more, but they want to be closer, geographically I mean, they're plenty close in other ways, a lot of history there though not as much as the older members of the group because Ricki was their Baby Dyke, but that was a while ago now, so Ricki got a job downeast at the school where Ann Marie teaches, she's passionate about grammar—Ricki is—think of *that* —and, well, anyway, the group is one member down and Petra and the others have been feeling for a while that they need some fresh—"

She can endure no more. "Why were you crying, Marlene?"

"Philomena."

"Oh."

They have arrived at the group.

"Hello, Michael."

"Hello, Wilma."

And to Marlene: "When did she—?"

Marlene's eyes fill but she doesn't actually cry. "Last night."

The two stand and look at each other. The others wait, respectful, apparently comfortable.

"Are you—?"

323

"I'm fine. It was the music. Danny's *good*—and that song—but I'm fine. It was time, she was ready, I was ready. Will you come over tonight, though?"

"I was intending to."

"You were intending to."

"I was intending to."

"Well, you're like that."

"Yes, I am."

"OK."

Marlene turns to the others. "We're finished. Thank you for your patience."

Petra smiles and says, "Our privilege. Wilma, we'd love it if—"

Marlene breaks in. "Petra invites people to the group on impulse. The last person she invited committed suicide. Nat felt obliged to add that to the invitation. Petra then felt obliged to poke her in the side. They're lovers. Nat's in DWELL too. Anyway, Petra felt like inviting us."

"I still feel like inviting you," says Petra.

Wilma nods. She's not ready to respond. She greets Raymond and the others who smile and nod and welcome her. She feels the counterpoint of the day, or is it polyphony, and is making her best effort to grasp how it all fits together. Petra is giving a quick sketch of the operations of Dykes Who Love Literature. "Our next poet is Emily Dickinson. None of us has read enough of her. We know she can be tangled and intriguing and we want to get past our high school—"

Another person is joining the circle.

"Hello, Michael."

Michael turns to Bob Smith.

"Hello, Bob."

"Robbie Lou, actually."

It takes Michael only a moment. Right. Robbie Lou.

"Everyone, this is Robbie Lou."

"Hello, Robbie Lou." A chorus.

What happens to Michael at this moment? Is he surprised? No, he is not surprised. Well, maybe a little, but this was almost predictable, wasn't it? And it's good, he can let go of whatever concern about suicide he might be suppressing. He's a sophisticated therapist, he knows he's probably been suppressing.

324

"Did you read the material, Michael? The material that I, or, that is, we—?"

"Yes. Yes, I did. Very interesting. Maybe we can talk about it—"

"I believe that will be possible on Thursday, *if* you happen to have the time."

"I have the time."

The two men look at each other. Michael is trying to recognize his client.

"Well," says Robbie Lou. He turns to the group. "Have you all seen this *wonderful* article in the Bangor Daily?" He reaches into his large purse.

Nat says, "Nice purse."

Dyke greeting faggot, thinks Michael, amused and impressed. Nat has her ways.

"Do you like it? I tried, you know, to find a *man purse* but they're so *terribly* expensive and I thought, why *not* this one? I do love it."

There is a bit of conversation about John Stone's article. John is praised by those who have read it—Petra, Marlene, and Michael. Robbie Lou distributes copies to all who have not—Wilma, Raymond, Danny, and Sephie. He says he regards spreading the word as his *work*. Also, he wants to tell everyone that he's *sure* this is going to be a *most* interesting performance, the unicorn is such a *powerful* figure, he's been to the Musée de Cluny in Paris—that is, his, um, friend, an art critic—well—at any rate—yes, he's seen the tapestries—*The Lady and the Unicorn*, you know—and they're *wonderful*—the *vivid* colors, the *intricacy* of the stitching—

Out of the corner of her eye Wilma sees Lyle Franklin, his slight limp, his one good eye. He stops to speak to a little girl, bending forward as they shake hands.

A microphone is tapped and Frank tells everyone the performance will begin in a couple of minutes. He thanks them for their patience. Wilma looks over at Gracie. She's alone now. Too, too alone. Wilma thanks Petra for the invitation to Dykes Who Love Literature and says that though she's not entirely sure about the word dyke—but that hardly matters, does it?—not that she objects, it's just that she has never—yes, she believes she'd like to be part of—but at the moment she does feel a need to join her new friend—

325

Marlene startles and says, "Oh, God, I was supposed to—I need to —we'll meet at the end, Wilma." And she starts to rush away.

To her back, Wilma says, "Is that your art?"

Marlene whirls around. "Yes! Everyone, that's my art up there!"

Appreciation and amazement are duly expressed. Marlene heads toward the stage. Wilma sees that Lyle has seated himself next to someone she doesn't know. He appears to be deep in conversation with a person whose gender is a bit uncertain. A customer? It occurs to her that she thinks of Lyle as friendless. This is possibly inaccurate. And of course, lately, she and he—

But the performance is about to begin. She takes her place beside Gracie who nods, but says nothing. A bit stiff again, Wilma notes. Well, never mind.

~ ~ ~

The performers stand on the raised platform, three presences in white tights and snugly-fitted white shirts, barefoot, rooted, motionless, silent. They must have worn their jeans and loose shirts over these stark costumes and stripped quickly at the last moment. Did anyone even notice? They stand transformed, waiting as the audience settles itself.

Silence comes over the audience like a huge slow bird, a solemn thing. The sparse Sunday traffic on Main Street might be moving in another world. Behind the performers, looming large, is a triptych of portraits, one mythic creature per panel. Not quite abstract, not quite figural, the creatures are recognizable enough as Unicorn, Minotaur, and Argus Panoptes. We seem to sense a connection between this triptych and Marlene's portrait of Young Henry, as if the artist longed to paint the mime again but was afraid of consequences. Are we about to see Henry mime a threefold expression of his own being?

Or might something less predictable take place?

Henry and Frank step quietly back and to the side. Milo, deliberate, self-contained, walks to the edge of the platform where Marlene is waiting. She hands him his guitar. Every movement is sculpted. The silence holds. Milo takes center stage, plays a few haunting notes, stops. Frank announces in a clear calm voice: "'Unicorn Sonnet' by Rainer

326

Maria Rilke, *Sonnets to Orpheus*, book two, number four." Milo sings, a cappella: "Oh this is the animal that never was..."

We see Marlene try to catch Wilma's eye.

Does Wilma remember their first afternoon together, how Marlene, after the rainstorm, after they shopped for food, after their separate baths, found this sonnet? How she read it aloud? It was their beginning.

Wilma remembers. The counterpoint of the day continues. Beside her is Gracie, mother of the boy with the angelic voice whose guitar enters and recedes, enters and recedes, small pure phrasings from the instrument alternating with the clear sweet unaccompanied voice. Gracie is stunned, unbreathing, seeing her son as if for the first time. It is the pain of more pride than she can manage. Wilma feels the intensity of the mother's being, feels the wonder of the boy's performance, and knows: Marlene made this happen, this sonnet, here, today. She is falling just a little further into an abyss of appreciation—appreciation for the strangely compelling quality of Marlene's unique being—while Rilke's animal that never was and didn't need actual existence is drawing near to the virgin, white and gleaming, and—here is the miracle—*enters existence*. The poet has reversed the myth. Not death, but new being. She turns to her new friend to share her pleasure.

Gracie, however, is unable to relate to any human just now.

Wilma understands, needs nothing from Gracie. Her ghosts are smiling. They love this day.

The sonnet has ended. Milo stands, holding his guitar, breathing, breathing. The audience is silent, unsure how to respond. Who expected poetry? It takes a moment but they decide they approve. It was, after all, daring. The applause comes, the volume increasing, increasing.

Milo grins and bows and moves to the side of the stage.

Frank steps forward. "Welcome, everyone—ladies and gentlemen— ladies and ladies—gentlemen and gentlemen—kids of all kinds."

Segments of the audience hoot and applaud.

"Thank you," Frank says, and bows. He turns as if to leave the stage. Many laugh. He looks up at the statue, cups his hands, and shouts, "H-e-l-l-o, Paul Bunyan! How ya' doin' today?" More laughter. He faces his audience and smiles dramatically and wipes his forehead with the back of his hand. "He's fine. Old Paul is fine, what a relief."

327

"Yay, Paul," someone yells from the audience. Scattered applause for Paul Bunyan.

"All right," Frank says. "Time for the serious stuff." He twirls in a complete circle, leans forward, peers out over the audience while shading his eyes with one hand, nods approvingly, and begins.

"Once upon a time, we say. Now, I've been trying to understand that. Up. On. A. Time. I know this is a time, right here, right now. How do we get ourselves up on it, though? Last night I had a dream and I might as well invite you into it since it sort of answers this sticky question. It's about mushrooms. I hope you like mushrooms. Yuck, some of you secretly say. Well, I'm not asking you to *eat* them."

"*I* like to eat mushrooms," says a little girl, jumping up and down.

Her big brother hushes her but Frank says he's very, very glad whenever anyone likes to eat mushrooms or watch them or even get on top of one, if it happens to be large and firm enough to hold an entire human being which is what some mushrooms, mythical mushrooms, can do. "There's one, right over there. I do believe it was in my dream. It stuck its head up at midnight and looked around and decided that Bass Park was fine place to be. It grew fast, mushrooms do that. In fact, it's already huge. It's a Time Mushroom. Wait. It's getting bigger. Bigger. Bigger. What a nice firm friendly giant mushroom! Let me see if I can get myself up on it."

He closes his eyes, gives a little hop, opens his eyes.

"I did it! Here I am, just this once, up on a time! Well, a Time Mushroom, but what's the difference? It's magic! A magic mushroom! Maybe some of you older folks are thinking of Puff, the Magic Dragon right now, but he's for another time and place, so behave yourselves. Anyone who wants to can get on top of the Time Mushroom. The trick is to close your eyes. Ready? All right. Close your eyes. Now up, up, up you go! That's right! Here we are! Open your eyes. See? We're almost as high as Paul Bunyan, up on our magic mushroom and we are in the Land of Myths. Three good myths today, the myth of the Unicorn, the myth of the Minotaur, and the myth of Argus of the Many Eyes. And we'll be making our own myth, too. Why not?"

Almost surreptitiously, Henry has begun to mime. Milo's guitar wanders in and out.

328

"Once upon a time," says Frank, "or a Time Mushroom, if you prefer, the people of Bangor, Maine looked around. From up on their giant Time Mushroom they looked and looked. What were they looking for? They were looking for a unicorn, of course. What is a unicorn? Some of you already know."

From the audience come the voices, not all of them belonging to children.

"A horse with a horn!"

"Yeah, one horn, pretty weird."

"It's not real."

"Yes it is."

"It's all white."

"Sometimes it's other colors."

"I saw one once."

"You did not."

"*I* want to see it."

"I think it's got pink around it."

"That's for babies."

"It's a myth, you can believe it or not believe it."

"Very good," says Frank. "You know a lot already. Yes, the unicorn of myth is a beast with one horn, a horse most of the time—though, in the way of myths, this is not entirely consistent. Never mind that. A horse with one horn, strong and wise. Unicorns are very shy and very innocent. They don't let themselves be seen by just anyone. Most of the time they're downright invisible. The great themes of appearance and reality slide onto the mushroom with us today, ladies and gentlemen, gents and gents, gals and gals, kids and kids—"

"Yay, Frank," someone yells.

Frank *has* these people, Michael thinks. Palm of his hand, very charismatic, I like him myself. Henry moves around the stage, decorating the edges of Frank's monologue, allowing Frank his moment, adding to it. Henry inhabits his body so completely when he's not off into his mind and his books. Michael loves to watch the work, the very speechlessness of it. And when they meet again at Pizza Hut, they'll have actual conversation. Where will they go with it this time? Their future feels suddenly challenging. A mystery. Almost dangerous.

329

"Yes," says Frank. "Well. As I was saying, most of the time unicorns are invisible, but let's look around and see what we can see. We'll need a lot of eyes. Have you ever heard of Argus Panoptes? You have! One, two, three, four people have heard of Argus. Well, let me tell you about him. He had hundreds of eyes. He was some seer. What a watchdog. Did he have to sleep? Of course he did, he worked hard. But he never ever closed all of his eyes at once. Well, not until later in the story when he was bored to death, so to speak, by one of those old gods who had it in for him. But Argus during his glory years slept with some eyes closed, getting a good rest, while his other eyes stayed open, open, open. But, wait. We all do that! Every night I go to bed. Do you go to bed every night? Every night I go to bed and close my regular eyes. I bet you do, too. We close our regular eyes and now we're sleeping and guess what? We have dream eyes! Our dream eyes are open and we see ever so many things. Maybe Argus wasn't so unusual after all. And I just thought of another thing. Here we are today, all of us, and we are all human, so we are All One, one giant human phenomenon—with, you guessed it, many eyes. And with our many eyes I just *know* we can see the unicorn. Yes! There he is! He's going into this place called a labyrinth—lovely word, isn't it?—where it's very easy to get lost. He's not worried, though. He'll find his way. He's going to visit an old friend of his, the Minotaur. Now this Minotaur fellow is quite unusual. Well, aren't we all? But the Minotaur is really quite, quite different, being part human and part bull, and he's not having the happiest time in his life because he has to live inside this labyrinth which is also called a maze and it has so many twists and turns that he'll have to pull off a miracle to find his way out, but our kind and loving unicorn..."

By this time Gracie is quite irritated. What about the hunters and how they're getting close and how the unicorn lays his head in the virgin's lap? Oh, dear Jesus, what if they don't follow the story?

She closes her eyes. She prays.

She must have missed a beat because Frank has finally stepped out of the way and now he's telling the real story from the sidelines. Thank you, Jesus. The mime and dear Milo are the important ones now and, just as the Guides predicted, the mime is the unicorn. The hunters are after him, he's evading, evading, veering here and there and everywhere, faster and faster, seeking a safe place. Milo's guitar is becoming almost frantic.

330

Suddenly the music stops. The unicorn stops, too, a statue now, balanced on one foot, leaning forward. Everything goes silent. Milo gives his guitar to the woman at the edge of the platform and slips into a skirt.

A skirt.

This is worse than she thought it would be.

The unicorn is moving again, trying to find safety. He looks terribly frightened. Well, he has cause. Now Milo is sitting down, his skirt spread out around him. Her own boy! The unicorn is circling, searching, but little by little it's getting closer and closer to Milo who is—she sees it— the *virgin*.

Oh, my God.

She's had her hand on the gun inside the bag for a while now. She pulls them out, hand and gun, and stands up. Her Guides are with her. She is firm on her feet, the gun is steady in both hands, time is slowing, making room for the holy deed.

Wilma barely catches the movement in her peripheral vision.

Gracie aims and fires. Down onto the platform falls the faggot devil. She got him before he soiled the lap of her virgin son. *Thank you, Jesus.*

Wilma realizes, almost, what just happened.

Gracie sits, gun in hand. She looks at the gun. She looks at the little stage. She hears a moan slip from her own throat. It is a growing moan-thing, it wants to get out of her. That's all right. That's certainly all right. What did she expect? After all—

Wilma turns to Gracie, everything in slow motion just now for both women. She gently takes possession of the handgun and puts her arm around Milo's mother. She looks to the stage and sees Michael and Marlene and Frank surround Henry. She sees Milo sitting, the circle of his skirt perfectly in place, his hands open, waiting for Henry, staring out at his mother. She turns back to Gracie. This is her place, with her new friend. The sirens would be loud if they could be heard but her ears have been producing a steady ring and now she is temporarily deaf. A Smith and Wesson .38 caliber will do that to a person, as she will learn some time later.

~ ~ ~

331

Marlene's bedroom. A clean sheet and light blanket cover Marlene and Wilma as they lie on their backs side by side, two women untouching. They have been through the hours together. This is the hiatus. Marlene sleeps, tears spent. Wilma does not sleep. She is moving in and out of the events, absorbing. She is not troubled. She might even be described as peaceful, or perhaps contemplative would be the better word. Her ghosts are nearby but quiet, as if sitting on chairs in the deepest shadows of the room. Her god is also quiet, but present as essence of all.

Henry lies in the hospital in a coma, surgery completed. The doctors cannot say whether he will live or die. His father and his new lover Frank and his former lover Michael will watch through the night at his bedside in ICU, one at a time, obeying the rules. Wilma and Marlene were urged, virtually ordered, to go home, get some sleep, they will be needed later. Michael will call, "should anything change."

Milo is with his incarcerated mother, begging anyone who will listen to please, please tell him how to get her transferred from the jail to a hospital, there must be a hospital where someone mentally ill can get help, she's not a bad person, she's such a good person. He has spoken briefly with a lawyer, someone gave him a number to call, but nothing will happen until morning. John Stone stands by—reporter, new friend to Milo—but what can he do? Wilma, knowing nothing of events at the jail, knows nevertheless that Milo is terrified.

Lying in bed beside Marlene, she brings sweet young Milo into her heart. She welcomes Gracie, the well-meaning shooter, into her heart. Frank has a place there, and the father, the poor father.

The others, Young Henry, Marlene, and Michael, are so firmly melded with her own being that there is no thought of heart. They are all one animal, they are living this thing together.

The details come and go. The hard gun in her hand as she took it from Gracie. Her arm around the woman who shot her dear Henry. Lyle suddenly there, his warm hand against her back, taking the gun, handing it to the officer. The face of the officer, a young woman. Too young. The other officers, joining her, one a large black man with presence, the other a white youngster, breathing hard. They all are so young—the officers, Henry, Frank, Milo. Even Gracie is young.

332

The ride to the hospital, Marlene driving, Michael and Frank in the back seat. The deafness receding, the sirens becoming audible as they speed through the streets. Marlene slips through the red lights, a car pulled forward in the wake of the ambulance in a world of sirens. Inside the ambulance are the patient, the EMTs, the father.

The Emergency Room parking lot.

The large doors opening.

The rushing, the sleek floors, the bright lights, the waiting.

The news: he has not died.

The drive away from the hospital. Wilma driving Marlene's car, Marlene allowing this, her tears having begun after hours of control. How surprising, how impressive Marlene became in the hospital, taking charge, making sure Henry's father was given information, making sure he was treated with respect, passing the information to the others, Frank and Michael and Wilma.

Wilbur. The father's name is Wilbur, echo of Wilma's own, or hers is an echo of his. She has never known a Wilbur. This one appears fractured in his essence, the pieces put together again and again over the years, never quite fitting; the pain leaking out, old pain; the new added in, another piece that won't fit.

Marlene, the death of Philomena so new, her Henry shot and in surgery, gets coffee for everyone. "No, let me do this," she says to them all. They sit in chairs. They make their introductions. Only Marlene has met Wilbur before this day. Wilbur Whitsun, her sometime mechanic.

They drink their coffee. They tell Frank the performance was wonderful, it was such a fine start, it's terrible that—

Well of course it is, what can they say?

They take turns getting up, walking away, coming back.

When the plans for the hopeful anguished nighttime bedside watch are made, when the drive to Marlene's is accomplished, when the two woman have climbed the stairs and entered the apartment, they walk to the portrait, as if in accord with a plan. They stand and look at him, Marlene's Henry. After a while Marlene says, "I know the painting didn't make this happen." Wilma nods. They stand looking, breathing. Marlene says, "I think I'll light a candle." She pulls a little stool close to the painting. She gets a candle, a tall red one, and lights it. "Sorry about the color," she says. Wilma shakes her head, laughs a little, says the color is

333

fine, solemnity is not required of a candle. They hold hands, standing there, the red candle with its steady flame, the portrait with its Henry essence. Marlene sighs. "No. Not right." She blows out the candle, takes it away, moves the stool back where it was.

"Come and sit," Wilma says. They sit on the couch and Wilma holds Marlene and Marlene cries some more, saying quietly again and again, "It's both of them." Wilma replies again and again, "I know." Peace, strange and necessary, comes. After a while Marlene says she wants warm milk and cookies. They have their snack and go to bed. Marlene sleeps.

Finally, having sufficiently acknowledged the realities, Wilma also sleeps. Her dream is of Young Henry's fine mind, intact, alert, disembodied, transmuting threads to father-philosopher Henry Schuh for the weaving of a vividly colored, intricately designed tapestry with a unicorn at the center. Her god is a pinpoint of near-light spreading with such subtlety through the atmosphere of the dream that she seems to breath it, or hear it as a low hum, a hum below the threshold of hearing. A sentence echoes in the background. *All is metaphor*. She erases the sentence as a thing far too palpable. The blackboard is from school days, the eraser is clapped clean by Alma's angel who walked into the sun. This is the wiping away of unnecessary words. She sleeps then, very soundly, beyond the place of dreams, having somehow, unknowing, taken Marlene's hand into her own.

Seven: Epilogue

the ever-active core of the Real, automatically lovable

Henry remained in a coma for two weeks, his father and his friends sitting beside him one after another through the days, through the nights, talking to him, reading to him, holding his hand; or reading their books silently, or holding their newspapers, solving crossword puzzles, staring into space; or (Milo) softly playing the guitar; or (Michael) humming, then trying a few harmonica chords; or (all) praying, or meditating; thinking, remembering, quietly weeping; or (some) dozing, but never deeply, and never for long.

Then, after two weeks, at three in the morning, with only young Milo present, Henry stopped breathing. No restlessness, no struggle for further breath, no sign, unless there was something to Milo's feeling—it was not something he saw, exactly, it more something he knew—that Henry opened one eye and closed it, quick as a lightning strike. It could have been a sort of wink, a wink in reverse, or a last stolen look at the world, or a bioelectric event, or nothing at all.

Those two weeks of sitting with Henry were precious to all. The beloved young man—offspring, lover, friend, fellow artist, model, inspiration—might die. Hope waxed and waned, a tide. If nothing else, they were granted this time with him, hour by hour.

But early, very early, Wilma and Michael understood that hope was beside the point—the sharp clear point they both could see, as Wilma put it, where Henry stood, ready to take flight. How they knew, they could not say. They followed one another quite often in the schedule. More than once one of them stood at the door, witness to the other. Wilma heard Michael make a joke: "I thought we'd be Platonic, Henry, but not *this* Platonic." He took Henry's hand then, and lifted it and kissed it, and dropped it, and walked to the window. The view was of the river, the Penobscot, their wide comfort, light-catcher, lovely. One evening she heard Michael playing *Swing Low, Sweet Chariot* as she walked toward the room. The tune was finished and he was weeping openly when she entered. She took him in her arms and held him for a while. Once he caught her reading Deleuze to the man in a coma. Deleuze! She told him she'd been reading Rilke earlier, for her own benefit, "*Duino Elegies*, Michael. The poet says murderers are easy to understand. I find this a balm. I believe our Young Henry would, too, if he happened to focus on the matter. I've been to visit Gracie. She tells me of a story in which the Minotaur knew the way out of his maze." Michael stopped her, reminded

337

her that Henry would have to die before Gracie would be called a murderer. She looked at him. "You know, as I do, that Henry will die." Michael met her eye and nodded. They understood they were the only ones. The others were thrashing around in hope, Wilma said, her compassion for the poor hopeful things in her voice. Michael pondered the idea that murderers are easy to understand. "That might be going a bit far for me, Wilma," he said. He could see she was ahead of him on that road and he told her so. She assured him his pace was just fine, but it was a relief to speak of death as a certainty, wasn't it? He nodded. Yes, it was a relief. They talked about Gracie, her unusual mind. "I find our minds touch at times, Gracie's and my own," Wilma said. "It's a satisfaction to me. I had my murder, you might remember." "Well, yes, Wilma. But there was a difference." "Oh, there is always difference," she said. "Young Henry led me to that, with his philosopher."

~ ~ ~

When Marlene was not at Henry's bedside, or painting compulsively, or with Wilma—they slept together every night now—she was tending to Wilbur, and to Milo, young visitor from Cambridge who, living nowhere, knowing no future, slept on Wilbur's couch. Soon it seemed only right for him to be there, he and Henry's father needed each other. It seemed they also needed Marlene who kept the place cleaner than it had ever been and made sure they ate. She laundered and folded their clothes and ran to the store to get supplies they hardly knew they needed. A woman's busy presence was a welcome thing and it was what Marlene was able to do. She could not, yet, think of visiting Gracie. She would not have understood Rilke's claim that murderers are easy to understand if Wilma had been imprudent enough to mention it to her. Murder would imply death and Marlene was unready, but of course that wasn't all. To forgive the shooter would not be in her, not yet.

The first time the two woman had sex was in the wake of an argument about whether or not Young Henry would die. It was after their first Dykes Who Love Literature meeting. DWELL, this group of older lesbians, took up Emily Dickinson's "There came a Wind like a Bugle." They took it up as if into their hands, as if it were a piece of fabric, its threads woven tight, a tough, flexible little piece of material. They put

338

their needles through it, their thought-threads. Their thoughts were sewn into the poem, a dimension added. This was something more than a simple reading for meaning, something beyond interpretation, or even appreciation, a multi-faceted group response to a tight flexible set of strangely woven words and images.

At one point the poem's green chill came over Petra—"And a Green Chill upon the Heat / So ominous did pass / We barred the Windows and the Doors / As from an Emerald Ghost"—and she talked about Sephie's terror at Bass Park, her prolonged shaking terror, and how they got her home and surrounded her, all of them, Raymond and Danny and Nat and herself, a wall of protection, for hours. But, yes, Sephie would be all right, she was a resilient soul. She was at the ocean with a friend's family for a few days now, away from any immediate reminder that her mime was shot and might die. She phoned Raymond and Danny often, said she was being brave. She cried a little but rallied and said she had to go, she really was having an OK time, the ocean was the right place to be. Sephie didn't know that the woman who had joined DWELL and then committed suicide had been her mother, didn't know a gun was involved in the carefully planned death which also included drugs and a severed artery, but the DWELL women knew and the old death, almost twelve years ago, had been brought back for all of them. Someone said this, they talked about it a little, and fell silent until it was time to end the group. Nat quoted the poem's final lines then in her firm calm voice: "How much can come / And much can go, / And yet abide the World!" Wilma and Marlene sat stunned and impressed. It was more than they had expected. DWELL would be a part of their life for years to come. They almost knew this then.

After the meeting, Marlene talked about Charlie Howard. She couldn't stop thinking about him, did Wilma know who he was? Yes, Wilma knew who he was, the young gay man thrown into the Kenduskeag stream by those three boys—high school students, weren't they?—and he couldn't swim. He died because he couldn't swim, and because he was gay. But it was a piece of news on the radio for Wilma, she was not one to get involved. Well, Marlene was one to get involved. She went on the walk to the Kenduskeag, threw flowers into the water, part of the quickly-formed group of gays and their supporters—how efficient that organizing effort had been—when suddenly, from nowhere,

Henry Whitsun appeared, her mechanic's son, standing beside her, watching as bunch after bunch of flowers hit the water. Henry, the boy who came home with her that time, the boy who was sent over to Wilma's for a cup of sugar, who sat in Wilma's kitchen and ate the cookie and drank the milk, the boy who, whether he knew it then or not, was gay. He must have been about eleven when Charlie Howard was killed. He talked about the murder when he and Marlene were planning the backdrop for the performance at Bass Park. He told her Charlie was part of why he came back to Bangor, a thing he couldn't explain. "It's as if he knew," Marlene said. "As if he had to come back to get shot. But at least he won't die."

Wilma felt something come over her. She took Marlene by the shoulders and said "Look at me. He will die. Prepare yourself, he is going to die." Marlene was rigid with anger and denial and they argued, neither woman feeling entirely like herself. They were objects of warring forces larger than themselves, the force of life, the force of death. They exhausted themselves and slept and in their sleep they reached around each other and woke from being touched and made love. They slept again, almost restored to their former selves.

The phone woke them. It was Milo. Henry had died.

~ ~ ~

That was the last day of August. September and October were task-oriented, transitional. Wilbur was grateful when Marlene suggested Henry's friends might arrange something for a memorial service. He was too broken up to think about it and anyway he wouldn't know how. John Stone wrote the service up for the paper and there were photographs, an entire page devoted to this single event at the Unitarian Universalist Church. On the next page was one of John's series of interviews with Gracie, accompanied by yet another photograph, Gracie the minister preaching to her tiny congregation back in Massachusetts. John knew about Wilbur now, but Wilbur refused to speak to him, nothing personal, a matter of holding himself together, he hoped the young man would understand.

Wilma finished the bookcase. She got Dickie, Marlene's cheerful brother, to bring his truck and they surprised Marlene who was just

340

leaving to meet with a gallery owner. There might be an exhibit, she might be part of it. "An exhibit in an upscale gallery. Me. Unbelievable," she said. They said it was perfectly believable, she was a very good artist. By this time Wilma had a key to the apartment and she and Dickie managed alone. When Marlene got back, her floor books were in the bookcase and Wilma had made muffins. Marlene burst into tears. The bookcase, the muffins, her chance as an artist, it was all too much. The exhibit was going to happen, it would be just her work and that of one other woman, it would last an entire month. The opening would be two weeks before Christmas, it couldn't be more perfect, how had this happened?

"And I've decided to do it," Marlene said.

This was confusing, of course she'd do it.

"No, I mean you."

"What?" said Wilma, but then she understood. Marlene was going to paint her portrait.

"If it turns out, it will be part of the exhibit. Don't look like that, I'll ask your permission. I might even listen to your answer."

While they waited for Gracie's case to clarify, Wilma posed, sitting naked, elbows on knees, hands clasped loosely, looking up with only her eyes, Marlene's first live model. Neither woman wanted conversation during what they called their work sessions. Marlene wanted music— Gershwin, Stravinsky, Satie—auditory input mixing with the visual. This was part of her recent transformation as an artist, hadn't she told Wilma? She hadn't, but that was fine, Wilma didn't expect to know everything in their first few months. She didn't expect to know everything about herself either. Why had she come to want this portrait so desperately? Why was it so satisfying? She only knew it felt as if the final piece of a large puzzle, long lost under an old couch cushion, had been found and fitted into place. She found a new way to relax her muscles and was able to hold the pose for longer and longer periods. When the weather cooled, Marlene brought a space heater into the studio and put it on the floor close to naked Wilma. She wore a t-shirt and shorts herself. They were both perfectly comfortable.

~ ~ ~

341

Gracie was charged with murder as soon as Henry died. She did not agree with the idea of mental illness but she didn't mind being moved to that place in Augusta for the time being if it was what everyone thought best. It was over an hour from Bangor, though, would Milo come to visit? Yes, he would. Well, fine then.

She settled into Riverview Psychiatric Center rather nicely. Not much changed for her after the trial during which, and not a minute before, she agreed she could say in good conscience that most humans, not understanding, would think she was both guilty and crazy when she executed that mime, though she herself could never entirely condemn an act ordered by her Guides. She might prefer one of those group homes on the hospital grounds, if the judge didn't mind. The judge minded, at least for the time being. She wasn't a bad judge, Gracie knew this. Look how graciously she accepted the spare Bible Milo had somehow located, such a good son. The handing over of the Bible—it went from Gracie to her patient lawyer, to the guard who stood straight in his uniform throughout the proceedings, to the judge—was a fine ending to the trial. The Guides agreed that the judge was not a bad one, though they had doubts as to whether she would read the entire Bible, she seemed a bit secular. But never mind, everything transpired in accord with the Will of God.

In exchange for her plea, Gracie was allowed to begin preaching on Sundays and, yes, all right, on Wednesday evenings also, but within the walls only. The congregation quickly became larger than the one back home and Gracie had no complaints. God has His ways. Milo came for the service once a month and played and sang. He knew all the hymns.

In Bangor, though, Milo was not exactly a Man of Faith. He and Frank went from place to place, speaking to whatever group would have them, about the ruinous effects of rigid belief.

~ ~ ~

The opening of Marlene's exhibit was a great success. John Stone's piece for the Bangor Daily had appeared the Sunday before, along with photographs of Marlene's two portraits, one of the murdered mime and one of her special friend Wilma. Marlene danced around her apartment exclaiming.

"Nudity in the Bangor Daily!"

342

"All power to the goddess of art!"

"Gay nudity!"

Wilma pretended no one would recognize her from the painting, which might have been true had her name not been in the title. *The Eyes of Wilma Schuh*, despite its title, was a whole body portrait of a woman, but a complex one. It started with Wilma posing naked on the chair, surged toward abstraction, added what Wilma called puddles of pure energy (pools to play in, Marlene said), and included a shadow portrait based on Wilma's cracked mirror art. Marlene had sketched this from an angle in the hallway early one morning while Wilma posed, standing naked, arms crossed under her breasts, in front of her hallway mirror.

Then she left Wilma to herself.

Wilma had begun to experience a hunger for solitude. She was unused to such a generously peopled life, as she put it. When Marlene was safely down the steps and could be seen getting into her car, Wilma stood at the window and let herself breathe. She would be alone until the next afternoon when Marlene needed her, please, if she could manage it. Would she come and sit, at least for an hour?

Still naked, on her way to getting dressed, Wilma passed the mirror in the hall. She was compelled to stop. *Nude by Way of Hammer on Glass.* She sat down on the floor. *Difference: the Sitter.* She tried posing sideways, knees up, arms around knees, looking over her shoulder at the mirror, a shy child. She laughed. There was nothing of the shy child left in her, old woman that she was. She stood up and messed with her hair and bent at a crazy angle and looked at herself. *Wilma Schuh in Cubist Dishevelment.*

Ah, it was good to be alone.

She dressed and sat on the brown couch and closed her eyes. She would meditate.

Images and memories, sounds and sensations, random phrases and stray ideas entered with the mantra. *Wedge, wedge, wedge*—Young Henry, collapsed and surrounded on the low stage—*wedge, wedge*—glimpses of Kali as she flitted around Bass Park—*wedge*—a wind blowing through the hospital corridors like the sound of a bugle—*wedge, wedge*—the needle entering Lorraine's arm—*wedge*—Alma's angel entering the sun—*wedge, wedge*—the universe quietly turning itself inside out—*wedge, wedge, wedge*—the splinters of many mirrors—

wedge. She took quiet breaths and waited. The silent void, familiar now, rose up and became a dance of the known and unknown, a subtle gusting, a descent. She slid down one dark side of the deep essential v-shaped geometry of existence and landed where the elements of everyone she had ever known sprang forth eternally. This was the ever-active core of the Real, automatically lovable.

It wasn't long before hunger pulled her to her feet. She opened a can of lentil soup and heated it, sliced a lemon and squeezed the juice into the soup. She thanked Marlene's Philomena, never met, for the secret of her recipe, then sat and slowly ate a late lunch while reading *The Severed Head* by Iris Murdoch. It was in many ways just another day.

~ ~ ~

In the months after Henry died, Wilma and Michael would sometimes see each other, shopping, watching gulls strut along the waterfront, walking the streets of Bangor in the night air. They both expressed an appreciation of the night skies. They would walk together or find a place to sit and talk. Henry was their link, as well as that bit of time when Michael was therapist to Wilma, a guaranteed conversant, as she put it. But she wondered if conversant could be used as a noun. It could not, but Michael understood her meaning: point number five, speak at least minimally to another human every day. She asked if he had her entire plan memorized. He said no, only that point, the one that applied to him. He grinned and labeled himself unforgivably self-centered. She took his hand and squeezed it and said, "Michael Chaim Solomon, you know better than that." They were on a bench, watching gulls, watching the river, not minding the chill in the air. She let go of his hand. They had a quiet time then, sitting and watching, nothing more to say at the moment.

~ ~ ~

Though they continued to sleep together most nights, neither Wilma nor Marlene wanted to merge households. "Too old." "Too set." "Too introverted." "Too peculiar." They laughed at their list and blessed the gods of compatibility. Nevertheless, when gay marriage became a reality

344

in Maine five years after the death of Young Henry they went to the city clerk, paid their forty dollars, and got a license. It seemed the thing to do. Marlene and Nat became ministers of the Universal Life Church, unbelieving but official. One entire DWELL meeting was devoted to the phenomenon of "old dykes getting hitched." Marlene officiated for Petra and Nat, Nat did the same for Wilma and Marlene. Everyone wore jeans. Gifts were forbidden. The poem chosen for the day was "Negotiations" by Rae Armantrout, because of the toes. Nat read the last lines with great fervor:

and a current
runs between us
where our toes touch.

Everyone applauded.

For the interested reader—

Twelve years ago...

Sephie (or Chippie, as she is then called) is a baby. Her mother commits suicide. Shirley Glubka's first novel, *Return to a Meadow*, tells the story of that suicide and how it changes the lives of all who know her, including Petra, Raymond, and Danny. Poetry, philosophy, and mystical writings are woven into what is essentially an intense psychological drama.

Works Consulted and/or Cited

Anonymous. *The Cloud of Unknowing* (*The Clowde of Unknowyng*), written in the latter half of the 14th century, edited by Patrick J. Gallacher. TEAMS Middle English Text Series. http://d.lib.rochester.edu/teams/publication/gallacher-the-cloud-of-unknowing

Bacon, Francis. *Painting, 1946.*
   http://piratesandrevolutionaries.blogspot.com/2010/02/accidents-at-butcher-shop-francis-bacon.html

_____ *Triptych, Studies from the Human Body, 1970.* http://piratesandrevolutionaries.blogspot.com/2010/01/paintings-cited-in-deleuzes-francis.html

_____ *Triptych, Three Studies of Figures on Beds, 1972.* http://piratesandrevolutionaries.blogspot.com/2010/01/paintings-cited-in-deleuzes-francis.html

_____ *Triptych, Three Studies for a Crucifixion, 1962.* http://piratesandrevolutionaries.blogspot.com/2010/01/paintings-cited-in-deleuzes-francis.html

Blake, William. *The Four Zoas*, unfinished work begun in 1797, in *The Complete Poetry & Prose of William Blake*, edited by David V. Erdman, commentary by Harold Bloom. New York: Anchor Books, a division of Random House, Inc. (1988)

Blake, William. *The Four Zoas.*
   https://en.wikisource.org/wiki/Vala,_or_The_Four_Zoas

_____ *The Ghost of a Flea.*
   https://en.wikipedia.org/wiki/The_Ghost_of_a_Flea

Bosanquet, R. G. "Remarks on Spinoza's *Ethics*," *Mind*, Vol. 54, No. 215 (July 1945)

Buber, Martin. "From the Hasidim" and *passim* in *Ecstatic Confessions: The Heart of Mysticism*, collected and introduced by Martin Buber, edited by Paul Mendes-Flohr, translated by Esther Cameron. Syracuse: Syracuse University Press (1996)

Crane, Hart. *White Buildings: poems.* Forward by Allen Tate. New York: Horace Liveright. (1926)

Deleuze, Gilles. *Difference and Repetition*, translated and with a preface by Paul Patton. New York: Columbia University Press (1994)

_____ *Expressionism in Philosophy: Spinoza*, translated by Martin Joughin. Brooklyn: Zone Books (1990)

_____ *Francis Bacon: The Logic of Sensation*, translated and with an introduction by Daniel W. Smith, afterword by Tom Conley. Minneapolis: University of Minnesota Press. (2005)

_____ *Nietzsche and Philosophy*, translated by Hugh Tomlinson. New York: Columbia University Press (1983)

Dickinson, Emily. "XXVI" in *Complete Poems* (1924) as presented at http://www.bartleby.com/113/2026.html

————"There came a Wind like a Bugle." https://genius.com/Emily-dickinson-there-came-a-wind-like-a-bugle-annotated

Durant, Will. *The Story of Philosophy: the lives and opinions of the great philosophers.* New York: Simon and Schuster (1933)

Harding, Elizabeth U. *Kali: The Black Goddess of Dakshineswar.* York Beach, Maine: Nicolas Hayes (1993)

Hesiod. "Amigos," poem attributed to Hesiod by some, most likely written between 750 and 650 B.C.E. Fragment at https://en.wikipedia.org/wiki/Argus_Panoptes

Julian of Norwich. *Showings.* Written c. 1373/1393, translated from the critical text by Edmund College, O.S.A. and James Walsh, S.J. with a preface by Jean LeClercq, O.S.B. Mahwah, N.J.: Paulist Press. (1978)

Kandinsky, Wassily. *Composition IV.* https://www.wikiart.org/en/wassily-kandinsky/composition-iv-1911

———— *Concerning the Spiritual in Art*, originally published in 1912, translated with an introduction by Michael T.H. Sadler. New York: Dover Publications. (1977)

———— *Concerning the Spiritual in Art.* Presented by semantics.com at http://www.semantikon.com/art/kandinskyspiritualinart.pdf

Kinsley, David R. *Hindu Goddesses: Visions of the Divine Feminine in the Hindu Religious Tradition.* Berkeley: University of California Press. (1986)

Lucretius. *On the Nature of Things*, written in B.C.E. 50, translated and with an introduction by Charles E. Bennett, forward by David Morton. Roslyn, N.Y.: Walter J. Black, Inc. (1946)

Milne, A.A. *Winnie-the-Pooh*, with illustrations by Ernest H. Shepard. New York: E. P. Dutton. (1926)

Modigliani, Amedeo. *Chaim Soutine*. (1917). https://commons.wikimedia.org/wiki/File:Amedeo_Modigliani_-_Chaim_Soutine_(1917).jpg

Murdoch, Iris. *The Philosopher's Pupil*. New York: Viking Press (1983)

———— *The Sea, the sea*. New York: Viking Press (1978)

———— *The Unicorn*. New York: Viking Press (1963)

Neff, Terry. *Getting Started with Ethics I*. http://home.earthlink.net/~tneff/e1begin.htm

Rilke, Rainier Maria. *Letters of Rainer Maria Rilke*, Vol. II, 1910-1926, translated by Jane Bannard Greene and M.D. Hester Norton. New York: W.W. Norton & Co. (1948)

———— *Letters of Rainer Maria Rilke*, Vol. II, 1910-1926. https://archive.org/stream/lettersofrainerm030825mbp/lettersofrainerm030825mbp_djvu.txt

———— *The Notebooks of Malte Laurids Brigge*, first published 1910, translated by Stephen Mitchell, introduction by Willian H. Gass. New York: Vintage Books, a division of Random House, Inc. (1985)

———— *The Selected Poetry of Rainer Maria Rilke*, works first published in late 19th and early 20th centuries, edited and translated by Stephen Mitchell with an introduction by Robert Haas. New York: Vintage Books, a division of Random House (1989)

Saville, Jenny. *Plan*. http://www.saatchigallery.com/artists/artpages/jenny_saville_4.htm

Shores, Corry. http://piratesandrevolutionaries.blogspot.com/2010/01/paintings-cited-in-deleuzes-francis.html

Soutine, Chaim. *Mad Woman*. (c.1919). https://www.wikiart.org/en/chaim-soutine/the-mad-woman-1

Spinoza, Baruch. *Ethics, Treatise on the Emendation of the Intellect, and Selected Letters*, written latter half of 17th century, translated by Samuel Shirley, edited and introduced by Seymour Feldman. Indianapolis & Cambridge: Hackett Publishing Co. (1992)

Walser, Robert. *The Assistant*, first published 1908, translated by Susan Bernofsky. New York: New Directions Books. (1985)

———— *The Robber*, first published 1925, translated and with an introduction by Susan Bernofsky. Lincoln, Nebraska: University of Nebraska Press (2000)

Werefkin, Marianne. *Anthill*. http://pictify.saatchigallery.com/1130164/the-athenaeum-anthill-marianne-von-werefkin

———— *La grosse Lune* (*Large Moon*). https://commons.wikimedia.org/wiki/File:Marianne_von_Werefkin_La_grosse_Lune_1923.jpg

———— *Der Kramer* (*The Chandler*). https://digitaltmuseum.se/011044501465/der-kramer-der-einsame-weg-malning

———— *Der Lumpen-sammler* (*The Rag-and-Bone Man*). https://theartstack.com/artist/marianne-von-werefkin/der-lumpensammler

———— *Stadt in Litauen* (*City in Lithuania*). http://www.schirn.de/en/magazine/context/between_life_crisis_and_world_war/

About the Author

Shirley Glubka is the author of *End into Opening: six sestinas and their humble companion poems*; and *Echoes and Links: poems*; and *Return to a Meadow: a novel*; and *All the Difference: poems of unconventional motherhood*; and *Green Surprise of Passion: Writings of a Trauma Therapist.*

Her poetry and prose have appeared in such journals and collections as *2River View*; *Conditions*; *Feminist Studies*; *The Ghazal Page*; *h.o.m.e. Words*; *Narramissic Notebook*; *Puckerbrush Review*; *Seems*; *Sinister Wisdom*; *Sun Dog* (*The Southeast Review*); *Tipton Poetry Journal*; *Lesbians at Mid-life: the Creative Transition*; *Mothers Who Leave: the myth of women without their children*; *Women in Culture: a Women's Studies Anthology*; and, under the name Shirley Starkweather, *Naming: poems by 8 women.*

Shirley is a retired psychotherapist living in Prospect, Maine with her spouse, Virginia Holmes.

Website: http://shirleyglubka.weebly.com/

www.ingramcontent.com/pod-product-compliance
Lightning Source LLC
Chambersburg PA
CBHW061312170626
46817CB00001B/152